MANFRONÉ

MARY ANNE RADCLIFFE is something of an enigma. The name may have been a pseudonym, a clever marketing ploy used to mislead readers into thinking she was the same person as the best-selling author Ann Radcliffe, although other possibilities include the writer of feminist tracts and memoirs, Mary Ann Radcliffe (1746-1818), or another Mary Anne Radcliffe of Durham. Further complicating matters is the fact that Louisa Bellenden Ker, applying for assistance from the Royal Literary Fund in 1822, claimed authorship of the book. Whoever the author was, her *Manfroné; or, The One-Handed Monk* (1809) was a terrific success, being reprinted numerous times through the nineteenth century, and it remains one of the foremost examples of early Gothic fiction.

Manfroné
or,
The One-Handed Monk

Mary Anne Radcliffe

INTRODUCTION BY
LISA KRÖGER

VALANCOURT BOOKS

Manfroné; or, The One-Handed Monk
Originally published in four volumes by J. F. Hughes in 1809
First Valancourt Books edition 2007
This edition first published 2021

Introduction copyright © 2021 by Lisa Kröger

"Monster, She Wrote" trade dress designed by Andie Reid,
copyright © 2019 Quirk Books. Used under license. All rights
reserved.

Published by Valancourt Books, Richmond, Virginia
http://www.valancourtbooks.com

ISBN 978-1-954321-01-4 (hardcover)
ISBN 978-1-954321-02-1 (trade paperback)

Also available as an electronic book.

Cover by M. S. Corley
Set in Adobe Caslon

INTRODUCTION

READERS, if this novel's title doesn't terrify, then you're not a fan of eighteenth-century Gothic novels. But since you're here, I'm assuming that you are. So, you already know the conventions of the genre: a virtuous heroine is held prisoner in a secluded castle by some lascivious character, who is usually using the heroine's body as a means to secure her fortune, probably through a forced marriage. Chills and thrills abound, but usually not the kind of violence that *Manfroné* opens with.

The villain of Mary Anne Radcliffe's book, like many Gothic novels, is a man dressed as a monk (remember this is a Gothic novel and Catholicism was always scary to those British readers). If you want to know how he lost one of his hands, read on. I promise you that it will not disappoint.

In *Manfroné*, Mary Anne Radcliffe has created a pitch-perfect Gothic novel. Every element is in place. The story opens on our heroine, alabaster-skinned Rosalina, who is pining away in her richly appointed bedroom chamber, in her castle in the verdant forest. She's a regular fairy-tale princess, as many Gothic heroines are, but she is in a sullen mood and is struggling with insomnia.

Predictably, Rosalina hears spooky sounds in her room, and because she is a woman in a Gothic novel, those sounds are not simply atmospheric or ghostly. Yes, she is trapped inside a dark and gloomy estate, and there very well may be ghosts. But the Gothic novel hinges on the threat of violence to the female body. Rosalina, before she even has a chance to investigate any of these strange noises, is blindsided by a man—her "midnight assassin," as he is called—attacking her in her bedroom. It's a violent scene. Within the first three pages, Radcliffe constructs a nightmare for her heroine. The first chapter starts with an attempted rape—and ends with a bloody hand on the floor.

Manfroné follows the familiar conventions of the Gothic novel in many ways: a heroine is under threat from a lascivious villain who wants to force her into marriage in order to secure her fortune; there's also a romantic subplot with a mysterious but handsome man who will prove to be her savior. But Radcliffe's novel has key differences from other contemporary Gothic novels. For one, Rosalina is not a heroine who shies away from a fight. From the opening scene, she is depicted as someone not given to fear or weakness. As an example, when the severed hand is discovered, Rosalina does not faint away. She finds it grotesque and sickening, but it is Carletta, her handmaid, who faints at the sight of it.

And while the novel gives Rosalina ample opportunity to faint like a good Gothic heroine (and she does so, many times, despite her strong constitution), Rosalina does manage to maintain goals and plans that are not connected to the aims of the men in the book. While she wants to honor her father, she still pushes back against the proposed marriage to Montalto, making her a kind of modern heroine that readers will relate to (and perhaps because of that, a heroine that readers will fear for when she is in danger).

The novel also doesn't look away from the horror. It starts with that bloody hand, of course, but there are enormously creepy moments, especially when Rosalina's body is contested. The book begins with an attempted rape—a rape which is foiled—but she is in constant danger until the end of the novel. In moments where Rosalina does faint away, her body is held uncomfortably in the male gaze of the villain (and sometimes falls victim to a stolen touch or kiss). It is the shuddering kind of horror. The kind that is often implied in other Gothic novels of the same time period, rather than displayed on the page.

Mary Anne Radcliffe, in these pages, has managed to write a fully fleshed out Gothic heroine and a thrilling plot that cuts directly to the punch. Unlike Ann Radcliffe (author of *The Mysteries of Udolpho*), whose novels contain rather large chunks of landscape description, sacrificing the tension of the plot,

6

Mary Anne Radcliffe focuses on the action, which helps the novel considerably.

Speaking of Ann Radcliffe, it is difficult to discuss Mary Anne Radcliffe without at least noting the authorship of this book. Critics have largely agreed that the book belongs to Mary Ann Radcliffe, a diarist who was actively writing at the time. Of course, it is plausible that *Manfroné* was written under a pen name, and this one would entice readers with its similarities to Ann Radcliffe, the undisputed Queen of Gothic novels at the time. One other contender is Louisa Bellenden Ker, who listed *Manfroné* as one of her published works in a letter to the Royal Literary Fund. Later reports would discredit Ker as the author, establishing instead that the book belonged to a Mary Anne Radcliffe from Durham. Scholar Dale Townshend has an excellent article on the authorship of *Manfroné*, which was published in an earlier Valancourt edition of this book.

Whoever Mary Anne Radcliffe was, I for one am glad that she took pen to paper and gave us *Manfroné; or, The One-Handed Monk.* Every time I read this book, I find that I am enchanted by the dungeons and castles, by the verdant and dark forests, and by the evil villains who want to stop true love. I will always root for Rosalina, the strong heroine of this tale, as she fights the cruel prince and the mysterious monk in order to be reunited once again with Montalto, the man of her dreams.

Readers, I hope you enjoy the adventure as it unfolds in this book as much as I do. I think you will.

LISA KRÖGER

August 2020

LISA KRÖGER, Ph.D., is the Bram Stoker Award and Locus Award winning author of *Monster, She Wrote*, as well as co-host of the *Know Fear* and *Monster, She Wrote* podcasts. She has contributed fiction and nonfiction to *Lost Highways: Dark Fictions From the Road, EcoGothic, The Encyclopedia of the Vampire*, and *Horror Literature through History*. Her essay collections include *Shirley Jackson: Influences and Confluences* and *Spectral Identities: The Ghosted and the Ghostly in Film and Literature*. You can find out more at www.lisakroger.com.

NOTE ON THE TEXT

This edition of *Manfroné; or, The One-Handed Monk* follows the third edition of the novel, published in four volumes by A. K. Newman of London in 1828. The novel first appeared in a four-volume edition published by J. F. Hughes in 1809, and was reissued in a second edition by Newman in 1819. It later appeared in a cheap double-column reprint in 1839 for John Cunningham's *The Novel Newspaper* and was reissued from time to time throughout the nineteenth century, sometimes erroneously attributed to Ann Radcliffe.

The Valancourt Books edition reprints the 1828 edition verbatim, except for obvious printer's errors in the original, which have been silently corrected here. In the original edition, Volume I comprised Chapters I-VI; Volume II, Chapters VII-XI; Volume III, Chapters XII-XVI; Volume IV, XVII-XXIII. For the present edition, the division into four volumes has been omitted.

MANFRONÉ.

CHAPTER I.

Rosalina, for some time lost in thought, rested her head on her white arm, till the increasing gloom of her chamber made her look to her expiring lamp; hastily she arose to trim it, for she feared to be left in the shades of darkness, as her thoughts were sorrowful, and sleep seemed not inclined to "steep her senses in forgetfulness."

Her apartment was spacious and lofty; the wainscoting was of dark cedar, and the ceiling was formed of the same. The uncertain light of the lamp, which doubtfully fluttered round the wick, scarcely shed its faint lumen farther than the table on which it was placed.

An almost nameless sensation, but in which terror held a share, disturbed Rosalina; for, as she gazed around, she almost fancied the distant shades as the shrouds of spectral forms, gliding along with noiseless pace; and fancy made her listen in idea to the hollow tones of their sepulchral voices.

She had some time dismissed her servant, who had retired to her bed; and whether it was the effect of the tale she had been perusing, or some presentiment of ill which arose in her breast, and which filled her bosom with a secret dread, is uncertain; but she was going to summon her domestic to remain with her during the night, when a noise at the further extremity of her chamber fixed her, trembling, to her seat.

The sounds seemed to be occasioned by the sliding of a panel through its grooves, and which appeared to move with difficulty, as if long disused. Terror deprived Rosalina of the power of action or speech; her lamp grew every moment more dim, and the gloomy shades which filled her apartment more dense.

The noise, however, soon ceased, and Rosalina began slowly to recover from her terrors. She was not naturally of a fearful disposition; but her imagination, heated by her disturbed ideas, made her that night somewhat timid; true it was, that the apartment she was in was solitary, and the lumen of her lamp served rather to make the darkness visible, than to chase away its solemn shades.

Rosalina, after some time spent in endeavouring to penetrate through the gloom, and listening for the renewal of the noise that had so much disturbed her, summoned up sufficient courage to advance to the lamp to trim it; having so done, she held it up, in order to examine the remote parts of the chamber, when, to her terror-struck vision, appeared a tall figure in a sable mantle, advancing towards her with a noiseless pace, whose features were not perceptible, for they were shaded by the dark plumage he wore in his barette.

Rosalina started back, for at the first glance she imagined the form before her was that of some supernatural visitant: her senses were fast congealing with horror, and the lamp dropped from her trembling hand; but, in a moment after she was terribly convinced to the contrary, for she felt herself seized by a firm grasp, from which she was unable to disengage herself. The lamp, when it fell to the floor, was extinguished; and thus, in utter darkness, Rosalina was at the mercy of some unknown assailant, whose base purposes soon became no matter of doubt.

Her piercing shrieks re-echoed through the vaulted corridors of the castello, and soon were heard by the duca di Rodolpho, her father, who, hastily taking his sword, rushed towards her chamber, the portal of which he burst open, and beheld his daughter in the arms of the daring intruder, her strength nearly exhausted, and her voice becoming every moment more faint.

Without laying down his lamp, he rushed on the unknown, who, leaving the trembling Rosalina, defended himself against the furious attack of the duca.

The lamp which the duca held was soon struck out of his hold, and they fought in utter darkness, till at length the stranger was disarmed, and, groaning deeply, fled; the duca would have pursued him, but could not discover which way he had gone, for his footsteps became suddenly silent, and nothing was now heard but poor Rosalina, who lay on the floor, gasping for breath, and unable to speak.

The servants, alarmed at the clashing of swords, and the screams of Rosalina, at length rushed into the chamber, where stood the duca, resting against the table, covered with blood, for he had been wounded in the violent contest; the sight of her father in that situation completely roused Rosalina from her insensibility, and she tottered forward to support him.

"My father!" she exclaimed, "my dear father! you are wounded.—Oh, Pietro! Gulieno! hasten away to procure assistance!"

"There is no occasion for your alarms, Rosalina," replied the duca; "my wounds are, I trust, not dangerous: but where could the villain have escaped? Search instantly the chamber, for I am almost certain he did not go out at the portal."

The servants instantly obeyed the command, but nowhere could they discover any trace of the person they sought; but Rosalina, who by this time was perfectly returned to her recollection, mentioned the circumstance of the noise she had heard; from which they concluded that there was a private entrance into the chamber, and on examining in the direction she pointed out, a loose panel was discovered, which, being forced from its holds, disclosed a small passage which terminated in a flight of steps; the drops of blood on the floor shewed that the unexpected visitant had certainly gone that way, and the servants were immediately ordered to descend the stairs, and to trace his steps. In this, however, they did not succeed; for after descending them, they found that they led into the subterraneous apartments of the castello, whose intricate turnings and windings they for a long time paced, till at last, satisfied that the object of their pursuit must have left the precincts of the castello by some concealed entrances to the vaults, they returned to Rosalina's chamber, to report their ill success to the duca.

After the departure of the servants, Rodolpho, faint with the loss of blood, had retired, and Rosalina was left with her favourite servant Carletta. Though repeatedly assured by him and father Augustino, confessor to the castle, who was greatly skilled in chirurgical knowledge, that none of his hurts were dangerous, yet she was not able to dismiss her fears on her parent's account, and sat in tears by the side of her couch, till a violent scream from Carletta, who was arranging the furniture of the apartment, which had been thrown into confusion during the late mysterious occurrence, made her start from her seat to inquire into the cause, when she beheld her attendant standing with her eyes fixed on some object on the floor, and her hands clasped together, while her trembling frame bespoke the agitation she endured.

"What is the matter, Carletta?" said she, advancing—"what alarms you so much?"

Scarcely had she concluded her question, when her eyes rested on the object that had caused the exclamation of affright from her attendant, and which, with horror, she perceived to be a human hand, blood-stained, and apparently but lately severed from its limb. She sickened and turned pale at the sight, and, sinking into a chair, covered her eyes with her hands, lest she should again behold so unpleasant an object; while Carletta, whose fears were still greater than those of her mistress, fainted away, and lay inanimate on the floor, close to the cause of her alarms.

In this situation they were found by the domestics, on their return from their fruitless search. Lupo, the castellain, entered first, and Rosalina, when she beheld him, gathered sufficient courage to point out to him the bleeding hand, which he immediately took up and examined; it was large and muscular, but no rings being on the fingers, they were at a loss to conceive who the owner could be.

"At any rate," said Lupo, "it will be easy to recognize him again, should he be any one belonging to the castello, and which I should almost conceive to be the case, by his being so well acquainted with the private passages of it. As to his hand, lady," continued he, "it shall no longer alarm you."

Thus having said, the castellain, opening a casement which overlooked the wide waters of the lake Abruzzo, threw out the hand of the mysterious intruder, and having fastened the panel, departed with his followers to the apartment of the duca, to acquaint him with this last circumstance.

Carletta, meanwhile, had been recovered from her state of insensibility, and Rosalina, who could not sufficiently compose her spirits as to remain any longer in that chamber, immediately left it.

The next morning various were the inquiries throughout the castello; the result of which was, that no one was missing, nor was any person able to give the least information which could throw any light on the events of the past night; neither could it be discovered where the person had left the subterraneous recess, for no outlet was found where he could possibly have had egress.

The duca was involved in a labyrinth of conjectures, but his suspicions rested on no one; for if, even for a moment, he harboured any, the person suspected having both his hands, was a certain proof that he was wrong.

Rosalina could not enter her chamber for some time, without shuddering at the recollection of the bloody hand; and so much did the remembrance disturb her, that she removed to another wing of the castello; but at length the lovely view that her former apartment commanded induced her to live there again, particularly as she had little reason to fear that another attempt would be made by the person who had paid so dearly for his temerity.

There was, perhaps, another reason why she preferred those chambers, for from them were seen the proud turrets of the residence of the marchese Montalto, whose son Rosalina had long loved, and who returned her tender passion with the sincerest adoration.

In order to disclose the commencement of that attachment it will be necessary to look back some years, and to relate events which took place both before and after the arrival of the duca at his castello, from which he had been absent on an expedition against the combined forces of the northern states of Italy.

CHAPTER II.

THE sun, arising from the bosom of the eastern waters, had just tipped with his golden reflexes the lofty turrets of the castello di Colredo, when, through the wide-stretched valley over which they proudly towered, echoed the martial tones of the shrill clarions; and from the extensive ramparts were a party of warriors seen winding amongst the passes of the distant hills, who displayed the well known ensigns of the duca di Rodolpho.

Spurring his fiery courser over the plains, a horseman hastened to the castle gates, and proclaimed aloud the arrival of the lord of the vast pile.

Hastily the warder ascended the highest turret, and blew his sounding horn, which, borne on the early breeze, was heard by the duca and his numerous retinue, who soon made the vallies resound with the merry notes of their trumpets, while the hollow drums and clashing cymbals increased the warlike harmony.

Awakened by the blasts of the shrill-toned horn, the lovely Rosalina raised her head from the pillow, and summoned her attendants, to know the cause of the unusual disturbance which seemed to be in the castello.

"The duca is approaching, signora," replied Carletta, "he is now entering the valley."

Delighted at this intelligence, Rosalina hastily arose, and prepared to receive her father, who had been absent some months with his vassals, in reducing to subjection the bands of ferocious marauders, who had taken their residence amongst the impenetrable recesses of the Pyrennean mountains, and their strength daily increasing, had threatened to carry the sword of desolation over Italy.

Alarmed for their general safety, the sovereigns of the neighbouring states united their forces, and at length, though not without much effusion of blood, reduced them to obedience.

Art was not requisite to adorn a form on which nature had been truly lavish. Rosalina's figure was rather above the common height; her black glossy ringlets sported over a bosom fairer than the Alpine snow; her dark eyebrows formed a beauteous arch over her expressive eyes; and on her lovely cheeks the blushing rose and pale lily dwelt,

> "Whose red and white
> Nature's own sweet and cunning hand laid on."

Scarcely had she numbered seventeen summers, each of which had strove to bring to perfection the loveliest of created beings.

Such was Rosalina di Rodolpho, who, now quitting her apartment, hastened on the eastern ramparts, which overlooked the valley, and from whence her eyes were greeted with the sight of her father.

The soldiers who had been left to guard the castello hailed with delight their comrades, who were returning, laden with the spoils of the well-earned fields of sanguine strife; and the huge folding gates were soon thrown open to admit them.

Rosalina from the ramparts heard the hoofs of the neighing steeds clattering on the ponderous drawbridge, and looking into the court of the castello, saw the troops enter it, preceded by the duca, by the side of whom rode a person unknown to Rosalina, but who, from the great attention paid him, she concluded was of high rank. While she was leaning over the stone parapet, she attracted the gaze of the stranger, whose beaver being up, she for an instant saw his features; they were not those, however, which could cause admiration, for they looked dark and gloomy, and as his large expressive eyes were fixed on her, an unaccountable emotion made her draw back, and leaving the rampart, she hastened to the grand hall to receive her father.

She had not long waited there, when he entered, accompanied by the stranger.

"Advance, my dear Rosalina," said the duca, "and welcome the prince di Manfroné, who has condescended to honour my castello with his presence."

Rosalina obeyed, but as her eyes met the glance of the prince, she trembled, and her faltering voice could hardly articulate her forced welcome.

To a colossal figure, in Manfroné was added a forbidding countenance; his black eyes rolled beneath his bushy exuberant brows, and seemed an index to the dark thoughts of his heart. Without seeming to attend to the faltering speech of the beauteous Rosalina, he employed those moments in gazing on her lovely features, till, deeply blushing, she turned aside to seek her father, but who had already left her, and was engaged in deep converse with Lupo.

Thus situated she was obliged to attend to the speech of the prince, who, with an appearance of forced condescension, replied—

"A welcome from you, fair signora, greatly adds to the pleasure I anticipated from my sojourn with your father: report, I find, has only done his charming daughter that justice which is her due."

The arrival of the duca at the moment relived Rosalina from the unpleasant situation she felt herself in.

"I congratulate you," said Manfroné, "on possessing such an inestimable treasure as you have in so fair a daughter."

"Your highness does me much honour," replied Rodolpho. "Rosalina will endeavour, with me, to prevent the time hanging heavy while you honour us with your presence—will you not, my child?"

"Certainly, my dear father," said the agitated Rosalina; "your wishes are ever my pleasure."

Thus having said, she departed from the hall with her attendant, and looking behind, as the portal was closing, saw the prince's eyes earnestly fixed on her. The happiness she had anticipated from the return of the duca was entirely clouded by his having brought so unwelcome a visitor; for an inquietude agitated her bosom, for which, indeed, she could scarcely account, at the sight of the prince, but which, fatally for her, was a foreboding of evil, which, as the ensuing pages may perhaps shew, was not without reason.

The castello di Colredo was a pile of buildings of immense extent, almost surrounded by the spacious lake of Abruzzo, which washed the craggy rocks on which it was erected, both on the northern and western sides. Fronting the east was the frowning walls of the barbacan, the embattled summits of whose towers, projecting over the base, defended the passage to the gates; and round the southern and eastern sides, a precipice denied all access to the walls, over whose yawning chasm a bridge was thrown, which communicated with the gates. Thus situated, the castello reared its frowning walls above the neighbouring hills, in stern defiance of the attack of an enemy, from which it was so amply secured both by nature and art.

From the gates a path, winding among the rocks, descended to the vale below; on one side of which the wide waters of Abruzzo reflected the splendour of the sun on its wavy surface; on the other an extensive forest waved its lofty summits with the blast, whose thick embowering shades denied access even to the meridian beams, and stretching over a large tract of country, was bounded by a long chain of mountains.

A monastery and convent dedicated to the Santa Maria, rose in the valley, from which was a subterraneous communication with the castello, to afford the means of escape and protection for the inhabitants, in case the troops of banditti, who infested the mountains, should dare to offer violence to them in hopes of plunder.

The shrill clarions and merry trumpets now proclaimed the hour of repast. Rosalina trembled at the sound, for it summoned her to the hall, where she must again be exposed to the meaningful glances of the prince. Hastily she arrayed herself in a long robe of white, which was confined to her slender waist by a circlet of diamonds, and her lovely hair, adorned with a band of the same, sported in glossy ringlets over her ivory neck.

She then descended to the hall, which having entered, the first object she beheld was the prince de Manfroné, who hastily advancing, took her hand, and led her, covered with blushes that bespoke her innate modesty, to the splendid board, where he placed her between himself and the duca. There she was obliged to attend to the speeches of the prince, who sought to engage her attention by his unpleasant flatteries.

The table was crowded with the principal officers belonging to the prince and the duca, who, as the minstrels swept the sounding chords of their lutes, and in their verses celebrated the martial deeds of heroes of other days, while at intervals the hollow timbrels and the warlike trumpets resounded through the hall, with stern and haughty look recalled to their remembrance their own prowess in the sanguine plains.

High was raised the goblet sparkling with the ruby draught, and joy reigned in every heart, save those of the duca and Rosalina: far different indeed was the cause, but great was the grief of both.

Affliction had found a passage to the heart of Rodolpho in the early death of the amiable duchesa, and fatally, in order to divert his grief, he had abandoned himself to every species of dissipation, which, at last, had made him commit deeds of sable hue, which darkened all his future days, and rendered him a slave to the horrors of an accusing conscience.

Rosalina had often noticed the wild and distracted sentences which the duca would at times utter, and the gloomy expression of his features; there were other circumstances too, which she almost dreaded to recall to her recollection. Lupo, the castellain, was the only person in the castello who seemed to be in his confidence; frequently was he closeted with him, and once Rosalina beheld them at midnight from the ramparts, when she was walking to enjoy the refreshing breeze, stealing along an unfrequented courtyard, apparently as if wishing to escape observation.

At length, when the disturbance that had some time been

caused by the northern banditti, had called the attention of the
duca and the sovereigns of the neighbouring states, to arm their
vassals in order to quell those dangerous insurgents, Rosalina
indulged a hope that his present occupations would lull the
sorrows and agitations of his mind, and which indeed made her
the less regret his departure; but when from the ramparts of the
castello she beheld his troops winding down the vale—heard
the sound of the martial music, which sweetly floated in soft
cadences, as its echo reverberated from the distant hills—and
saw the departing beams of the sun glitter on the arms of his
followers, as the train entering the extensive forest were lost
to her view, then mournfully she turned around, and tears of
heartfelt grief coursed each other down her lovely cheeks. Her
faithful Carletta remarked her deep sorrow, and as she attended
her back to her apartments, with kind solicitude endeavoured
to comfort her afflicted mistress.

At length the lenient hand of time calmed the excess of her
grief, and attended by Carletta, she would often wind down
the road that descended from the gates of the castello to the
valley, and enjoy the cool breeze of evening, as it floated over
the ruffled surface of the spacious lake.

The monastery of Santa Maria was a venerable pile, and
had been erected before the Castello di Colredo. Rosalina felt
a melancholy pleasure in pacing the long and lofty aisles of
its chapel, and in viewing the monuments of departed worth.
The tombs of her ancestors here rose in proud magnificence,
adorned with all that human art could bestow, while their
inmates had long since returned to their original earth, as in a
few revolving years would the time-worn marble that served to
record their virtues to their posterity.

Fresh, however, were the adornments of the monument of
her mother, the duchesa de Rodolpho—fresh were the characters which were engraved on the marble, a small tribute to the
numerous virtues she possessed when alive—and fresh was the
recollection of them in all who had known her.

By the side of the tomb, often would Rosalina kneeling raise
her lovely eyes to the abode of the Ruler of the Universe, while

a fervent prayer for the repose of her mother's soul would be breathed from her coral lips, which, wafted in the bosom of the rose-scented zephyr, ascended to heaven.

Rosalina, invited by the beauty of the weather, attended by Carletta, strayed one evening along the verdant margin of the lake, till she found herself on the skirts of the forest. The sun had some time sunk behind the mountains which bounded the western horizon, and was gladdening other worlds with his bright beams—the grey-robed twilight descended around, and Rosalina, who had been deeply ruminating on her parents, at length became sensible of the increasing gloom, and somewhat alarmed, began hastily to retrace her steps towards the castello.

A sudden rustling among the underwood caused Rosalina to turn around, when to her fear-struck eyes appeared two men, who instantly darted towards her.

Screaming with affright, she fled on the wings of terror towards some peasants' huts which were near the entrance of the forest; but the distance was great, and one of the men had just got her in his firm grasp, when he was struck to the earth by an unseen hand.

Rosalina turned round, beheld a cavalier fiercely engaged with the other man, who at length fled into the forest, and was soon lost in its mazy intricacies.

Scarcely believing what she saw, and supporting herself on the trunk of a fallen tree, she gazed on the ferocious countenance of the man who lay extended on the earth, groaning in a dreadful manner, for the sword of her deliverer had been deeply sheathed in his body, and the current of life was fast streaming from the wide gaping wound.

Sickening at the horrid sight, Rosalina, nearly fainting, was sinking on the ground, when the stranger came to her assistance.—"How happy am I, signora," said he, "to have been so fortunate as to be near you at so important a moment! Those men who pursued you had certainly some other motive than the hopes of plunder; their appearance is not that of common banditti. Yonder wretch seems still to breathe; humanity must, however, make me wish to preserve his life, though he has so richly deserved to forfeit it."

Having said this, he left Rosalina to the care of Carletta, who had arrived at the place, and proceeded to the wounded man, who appeared to be nearly lifeless. Hastily he raised him up, and endeavoured to stop the sanguine stream of life; he at length succeeded, and the man opening his eyes, in a feeble voice said—"Your endeavours, signor, are useless—I am dying; yet I would do one good act before I depart this world. The signora Rosalina has a secret enemy; bid her to beware of— of——"

Here, without allowing him to conclude the important information he was on the point of disclosing, death stopped his further speech, and the signor remained in uncertainty as to the person.

Rosalina had listened in breathless expectation to the speech of the man, which filled her with dread. That it was true she could hardly doubt; for what motive could the dying man have to deceive her? But she had not the most distant idea who could be the person he alluded to, for hitherto she knew not what it was to have an enemy.

"Signor," said the trembling Rosalina, as soon as she was able to speak, "the important service you have rendered me deserves my most grateful thanks. To whom is the daughter of the duca de Rodolpho indebted for her deliverance?"

The stranger turned pale at the conclusion of her speech: awhile he seemed to be plunged in a deep reverie; then he raised his eyes on her, and deeply sighed, while Rosalina heard him say in a low voice—"Cruel fate!" Again his eyes were sunk on the ground, and again did a sigh escape his lips.

Rosalina, on finding that an answer was not returned, raised her eyes on the cavalier, and noticed the agitation he was in at her question, which she felt sorry had proceeded from her; the remark of Carletta, however, served to recover her from the confusion she felt.

"Dear signora, only see how dark it is getting, and we are so far from the castello. Holy Virgin! I am terrified to death."

"There is no reason for your fears, Carletta," replied Rosalina; "the peasants' huts are near, and we can easily have an escort to the castle."

"Permit me, signora," said the cavalier, "to attend you there; it is likely the peasants are now retired to rest. Reflect on the danger you have escaped, and do not make me unhappy by a refusal."

"Were my father at his castello," replied Rosalina, "I should accept your courteous offer—happy would he be to entertain the protector of his daughter; but in his absence, I must decline your kindness."

The stranger sighed, and Rosalina, as she raised her eyes for a moment, beheld his expressive features assume a melancholy look. She was sorry that she had refused his request—he to whom she was so greatly indebted, and that regret came from her heart.

"In rescuing you, signora, I merely did my duty," said the stranger, "and for which the happiness I feel is an ample return. Reflect, I entreat you, that one of your assailants is yet in all probability lurking about this spot, or gone to seek his confederates; in such a situation, excuse my earnestness in again troubling you with my request."

Rosalina, whose fears were excited by his last words, did not think it prudent to refuse his offer, and leaning on the arm of Carletta, proceeded towards the castello, the cavalier walking by her side. Frequently was his discourse interrupted by deep sighs, which he apparently strove in vain to suppress. Concerning who he was, he was silent, but from some part of his conversation, Rosalina judged his habitation was not far distant.

When he had conducted her to the castle-bridge, he took his leave, but he lingered on the road, till entering the gates, she was hid from his view.

Rosalina sighed as from the ramparts she beheld his interesting figure gliding down the path. Often he stopped, and turning, gazed on the lofty battlements, till the condensing shades of night wrapped him in their murky veil.

Her memory, however, still retained his manly graces and his interesting converse; she remembered him also with gratitude as her preserver, and often sighed because she recollected that he had done so.

From that time she used frequently to wander along the verdant margin of the lake, and ponder on the words of the dying man, which the more she considered, the more she was inclined to put less confidence in. From them, her thoughts would carry her to the confusion so visible in the countenance of the stranger when she disclosed her name, and requested his.—"There must certainly," she thought, "be some great cause for his concealing it, for his air is noble, and bespeaks him of an origin he should be proud to own."

One evening she saw the object of her thoughts walking with a melancholy pace near the lake; his arms were folded, and his eyes bent on the ground. Once he stopped, and raised them on the lofty walls of the castello de Colredo, and then again cast them down, and dejectedly continued his walk.

But when he saw Rosalina, his whole frame seemed agitated by emotions of the most violent nature, and which he appeared to have great difficulty to subdue sufficiently to enable him to address her.

Their conversation at first turned on beauties of the surrounding scenery, and while thus engaged, their steps almost insensibly led them towards the venerable walls of the monastery. The monks were then chaunting the vesper service, and they entered the chapel, and there staid till it was concluded.

The nuns and monks then withdrew, and Rosalina, attended by Carletta, still remained with the stranger, pacing the long and lofty aisles, which now echoed with their footsteps. A monk with his cowl drawn closely over his face, suddenly crossed the aisle they were in; he seemed intently to direct his gaze on them, and, as if shocked with some sudden recollection, started away, and left the spot.

Rosalina could not help remarking to the stranger his singular conduct.

"If I mistake not signora," said he, "I have seen that mysterious form before, and under circumstances which make me anxious to know whether it really is one of the fathers, or a spirit that has some time attended my steps, and embittered the dearest hope which my bosom had dared to entertain."

Thus having said, he cast his eyes on Rosalina, and deeply sighing, darted after the monk.

The gloom of evening soon obscured him from the view of the astonished Rosalina, who listened to his receding paces till she heard a distant portal hastily close. All was then silent; once, indeed, she thought she heard a hollow voice, but it might have been only imaginary, or the effect of some distant echo.

She was now going to leave the chapel, when an approaching footstep made her turn round, and she soon recognized the form of the stranger; his countenance was pale, and his eyes were dilated to their utmost. She started at beholding his agitation, when in hurried accents he thus addressed her:—

"The form has eluded my pursuit, but again have I heard its warning voice—you, signora, are implicated in its threats. At present, I am unable to relate the particulars, but if you will meet me to-morrow at sunset in the valley, Montalto will unfold to you the cause that agitates his bosom. Till then adieu!"

Having said this, he suddenly left the astonished Rosalina, and hastened out of the chapel. Astonished indeed she was, for the name of Montalto she had heard before, and that in a way that again hearing it caused sensations of the deepest terror and agitation to take possession of her bosom.

She leaned for a few moments on the arm of Carletta to recover herself, while she fearfully looked around, expecting again to see the monk starting from the concealment of some of the columns which supported the fretted roof of the chapel. No such object, however, met her view: all was silent, and the increasing gloomy obscurity of the chapel, terrifying Rosalina, she exerted her strength, and slowly left it.

It was some time before she could reach her apartments in the castello, when sinking into a seat, she again ruminated on the events of the past evening, and also other circumstances, which, fatally for her peace of mind, were too deeply imprinted on her memory to be eradicated from it while she existed.

She would often endeavour to chase them from her mind, and to consider what she had heard as a delusion of her imagination. She now longed anxiously for the next evening, when the mysteries which for some time had been clustering around her might perhaps be elucidated.

Slowly wore away the tedious hours of that night, for Rosalina could not close her eyes—sleep would not lull to rest her perturbed senses; and scarcely had the beams of the morning shone over the eastern hills, when she arose and inhaled the early zephyr, impregnated with the fragrance of the opening flowers.

Rosalina that day thought the sun unusually tardy in his progress, and with impatience watched the lengthening shadows of the lofty turrets of Colredo, as he slowly declined from his meridian altitude.

At length his beams faintly brightened the summits of the distant mountains, and Rosalina, throwing a thin veil over her, attended by Carletta left her chamber, and entered the extensive corridor which communicated with the apartments in that wing of the castello.

The bright reflexes of the clouds, tinged with the beams of the departing sun, shone on the casements of the corridor, and dispersed the sombrous gloom which reigned in its interior. At the further extremity of it was a passage to the staircase, which rose from the hall vestibule. Rosalina descended the marble steps, and as she was crossing it, for the first time began to reflect on the improper step she was taking, in thus attending the wishes of a stranger, and which was not only derogatory to her high rank, but also inconsistent with the strict rules of propriety. His name might not be Montalto; and even supposing it were, the way in which she had heard it mentioned on a former period ought rather to cause her to shun the conference, than by an ill-timed curiosity to embitter her life, and look with horror and detestation on the source from which she sprung. She had nearly determined on not going, when she again reflected on the mysterious words of the stranger, in which he seemed to infer that she was implicated in the threatenings of the form which he in vain pursued in the chapel of Santa Maria; and she also brought before her visual senses his interesting figure, the candour and sincerity which appeared in his countenance, her promise given to meet him, and lastly, that she certainly ought not to regard as a stranger one who, at the hazard of his own life, had preserved her from the dark designs of some secret enemy, and which, in all probability, from the converse she should have that evening with him, she would be enabled to trace to its source, and guard against further attempts. The impulse of all these reflections was irresistible, and Rosalina, who, while thus employed, had continued proceeding through the hall, now found herself near the castle gates, which she soon passed through, and winding down the road, arrived on the banks of the lake.

The evening was beautiful. The clouds had lost their borrowed lustre, and now resuming their fleecy hue, floated gently through the vast aërial expanse; the evening breeze just curled the wide-spreading waters of the lake, and cooled the sultry glow of day. It was an evening that disposed the mind to enjoy the beauties of nature, and the pleasures of meditation, and lulling the ever-increasing cares of life, left the senses in that sweet tranquil state, which is so dangerous to a heart endued with sensibility.

Rosalina soon beheld the interesting form of her preserver approaching. She was greatly affected at the melancholy which was but too clearly portrayed in his countenance, and which indeed so much agitated her, that she could hardly reply to the expressions which he made use of to shew his gratitude for her kindness.

Seated on the trunk of a fallen tree, he thus addressed the astonished Rosalina:—

"You, no doubt, signora, were surprised at my hasty departure from the chapel of Santa Maria, but the distracted state of my ideas at that moment must be my excuse; those only whose feelings are so deeply interested as mine are, must be my judges. It is now three months since I arrived in these parts to take possession of yonder castello, which belonged to my father, the marchese di Montalto, who has been dead nearly two years."

Rosalina here turned pale; her limbs trembled beneath her, and she could scarcely prevent herself from falling to the earth. The stranger was, however, so deeply engaged in the relation of his tale, that, fortunately indeed for her, he did not notice it, and thus proceeded:—

"The grief I endured for the loss of my father was excessive, and which was greatly increased by the unfortunate manner in which he met his death. A peasant was returning home late one evening, when he saw him struggling with the waves, endeavouring to cross a ford, which had been rendered impassable by reason of some violent rains. The man was unable to assist him, and he perished; the horse came safe to the shore, but the body of my father never could be found, notwithstanding every exertion was made to recover it from its watery tomb. Such was the report of the man; but there were suspicions entertained of the truth of his relation, and when I arrived at the castello I made every inquiry; but in vain, for no other account could be obtained, nor could the peasant be found. Indulging my melancholy thoughts, I have often wandered along the skirts of the forest and the banks of the lake. In those solitary walks I first beheld you, signora—first saw those beauties which from that moment have never been absent from my recollection.—Fearful of creating suspicion by my inquiries, and ever wanting resolution to address you, I was ignorant of your name; nor did I even know that the duca di Rodolpho possessed so incomparable a treasure as yourself. Thus did the time pass away, till, near a week ago, as I was concealed behind a myrtle hedge, watching you as you passed along, deeply engaged in that dear occupation, I did not notice a person in the dress of a monk, who was standing by my side, intently observing my actions. When, however, you had passed, suddenly a deep sigh was breathed near my ear. I turned round, and then beheld the monk. Greatly surprised at that circumstance, I was on the point of questioning him concerning his motives, when he suddenly glided from the spot, and left me full of wonder at his singular conduct.

As I expected that on your return from your walk, you would again pass by the place where I was, I still remained there, and in that sweet expectancy the recollection of the monk faded away. You again approached, signora; again I viewed your lovely form—again beheld those fascinating graces. Lost in delight, I remained rivetted to the spot, but was roused from my reverie by the following words, which were uttered in a deep hollow voice:

'And does the son so little regret the loss of his parent? Can the heir of Montalto rest in peace, while his death is involved in mystery? Degenerate boy! shun the house of Rodolpho, and all the scions of that accursed stock.'

"I looked around me, struck with terror and amazement, and again saw the form of the monk gliding away. I followed, resolved to make him explain the meaning of his ambiguous sentences; but he eluded my pursuit, and was lost in the increasing gloom of evening.

"It was but a few days after that circumstance had occurred that I was so fortunate, signora, as to be near you when you were pursued by the two ruffians. How happy did I feel at so fortunate an opportunity of making myself known to you! But when you disclosed to me your name—when I found that you, whom I so much adored, was the person whom I had been so mysteriously cautioned to avoid, how great was my sorrow and distress! You, no doubt, observed it, and that I concealed from you my name, for I wished to meet the monk again, and to force him to disclose his reasons for his mysterious warning, before I should again behold you. I frequented the chapel of the monastery of Santa Maria, to which order, by his dress, he belonged; but amongst the whole train of fathers, I did not observe any one whose form seemed like his. You were present the next time I saw him, when in the chapel; and you will now easily account for my conduct on that occasion. I hastily followed him down the grand aisle, and saw him pass through an open portal at the extremity. I was then but a very short distance from the object of my pursuit; and scarcely had the door closed on him when I threw it open, and entered a large gloomy apartment.

All was silent within. I looked around: no other door met my view which could have afforded to my tormentor the means of departure from the chamber, which however contained him not. My imagination already had made me conclude him some supernatural visitant, when again the well-remembered voice hollowly gave utterance to the following words:

'The caution you received you have neglected. You love the daughter of Rodolpho—Rodolpho, who leagues with the midnight assassin. Vengeance shall pursue him. Rosalina shall be the victim which shall appease the wrath of the injured—that Rosalina whom you love.'

Here Montalto stopped. Rosalina fainting had sunk on the earth. Carletta was at some distance; hastily he raised her up, and supported her in his arms, while she ran to the lake to procure some water. Slowly did the suspended powers of animation return to their natural functions; Rosalina at length began to breathe; meanwhile Montalto in silent ecstacy gazed on her beautiful features, where the pale lily usurped the place of the rose. Gentle deity of the tender passions! even in that moment when his bosom was agitated by the recital of his tale, and the terrible denunciation of vengeance which was hollowly breathed in his ears by the monk, how deeply did the tender emotions of love and sympathy take root in his heart! He pressed her to his bosom, and kissed her unconscious cheek; when at that moment again did the gloomy form of his tormentor appear before him—Montalto started. Had Rosalina been able to assist herself, or had Carletta been near to take care of her mistress, he would have satisfied himself who the person was that thus watched his steps and actions; but to leave her was impossible.

"Beware!" said the well remembered sepulchral tones, as in threatening gesture the form raised its arm, and instantly retired to the shady concealment of the forest. While it was visible, Montalto pursued its course with his eyes; and when the gloom of evening and the clustering foliage hid it from his view, he deeply sighed, as turning round to Rosalina, who was now fast recovering. She opened her beauteous eyes, but on finding herself in the arms of Montalto, a blush crimsoned her lovely cheeks, as she endeavoured to disengage herself.

"Leave me," she faintly exclaimed—"leave me to my own sad fate. I fear not the vengeance of your mysterious monitor, for Rosalina is innocent; be then directed by its warning voice, and shun the daughter of Rodolpho."

"Shun you!" exclaimed Montalto, as he threw himself at her feet. "Lovely Rosalina, why should I shun you? Oh, recall those cruel words! Supposing even that it were true what the monk seemed so darkly to hint at, you are innocent."

"Indeed I am," returned Rosalina, overcome at that moment with the cruel recollection of past events; "I am indeed innocent."

"From the inmost recesses of my heart I believe you," said Montalto: "perhaps, after all, the monk is only the instrument of malice—some enemy to the duca, your father, who thus wishes by his dark insinuations to hurt his fair fame."

Rosalina trembled, for again was she tortured with the remembrance of circumstances which had continually preyed upon her spirits, and which made the sight of Montalto painful to her: but were it indeed true what she feared, she reflected, that perhaps it might be in her power to make some compensation for his wrongs. At that time she found it impossible to support the increasing agitation of her bosom, and she determined to end the conference.

"Heaven knows all things, signor," she replied; "its retributive vengeance will doubtless soon or late fall on the guilty, and disclose their evil deeds to the world. The high station of life which the duca my father holds, doubtless has made him many enemies; be cautious therefore how you judge of his conduct, or listen to the secret whisperings of malice. Their secrecy is surely a proof that he is innocent; for if it were otherwise, what cause could there be for the accuser to shun you? Would he not rather step boldly forward, and blazon his crimes to the world, than thus endeavour secretly to rouse filial vengeance, and to witness the effects of his insinuations without increasing the danger of being called to an account for them when their falsity is discovered?"

Thus spoke Rosalina, but while she spoke she deeply sighed, for her heart was full of sorrow and melancholy forebodings. She arose from her seat and was departing, when Montalto restrained her.

"Lovely maid! you have spoken the sentiments of my own breast. Rosalina never can be the offspring of one who is capable of a bad act; the Heavens would not have allowed him so great a blessing. No, sweet possessor of my affections! your father is innocent; but his accuser shall be found—he shall be made publicly to recant his base assertions; I will not rest till he has ample satisfaction of this secret enemy. Meantime, permit me, dearest possessor of my heart! to see you, that I may inform you of the event of my researches."

"I feel too much interested in them, signor," replied Rosalina, "to refuse your request. Adieu! the dews of evening are descending, and my mind, ill at rest, has communicated its agitation to my trembling frame."

Thus saying, ill indeed at rest, both in her mind and body, the hapless Rosalina, leaning on her domestic, returned to the castello.

"Ah!" said she, as reclining on a seat she was ruminating on the events of the evening, "what I so much dreaded is about to come to pass. Still, however, there is hope, and while that remains, I will not abandon myself to misery. Montalto, though noble and generous, as are his sentiments, would turn from me with horror and detestation, and the moving finger of scorn would point me out as the daughter of a——"

The word she was going to utter proceeded not from her lips. She shuddered as she pondered on its dreadful meaning. Tears bedewed her lovely cheeks, for an affection, besides that she fostered for her parent, was now taking root in her heart, and which hourly increased. The subtle deity of love had hitherto in vain aimed his arrows against her bosom, but watchful of an opportunity, he now began slowly to twine around her gentle heart golden toils: at first she imagined it was no more than friendship which she cherished for Montalto, and which she thought he so well deserved, but was soon convinced to the contrary.

Often did they meet on the verdant margin of the lake, and pursue its winding course, or ascending the hills together, admire the lovely prospects which presented themselves to their admiring gaze; but though fascinated with the beauties with which an indulgent Creator has adorned the surface of the globe, yet in each other they beheld those graces, those charms which rivetted their kindred spirits in the sweet bondage of love. Their views and sensations were alike: if Rosalina heaved a sigh at the suspicions which seemed to be attached to the conduct of the duca, her father, Montalto sighed also to think that the slightest imputation should rest on him, and at length began to conclude it impossible that it could be so. Still, however, whenever he thought of his return to his castello, he could not form a resolution of calling on him, or soliciting from one on whom so dark an accusation seemed to hang, even so great a blessing as the hand of his daughter Rosalina.

Montalto had often wandered in the precincts of the monastery of Santa Maria, and often had he lingered in the lofty aisles of its chapel long after the hour of vesper service, in hopes of again seeing the monk; but his endeavours to meet him were fruitless, for he either avoided him as being aware of his intention, or else was not there: thus he was unable to ascertain the reasons which had induced him to make use of those mysterious expressions which had so much disturbed both himself and Rosalina.

So passed the days that brought on the arrival of the duca at his castello; thus have we partly accounted for the unhappiness which disturbed both him and his daughter, while all around them were joyous, and indulging in the pleasures of the festive board. Even the dark meaning countenance of the prince di Manfroné had begun to assume a gayer tint, as in full bumpers he drank to the healths which echoed round the hall.

At length, when the voices of the banqueters had increased in frequency and sound, Rosalina arose to depart; the prince starting up, followed her to the hall portal, and as he rudely pressed her hand, endeavoured to raise it to his lips, but by a sudden effort she disengaged it, and darting a look at him, which expressed her dislike of his conduct, opened herself the portal, which hastily closing, shut the prince from her view.

Rosalina, fatigued with the occurrences of the day, gladly sought her chamber; but no quiet awaited her there. One time she sat down and indulged the thoughts which arose in her bosom concerning Montalto; then when she thought of the miseries and imputations which seemed so directly to point at her father, and also of the prince, who seemed almost licensed in his conduct by him, she would start up and pace the confines of her chamber with a disordered hasty step.

CHAPTER III.

AFTER some time so unpleasantly employed, the beauty of the evening induced Rosalina to walk on the castle ramparts. Passing by the portals of the grand hall, she heard the loud voices of the revellers, who had not yet left their brimming goblets. Fearful that the portal might be opened, and she should be discovered there, she hastily left the spot, and entered a long narrow passage which led by the side of the hall into the courtyard, from whence she could gain the ramparts. Having passed through it, she ascended the walls, and slowly traversed them, till the increasing gloom and damp mists that began to hover over the vallies warned her to depart. She was retiring the same way she had come, when, just as she was passing the portals of the great hall, they were suddenly thrown open, and the prince di Manfroné staggered out, apparently overcome with wine. As soon as he saw Rosalina, he attempted to seize her hand, but greatly frightened, she hastened away as swiftly as she was able, the prince pursuing her.

Rosalina, hardly conscious of what she did, fled along the passage till she came to the foot of the grand staircase, which led to the corridor that communicated with her apartments. A moment's consideration made her determine not to ascend the stairs, but to continue along some of the numerous passages, amongst whose intricate windings she doubted not she should soon escape her pursuer. The echo of her steps, however, betrayed her, and Manfroné was several times on the point of seizing her. Rosalina began to repent that she had fled at all, since she was now doubtless traversing some of the uninhabited parts of the castello, where she would be the more exposed to the insolence of the prince, the apparent natural ferocity of whose disposition, when heated with wine, might induce him to insult her more than he had already done by his pursuit. That fear made her increase her speed, and she soon distanced her follower, when, arriving at the extremity of a long dark passage, she suddenly stopped, for she was not able to discover any way by which she could leave it, other than by retracing her steps, which she could not do without danger of being seen by Manfroné. Tremblingly she listened if she could hear him approach; no sound, however, broke on the silence of those dreary passages, and Rosalina began to hope that he had taken a wrong direction, and had missed her.

After waiting some time, and still not hearing any thing of him, she began to be more composed, and to turn her steps towards her own apartments.

This however was a matter of more difficulty than she imagined, for unacquainted with the part of the castello she was in, the more she wandered about, the more she was perplexed to find her right road, and she was fearful of calling out, lest the sounds of her voice should guide the prince to her.

The gloom around her was fast increasing, and the surrounding objects became every moment more indistinct. Rosalina began to be much alarmed at her situation, and endeavoured, but in vain, to recall to her memory the passages she had passed through.

While she was wandering about, she beheld at the farther extremity of a chamber, the portal of which was open, a casement which was sufficiently near the ground to allow her to look out of it. Hastily she approached it, and loosing the rusty fastenings, threw it back, and found she had nearly traversed the whole of the southern wing, and that when she had got rid of the prince's pursuit, instead of returning, she had unknowingly increased her distance from her apartments. The casement opened on a part of the ramparts erected on the verge of the precipice, the base of which was washed by the waters of the lake, and owing to their inaccessible situation, was unguarded, or else Rosalina could have procured assistance from the soldiers. While she was considering what course to take, she heard some persons approaching on the ramparts. It was now so dark that she could hear them talking before she discovered their features, when her own name pronounced made her listen to their conversation, which she soon found proceeded from the duca her father, and Lupo the castellain.

Curious to know what it could be about, she withdrew from the casement, and standing close by the side, heard the following discourse, as they slowly paced the ramparts:—

"And you are certain," said the duca, "that Rosalina is acquainted with Montalto?"

"Perfectly so," replied the castellain; "I have often seen them walking together in the valley."

"How long is it since his first coming?" said Rodolpho.

"It was not long after you left the castello. He has made frequent inquiries about the marchese; our precautions in sending away Parozzi have left us in security, but he suspects——"

"Ha! suspects, did you say, Lupo? What cause can he have of suspicion? No earthly being but yourself knows the events of that dark hour."

"Rumours have gone abroad, your excellenza: 'tis true, he can have no confirmation, but——"

"But what? You torture me," said the duca hastily: "proceed."

"Passing along the forest late one evening, I saw at no great distance the signora Rosalina and the young marchese in earnest converse; curious to know what was the subject, I concealed myself behind some thick underwood, and——"

Here distance prevented Rosalina from hearing the remainder of Lupo's speech, and she was about to retire from the casement, when she thought she heard them returning.

"'Tis very strange," said the duca. "Lupo, there is somewhat to be feared in this: mark me—Montalto must——"

The concluding words of his speech were spoke in so low a tone, that Rosalina could not distinguish what was said. She now drew back, for her father and his confident were passing hastily beneath the casement. They did not speak to each other in her hearing, and she concluded that they had made their determination, and were now returning to the hall.

Greatly agitated, Rosalina leaned on the stone frame of the casement for support. She did not entertain a doubt but that some dark plan was in agitation which threatened her lover; and that idea made her truly miserable. How to avert the impending danger she was ignorant, for it would be a matter of some difficulty for her to obtain an interview with him without danger of being discovered. Perhaps it was not till this moment that Rosalina felt how very dear Montalto was to her, for the thought of any sinister event befalling him was more than she could support; tears at length came to her relief, and when she had formed a resolve to acquaint Montalto with the occurence of that evening, she felt somewhat composed, and even began to think the conduct of the prince fortunate, since it had given her an opportunity of being of service to her lover.

The knowledge she had gained from the casement, of her situation, enabled her to find out the way to the grand hall, and from thence she ascended to her own apartments, where Carletta had long waited for her, and had begun to be very uneasy at her absence.

Rosalina, miserable about Montalto, could not sleep; she pondered, during the remainder of that night, on the best means of seeing him, unknown to her father or the vigilant Lupo. The conversation she had heard, and the dark hints thrown out against the old marchese di Montalto, could hardly leave her in doubt as to her former suspicions, and which made her truly miserable. Pale and ill, she arose in the morning, and was sitting deeply absorbed in pensive ruminations at her casement, which overlooked part of the courtyard, when she saw the duca crossing it, in earnest conversation with the prince di Manfroné. By their gestures, they appeared to be arranging some important affair, and once or twice the eyes of the prince were directed towards that wing of the castello which contained her apartments. She hastily withdrew from the casement, for the sight of Manfroné was from the first unpleasant to her, and his rude conduct the preceding evening had rendered it doubly so. In order to divert her thoughts, she took up the ancient manuscript of Legendary Tales, and was going to peruse it, when the duca entered her chamber.

Impressed with the recollection of the conversation she had overheard between him and Lupo, and fearful that he was going to tax her with her acquaintance with Montalto, Rosalina's agitation was so great that she had scarcely power to receive him. Her surprize was, however, greatly excited, when instead of beholding his countenance covered with frowns, she saw it lit up with a smile of satisfaction.

"I have news for you, Rosalina," said he, "which doubtless you will be happy to hear; it has given me the greatest pleasure. The prince di Manfroné has declared himself your lover, and has solicited your hand, which I have promised he should possess."

Rosalina at the first mention of the hated prince trembled and turned pale; but when her father had concluded his speech, her emotion was so great, that she was obliged to hold by her seat to prevent her sinking on the floor. The duca frowned.

"You do not receive this intended honour, Rosalina, as you ought; or perhaps you have already disposed of your affections? Tell me in one word, have you been so unmindful of your duty as a daughter, during my absence from the castello?"

"The conduct of the prince last night," said the terrified Rosalina, "was sufficient not only to make me dislike him, but also to rouse the anger of the duca di Rodolpho."

"My anger!" said the duca. "What is it you mean?—what has Manfroné done?"

Rosalina then informed him of the prince's rude behaviour on the preceding evening, and the terrors she underwent at losing herself in the gloomy intricate passages of that part of the castello. She was, however, greatly distressed to find her relation produced no other effect on her father than a smile of contempt.

"And this, Rosalina, is the mighty reason you have for disliking the prince di Manfroné—because he wished to speak to you, and you, like a giddy girl, ran away? No, Rosalina, do not think to deceive me; I have heard of your *prudent* conduct in making an acquaintance with a stranger. On that subject, I shall talk to you further if you do not comply with my wishes and those of the prince, whom I order you to consider as your future husband."

Thus having said, he hastily left the chamber, without deigning to hear Rosalina's reply, had she been able to make one; but his last words robbed her of all power of action, and she had but just strength to totter to her couch, on which she sunk, insensible for a while to the miserable anticipations of her care-worn bosom.

The duca di Rodolpho was greatly disturbed at the dislike his daughter evinced to the proposed alliance, for to support the wild extravagance of his dissipated hours, he had borrowed immense sums from Manfroné, in order to pay which he must have disposed of a large portion of his territories: but the dark-meaning prince, who had before, by accident, seen Rosalina, was struck with her charms, and knowing how unwilling the duca would be to give up any of his lands, now made a proposal of cancelling the pecuniary obligations he was under to him, if he would give him Rosalina in marriage. To such a request the duca with joy acceded, and hastily informed his daughter of it; and conceiving that the rank of Manfroné would obliterate all partiality she might have entertained for any other person, he little dreamt that any resistance would be made on her part.

In this, as has been stated, he was mistaken; and he began to fear that his new-formed hopes of aggrandizement, and emancipation from his pecuniary difficulties, would, in consequence of her seemingly rooted aversion, or partiality for Montalto, vanish, and he should be in a worse situation than before, for he knew sufficient of the prince's disposition, to be well assured that he would ill brook a refusal, and that he should have every thing to fear from his dark resentment. One while he determined to drag his daughter to the altar, and force her to accept the hand of the prince; but he then feared that Manfroné would object to such compulsive measures. Another time he was going to Rosalina, to lay open his situation to her, to state the immense pecuniary claims the prince had on him, and to entreat her compliance with his wishes; but this step, which would have prevailed on the gentle and affectionate heart of his daughter, his pride forbade him to do. The third and last thought that entered his bosom was, to do a deed which would remove the object whom he had every reason to suppose had gained the affections of his daughter, and in all probability was the chief obstacle to his wishes. There were also other reasons which made this last step necessary, perhaps, even to his personal safety, and he instantly formed his dark resolutions.

The prince di Manfroné, anxious to know how Rosalina had received the intimation of his wishes, now entered his apartments; he started when he saw the confused manner in which the duca received him, and the dark characters which were but too legible in his countenance, as he pondered on a deed at which human nature starts with horror.

"The lady Rosalina, I fear, duca," said Manfroné, "is averse to the projected alliance?"

The duca attempted to smile.

"Your highness must make allowances for the timidity of a female; but I trust my daughter knows her duty too well to disobey my wishes. At first some allowances must be made; she is young, and marriage is perhaps what she has little thought of. Your highness may rely on my promise, that Rosalina shall be yours."

Manfroné appeared satisfied, and after a short conversation he retired; the duca then sent for Lupo, who remained a long time with him in his apartments, during which no one was permitted to enter.

Meantime Rosalina slowly recovered from the state of insensibility into which the unwelcome intelligence brought by the duca had thrown her. She opened her lovely eyes, and gazing around her apartment, found herself the sole inhabitant of it.

Tears bedewed her cheeks, while unkind memory made her long ponder on the harsh commands of her parent. What to do to evade his determination she knew not, for unfortunately she was but too well acquainted with his inflexible disposition, and that he little recked the means, so that by them he could obtain his ends. Her anxiety about Montalto increased every moment, for in the conversation the duca had held with Lupo, she had heard enough to make her fear the worst. Thus was the unfortunate Rosalina rendered doubly miserable, through her fears for her father's tyranny, and the safety of her lover. Concerning the prince di Manfroné, she had little hopes that he would relax from his suit, or that her candidly explaining the situation of her affections would have any weight on a heart that appeared hardened to the perpetration of any act of cruelty.

She found herself unable to attend in the hall at the hour of the banquet, and therefore sent an excuse, at hearing which the duca frowned, and the prince looked displeased. Neither of them could at that time express their sentiments, as the hall was full of the officers and other signors who had attended the prince and duca to the wars, and both sat down sullenly at the splendid board, for each, though from far different causes, was vexed.

When Rosalina, according to her usual custom, was taking her evening walk on the ramparts, lamenting her unfortunate situation, and considering how she should extricate herself from it, she saw advancing towards her the duca, accompanied by the prince: to avoid them was impossible, for in an instant the gigantic figure of Manfroné stood by her side.

"Lady Rosalina," said he, while a dark meaning smile illumined his sallow countenance, "I am happy to find you are so soon recovered from the indisposition which prevented me the pleasure of seeing you at the banquet."

"Your highness is kind, to concern yourself about me, who have so little pretensions to such a distinction," replied Rosalina, in a cold distant tone of voice, and was going to continue her walk, when the prince, striving to unbend from his natural haughty deportment, detained her hand, while he said—

"The duca, fair Rosalina, has already acquainted you with the sentiments I entertain for you, and he has given me his solemn promise that you should be the princess di Manfroné. I trust that your inclinations go along with our joint wishes?"

"The shortness of the time that has elapsed, since my father first informed me of your highness's interest in my favour, will, I hope, be my excuse for not directly answering your question in a point of so much importance," replied the trembling blushing Rosalina.

"At least," said the prince, "allow me to entertain the hope that you will soon overcome your scruples. The duca is as impatient as myself for so desirable an end."

"No doubt she will," said the duca, who had joined them during their discourse; "your highness will remember my words of this morning. In three days I promise you your fair bride."

"Rosalina," said he, in a low tone, unheard by the prince, while his eyes glared darkly on his hapless daughter, "beware of my eternal, heaviest curse, if you do not comply."

Having said this, taking the arm of Manfroné, he left his beauteous offspring a prey to unutterable distress. A feverish glow pervaded her trembling frame, and with an uncertain step, after much exertion, she gained her apartments, where, a prey to the deepest misery, she sunk on her couch, and but for a timely flood of tears, which relieved her bursting heart, her senses might have been endangered.

Rosalina at length began to be herself. Sorrowing and lamenting would avail but little in so desperate a case as hers was. It required all her energies to ward off so terrible a blow to her earthly happiness, and to contend with the furious dispositions of two such men as the prince and her father, who were each bent on the attainment of one object, to which she was to be sacrificed.

After a sleepless night, passed in ruminating on what course she should take, she at length came to a determination to see the prince, and acquaint him with her refusal of his suit, and throw herself on his generosity, if he possessed any, to allay the fury which her conduct would excite in the duca.

Thus resolved, and trusting she should succeed, she endeavoured to compose her agitated spirits sufficiently to allow her to attend in the hall that day; and when at length the hour came, she descended the grand staircase, at the foot of which the prince, who had observed her, was waiting to receive her.

She was seated between Manfroné and her father, who seemed pleased to observe, that the traces of sorrow, which were before but too apparent on her lovely cheeks, had now given way to the delicate tint which her hopes of success had suffused over them. The prince was in high spirits, and once or twice hinted his impatience for the arrival of the appointed day, on which he was to lead Rosalina to the altar.

When at length the banquet was concluded, Rosalina retired, glad to be out of the presence of the detested prince, and, fearful lest she should meet him if she went out, determined to remain that evening in her apartments.

The next morning she had fixed on for her interview with Manfroné, and with much anxiety she awaited its arrival, which would unfold to her what she had to encounter, to avoid the miseries that were impending over her. Of Montalto she frequently thought, and often were her eyes directed to where the lofty turrets of his castello rose in proud magnificence over the summit of the surrounding forest; but in vain did her earnest gaze endeavour to pierce its dark recesses, for his interesting form was not to be seen.

Night, that shares with day the empire of the world, now spread her sable mantle over the hemisphere; and Rosalina, weary and exhausted, sunk on her couch, and gladly resigned her senses to the composing influence of the somnific deity.

The next morning Rosalina sent a message to the prince, to request his presence in her apartments, and when she heard his approaching steps along the corridor, notwithstanding she had summoned up all her resolution, she trembled, and the roseate hue forsook her downy cheek.

The prince, struck with the visible agitation of Rosalina, was going to inquire the cause, when she thus addressed him—

"I sent for your highness on a subject of the utmost importance to both of us, and I hope for your indulgent hearing. My father has acquainted me with your predilection in my favour, and without ever consulting my inclination, has peremptorily ordered me to prepare for our union. I attempted to remonstrate against his sudden disposal of me, but in vain; and he has threatened me with his heaviest curse if I do not comply. Your highness's generosity will doubtless pity my situation, and cease from your suit, or else you will render me wretched, and the object of my father's hate; for to be candid, I do confess that my affections are already disposed of, and such is my hapless situation, that I cannot even indulge a hope that the duca will ever consent to my union with the object that possesses them. Thus situated, to wed you while my heart was another's, would be acting ungenerously towards you, and would make us both miserable. I hope that your kindness will induce you to conceal this candid avowal from my father, as it could answer no end than that of increasing his anger against me."

The dark meaning countenance of Manfroné blackened, as the trembling Rosalina addressed him; his brows protended over his scowling eyes, whose gaze was bent on the ground; his lips were of a livid hue, and closely pressed together. He seemed to be revolving in his mind, and determining on the commission of some dark deed. When she concluded her speech, he raised his eyes on her, and endeavoured to assume a calm look.

"Your candour, fair Rosalina, does you honour, and makes me doubly lament my unfortunate situation in being deprived of so much excellence; but as it is so, I will cease my suit, and endeavour to reconcile the duca to my so doing; but the hints you have thrown out, respecting the engagement of your affections, I must confess, somewhat surprises me, for surely the daughter of the duca di Rodolpho has not placed them on a low-born or undeserving object. May I know, Rosalina, who it is?"

Full of gratitude at the seeming ready acquiescence of the prince to her wishes, and feeling her bosom lightened of a load of care, Rosalina did not hesitate in her answer.

"Your highness," she replied, "is right in your ideas, for no unworthy person could for a moment engage my affections. The marchese di Montalto."

"Montalto!" furiously exclaimed the prince, starting from his seat, his eyes gleaming with rage; "hated name—Montalto my rival! Rosalina, I retract my words; I shall hold the duca to his solemn promise, and though Montalto has your affections, Manfroné will possess your person: to-morrow is the day appointed for the nuptials; then shall I triumph over Montalto; but that is not all, for my hatred shall pursue him while he exists."

Having said this, he left the apartment, and Rosalina in a state of agony not to be described; even hope, that consoler to the afflicted, had deserted her, and now grim and black despair pervaded her bosom. To add to her sorrow, from her casement she beheld Manfroné in earnest conversation with the duca, and from the vehemence of his manner, she little doubted but that he was relating what she had so imprudently confided to him. She was not long left in suspense, for shortly after the door of her apartment was rudely thrown back, and the duca entered.

He looked at his trembling daughter for some moments, while his brows were contracted into a dreadful frown, and then waved his hand for her to follow him. Rosalina with difficulty obeyed, for her limbs were scarcely able to support her, and she expected every moment to fall to the floor.

The duca leaving the apartment, entered on one of the corridors which led to the east side of the castello, followed by Rosalina, who mournfully anticipated some dreadful event to be on the eve of taking place.

At length, after having traversed a long range of intricate passages, the duca at the extremity of one opened a door.

"This," said he, in a voice of thunder, "is your abode, till at the altar you become the princess di Manfroné. My resolution is fixed, and since you are blind to your own interest, it is necessary that I should force you to be observant of it."

"Oh, my father!" said the weeping Rosalina, "have pity on me! I cannot love the prince; and would you wish your daughter to be made miserable during her life?"

"Idle talk!" vociferated Rodolpho, "it is to Montalto's cursed arts I am indebted for having a disobedient child; but dearly shall he rue the lessons he has given you, Rosalina. Now mark my words: I give you two more days to consider whether you will go willingly to the altar, or be dragged to it."

The furious Rodolpho, without awaiting her answer, now left the apartment, and fastening the portal, the hapless Rosalina became a prisoner.

She sunk on a seat, and gave vent to her sorrows in a flood of tears, lifting up her swollen eyes to the azure canopy of the world.—"Good Heavens!" she exclaimed, "what crime, what deed so dreadful have I committed, that my whole life is to be one scene of wretchedness? Ah, Montalto! dearly have I purchased the few hours of happiness I enjoyed in thy society—hours which I fear are destined never to return. Ever shall thy Rosalina be faithful to thee; for never with my own consent, though these walls were to become my tomb, will I wed the cruel deceitful Manfroné."

When the first emotions of tumultuous sorrow had somewhat subsided, Rosalina surveyed the apartment; it was of great size, and lighted by casements which were so high that she could not reach them. The chamber had apparently been long in disuse, for the walls were damp, and the ivy was fast creeping round the stone framework of the casements, which, obscuring the little light that even in mid-day pierced through the tinted panes, now covered with the snaring labours of the spider, made it gloomy and cheerless. The furniture was old, and some of it seemed almost dropping to pieces. A large mirror at the farther extremity of the chamber attracted her notice; she approached it, but started back with terror, for as she was looking at it, whether her fears made her imagine it, or what she saw was a dreadful reality, but the glass reflected a tall figure gliding along the further end of the chamber opposite to it, and which instantly vanished; for as she turned round, no sound of footsteps could she hear, or discover any place where the person, if such it was, had left the chamber. Again she stopped and listened, but the silence around was only disturbed by her agitated breathings. Superstition with her ominous voice, had never breathed her fearful tales into Rosalina's ear, for her natural good sense made her reject what could only have effect on the weak and credulous; but what she had just witnessed staggered her belief, that spirits were not allowed to visit the world.

Rosalina slowly approached the seat she had so lately quitted, on which she remained some time, gazing fearfully on the spot where the singular figure had been in a moment hid from her sight; but nothing occurring which could occasion her the least alarm, her terrors somewhat subsided, and she began to think that her disturbed imagination, and her sight dimmed by her frequent tears, might have formed the alarming vision.

Her mournful thoughts were now interrupted by the sound of paces in the corridor, and presently after the door of her apartment was opened, and a domestic entered carrying a basket.

"The duca, signora, has ordered me to bring you some refreshments," said the man, laying down his burden on a large marble table, "and he wishes to know if there is any thing else you want before to-morrow morning."

Rosalina at that moment first reflected that she was to pass the night there, which, influenced as her senses had been by the ideal or real spectral figure she had seen, became a circumstance of terror to her, and in a faint voice she replied—

"The duca, Pietro, surely does not mean I should pass the night here, for there is no bed in this chamber?"

"But there is one in the next, signora, of which he has given me the key."

Thus saying, he advanced to a portal of ancient construction, which was concealed in a dark recess at that end of the chamber where Rosalina, by means of the mirror, had beheld the object that had so much alarmed her. The door easily opened, and disclosed to her view another chamber, somewhat similar to the one she was in. A lofty canopied bed, the hangings of which were green velvet, fringed with gold, but in a decayed and tarnished condition, stood at the further end; a few old chairs and a table were the rest of the furniture. This room was much darker than the one she was in, for the mantling ivy had completely grown over the casements.

"I have brought you a lamp, signora," said Pietro, "because this is a gloomy place to stay in at night, for no one has lived at this end of the castello for many years."

Rosalina sighed, but replied not; and when the man repeated his former question, she answered in the negative, when he withdrew and joined his companion, who was waiting for him at the portal.

Of that man Rosalina had a slight glimpse, but the partial view she had of his features was sufficient to alarm her, for she was almost certain that she had seen them before; and though it was at a time when she was under the influence of terror, yet the malign dark expression of his countenance, though viewed but for a moment, could not be obliterated from her recollection; yet as it certainly appeared very improbable, were he indeed the person she suspected; that he should hold any situation in the castello, she resolved not to think more about it till she had made some inquiries concerning him.

In her gloomy apartments, the shades of evening soon condensed into the sable mists of night; Rosalina then lighting her lamp, retired into the bedchamber, and having locked the door which communicated with the outer apartment, threw herself on the couch, not to sleep, but to ruminate on the miseries that seemed gathering around her.

In this melancholy employ the hours slowly rolled away, which brought on midnight. Rosalina, fatigued, and her senses harassed by her miserable reflections, at length slumbered, but unquiet dreams still agitated her bosom, and the long tolling of the last hour of night awoke her.

During her sleep, her lamp had gone out, but the moon, pale rolling along the heavens, darted her silver beams through the ivy clad casements, and partially illumined her chamber; and as Rosalina cast her gaze around, her eyes were caught by the soul-harrowing appearance of a tall form, which, standing on the side of her couch that was involved in darkness, with threatening gestures brandished in his grasp a naked dagger.

Rosalina groaned, as suddenly she raised her hand to prevent the seemingly intended blow of death, but at the sound of her voice the form glided away, and with noiseless paces retiring into the distant gloom, was lost to her view.

This was no illusion of her senses—no cloud-formed spectre of her imagination; she no longer doubted but she was conveyed into those remote apartments, for a purpose she shuddered to reflect on, when she remembered that it was her father who brought her to them. But from her death what benefit could he reap? On the contrary, he would destroy his seemingly long-formed plan of her union with the prince. Unable, therefore, to reconcile such a contradiction, she at length concluded her father innocent of any design against her life.

In proportion as the difficulties and terrors of her situation increased, Rosalina's fortitude also increased; she trusted in that All-seeing, All-beneficent Power, who, watchful over his creatures with unceasing care, protects them from the dark plots and base machinations of the wicked.

The long wished-for morning at length dawned, and Rosalina arose as soon as her chamber was sufficiently light for her to examine the wainscoting, where, if the person was an inhabitant of this world, she was certain he must have passed through, for she had kept her aching eyes stedfastly fixed on the receding form till it suddenly vanished. With diligent inquiry, she gazed on the panels, and as her hand wandered over the frames, she touched a spring, which on the instant silently released one of them from its holds, and it ran back in the groove. Rosalina started, for she could scarcely believe but some person had opened the panel on the other side, so gentle was its motion. No one, however, appearing, she took courage, and looking into the aperture, beheld a small closet. Rosalina paused before she ventured in it, till at length, convinced that had the nocturnal intruder intended to take her life, he would not have delayed his dreadful purpose, and that from him she had not now any thing to fear, she took courage, and entered the apartment, which was entirely destitute of furniture. A cavity, which seemed formerly to have been covered by a door which was lying near it, attracted her attention; a long flight of stone steps led down from it to some place below, but whither she was afraid to examine at that time, and leaving the closet, entered the bedchamber, and closed the panel, carefully marking the secret spring which opened it.

Rosalina's spirits were somewhat elated by this discovery, for she reflected that as that concealed passage probably led to some subterraneous outlet, should the duca persist in his unnatural resolution to unite her to the prince, she could by it effect her escape, and seek the protection of the convent of Santa Maria, which in such a case she thought she would be well warranted in doing, and she determined, as soon as it was night, when there would be little danger of her having left her apartments being discovered, to examine that concealed passage.

About the close of the day, Pietro entered the chamber; he brought with him a fresh supply of provisions.

"The duca," said he, "desired me to acquaint you, signora, that he intends seeing you to-morrow morning."

Rosalina, who too well knew the purpose of his coming, sighed deeply, and the man was going to quit the chamber, when suddenly recollecting the question she wished to ask him concerning the man who accompanied him on the preceding day, she beckoned him to return.

"Was the person who was with you yesterday, Pietro, a vassal of my father's?"

"No, signora; he is one of the prince's attendants."

"Good Heavens! how long has he been with him?" hastily demanded the agitated Rosalina.

"More than a year, signora, to my knowledge, for he was with us at the wars."

"That is sufficient," said the trembling Rosalina. "Good Pietro, let my present inquiries be kept a secret from the subject of them; I have reasons for this request, and as you faithfully observe it, so you will be rewarded."

The man bowing, quitted the chamber, and left Rosalina deeply involved in distressful ruminations, for the gloomy prospect before her was greatly darkened from the result of her inquiries.

It however inspired her with that resolution and courage which it was necessary she should possess, to assist her while traversing the subterraneous passages and dreary dungeon-vaults which were beneath the castello.

Night now came rolling on in all her sable mists, and rested over the silent hemisphere. Rosalina having lighted her lamp, prepared for her unknown wanderings. She listened, but no sound came to her ear; even the breeze of evening softly slumbered, and the clouds hung motionless on its tranquil bosom.

With a trembling but cautious pace, Rosalina descended the steps within the cavity in the closet; they wound round a large stone column, and terminated in a passage seemingly of great extent, for as Rosalina raised her lamp, she could not perceive any of its boundaries. Uncertain which way to direct her course, Rosalina advanced, and after she had proceeded some way, the passage became narrow, and at the extremity were several doors.

Concluding that one of them might communicate with the passage that led to the monastery, she drew back the bolts of one, and examined the interior; but the gloomy walls of a vaulted chamber met her view, and as she was retiring, her eyes glanced on a bundle of straw. She momentarily paused, for she thought she heard some one breathe. At first, greatly alarmed, she was hastening from the place, but at length, taking courage—"If the breathing I hear," thought she, "proceeds from a human being, it must be some wretched captive, who in this dreary cell is doomed to linger out a miserable existence, and Providence has doubtless sent me to his rescue."

Thus saying, she slowly advanced, and as the reflexes of her lamp flashed on the straw, she saw a man stretched on it, apparently asleep. His features were nearly hid by his cloak, but as she stood by his side, and lowered her lamp with trembling agony, she recognized the well-known countenance of Montalto.

CHAPTER IV.

THE sudden glare of the lamp which Rosalina held awoke Montalto, who started up, and gazed on her.

"Are my senses deceiving me, or do I really behold my adored Rosalina?" said he.

"'Tis indeed too true," replied the hapless fair: "alas! that we should meet in the dungeons of my father's castello!"

"How, Rosalina! Recall your words—or am I indeed the victim to Rodolpho's arts? Till now, I knew not my secret enemy; he is then indeed the infamous, base, midnight assassin, who——"

"Hold!" said the agitated maid; "do not add to the anguish of a breaking heart. Though my father may be guilty, spare his daughter the pain of hearing his actions called in question. Let these tears shew you my heartfelt sorrow, and let my being the instrument of your deliverance atone in some measure for his conduct."

"Dry, my Rosalina, dry those tears," returned the agitated Montalto; "your wishes shall be complied with. But you, my love, how came you to visit these gloomy subterraneous abodes at this silent hour, when doubtless the inhabitants of the castello are buried in sleep?"

"The detail of my present melancholy situation is long," replied Rosalina, "nor suits it with your situation to waste the precious moments; suffice it to say, that my father wishes me to marry the prince di Manfroné, and in consequence of my resistance has confined me in some apartments in the eastern wing of the castello, under which we now are. Through a mysterious circumstance, I discovered the entrance to a private passage which led me to this place; my intention was to find the means of escape, should it be necessary."

"To escape! Oh, my angel," said Montalto, "let me be your

protector—let us hasten to the monastery, and there repeat those dear vows which will make me the happiest—the most blest of men."

"No, Montalto, without a parent's consent Rosalina will never dispose of her hand; but this I promise you, that unless force is made use of, no one else shall possess it than Montalto. If by my father's conduct I am obliged to fly these walls, I shall, I trust, find a shelter in the convent; but never will I forget that I am a daughter."

"Alas! how unworthy he proves himself of such a treasure!" said the marchese, deeply sighing.

"Spend not the time in useless regrets," said Rosalina, "but let us hasten from this place; perhaps, after all, we may not be able to find an outlet, and you may still remain in my father's power."

"Part of the way I well recollect," replied Montalto, "for though I was conducted to the castello with a bandage over my eyes, it was taken off as soon as the gate was closed on me, which I imagine opened into the passage leading to these dungeons. Our way lies to the right: but, dear Rosalina, let me conjure you to proceed to the convent, now that you have it in your power. Oh! what tortures will rack my soul when I reflect that you are left here, the destined victim to an ambitious parent and the ferocious Manfroné!—Base, unmanly wretch! would that I could meet thee face to face! By Heavens, the last drop of thy heart's blood should hardly serve to appease my just revenge!"

While he thus spoke, the furious conflict of contending passions that warred within his breast shook his frame, and his intelligent countenance at one time was flushed with a crimson tint, while he thought of the prince and the duca, and the next moment it became pale and sorrowful, as he reflected on the dangerous situation of Rosalina.

He now, followed by that trembling maid, left his late dreary abode, and passing along the passage at the extremity, descended a long flight of steps; these led into other vaulted communications, till their progress was stopped by an iron portal.

Hitherto they had preserved a profound silence; but now Montalto, as he drew back the ponderous bolts which, forced deep into the stone frame, secured the gate, again conjured Rosalina to leave the castello; she, however, was deaf to his earnest solicitation, and when the portal was thrown open, and to her delighted gaze appeared the silver lamp of night, and the firmament thickly glowing with myriads of scintillating stars, she thus addressed him:—

"Montalto, I conjure you, before we part, to promise me that you will not seek to revenge yourself on my father! such a step would separate us for ever. For my sake, bear your wrongs patiently; and if you love me as much as you have often declared to me you do, you will find little difficulty in acceding to my request."

Montalto faithfully promised, and deeply sighing, took his leave. Rosalina then closed the heavy portal, and slowly began to retrace her steps, for her heart was sad, while she reflected on the unprincipled conduct of her father; she was, however, pleased beyond measure that she had thus fortunately been able to counteract his plans respecting Montalto, which from the conversation she had overheard between him and Lupo, threatened little less than his life. While thus ruminating, she had nearly gained the bottom of the spiral staircase which led to her apartments, when the light of her lamp flashed on a distant form slowly moving in the gloom. The view she had of it was momentary, for it soon became indistinct, but from the height and appearance of it, she was almost convinced that it was the same that had twice so greatly alarmed her. She hastened up the steps, and exerting her strength, drew the door over the cavity in the closet, and passing through the panel, she closed that, and placed some of the furniture of the chamber against it, in such a manner that the slightest movement of the panel would cause them to fall, and the noise would prepare her for the approach of the nocturnal visitant. This done, fatigued with her exertions, Rosalina now lay down, and sleep closed her eyes till morning again dawned brightly on the earth.

Neither the panel nor the trap-door had been disturbed, and

Rosalina, having replaced the furniture, sat in her outer apartment, waiting with anxious expectation for the arrival of the duca, and pondering in her mind what she should say to induce him to change his cruel intention.

While thus ruminating, the noise of footsteps along the passage indicated the approach of her father. Notwithstanding all the resolution and fortitude she had armed herself with to encounter the coming storm, she trembled and turned pale when she saw him enter.

"Well, Rosalina," said he, "I hope you have by this time learned to comport yourself according to your father's will, and that you will now freely and joyfully consent to mine and the prince's ardent wishes."

"My dear father, how great would be my delight were it in my power to make you happy! but you, who have been so kind a parent to me, would not surely wish to see your Rosalina for ever miserable? such would be my case were I to wed the prince. Oh, my father, urge me no more on this subject! indeed I cannot—cannot love him."

"Rosalina, hear me: he who possesses your love, whom you dared to meet without a parent's sanction, now lies a captive in the dungeons of this castello. The moment you are united to the prince, he is free; but if you obstinately refuse his hand, Rosalina, mark my words—then Montalto dies."

Rosalina's eyes were at the conclusion of the duca's speech raised to Heaven, full of gratitude for her having so happily rescued her lover from the fate that awaited him, for she was but too well assured, whether she was united to the prince or not, his death would have been certain. Fearful, however, lest her father should have any idea that she was privy to his escape, she affected to be shocked at his speech.

"Surely," said she, "you would not, could not be guilty of so dreadful a deed? What has Montalto done to deserve it?"

"No matter, such is my resolve," hastily replied the duca, while the varying colour in his cheeks bespoke the sudden agitation of his mind: "now Rosalina, your final determination?"

"My dear father, believe me it makes me miserable to refuse

you, but never willingly will I wed the prince; and should force compel me to the altar, that hour shall be my last."

"Then is your last hour soon," said the frowning Rodolpho, "for before midnight you shall be the prince's bride."

Thus having said, he left the chamber and his hapless daughter, who almost repented that she had not made her escape to the convent the preceding night, when she might securely have done it under the protection of Montalto; now, there might be both danger and difficulty in the attempt, for if his flight should have been discovered, the faults and subterraneous recesses might be more strongly barricadoed, and it would therefore become beyond her power to release herself.

She opened the panel, intending to remove the trap-door, but to her astonishment, that had been already done. She listened, but could not hear the sound of any paces below; that the mysterious person had been there she could not doubt, and in all probability, but for the duca's being in the apartments at the time, she would again have beheld him. Her present miserable situation prevented her from reflecting long on that circumstance; her escape from the castle was now become a matter of necessity, and she waited with the greatest anxiety for the evening.

When Pietro brought the provisions, Rosalina observed that he omitted the usual supply of oil for the lamp, a circumstance which greatly distressed her, as the small quantity which remained, she feared, would not be sufficient to enable her to find her way through the subterraneous passages; she however forbore to make any remarks to Pietro, fearful lest they should create a suspicion of her intention.

As soon as the sombrous hue of evening darkened her chamber, Rosalina prepared for her escape. Trembling, and anxious for the result, she fervently petitioned the Guardian of the oppressed to aid her at that perilous moment. A glow of increasing confidence animated her frame, and raising from her knees she illumined her lamp. Scarcely had she done so, when Pietro again made his appearance, bringing a bundle of clothes with him.

"The duca desires, signora, that you will lose no time in dressing yourself, as he will be here in less than an hour to conduct you to the chapel."

Thus saying, leaving his parcel on the table, he departed, and Rosalina casting her eyes on it, found that it contained a most elegant dress, with a casket, which held her most valuable jewels. Till now, it never had occurred to her that she was without the means of procuring admission into the convent, and this unexpected circumstance, which so amply put it in her power, animated her with a hope that she should succeed in her attempt to escape.

The moments were now precious, for should she use her utmost speed, her flight must be discovered before she could have traced the extremity of the subterraneous passages, and she might, in her hurry and anxiety to escape, miss her way, or be otherwise detained. Taking up her lamp and her jewels, she hastily opened the panel, and descended the spiral staircase. Scarcely, however, had she proceeded many paces, when a light flashed along the extremity of the passage, and she distinctly heard the sound of many voices and steps, which seemed advancing towards her. Terror-struck, Rosalina fled, and her sudden motion extinguished her lamp.

The footsteps approached, and Rosalina, who had observed some large columns near her, which served to support the roof, concealed herself behind one while they passed, and from their discourse found that they were caused by some of the domestics, who had but just discovered the escape of Montalto, and were proceeding to the duca to inform him of that circumstance.

Dreadful was the situation of the hapless Rosalina, and scarcely could she prevent herself from fainting. The party, however, passed on without observing her, and soon quitting the place she was in, left her involved in darkness.

Rosalina endeavoured to recollect the way she had come, but in the dark she found it utterly impossible. Deeply did she repent not having proceeded with Montalto to the convent; she would now have been safe from the cruel wishes of her father, and the dark designs of the hated Manfroné. Her regrets now, however, were too late, her agitation increased every moment; the visible darkness of the place, the deathlike silence that reigned throughout these subterraneous passages, the dampness of which coldly struck on her trembling frame, made her almost wish to return to her chamber, there to await the coming of the duca, and trust to an All-protecting Power to avert the impending storm; but she was as unable to do that as to escape from the castello, having, in her fears of being discovered by the people who had so lately passed her, wandered into several to her unknown passages.

She had been in this distressing situation some time, when she heard a confused noise at a distance, and her name repeated several times; the light of torches gleamed on the distant walls of the extremity of the passage, and she now plainly recognized the duca's voice.

"Merciful Powers!" said she, mournfully, "have pity on me! and if ever my lips gave utterance to the pious effusions of my heart, aid me at this dreadful crisis of my fate!"

At that moment Rosalina heard a gentle rustling near her; she started, and looked around, but the gloom was so dense, no object could be discovered, while in her ears was breathed, in a deep hollow voice—

"Rosalina, fear not—I will protect thee."

"And who art thou?" said the trembling Rosalina. "Alas! I am indeed in want of a friend, but thou who shunnest the light, whose deeds are dark and mysterious, what confidence can I place in thee?"

"Thou shalt again see me, Rosalina; be not afraid," returned the voice.

The duca now approached, and the light of the torches his people carried quickly darted through the gloom. Rosalina gazed around, for though astonished and terrified, yet she was somewhat comforted by the import of the words she had heard, and wished to see the person who had uttered them; but when the place was sufficiently light, she could not discover him; and while thus employed, her white garments had attracted the notice of her father, who starting forward, seized her by her trembling arm.

"Disobedient girl," he exclaimed, "have I at last found thee? Tell me this instant, where is Montalto?"

"I know not," replied Rosalina, "but I trust in safety."

Not if he is within the walls of this castello," said Rodolpho, gloomily. "Dread, Rosalina, dread my utmost vengeance if you hesitate to inform me where you left him!"

"Indeed, dear father, I have not seen him this night," she replied.

"Well, it matters not," returned the duca, "the prince now waits, Montalto's escape shall not impede his nuptials. Come," said he, dragging along his feeble unresisting child, "come to the chapel; to-morrow I will think of Montalto."

Preceded by the domestics, the hapless Rosalina, impelled on by her unnatural father, hastened along the subterraneous passages, and at length, ascending a long flight of stairs, entered a corridor which led to the chapel.

A lamp on the altar was the only light in the chapel, and as Rosalina anxiously gazed around, she saw the prince slowly pacing the aisle; he hastily advanced towards her, and attempted to take her hand, which she drew quickly away, and collecting all her fortitude, she thus addressed him:

"My hand, prince, can never be yours but by unwarrantable force, nor will Rosalina ever live to call Manfroné her husband. You have ungenerously taken advantage of the confidence I unsuspectingly placed in you, to incense my father against me, who, little knowing your real character, or the base means you formerly employed to get me in your power, has consented that I should be your bride."

"Your words astonish me," said Manfroné. "What can you mean?"

"Would you wish me to tell you, prince? Would you wish to have Bertoldo called to relate how he was foiled in his mission, when by your orders he lay in wait near the forest with his companion, to seize me as I was taking my evening walk?"

"What is all this discourse about?" said the duca, impatiently.—"Where, Pietro," said he to the man who attended him—"where is father Augustino?—is he able to come?"

"I went to his apartment, your excellenza," replied Pietro; "but he was too ill to attend, and I sent Paolo to the monastery as you ordered me."

During this discourse the prince fixed his stern glances at the trembling Rosalina.

"Why, signora," said he, in a low tone, "would you accuse me falsely. You know I am innocent of the transaction you allude to."

"What if the man slain by the marchese di Montalto owned it with his dying breath?" replied Rosalina.

"Ha! did the caitiff betray me?" said the prince, put off his guard by the answer of Rosalina; "then am I glad he met his reward."

"You have betrayed yourself, prince," said Rosalina; "the man would have done it, but death stopped his further utterance: the ruffian features of Bertoldo remained in my recollection, and thus your daring insolence became known to me. And do you really imagine that I will ever become your bride? My father may drag me to the altar, but never shall the lips of Rosalina utter other than vows of constant detestation and abhorrence of the prince di Manfroné."

The duca, who had during their discourse been pacing the aisle of the chapel, awaiting anxiously the arrival of the monk, having heard Rosalina's last words, drew her aside, and with a look of determined ferocity, which made the life blood of Rosalina trickle coldly through her veins, breathed against her the most horrible imprecations, if she did not consent to be united to the prince.

Rosalina replied only by her tears and imploring looks, for her heart was ready to burst with the agonizing sensations she endured, and which denied her the power of speech.

Paolo now entered the chapel, accompanied by a monk, at the first glance of whom, Rosalina, recovering the power of speech, sunk on her knees before her father, and in the most piteous manner implored him to delay the time till she could conquer her aversion to the prince; but the duca sternly denied her even a day's preparation, and seizing her arm, forced her along the aisle, the savage Manfroné following with deep exulting malice portrayed on his dark features.

"Father," said Rosalina, addressing the monk, "I solemnly conjure you not to wed me against my will, as you hope for mercy at the last dreadful day of retribution."

The monk, who with slow and measured paces was proceeding along the aisle with his arms folded, and his head covered with his cowl, seemed not to pay the smallest attention to the words of Rosalina, but placed himself at the altar at which she now stood, supported on one side by her implacable parent, and on the other by the stern Manfroné.

One domestic only remained in the chapel, who held a torch to dispel the dark gloom of its interior, and the duca, who was standing next to the monk, becoming impatient at his seeming negligence, for he had not as yet made any preparations for the ceremony, said in a hasty angry tone—

"Father, why this delay? Proceed instantly with the service."

"No, duca di Rodolpho, I will not proceed in such a cruel act; nor, as you dread my re-appearance, do you dare attempt to unite your daughter to Manfroné," said a hollow voice which proceeded from beneath the cowl, which the mysterious utterer now slowly raising, disclosed to the duca, and to him only, his features.

Dreadful was the effect the sight of them had on Rodolpho: his eyes gradually dilated to their greatest extent; his mouth opened, and his lips quivered, as if he would have spoke, but wanted the ability. A terrible convulsion seized his limbs; he staggered back from the altar, and fell on the pavement.

Forgetful of her own dreadful sensations, Rosalina hastened to the assistance of her father, as did also the prince di Manfroné, while the man who bore the torch ran out of the chapel to summon the domestics to it.

The senses of the duca had fled, nature was not able to sustain the warring conflict of contending emotions which agitated his breast. The trembling Rosalina, whilst she waited anxiously for the arrival of the domestics, once ventured to raise her eyes, and look around the chapel, but her mysterious preserver was no longer to be seen.

The attendants now entering the chapel, conveyed away the inanimate form of the duca to his chamber, whither Rosalina followed, while the prince, mad with his disappointment, which evinced the force it had on his mind in his disturbed gestures and pale quivering lips, for some time continued pacing the gloomy aisle.

Life slowly revisited the form of the duca, and as soon as his recollection returned, he opened his eyes, and with evident sensations of horror, looked around him. The object which he sought, however, met not his gaze, and he appeared to be somewhat less agitated.

"Rosalina," said he, in a voice scarcely audible, "is that horrible spectre gone?—or was it only a delusion of my imagination, which shaped to my mental view that dreadful well-remembered form? But no—it was real, the same tone of voice as when alive, the——"

Here Rosalina, who began to fear lest any unguarded expressions should escape the duca in the hearing of the several attendants who were in the apartment, hastily dismissed them, and when she was alone with the duca she endeavoured to compose his disturbed senses, under the idea that the words of the mysterious being would have the desired effect on the duca, to prevent him from uniting her to the prince. She concealed her having before seen him, but dwelt strongly on his threats of again appearing, should her father persist in his intentions; and she concluded her discourse with an earnest entreaty that he would not; and then, for the first time, disclosed to him the circumstance of Manfroné's having sent two men during his absence from the castello, to seize her; adding, that it was on that event she first became acquainted with Montalto.

Whoever it was, whether belonging to this world, or the air-formed resemblance of some departed being which had disclosed its features to the view of the duca, and hollowly breathed those threatenings in his ears, cannot at this time be unravelled; but certain it is, that the dread of his re-appearance, and that restless monitor conscience, which loudly and unceasingly vexed the soul of Rodolpho, made him resolve to comply with its demands respecting his daughter, for he felt he could sooner dare all the rage and vindictive malice of the prince, than again behold that terror-striking form. The disclosure that Rosalina now had made of Manfroné's former insulting conduct to her served as an ostensible reason for his declining his alliance, though from the evident alteration in his features, and contraction of his brows when Rosalina pronounced the name of Montalto, it was evident the duca was vexed that it was to him she was indebted for her safety.

He now assured the delighted Rosalina that she should not be allied to Manfroné, words which caused such a sudden sensation of heartfelt rapture to pervade her frame, that for some moments she was not mistress of her actions; and while she was in that delirium of joy, a domestic entered the apartment, announcing the approach of the prince di Manfroné.

Unwilling to be present at their meeting, Rosalina requested permission to retire to an adjoining chamber, to which the duca consented, whose strength having, by this time, in some measure returned, was slowly pacing the apartment, revolving in his mind the probable consequences of his refusing the prince's alliance.

CHAPTER V.

WHEN the prince di Manfroné entered the duca's apartments, and saw him pacing his chamber, the dark frown of disappointment which had contracted his brows gradually disappeared.

"I am glad to see you so soon recovered," said he, addressing himself to Rodolpho. "Have you any idea who the insolent monk was, that dared to dictate to you? He shewed you, I think, his features?"

"He was no monk," replied the duca, greatly agitated, "nor is he an inhabitant of this world. Would to God he were!"

The prince started.

"Your senses," said he, "are surely wandering."

"No," returned Rodolpho, deeply sighing, "it could be no delusion of my imagination. You heard the words it uttered, and saw the form, which only to me unveiled its ghastly too well-remembered countenance."

"Well," said the prince, in an impatient tone, "it is now gone: cannot you send to the monastery for a father to perform the ceremony? The night is fast wearing away."

"It is impossible," returned the duca.

"Impossible! why so—what is your reason?" said Manfroné.

"My daughter is averse to the union."

"How! averse, duca?—Am I to remind you of your solemn promise—a promise which may not be broken with impunity?"

"When I made you that promise, prince," said Rodolpho firmly, "I was under the influence of my private interest—I looked on you as one who would not do a dishonourable act; and that I meant to perform my promise, you certainly must allow, had I not been prevented by that awful soul-harrowing form."

"Which doubtless," said Manfroné indignantly, "was some trusty agent of your own, in order to give a colour to your proceedings."

"They who are guilty of base acts are ever ready to suspect others. You, prince, are one of those; Rosalina has informed me of the attempt you made to seize her person during my absence, and that conduct, joined with the awful warning voice, has made me determined that she shall never be your bride."

The countenance of the prince, as the duca spoke the preceding words, assumed each moment a darker tint; his eyes darted their infuriated glances on him, and his hand firmly grasped the hilt of his sword; but soon the ideas that were generating in his dark plotting soul made him loose his hold, and he then, in a voice almost rendered inarticulate by rage, replied—

"'Tis well—Manfroné disdains to sue. Reflect, duca, from this moment I am your bitterest enemy. Rosalina only can repair the breach between us; and while you withhold her, dread my most deadly hatred and revenge."

Before the duca could reply, the prince had left the chamber, and Rosalina, leaving the apartment from which she had heard the conversation between him and her father, and which had filled her with a thousand nameless alarms for his safety, entered the chamber in which he was, pale and terrified.

"My dear father," she tenderly exclaimed, "how miserable it makes me to think that I should be the cause of so much uneasiness to you! But surely you cannot blame me for my invincible aversion to the prince, now that you see his real character?"

The duca, involved in thought, replied not for some time, but at length, without adverting to what his daughter had been saying, he thus addressed her:—

"Rosalina, I charge you, as you fear my heaviest resentment, that you never more hold converse with Montalto: if I once find you disobey my orders, the prince di Manfroné may perhaps obtain his wishes. Retire now to your apartments."

Rosalina, sighing, obeyed, and entering her own chamber, threw herself on her couch, where she remained till the morning beams entered her casement, deeply pondering on past events, when a confused noise in the courtyard of the castello made her hastily arise to see what it was occasioned by, and she perceived the numerous attendants of the prince, some mounted on their horses, and others getting ready to do the same. Shortly after, Manfroné appeared, and vaulting on his steed, rode through the gates, casting on the lofty towers of the castello, as he passed, a look of black determined malice.

Rosalina watched with pleasure his train winding through the valley, till at length, entering the forest, they were hid from her sight in its umbrageous recesses; and her mind, notwithstanding the cruel mandate of her father respecting Montalto, gradually recovered a degree of composure, since she had escaped so horrible a misery as would have been her certain lot had she been married to the savage Manfroné.

The duca di Rodolpho long paced his chamber, while the reflections produced by the mysterious appearance which, in the habiliments of a monk, had so much alarmed him, together with the dark threatenings of the prince, left not a vacancy in his mind unfilled by dismal presages. The immense sums he owed to him would take more than the value of half his estates to liquidate, and the expence of his deranged affairs in being obliged to dispose of them, was a circumstance too humiliating for him to reflect on without the greatest vexation. Nor was that all, for as his vassals would be consigned with his territories to the purchaser, he would thereby so much weaken his troops, that his helpless condition would subject him to the attacks of the neighbouring potentates, and most of all, to the prince di Manfroné, who doubtless would avail himself of the opportunity, and wreak on him his threatened vengeance.

He therefore determined to subject himself to any imputation which might be made on his honour in not discharging the sums he owed the prince, rather than to leave himself destitute of the means of defence against his dreaded adversary.

The unfortunate escape of Montalto from the dungeons of his castello had also given him another enemy, but from him in the strong walls of Colredo he had little to fear, as his resources were contracted. He however determined to attack the castello di Montalto, in order to take him, since the marchese had eluded the search of Lupo and his confederates, who had diligently sought him from the moment that his escape was discovered; for from his conduct to Montalto, he could not but be well assured that he had made him his bitter enemy; his motives for it were perhaps known only to himself and Lupo, though conjectured by Rosalina from the too well remembered events of a former night.

Some days now passed in melancholy tranquillity. Rosalina, unable to make any inquiries concerning Montalto, was no less miserable about his situation than he was about hers; the dreadful idea continually tormented her that perhaps he was a second time confined in the dungeons of the castello, from which he would in all probability be emancipated only by death. The first two days after the prince's departure, she saw little of the duca; he scarcely ever left his chamber, in which no one but Lupo was admitted. On the third, he took his usual repast in the hall. He conversed a little with Rosalina, but never once mentioned the name of the prince, or any of the past events; his faculties seemed absorbed in dark ruminations, the melancholy effects of which were too plainly evinced by his pallid countenance, and the frequent sighs which escaped him.

It was not till the evening of the fourth day that Rosalina ventured to leave the castle. Deeply did she sigh while retracing those well-remembered walks where she had enjoyed the converse of Montalto—where she had listened to the sweet declarations of his sincere attachment. The agonizing sensations, which since that period she had endured, made her think on those happy moments with increasing regret. Alas! she had every reason to fear that they would return no more—that they were like the peaceful visions of the slumberer, disturbed by the midnight tempest, who, while he imagined himself revelling in ecstatic scenes of delight—while pleasure hovered over him with her airy pinions, suddenly is awoke by the howling blast; his dream of joy is fled, but the remembrance of it painfully vibrates on his soul, while he contrasts his ideal scenes of tranquil delights with the furious conflict of elemental warfare.

Alas! Rosalina had still greater evils to experience. The path she had to tread in her weary pilgrimage was full of craggy rocks, precipices, and quicksands, where the least false step would consign her to destruction; the temple of happiness appeared far, far distant, and at times seemed but a cloud-formed fabric.

The beauty of the evening—the sweet tranquillity of nature—the crimson tints of departing day, fast sinking into the meditative gloom of twilight—the gentle cooling zephyr—the last soft twittering of the feathered race, as extending their wings over their downy nests, they protected their young from the damp mists of approaching night—the pale nocturnal regent, slowly rising above the rustling summits of the forest, as yet nearly rayless, but each moment increasing in her borrowed beauty, with here and there a twinkling star momentarily visible—the busy hum of creation dissolving into solemn silence—all served, in some measure, to lull the sorrows of Rosalina. She was seated on the trunk of that well-remembered tree where first Montalto had avowed to her his love; and so deeply was she involved in ruminations, that she became unconscious that the gloomy mists of night were thickly rolling over the hemisphere, shrouding the objects around in their sable investiture.

At length the cold chill of night warned her to depart. She started as she gazed around, and beheld the shades of night: but now the clouds, which had some time intercepted the rays of the moon, sailing swiftly along, she darted her silver radiance on the earth, brightening the frowning walls of Colredo, and trembling on the undulating surface of the wide waters of Abruzzo.

Rosalina, vexed that she had strayed out so late, was hastening onwards to the castello, and had almost gained the winding road which led up to its entrance, when three men darting from the covert of a thicket, caught her rudely by her arm, and at the same moment, another prevented her screams by putting a handkerchief before her mouth.

Rosalina struggled for liberty, but her efforts were of no avail; the men dragged her along towards the thicket, where they seated her on a mule, one of them still holding her hands, and keeping the handkerchief so close as to prevent her breathing, only removing it now and then for a moment, that she might not be stifled.

In this manner the party proceeded some time, till the harassed senses of Rosalina became for a while suspended, and she dropped inanimate into the arms of the man who had held her on the mule.

The party immediately stopped; Rosalina was placed on the rugged rock which formed one side of the road, and one of the men was sent to get some water from the lake below.

The path which they had taken, ascending from the valley, wound along the sides of a lofty ridge of rocks, at the foot of which rolled the waters of the lake; and where they now had stopped, the road was formed on a part of the rock which far overhung its base. The moon brightly shining, disclosed the dangers of the place, and shewed the lofty summits of the rocks which rose above the road, and the various paths made to facilitate the pursuit of the izard, or bounding chamois, by the hunters, whose cabins were erected on some of the verdant spots which were scattered about.

The cool gale of night tended to reanimate Rosalina, whose recollection returning as she opened her eyes, she wildly shrieked aloud, and attempted to leave the place, but her feeble limbs trembled beneath their burthen, and denied her the power.

The tall figure of a man now hastily approached her.

"Rosalina," said he, "your screams are useless; you are now in my power, hid far from the hearing of Rodolpho or his myrmidons."

Affrighted at the sound of that dreadful voice, Rosalina looking up saw the countenance of Manfroné, on which the moon shining, disclosed the revengeful smile of exulting malice which played darkly on his features, while he gazed on the trembling form of his intended victim.

The cold chill of terror had nearly a second time stagnated the vital current which slowly crept through the veins of Rosalina as she beheld her most dreaded enemy, and reflected that she was in his power.

"Oh, merciful Power!" said she, raising her lovely eyes to the blue vaulted firmament of heaven, "have pity on me, and confound the base plans of the wicked!"

While thus employed, her eyes were attracted by the form of a man who was slowly winding along one of the rocky paths above; and when Manfroné, impatient of delay, hastily approached, and taking her in his arms, was placing her on the mule, she again screamed aloud, and Echo, with her busy responsive train, long repeated the sounds of her voice amongst the recesses of the rocks.

That the person whom Rosalina had perceived had heard her cries was evident, for she now beheld him rushing down the path with inconceivable velocity. Somewhat comforted by the hopes of assistance, Rosalina gained fresh strength, and loosing her hands from the grasp of the prince, ran towards the path which wound up the rocks, at the same time loudly supplicating for assistance.

Swift as the meteor glides along the vaulted firmament, so rushed the solitary wanderer on the prince, who hastily desisted from pursuing Rosalina, to defend himself from his furious attack, while his attendant ran up to his assistance.

Though opposed to two, the unknown declined not the combat: quickly he sheathed his sword in the bosom of the domestic, who sunk groaning on the blood-stained rock; and now the prince singly opposed him, but unable to bear up against his furious assault, terrified he began to retreat. The unknown pressed on, and now they both approached the verge of the dreadful declivity; the prince was ignorant of his danger, for his back was to it, and as the stranger aimed at him a death-dooming thrust, he started back, and his foot slipping, he fell down the precipice.

Rosalina, who had attentively surveyed the combatants, uttered a scream as the prince disappeared, and then listening for a moment, heard his body dash among the waters of the lake. The stranger now hastily approached her, when the light of the moon gleaming on each other's faces, she instantly recognized her beloved Montalto, and he his adored Rosalina.

To describe the sensations of either would be impossible. Overcome with the excess of delight at being rescued from the prince, and that by Montalto, she almost sunk insensibly in his arms, while he, no less transported with joy, hung over her enamoured, and as he exclaimed—"My angelic Rosalina!" pressed her closer to his bosom, and touched with his trembling lips her lovely cheek.

Rosalina's feelings sympathized with his. Theirs was indeed the union of souls and sentiments; each was to each a dearer self—love in all its heavenly purity glowed in their bosoms, unmixed with the base dross of sensual passions.

"The enemy of our peace," said Montalto, as Rosalina, gently disengaging herself from his arms, rested her agitated frame on a projecting rock, "is now no more: you are happily for ever safe from his malicious intents."

"The saints be praised for it!" replied Rosalina; "but tell me, Montalto, by what wonderful circumstance was I so fortunate as to meet with my preserver in a situation so wild and remote as this appears to be?"

"Alas!" replied Montalto, "you cannot, my dear Rosalina, but know that the emissaries of the duca di Rodolpho are busily employed in endeavouring to find me. To evade them, I retired to this sequestered spot, where I have indulged the sadly-increasing griefs of my bosom; for, ignorant of your situation, I surmised the worst, and concluded that the duca had forced you to accept the hand of the base Manfroné; your present situation, however, has filled me with hopes that my fears were unfounded. Tell me, loveliest Rosalina, am I right? Oh! relieve me from a suspense too painful for me long to support!"

"When dragged to the altar by parental tyranny," said Rosalina, "and no hope was left of escaping, but by death, from the cruel fate that awaited me, the mysterious monk who so much disturbed your peace of mind, who warned you not to hold acquaintance with the daughter of the duca, was himself my preserver; his countenance, which my father alone beheld, and the mysterious words he uttered, had the desired effect; and the prince, unable to prevail on the duca to complete his promise, left the castello, and, as I conclude, secreted himself near it in order to carry me off, in which, but for you, he would too surely have succeeded. The great service you have rendered me will doubtless be the means of reconciling the duca to you, and make him desist from his unjust and groundless persecutions."

Montalto sighed, while a frown at the recollection of his unmerited wrongs momentarily contracted his brow.—"My injured feelings," said he, "unceasingly impel me to demand that satisfaction from the duca di Rodolpho which I am fully entitled to from his unprecedented conduct; but the promise I made you, my adored Rosalina, alone restrains me. Could I but see that mysterious being—he doubtless is well acquainted with the reasons of Rodolpho's seeking my life. Alas! I do but too strongly surmise the cause."

Here his agitation became so great that he stopped, and Rosalina looking at him, beheld his eyes raised to the heavens, while a tear silently rolled down his pallid cheek. Alas! she knew too well to what he alluded not to feel emotions almost as acute as his.

For some time both were silent, till at length Montalto interrupted it.

"And what, dearest Rosalina," said he, "are your present intentions? Do you mean to return to Colredo, or seek the more certain protection of the convent?"

"The prince being no more," returned Rosalina, "there can be no danger attendant on my return to the castello; I hope too, that my father, impressed with a sense of gratitude for the important services you have rendered me, will seek to make you ample amends for his conduct."

Montalto sighed, while sudden recollections crossed his mind. Rosalina heard him faintly utter—"Oh, impossible! What amends can be made for such a deed?" Then turning away, he walked forwards a few steps, seemingly greatly agitated, till the sight of the body of the prince's attendant disturbed him from his mournful ruminations: he examined it, but the spark of life was extinct.

The moon now began to be obscured by a fleecy veil of clustering clouds, and the breath of morning chilly sighed around. Rosalina arose from her seat, and Montalto instantly joined her.

"Will you ascend yonder path, lovely Rosalina," said he, "which will conduct you to my humble abode? The peasant and his wife who inhabit it will procure you refreshments, which are absolutely necessary for you in your present weak state, and in the morning you can proceed towards Colredo."

"The anxiety of my father concerning me must be great," replied Rosalina, "and I therefore am anxious to return immediately to end his fears on my account; I am able to ride on the mule the short distance we have to go."

"It is nearly two leagues from this to the castle," replied Montalto.

This information greatly surprised Rosalina, but she concluded that her senses had been so harassed, that she was totally ignorant of the distance she had travelled, and which having to return made her the more anxious to proceed without further delay. Montalto, at her solicitation, brought the mule, which she mounted, and slowly wound down the road which led to Colredo.

The ruddy streaks of morning soon began to illumine the eastern horizon, and the lively strains of the feathered creation echoed around; the mists of night yet hung over the lake and distant valley of Abruzzo, but soon the sun, red rising from the wide world of waters, chased away the nocturnal vapours, and gladdened the face of nature with his orient beams.

Swiftly passed the fleeting moments in the sweet inter-change of their mutual sentiments of love, for Rosalina forgot the duca's stern mandate that she should not hold any converse with Montalto, and enjoyed without alloy the present oppor-tunity.

At length the lofty turrets of Colredo rose to the view, and Montalto sighing, took his leave of Rosalina, who, as she was proceeding to the gates of the castello, saw an armed party emerging from them, headed by the duca. At the sight of her they halted, presently after returned to the castello, which she soon entered, and received a message from her father to attend him instantly in the hall.

Though greatly fatigued, Rosalina immediately obeyed his summons. He was alone; his countenance was pale and agitated; he seemed to have anticipated what had happened to Rosalina, for he hastily asked her if the prince had a large party with him?

"No," replied Rosalina, "he had but two domestics."

"Only two! and which way did he go? Do you think there is a possibility of overtaking him?—This is indeed a glorious opportunity," said the duca, hasting forward to the hall portal which opened to the castle courtyard, where the troops were still waiting his orders.

"The prince di Manfroné," replied Rosalina, "has met the due reward of his atrocious acts—he is no more."

"No more!—dead, say you?" returned the duca. "Repeat those words again. Dead!—is it possible?—are you certain?"

"The waters of Abruzzo now flow over his remains," returned Rosalina: "he was thrown from the precipice of Salerno into the lake."

"From Salerno!—a dreadful height! Then are all my fears over. Rosalina, my child, embrace me—my bitterest enemy is no more. But tell me, how did it happen—was it the effect of chance, or were you rescued?"

"Yes, by one who had little reason to interfere on behalf of the daughter of the duca di Rodolpho," replied Rosalina, in a mournful tone.

"Why did he not attend you to the castello?" said the duca. "The preserver of my daughter should have been loaded with honours and rewards."

"Your daughter's preserver," said Rosalina, firmly, "wants only justice, and that he requires from the duca di Rodolpho."

"From me!" said the duca. "Who is he? Let me know his name?"

"You will be sorry to hear it," returned Rosalina. "'Tis Montalto."

A slight suffusion was indeed perceptible on the countenance of Rodolpho, for he remembered but too well the injurious treatment Montalto had received from him—he remembered how greedily he had sought his life, who had twice rescued his daughter from the base designs of the prince, and above all, had released him from a thousand fears in the destruction of his most bitter enemy. There were perhaps other ideas which crossed his mind, but those he forbore to dwell on, for his conscience too often brought them to his recollection.

"Perhaps," said he, after a pause of some minutes, "I have been too hasty with respect to the marchese Montalto; perhaps his conduct has been misrepresented to me. Be it as it may, in consequence of the important services he has rendered me, I will no longer seek his life; nay, I would even wish to be on terms of friendship with him. You may inform him of my words, Rosalina."

It was not without sensations of the greatest delight that Rosalina heard her father's resolution, and she blessed the happy circumstance that was likely to produce a reconciliation between Montalto and the duca; nay, she fondly anticipated more, and that with a parent's approving consent her life would be passed in blissful union with the beloved of her heart.

The duca now questioned her about the particulars of her escape, and Rosalina felt the greatest delight in expatiating on the valiant conduct of Montalto in attacking the prince and his domestic. She dwelt perhaps on that loved theme longer than pleased the duca, for his brow was contracted with a frown, and he moved towards the portal to dismiss his armed followers.

As he threw it back, a confused noise was heard in the court. A crowd of people were heard advancing through the gates. The duca repeatedly desired to know the occasion of the disturbance, but the centinels who guarded the hall entrance were ignorant of it. Rosalina, anxious to learn what it was, advanced to the edge of the marble steps which led to the portal, and looking forward, saw, environed by a crowd of her father's people, and ignominiously confined by heavy chains, her preserver, her beloved Montalto.

A party of the duca's people who had been sent out in search of Rosalina, on their return amid the passes of those mountains which she had so lately travelled over, found the marchese di Montalto, who, weary with his late exertions, had thrown himself on a grassy knoll, where he was slumbering.

In that situation they easily secured him with chains, and knowing how acceptable the capture of Montalto would be to the duca, returned exultingly to the castello: while he, indignant at the base treatment he received, regarded his conductors with a fierce and threatening look, which awed them into some respect for their unfortunate captive.

CHAPTER VI.

THE duca, from the sudden exclamation of Rosalina, as soon as she recognized her deliverer, learning who it was, instantly issued orders for his liberation, and retired from the hall, leaving his daughter to receive him.

The stern looks with which Montalto regarded his conductors instantly vanished at the sight of Rosalina, while that lovely maid, animated with the sweet hope of that day being the commencement of happier hours, received him with a smile.

"I did not expect, lovely Rosalina," said he, "that I should so soon have the pleasure of seeing you again."

"Nor I, signor, to be the bearer of so pleasing a message as it is my father's desire I should deliver to you; he wishes you to forget what is past, assures you that his conduct was occasioned by misrepresentations, and hopes that the friendship which once existed between him and your father may be revived in you."

At the first part of Rosalina's speech, Montalto's intelligent countenance spoke the joy of his heart, but when she mentioned his father, a sudden melancholy seized him.

"Impossible!" said he, with a deep sigh, "dearest Rosalina, it is impossible: you know, or you perhaps conjectured, what I would say—that inexplicable mystery—till that is solved, oh, Rosalina, I must be a stranger to these towers."

Rosalina was affected even to tears, for all the past rose to her remembrance. She took the hand of Montalto—"But not to Rosalina," said she, in a low trembling voice—"you will not be a stranger to your grateful Rosalina?"

How much were the feelings of Montalto agitated by her tender reply!

"A stranger to you," said he, "sweet maid of my heart! Oh no, no—your dear image is too deeply implanted in my breast;

your fascinating manners—all, all, Rosalina, dwell in my soul; but for you, how different would be my conduct! You have disarmed me—you have rendered me incapable of pursuing those measures which filial duty and my unmerited wrongs require. This forbearance my Rosalina well knows is no small proof of my love."

"As such I consider it," replied Rosalina; "perhaps the cloud that hitherto has enveloped your father's fate may be at last dispersed; and may heaven grant that your present suspicions be wrong placed!"

"To find the mysterious monk," returned Montalto, "shall be now my care; doubtless he is acquainted with the circumstances of my father's death."

"He knows the whole of that horrible transaction," said the monk's well-remembered voice.

Both started and looked around, but no one was near them; they were walking beneath one of the galleries which were erected on each side of the hall. A door which was close to them attracted the notice of Montalto, and imagining that the monk might be concealed in the place to which it communicated, he hastily threw it open. Nothing, however, but a long empty corridor met his view: disappointed, he turned to Rosalina.

"This incomprehensible being," said he, "has surely the power of rendering himself invisible; the voice appeared close to my ears, but nowhere can I discover the utterer. His keeping himself concealed almost makes me think that he is some enemy of the duca's, and through fear of punishment obliged to have recourse to privacy to effect his plans: yet his conduct has been so contradictory; he has warned me to shun you, my beloved Rosalina, but he prevented your being united to Manfroné, an event which, had it taken place, would have completely done away any possibility of our further acquaintance. To reconcile these circumstances is almost impossible; time alone will unfold the mystery."

"And may that time be not far distant!" replied Rosalina, who had during the speech of Montalto recovered from the alarm occasioned by the voice of the monk; "for to exist in this state of torturous uncertainty is worse than the knowledge of the reality itself. Adieu, Montalto!" said she, holding out to him her lily hand, "let us pray for happier times. We will meet sometimes in the chapel of Santa Maria, where thou mayest make me acquainted with the results of thy researches."

Montalto put her hand to his lips, and deeply sighing left the hall, and crossing the courtyard, wrapped in melancholy ruminations, proceeded to his castello.

Weary and miserable, Rosalina retired to her chamber. It was, however, some consolation to her, amidst all her accumulating distresses, that Manfroné could no longer disturb her, though she rather wished that desirable circumstance had been effected by other means than the forfeiture of his life by the hands of Montalto.

The duca di Rodolpho, in the death of the prince, seemed to have attained the summit of his wishes: he was now freed from the distresses that threatened him, in being obliged to repay the immense sums he was indebted to Manfroné; and that he might be entirely secure in every quarter, he hoped that Montalto would accept of his proffered friendship, and bury all past transactions and present surmises in oblivion; but in that he was mistaken. Montalto, though he adored his daughter, yet could not forget that he was a son. Happy indeed would it have been for the duca could he have taken a Lethean draught, for his past deeds were green in his recollection, and took each hour deeper root in his bosom, while the sharp piercing thorn of an accusing conscience rankled to his heart's core, embittering his most festive hours; and when at night he slumbered, horrid dreams would disturb his repose, and the momentary gleam of happiness he enjoyed at the destruction of the prince soon faded away, and left him as miserable as ever.

It was at this period that the event which is recorded in the first pages of this work took place, and which gave rise to such a variety of conjectures.

After many attempts to fix her suspicions, Rosalina at last concluded that it could be no one but the monk who had refused to unite her to Manfroné; but when she communicated her ideas to the duca, he replied, in rather a confused manner, that it was impossible it could be him, as from the circumstance of the daring invader's having lost his hand, there little doubt but that in time he would be discovered. Rosalina contented herself with awaiting in patience the disclosure; and having had the secret communication with her apartments closed up, she again resided in them.

For some time nothing material occurred. Montalto, though indefatigable in his endeavours to see the monk, did not, however, succeed. He frequently now had opportunities of seeing Rosalina, and each interview served but to increase their mutual love.

The venerable father Augustino, who for many years was confessor to the inhabitants of the castello di Colredo, had for some time been confined through indisposition to his chamber; and now his soul seemed impatient to quit its mortal tenement, and to wing its flight to those blessed regions where it would meet the bright reward of a well spent life.

Every one who knew him mourned his approaching disso-lution, but none more than Rosalina; she often visited the old man's couch, and by her tender assiduities anticipated his few wants, till, resigned to the will of Heaven, without a groan he sunk into the arms of death.

What a pleasing, soul-elevating sight is to behold the last sighs of the just! No painful retrospections cloud their hopes of eternal joys; with confidence they look forward to their last sigh, as the welcome passport to heavenly bliss.

It was father Augustino's last request, that his remains might be entombed in the chapel of Santa Maria, and Rosalina deter-mined to see his wish performed herself.

The ceremony took place at midnight, when the mournful train, lighted by torches, issued from the castle gates. At the bottom of the rocks they were met by the monks of the monas-tery of Santa Maria. A long black veil covered the lovely form of Rosalina, who, leaning on the arm of Carletta, accompanied the procession, which now entered the chapel, and arranged themselves round the grave.

Rosalina dropped a tear over the senseless remains of the father before the ceremony was concluded, and, satisfied in having performed his last request, she raised her eyes to observe if among the monks she could perceive that mysterious person who had given her so much uneasiness, and had also been so materially her friend; but after she had, as she supposed, seen all of them, she met not his well-remembered form; and while thus deeply engaged in her scrutiny, she did not notice one of the fathers, who, with his cowl closely drawn over his face, and arms folded within his long garments, had stationed himself by her side, and seemed intently viewing her through the narrow aperture of his cowl. The unusual height of the monk, his silent motionless posture, made Rosalina start, which it was apparent he observed, for turning round, he slowly traversed the aisle, and was soon lost to the sight in the surrounding gloom.

At first she thought that this person must be the monk that Montalto so much wished to find, but on recollection, the height and figure of the father she had just seen were so widely different from his, that she was well assured he was not the one who had preserved her from her union with Manfroné.

The attendants being now ready, Rosalina returned to the castello, and repaired to her chamber, where she sat some time before she retired to rest, ruminating on the singular conduct of the monk.

The crimson tints of approaching morning at length warned her to seek repose. Soon she closed her eyes, but her imagination rested not; the events of the past evening again appeared before her mental view. She thought she saw the monk whose conduct had so much surprised her, again standing by her side, his features still obscured by his cowl; he was seemingly engaged in contemplating a mangled corpse, which appeared to afford him the greatest satisfaction. Suddenly the scene changed, and she imagined herself in a small boat, with the monk seated by her side, gliding along a muddy lake; torrents of water falling all around her from the heavens obscured the view. Again, by one of those transitions so natural in dreams, she conceived herself dragged by the monk across an immense hall, and forced down a long flight of stairs into a subterraneous dungeon. He then was slowly withdrawing his cowl, but at that moment Carletta knocking at the door awoke her from her uneasy slumbers, and dispersed her mental visions.

She arose pale and unrefreshed, and sat for some time endeavouring to collect all the circumstances which had occurred in her dream, for there was a consistency in them which made her regard it as if sent to warn her from some evil designs of the monk, and she lamented her having been disturbed at the very moment when the sight of his features might perhaps have explained the whole. Her regrets were, however, now of no avail; but in order to satisfy her curiosity, she determined to attend the service in the chapel that evening, when she would possibly again behold him, and learn from some of the fathers who he was; "though, after all," thought she, "the dream may be merely the result of my mind, disturbed by the melancholy scene I had just witnessed, and the singular conduct of the monk, which, however, might not be occasioned by any other motive than curiosity."

Such were the ideas of Rosalina, who, when it was near the time that the vesper service commenced again, repaired to the chapel; but her curiosity to see the monk had brought her there before the fathers had entered it.

The beams of the setting sun faintly penetrating the saint-enciphered glass, illuminated with a mellow light the dusky aisle. The chapel presented a scene well calculated to inspire holy meditation; its long aisles and lofty columns, that in some places were worn by the crumbling hand of time, which long since had consigned to dust the relics of the mitred saints, whose statues mouldered in the gloomy niches, where the marble, no longer faithful to the efforts of the sculptor, had long ceased to record to posterity their virtues; and now nameless were they as the crowd who had craved their benedictions, and who like them, had long since sunk to rest.

Rosalina, whose heart, softened by love and the ideas produced by the surrounding objects, wrapt in serious musing, had strayed to the further end of the grand aisle, where, beneath a deep and gloomy archway rose the monument of the illustrious chieftain who had been the founder of that religious edifice; and while she surveyed the fragments of the mouldering tomb, she could not help reflecting on the instability of human grandeur.

"Ah! what avail him now," thought she, "his crowding vassals and wide extending domains, his train of hardy valorous knights, or his castle, whose towering turrets divided the airborne clouds, and, deemed invincible, frowned defiance on the desperate foe, though now perhaps, conquered by time, the fabric, as well as the founder, are levelled with the dust? There, where once the lyre or lute gave their soft harmonious sounds to the air, now perhaps the solitary owl, or harsh croaking raven, foul birds of discord, dwell; and where society with all her laughter-loving crew—where beauty with her train of graces dwelt, now eternal solitude has fixed her dreary cell. How vain in man to raise the lofty pyramid! how vain the sculptor's labour on the mottoed stone! for soon the hand of time confounds the monumental trophies with the crumbling bones. The peasant's head, beneath the lowly turf, rests as soft as his who once ruled over him with despotic sway, though inurned in the laboured tomb: the grim tyrant Death levels all distinctions; beyond the grave no vassal owns his lord—no haughty ruler demands obedience from the peasant."

The vesper service was now commencing; Rosalina desisted from her melancholy ruminations, and joined in the choral train. She looked around her, but did not see the tall figure of the monk amongst the fathers; but as her eyes were wandering about, she thought she saw him kneeling before an altar which was placed in an obscure corner of the chapel; his motionless posture and figure made her at last certain that it was him, and she watched his form, till slowly rising he glided amidst some tombs, which thickly rising around, obscured him from her sight.

When the service was concluded, Rosalina, as was her constant custom, passed on to the tomb of her lamented mother; there, while as she was silently offering up her usual prayer, she happened to glance her eyes around, they again encountered the figure of the monk: his colossal form standing erect and motionless in the dark shadow of a large column, his features still concealed, his arms folded, and the solemn silence he still preserved, was more than the spirits of Rosalina, weakened by the mournful reflections she had been so long indulging, could support; and hastily arising from the suppliant posture in which she had directed to Heaven her prayers for the repose of her mother's soul, she left the retired part of the chapel she was in, and seeing the venerable abbot at a short distance, advanced towards him, in order to make the inquiry she so much wished concerning that mysterious monk, whose actions had taken such hold of her recollection as to make him the subject of her thoughts when her slumbering senses gave place to the imagery of fancy.

The abbot of Santa Maria had numbered near a century; he had been the tried and esteemed friend of the late duchesa di Rodolpho, and as such Rosalina considered him to herself.— The venerable father possessed that pleasing garrulity natural to years, but his conversation was both amusing and instructive, and Rosalina always attended to it with pleasure. He smiled when he saw her approaching; but when he beheld her pallid countenance, and concluded that something unpleasant had taken place, the smile instantly was banished, while with a look of concern he questioned her about it.

"Fair daughter," said he, "I am sorry to see you look so pale: has any circumstance taken place to cause it which I can remove?"

"Nothing of very particular import, holy father," returned Rosalina, "but yonder monk has roused my curiosity; twice have I beheld him gazing on me: you can inform me who he is, and perhaps also his reasons for his silent mysterious deportment?"

"I know but little of him, daughter," returned the abbot; "he has not been amongst us very long. I believe he has met with many misfortunes, which have caused him to withdraw from the world. His manners are singular; he never mixes with us at the hour of repast, but takes his food to his own cell, where in solitude he eats it. He does not even pray with us, but always retires to a private altar, which you might perhaps have taken notice of this evening. With none of the fathers has he scarce ever exchanged a word; he wanders by himself in the gardens, and never admits any one to his apartment. In his devotional exercises he is most exemplary; all his thoughts seem directed to heaven, and to have excluded for ever worldly matters. Perhaps in you he may have traced a resemblance to some regretted object, which doubtless was the reason of his regarding you so particularly, a circumstance which I observed myself at the interment of our lamented brother Augustino: but that is mere conjecture. Strange as you may suppose it, it nevertheless is true, that there is not one of us who have as yet seen his face.

"It was late one evening," continued the communicative abbot, "as I was sitting beneath the cloisters, that I beheld approaching me a tall figure enveloped in a large mantle."

'Holy abbot,' said he, 'a man weary of the world wishes here to find that repose which hitherto has been denied to his researches. Want of the means of existence is not my motive for seeking an asylum here; but I wish to detach my thoughts from the world, to dedicate my remaining days to Him who gave me being. With my treasures I will endow the monastery, for I shall no longer need them. I fly from society with a heart torn by contending passions. You shall know my history, but all I entreat is, to allow me to live agreeably to my own wishes, and to act as I please.'

"There was something," continued the abbot, "so singular in the request of the person, who seemed to have such laudable motives for retiring from the world, that I granted his request, and admitted him into the monastery, since which time he has ever conducted himself with the greatest propriety; he seems to be consumed with some inward grief which we respect, and as he appears to dislike society we do not force ours upon him, or even seem to take the smallest notice of him; for whenever spoken to he betrays an evident uneasiness, and a wish to be left to his own thoughts."

"Do you know his name, father?" demanded Rosalina.

"Grimaldi is that by which he is distinguished here," returned the abbot; "his real name is Romellino."

"You know his history then?" said Rosalina. "Your pardon, father, for being so inquisitive, but I must own that this monk has roused my curiosity so much, that I have even dreamt of him."

The abbot smiled.

"Since it is so with you, my fair daughter, you shall be satisfied. I will bring you the manuscript he left with me, which you may peruse at your leisure; that done, let me again have the papers. Wait here awhile, and I will enter the monastery, and procure them for you."

Rosalina expressed her gratitude to the abbot for his goodness, who, leaning on the arm of an attendant, left the chapel. While Rosalina was awaiting his return, she again directed her gaze after the monk who had been the subject of her conversation, but he was not to be seen; once indeed she had imagined she saw a form like his slowly retiring amongst the shades of the columns that supported the fretted roof of the chapel; but the increasing gloom rendered it impossible to distinguish any distant object.

The abbot was not long before he again returned, bringing with him a small roll of papers, which he presented to Rosalina.

"In this manuscript, my daughter," said the venerable superior, "you will find the history of the father which you so much desire to learn: and I hope," added he, with a smile, "that you will not let their contents disturb your slumbers. It is not my wish that it should be known that I have submitted them to your perusal, yet as the father Grimaldi did not restrict me in that respect, I conclude that there is no impropriety in what I am doing."

Rosalina promised that not only the contents, but also her having the papers, should be kept a secret by her; and pleased with the success of her attempt to discover who the monk Grimaldi was, she took leave of the abbot, and hastened out of the chapel.

The shades of evening were fast condensing into the gloom of night, as Rosalina, unaccompanied, contrary to her usual custom, even by Carletta, was winding up the rocky path which led to the castle bridge, when again she encountered the fixed motionless form of Grimaldi, who was standing in a recess in the rock close by which she was obliged to pass.

If Rosalina had not had the conversation above related with the abbot, her again seeing him still in the same motionless posture might almost have made her suspect that he was some supernatural attendant on her footsteps. As it was, the lonely place she was in, almost out of hearing of the guards who watched at the gates of the castello, and without any domestic with her, made her susceptible of fear, and she hastened along the winding ascent, without even daring to turn her eyes to where the monk was standing. She, however, took courage when she had passed the recess in the rock, and looking back, saw him still apparently gazing on her; he made a faint inclination of his head when he observed that she stopped, and then slowly pursued his way towards the monastery.

Rosalina watched his tall figure till the mists of evening obscured him from her view: that he had placed himself in the recess in the rock for the purpose of seeing her she could not doubt, for he had not had sufficient time to reach the castello, while she was engaged in conversation with the abbot; and she began to conclude that he had some sinister designs respecting her: yet she banished the thought almost as soon as it had taken place in her mind; and what the abbot had said concerning the miserable solitary life he led, and his opinion that he was labouring under some heavy calamity, now occurred to her. Pity for the unfortunate ever found a ready place in her bosom. "It is probable," thought she, "he mourns a friend departed from this world, or some crime, which, though perhaps involuntarily committed, calls for years of penance to extenuate: perhaps love is the cause of his melancholy—a passion unreturned, slighted by the object he adores. Ah!" thought Rosalina while the loved remembrance of Montalto rose freshly in her mind, "if that is his situation, I do indeed pity him."

The packet she had obtained from the abbot would in all likelihood solve the mystery which attended his conduct, and she continued on her way to the castello, intending that night to peruse it.

In the hall she met the duca, who detained her in conversation to a late hour: he had of late been more kind and attentive to her than she had ever recollected him; but he never, from the day that the prince had attempted to carry her off, and she was rescued by Montalto, mentioned her deliverer's name—a circumstance which gave her the greatest uneasiness; for though, under the circumstances which she too well recollected, she could not imagine that till the imputation which had been cast by the monk on her father's character, and his subsequent conduct to Montalto, should be done away and forgot, that he would even enter the castello, yet she thought her father bound to repair his injurious treatment by every conciliatory measure he could adopt, particularly as not only justice but gratitude called for it, since he had rid him of his bitterest enemy, and had saved her from impending destruction.

When the duca retired it was too late for Rosalina, fatigued by her evening's excursion, and the unquiet night she had passed, to peruse the manuscript; she therefore carefully deposited it in her cabinet, and sought the gentle deity of slumbers, who, propitious to her wishes, steeped her senses in forgetfulness, till long after the lark, the early precursor of day, had soared on the fresh breath of morning, and had hailed with his blithe notes the sun, as he rose in majestic splendour from the eastern wave.

CHAPTER VII.

IT had been of late the duca de Rodolpho's custom to walk every evening, either in the wood near the castello, or on the banks of the lake; in these excursions, he very frequently went unaccompanied, or sometimes with the castellain, who, it has before been observed, was the repository of his secrets.

It was on the evening following that on which Rosalina had obtained the manuscript of the ill-fated Romellino from the abbot, that the duca, who was walking alone in the forest, observed at some distance behind him one of the fathers of Santa Maria: concluding that the monk was, as well as himself, enjoying the refreshing shade, he still continued his walk, and in the ruminations which he was deeply engaged in he soon forgot that circumstance.

The duca was reflecting on the situation of the principality of Manfroné, which, by reason of there being no regular successor to the government after his decease, was now become a scene of contentious strife, the partizans of the prince declaring that they would not submit to another ruler, till more authentic information could be obtained of his death; while another party, who wished to place on the regal seat a noble of their own election, sought to obtain their ends by acts of open violence. Great had been the effusion of blood on both sides; but as yet no important advantages had been gained by either. Such was the present situation of affairs, and the duca determined to enter into a private negociation with the noble, and to make him an offer of a large body of troops, in order to secure his election, provided he would, in that event taking place, cede to him a certain portion of the domains attached to the principality. He regretted at this moment the continued absence of Montalto, which proved that he had no inclination to be on friendly terms with him, and in all probability forbore attempting to resent his wrongs, out of the love he had for his daughter; for his valour and skilful conduct were well known, and to him he could have offered the command of the troops which he designed to send on the above-mentioned scheme. Or if the noble should reject his offers, he then determined to enter the province, and taking advantage of the disjointed state of the people, seize on the country himself.

Such were the schemes of aggrandizement which now were planned by the duca de Rodolpho, when he was disturbed by a footstep which appeared close behind him, and turning round, again saw the monk.

"A pleasant evening, father," said the duca; "the cool air that breathes amongst these woods is refreshing after the heat of the day."

"It is, duca," returned a slow deep voice, which made Rodolpho start, particularly as the form beside him did not attempt to withdraw the cowl from his face, or to pay him that respect to which he was accustomed, and he almost began to conclude that the person had some design on him, which made him almost instinctively grasp the hilt of his sword; the monk, however, did not seem to notice the effect his appearance had on the duca, and thus continued:—

"The air is cool, as you observe; but still there are hot conspiracies abroad, which soon will burst into a flame."

"You speak in such ambiguous terms, father, that I do not comprehend what you would mean. Perhaps, indeed, you are alluding to the contentions about the prince de Manfroné's vacant seat?" returned the duca, somewhat surprised that the unknown person should apparently allude to a subject so nearly related to the ruminations he had just before been indulging.

"No," replied the monk; "it is the duca de Rodolpho whom I would warn of an impending danger."

"Me!—What do you mean?" said Rodolpho. "What danger? I am unconscious of having an enemy."

"But I," returned the monk, "know that you have one—one whom you have little conception of; and I have long sought you to caution you against him."

"Your attentive kindness, father, merits my warmest gratitude. Who is this person?"

"I will shew him to you; nay more, I will deliver him into your power."

"Indeed!" said Rodolpho; "this is being a friend. And when will you perform your promise?"

"Meet me in the northern cloisters at the hour of midnight."

"At midnight!" said the duca, who began to suspect that some plan was forming against his safety; and the more so, as his fears had been excited by the mysterious information of the unknown monk. "Why is so silent an hour chosen?" continued he; "in the north cloisters too? To whom, father, am I indebted for this information?"

"It is of little consequence," said the monk, slowly moving from the duca; "your fears will unfit you for the part you have to act; my wish to render you an important service has therefore been fruitless."

"Stay, father," said the duca; "excuse the apprehensions you have yourself been the cause of."

"And what apprehensions could I be the occasion of? Had my purposes been of a sanguinary nature, the gloom and retirement of this forest would better have suited my purposes than the northern cloisters at midnight. You interrupted me in my discourse, duca—I was going to add, that it would be necessary you took with you a domestic in whom you could confide. One condition only shall I exact from you, as a return for my solicitude on your account."

"Name it, father," said Rodolpho; "I will conform to your wishes."

"When I entered the monastery of Santa Maria, I was disgusted with the world; I wished to fly from those parts where I had passed my life, to where I should not be known. My own name is hateful to me, as well as my features, which remind me of myself, for I wish to forget what I was, and only to think on what I now am—a poor monk of Santa Maria. The abbot has my eventful tale; it was necessary that he should know to whom he had granted admission into the monastery. You have hitherto been the object of my care and attention; but if ever you demand to see those features, which I myself abhor, that moment you lose a disinterested friend."

"You may depend on my promise that I will not," returned the duca.

"Am I then to expect you tonight, in the north cloisters?"

"Most assuredly," replied Rodolpho.

"Forget not to bring with you an attendant, such as I described."

"I will not fail," returned the duca; and the monk entering another path, soon disappeared from his inquiring view.

Although the duca had promised to be in the cloisters at the time appointed, yet as he returned to the castello, his resolutions began to waver.—"Might it not, after all," thought he, "be only a scheme to entrap me—a plan, perhaps, of this very enemy against whose attempts I am merely warned, to blind me from seeing the danger I am falling into? Yet, certainly, if there had been such a scheme existing, it might, as the monk observed, have been as easily effected in this wood, which is so much more retired than the cloisters of the monastery: this singular affair I will entrust to Lupo, who, if I go, shall accompany me."

Thus resolved, the duca, when he returned to Colredo, ordered the castellain to attend him in his apartments; when, having informed him of the events of the evening, it was resolved that they should attend the appointment well armed, and Lupo provided himself with a horn to alarm the soldiers who watched on the castle walls, in case their assistance should be required.

The midnight hour was now near at hand, and the duca and Lupo, muffled up in their long mantles, which concealed their swords and other weapons of defence, entered the northern cloisters of the monastery.

The waning moon's faint reflections only allowed them to trace the path, and to disclose to their view the nearer objects: beneath the cloisters all was shrouded in darkness, but at the further end a glimmering light directed their course: they concluded that when they were arrived at it, they should see the monk, but were disappointed, for the light proceeded from a small lamp which was fixed before the shrine of a saint, and the place was solitary.

"Surely," said the duca, "it has struck the midnight hour?"

"I do not think it has yet, your excellenza," returned Lupo, "but it cannot be far distant from it."

At that moment the deep sounding clock of the monastery tolled twelve; the echoes reverberating among the cloisters alarmed the duca and his domestic; the place chosen for the meeting was at the farthest extent of the building, and perhaps seldom visited even in the day; the cold gales of night began to sigh amongst the columns that supported one side of the vaulted roof, and chilled the duca, who closely wrapped his mantle around him.

Some distant footsteps were now heard, but so much were they multiplied by the echoes, that the duca and Lupo, imagining that several people were approaching, drew their swords, and silently awaited the event.

A sudden blast extinguishing the before almost-expiring lamp, left them involved in darkness; the footsteps seemed nearer, till at length a light illumined the distant walls of the cloister, and the figure of the monk was shortly after visible.

He seemed surprised at the hostile appearance of the duca and Lupo, for he started and drew back at beholding through the small aperture in his cowl their swords, on which the light of his lamp gleamed.

"This caution, duca, is needless," said he, "against an unarmed monk; your suspicions, too long continued, will hurt you in my opinion; and I believe I need not add, after what I have told you this evening, that the consequences of such a circumstance would be fatal to you."

The duca replied, "Your pardon, father; but implicit confidence is not the result of an acquaintance so short as ours has been; I own I was wrong in my suspicions, and I will from henceforth banish them."

"The failings of human nature are many," returned the monk: "would that like you I had been of a suspicious disposition! I had now been happy; but, credulous and compassionate, I became the tool of others: all these are failings, though of opposite natures, when carried to extremes; the suspicious infect others, making them deaf to compassion—blind to the calamities as well as to the virtues, good deeds, and good intentions of those who would be their friends, while the too credulous and compassionate teach mankind that foul crime, hypocrisy, in order to excite their feelings and attention, and thereby to obtain their ends. Hard and difficult is it to form a medium by which to regulate our conduct; but you, duca, I trust, will, at least with respect to me, divest yourself of suspicion: consider for a moment, what end could it answer to one detached from the world, whom no ambitious motives of self aggrandizement can await, to deceive or lead you into any error?"

"Your words," replied the duca, "carry conviction with them; I am satisfied; you shall not have cause again of complaint."

"You must now," said the monk, "accompany me to the altar, for though I have promised to deliver your most bitter, and, sorry am I to say, duca, your much-wronged enemy into your power, yet, without the most solemn assurances of his personal safety, I will proceed no further: as far as the detention of his person, which will answer every end, and insure your safety, I will allow you free permission to act as you may conclude best; but as my motives are for your good, the crime of blood shall not sully even your thoughts. What is your answer—will you accompany me to the chapel? or are you so fearful of your passions, that you waver between the giving of a solemn promise, and the eternal horrors of breaking it?"

"No," replied the duca, "as long as you make no restrictions respecting the detention of the person who, it appears, you are so well convinced is my bitter enemy, I will make you that solemn promise which will enable you to pursue your good intentions for my security, without the interruption of a moment's reflection on yourself for what you have done on my account."

"Recollect," said the monk, "that in our way to the chapel we must pass through part of the monastery; it will therefore be necessary that you keep a strict silence."

Saying this, he slowly turned round, and the duca and Lupo following him, they proceeded nearly the whole length of the cloisters, when the monk, opening a small portal, entered a long narrow passage, which apparently was seldom used, for the walls were green and damp; at the extremity of this, another door opened to a large corridor, on each side of which were many portals, which the duca concluded belonged to the chambers of the fathers, for here the monk softly trod, and the duca and Lupo followed his example, till they entered the chapel, when the monk, who was some paces before them, stopped and motioned his followers to retire behind a long row of columns, between whose spaces some lofty tombs afforded a secure recess for concealment.

"When I looked towards the altar," said the monk, in a low voice, "I beheld one of the brethren deeply engaged in prayer; we must therefore wait here till he retires."

The clock of the monastery had some time announced the first hour of morn before the father had concluded his midnight orisons: the monk watched him till he left the chapel, and when he, accompanied by the duca and Lupo, had reached the altar, he thus addressed Rodolpho:—

"You may now make that solemn promise respecting the person whom I shall put in your power. Swear then, that as you hope for Heaven's mercy, no circumstance whatever shall induce you to take away his life, either directly or indirectly; and that the most horrible curses, continually increasing, may be your portion, both here and hereafter, if you should break this solemn covenant."

The duca and his attendant took the oath, and they left the altar; but before they had got out of the chapel, the clock struck two—the monk stopped.

"It is now," said he, "too late; in another hour my presence will be required; we must defer this important affair till the next night."

The duca, whose curiosity, as well as desire to have his enemy in his power, was roused to the greatest extent, was vexed at the delay.

"Is there not time enough, father, for your purpose? Consider what bad consequences may be the result of putting off for a day my security."

"You may depend," replied the monk, "that nothing shall happen during that time—I will watch over your safety; be in the cloisters to-morrow night at the same hour—I will be punctual."

While he was saying this, he set down the lamp, and drew

back the bolts of the outer portals of the chapel through which the duca and his attendant passed, and entered on the road leading to the castello de Colredo.

The events of that evening crowding thickly on his recollection, deprived the duca of repose. The same question he so often put to himself still remained unanswered, which was, who the person could be that had fostered such bitter designs against him? At times he conjectured that it was the young marchese de Montalto; but that, however, he did not, on reflection, think probable, and the promise of the monk to put his enemy in his power made him certain that it could not be him. He arose with the dawn, and impatient for the return of the appointed time, its approach seemed every hour more distant.

When at length it came, with all its train of gloomy shades, and night had resumed her sable empire over the silent hemisphere, the duca, with his trusty attendant, again repaired to the cloisters, where they found the monk waiting their arrival.

He did not speak, but slightly bent his head as the duca approached him, and immediately crossing an ancient courtyard, directed his steps to a solitary tower which stood at its farthest extremity. The portal was only secured by a latch, which he directed Lupo to raise, and the party then entered a ruined chamber; the casements were broken, and in some parts the mantling ivy filled the spaces where once the tinted panes had glittered in the beams of the sun.

"In the next apartment, to which that door leads," said the monk, "is a concealed entrance to a subterraneous passage; it is there we must descend, for there the object of our search resides."

Lupo having opened the portal, the monk shewed him a trap-door, which was so artfully contrived as not to be perceptible to a common observer; when this was raised, a flight of stone steps appeared, down which the party descended; they led to a long passage, which was apparently formed out of the solid rock, for at different parts were placed large misshapen pillars to support the roof.

At the extremity of this passage, the monk pointed to a door, and in a low tone said—"In that place is your enemy; perhaps he now slumbers—enter softly, and surprise him."

The monk now shrouded his lamp with his long garments, and Lupo having opened the door, listened, when both he and the duca distinctly heard the breath of some person who appeared to be asleep.

Both drew their swords and entered the chamber; the monk in the meantime advanced to the door, and permitted a ray of light to fall on the countenance of the slumberer, when recognizing his features, he started and drew back; Lupo, as terrified as the duca, hastily followed his master out of the chamber, whose countenance, as he leaned for support against the wall, shewed the horrible sensations that tortured his bosom.

All this time the monk, who seemed deeply involved in ruminations, took no notice of the agitation of the duca, who, scarcely breathing, directed his steadfast gaze to the interior of the chamber; the slumberer, however, had not been disturbed.

"You seem surprised," at length said the monk. "I expected it—it is no air-formed vision you have beheld; by what miraculous chance he still exists, I know not. You have every reason to think that his concealing himself here is to carry into effect his schemes of revenge. I know that it is so; but you will be guided by your own judgment what course you will now pursue. I have acted the part of a friend, and I am satisfied."

The duca, during the speech of the monk, seemed to have recovered from his agitation, and to be debating with himself what he should do.

"You are right, father," said he, at length; "my astonishment had nearly overcome my senses. A circumstance which some time ago took place is now explained. Lupo, this is no time for vain fears—we must seize him: the runaway shall at last be stopped, if the dungeons of Colredo are strong enough to hold him."

"But how, your excellenza," said Lupo, "shall we convey him there? It is doubtless some distance from hence to the private postern in the wood."

"That need not trouble you much," replied the monk, "for

you are now, duca, in the subterraneous recesses of your own castello."

"Is it possible?" said Rodolpho. "Till now I never knew of this communication with the monastery."

"That knowledge is then confined to two," returned the monk—"myself and your intended prisoner."

"Lend me your lamp, father," said the duca—"Lupo, you enter and secure his arms—what further assistance you may require I will give you."

Alas! their intended victim still slept: perhaps at the moment when his deadliest enemies were slowly stalking towards his lowly couch, fancy, with her gay imagery, was depicting to his mental vision scenes of happiness. He awoke, and found himself in the firm grasp of two men, his arms pinioned, and unable to make any resistance, for by the uncertain light of the lamp he saw the well-known features of Rodolpho and Lupo; yet still, as he imagined his destruction certain, he was resolved not to part with life without some efforts for his deliverance, and seizing an opportunity, disengaged his hand, and felled Lupo to the ground; the duca sprang upon him, and the domestic quickly rising, he was again secured and dragged out of the subterraneous apartment.—When in the passage, his eyes glanced on the figure of the monk: he started, and exclaimed—"Ha! I see my betrayer! the vindictive—But no, I will be silent, for that will be some revenge on the base duca di Rodolpho."

The monk made no reply; he walked forward, and pointing out to Lupo a secret panel, said—"Now, duca, you remember your oath respecting the personal safety of your captive: that opening will bring you into the known passages beneath your castello. I will await here your return."

The duca and Lupo then passed through the concealed entrance, and found themselves in the vaulted corridor beneath the eastern chambers; they then secured their prisoner in one of the dungeons, and returned to the panel.

"Have you had any conversation with your prisoner?" said the monk, in a tone somewhat more hasty and disturbed.

"No, father," said the duca; "he has not spoken since."

"My wish to render you secure against his attempts has at length succeeded," returned the monk.

"It has, father, and my gratitude is boundless for your disinterested kindness. I know not in what way to shew it. I am at present without a confessor; will you give me a further proof of your friendship, and accept of that situation? That will give me an opportunity of frequently conferring with you on various circumstances in which I need the advice of a friend like you."

"My advice you shall always have," returned the monk; "but I must decline the situation you offer, though to be near you would perhaps lighten the load of care and anxiety that weighs me down to the grave's dreary brink: but I must then be exposed to the eye of insolent curiosity; I should, perhaps, be induced to violate a sacred and solemn vow which I have made, never to partake of the pleasures of society, and to eat by myself my scanty meals; I should not then be able to wander for days and nights in the gloomy forest, to meditate on the instability of human happiness—on past joys never more to return—on those glowing anticipations of felicity that once occupied my thoughts, but which now no longer occur, for all my hopes of earthly comfort are for ever blighted."

"If you will consent to reside in the castello, father, I will promise you that you shall pass your time as you wish. Whatever vows you may have made, it will be your own fault if you infringe on them. Your apartment shall be, if you desire it, in the most retired part of the building, from which, through these vaults, you may at all times have egress, without being perceived by any one."

"As long as you continue faithful to your promise, duca, I consent to reside in the castello; but it is only under the hope that there I may have an opportunity of being useful to you: but if you will not allow me to act as I please, I shall in that case again retire to the monastery."

The duca, pleased with having succeeded with the monk, in whom he hoped to find, not only a friend and adviser, but also a confederate in his future schemes, again repeated his promises that the monk should pass his hours agreeably to his vow.

"I am satisfied, duca," replied the monk; "you will hereafter see that you should do so from motives of interest, for in me you will find an adviser who, through mere accident, am intimately acquainted with your most private thoughts, and in particular with the schemes you are now forming concerning the attainment of the principality of Manfroné."

The duca started—"Every word you utter," said he, "increases my astonishment. That idea, which I own I had formed, was known only to Lupo; and he, I am well assured, would never mention it to any one."

"Nor did he," returned the monk, "and yet you see I am privy to that circumstance; and perhaps I may be able to advise you how to obtain that elevated post, but the time is yet too green—the circumstances which will doubtless occur to render it feasible are not yet sufficiently matured."

They had, during this conversation, been returning through the passage that led to the flight of stairs, which as soon as they ascended, the duca, pressing the monk to take his abode as early as possible in the castello, added—"Let me expect you, father, to-morrow."

"I will certainly be with you then," said the monk: "but there is yet one thing which, amongst many others, I wish to undertake myself, and that is, the attendance on your captive. There is no one but your present domestic whom you can put sufficient confidence in, to undertake so important an office."

"Certainly," replied the duca; "I will deliver to you the keys when you come to the castello."

"You will need my lamp to return through the passages, and I can find my way to my cell without its aid. Expect me to-morrow at sunset." This said, the monk closed the trap-door, and retired.

Rodolpho and the castellain passed the remainder of the night in conjecturing who the monk could be:—all their conclusions were, however, unsatisfactory; nor were they likely to obtain the information they so much desired, for the duca was restricted from making any inquiries by the promise he had made the monk to that effect, and he was obliged to be content with what he had partially related were his reasons for monastic seclusion.

The next evening, agreeable to his promise, the monk entered the grand hall of Colredo. The domestics having been apprised of his coming by Lupo, from whom they had been instructed how to act, received him with the greatest attention and respect, and went instantly to the duca, to acquaint him with the arrival of the confessor.

Rodolpho immediately requested his presence in his apartments, and when they were alone, delivered him the key of the dungeon.

"The prisoner, father, has not been visited as yet: will you go now, or wait till it is later?"

"I think you told me, duca, that in the apartment you had ordered for me, there was a communication with the dungeons; let your attendant, Lupo, shew me them, and provide some provisions in a basket. To-morrow I will confer with you at what time you may appoint."

"Use your own discretion, father, in that respect. I will give orders to Lupo to do whatever you may require—he now waits in the corridor."

The monk left the apartment, and as he was slowly pacing the corridor, in expectation of meeting the castellain, Rosalina, who was returning from her evening walk, was at that moment crossing it, in order to reach her apartments, when the unwelcome figure of the monk met her view. She stopped, almost doubting the evidence of her senses, so little did she expect to find the padre Grimaldi in the castello.

The monk bowed as she approached, and seemed as if he meant to address her, but at this moment Lupo making his appearance, he passed on, and Rosalina proceeded to her apartments.

Anxious to know what his business could be at the castello, she called for Carletta, but she was nowhere to be found, and her other attendants could not give her the information she desired.

After she had waited for near two hours, the door of her

chamber suddenly opened, and Carletta, pale and terrified, entered.

Rosalina, alarmed at the agitation of her domestic, repeatedly demanded what had occasioned it; but all the information she could get was Carletta's repeated exclamation of—"Oh, signora! signora! the monk! the monk!"

"What of the monk, Carletta?" demanded Rosalina; "what has he done to alarm you?"

Carletta at length replied—"Oh, signora. I saw him—I saw his face. I never was so frightened in all my life; and he is to be the confessor to the castello—Oh, signora! I never shall be able to confess to him; indeed I shall not."

"Confessor! indeed! has my father chosen that mysterious man to supply the place of the good Augustino?" said Rosalina. "Impossible! it cannot be!"

"Oh yes, indeed it is so," replied Carletta, "and you shall hear all about it.—Just before you went out, signora, I met Pietro. 'Ah, Carletta,' said he, 'have you heard the news?'—"What news?" said I.—'Why, about the confessor that is coming to the castello?'—So I replied, signora, that I had not."

"Well, Carletta," said Rosalina, impatiently, "you need not be so particular in describing your conversation: do, pray, proceed to the circumstance that caused you so much terror."

"I will tell you every thing, signora, but I shall not know where to begin, without I relate the whole."

"Do, then, let me have your wonderful story as quickly as possible, in your own way."

Carletta then proceeded—

"So, signora, when I told Pietro that I had not heard any thing about the confessor, he replied—'Then I will tell you:— you must know that no one knows any thing about him—who he is, or where he came from: we have all strict orders to pay him the greatest respect, but we are never to look at him, for they say he does not like it; and none of the monks, or any one else, have ever seen his face, or scarcely heard him speak. This I heard from the old porter at the monastery.' So, signora, when I found this, I felt curious to see him. "And where will he live?"

said I to Pietro.—'In some of the eastern chambers, I have heard Gulieno say,' he replied. Well, signora, I said nothing to Pietro, but away I went as soon as I heard he had arrived, to the corridor that leads to them, and concealed myself behind some large pillars, where I knew he would not see me. So, soon after I heard somebody coming, and sure enough it was the monk, and Lupo after him, carrying a basket full of something, which I could not see, for it was covered all over with a cloth. But the monk—oh, such a tall great ugly figure, with his cowl all over his face. Oh, signora, I never was so frightened in all my life."

"Indeed!" said Rosalina; "you were then easily alarmed, for I cannot discover the smallest reason you had for your fears."

"Oh, but signora, I have not told you all. Well, as he was passing almost close to the columns, the cowl opened, so that I had a sight of part of his face for a moment, for I had not courage to look at it any longer: and what do you think, signora?—it was all black!—and his eyes—oh! I never saw such eyes in all my life!—so fierce and frightful."

"You could hardly be a judge in the momentary glimpse which you say you had of them," replied Rosalina.

"Oh, signora, but indeed I am almost sure they were as I said; and as to his face, I am certain of that, for I saw it plain enough," replied Carletta. "And when he had passed, I ran as fast as I was able, and never stopped till I came here."

"As you do not seem quite certain about his eyes," said Rosalina, smiling, "I conclude that it was your fears, or the shade of the cowl, that darkened the father's face, and as such I would advise you to think it, and to compose your causeless alarm."

Carletta, however, did not seem to be of the same opinion as her mistress, and retired from the apartment, saying, as she went out, that she was sure his face was black, and she should never think otherwise till she had seen it again.

CHAPTER VIII.

Rosalina, after the departure of Carletta, sat some time ruminating on what she had informed her about Grimaldi. Her astonishment at his being appointed confessor to the castello was great, since it proved to her that he was known to the duca; and her desire to know who he was being greatly increased by that circumstance, she hastened to her cabinet, where lay, as yet unperused, the "History of the Monk." She took it out, and having unfolded it, read the following lines:

"THE HISTORY OF ROMELLINO.

"My hand trembles as I take up the pen, as I anticipate the renewal of my sorrows, while I detail the events of a few past years. Angelica, dost thou behold me from thy bright abode? Do thy beaming eyes gaze on thy Romellino? Perhaps thou art insensate to my woes: happy if so, for it would pain thy tender bosom to know the grief which swells that heart, which when thou didst inhabit this globe, was irrevocably thine—now insensible to love, it is alive only to unutterable grief.

"In the principality of Otranto lived the compte Romellino, my father: brave and generous, every one loved him. His greatest friend was Tancredi, prince of Otranto. When war with its deadly breath convulsed the state, they fought side by side; each would gladly have opposed his bosom to receive the wounds aimed at the other; and when the trumpet's shrill clangour no more was heard, when peace dwelt around, still they were inseparable. Death at last parted them: my father, with his dying breath, bequeathed me to Tancredi's care. I was then at that age when the boy verges to manhood—when the heart, unadulterated with the vices of the world, begins to indulge in the unsophisticated delights of love. Tancredi had a daughter: never did my eyes behold such perfect beauty—such winning gentleness—such attractive charms! Sure if a soul ever animated an angel's form on earth, it was hers. Our love was mutual, and Tancredi beheld it with pleasure.

'Yet a few years,' said the good Tancredi to Angelica and myself, as he placed my hand in that of his lovely daughter—'yet a few years, and Romellino shall be my son. But it is necessary that you should be known to the world: go, my boy; for awhile forget the soft indulgences of love in the rough duty of a soldier. The Turkish confederacy against our states calls forth our youth to repel the fierce invaders: would that I could accompany you to the field! but this arm is now enervated by age; I am but the shade of what I was when, with your valiant father, hand in hand, we reaped the sanguine harvest of the field. Peace now suits Tancredi's feeble years, and soon the hand of death will lull him to repose: but before that happens, I trust I shall see my Angelica thy bride.'

"Thus spoke the parent of my love, and the fire of a warrior kindled in my veins.

'I go, my prince; I burn to shew myself worthy to be called your son, and to be blessed with Angelica. Where glory can be gained I will be foremost; the danger of an undertaking shall be my greatest incitement to perform it.'

'But do not be rash,' said Tancredi, 'do not expose yourself more than your honour, your duty calls, lest I have to regret the loss of the son as well as the father: and who shall protect my Angelica when I am no more?'

"The prince sighed deeply while memory recalled to his mental vision my father, and he left the hall, to indulge in private the rising sorrows of his bosom.

"Angelica was in tears; she covered her lovely face with her lily hands, but the pearly drops of grief rolled from beneath them. I approached her; I knelt before her.—'My Angelica! soul of my existence!' I exclaimed, 'why this grief?'

'Romellino is false,' said the beauteous maid; 'he loves not Angelica; gladly he leaves her to endure the toils and dangers of war. Go, then, ungrateful man, and forget me for ever!'

'Forget you!' I exclaimed. 'Oh, Angelica! rend not my heart by such unkind expressions! In the hour of the battle, it is the thoughts of rendering myself worthy of Angelica that will nerve my arm. My watchword shall be Angelica; the signal for the attack shall be the name of my love. Would the heiress of Otranto be united to one who, when his country was in danger, rushed not to its aid, but shrunk inglorious from the toils of war? Would she not rather see her Romellino returning, honoured with the praises of the multitude, and hailed as the saviour of his country? Oh, how would your bosom beat when you clasped to your heart your warrior, and welcomed him back to your arms! Such a moment would be worth ages of common life.'

'Go, then,' said the weeping maid: 'your glory, Romellino, is far, far dearer to me than life; but when you think of your Angelica in the hour of danger, let not her remembrance nerve your arm to acts of desperation, but make you careful of a life she loves far dearer than her own.'

"I promised to comply; I soothed the lovely fair; I dried up the crystal sorrows of her eyes. We passed the evening in sweet anticipations of future happy days, for we little doubted but that when the war was over, we should be blessed in the possession of each other.

"Soon the war-trumpet was heard; its shrill blast animated each warrior's heart. The fields were deserted to fill the camps; mothers sighed for their sons—wives for their husbands—and children for their fathers. The martial preparations were soon completed, and the galleys were crowded with warriors. The day, the hour was fixed when we were to depart, and I came to bid adieu to Angelica. In spite of all my ardour for the field—in spite of all my wishes to render myself worthy of my love, my heart was distended with grief.

"She saw the settled sadness of my soul, and smiled on me through her fast-falling tears. She took an embroidered belt, from which suspended a costly sword, and placed it by my side. 'Go, my soldier,' said she, in a faltering voice; 'go—be brave, but remember your life is not at your own disposal; be careful of that, that you may bless your Angelica when the dreadful business of war is over.'

"She could not say more; her grief impeded her utterance. Long we held each other in a close embrace, till the last moment arriving, I tore myself away.

"On the beach stood the venerable prince Tancredi; he saw the varying colour in my cheeks, and divining the reason said— 'Do not give way to grief, Romellino: the joys of your meeting will richly repay the pangs of absence. I will endeavour to comfort Angelica. We shall hear from you often—we shall hear that you are acquiring glory and renown, and that will console her.'

"Our banners now wantoned on the bosom of a favouring gale. I embraced my future parent, and hastening on board the admiral's galley, we spread our canvas to the breeze, and soon the loved shores of Italy lessened to the sight.

"As long as they were visible, I kept my gaze fixed on the part where my Angelica dwelt, while deep sighs rose from my bosom; and when at length Italy, diminishing to a speck, was lost in the clouds, still I could not turn away, but kept looking towards the sky-mixed waves.

"Perhaps Angelica, from the towering turrets of her father's castle, had been watching my vessel—had seen the gilded hull sinking, as it were, in the waters, which at length obscured even the tall masts.

"The next morning we descried the enemy. Our hearts beat high for the combat—our bosoms panted for glory—each warrior felt himself an host, and half unsheathed his sword, impatient for the battle. We urged the rowers, who, exerting their whole strength, the ocean foamed before the quick-gliding prows.

"The combat was dreadful. Many a turbaned head lay low, and streams of blood flowed from our decks. Boarded by the Turkish commander on one side, and one of his captains on the other, hemmed in between the two vessels, our situation was desperate. Each moment witnessed the death of our people; but they fell not unrevenged, for twice their number of the Turks groaned out their souls.

"Floreski, the admiral, was furiously attacked by the Turkish leader; but his strength was not equal to that of his fierce antagonist; scarcely at length could he parry his reiterated blows. I saw his danger, and rushed to his aid. Fortune attended my sword—the Turk fell, and his people seeing the death of their leader, retreated to their vessel.

"Enraged at being indebted to me for his life, Floreski sternly demanded why I had dared to interfere? Surprise at such a question, when I expected to have received his thanks, kept me silent. He imputed it to fear, and openly censured my conduct, and intimated, that wishing to acquire at an easy price the thanks of Tancredi and the prize of valour, I had stepped in, and by subduing the nearly vanquished Turk, had basely endeavoured to take from him the glory of the conquest.

"My anger rose at his vile assertions; but it was not a time to seek revenge, for the heat of the battle increased, and the rapacious tyrant Death was sated with the blood of thousands.

"Victory at length smiled on our fleet; the Turks fled, and we pursued. Three days we ploughed the liquid waves; on the fourth our enemies abandoned their vessels, and sought the protection of their own shores, where, strongly entrenching themselves behind their barks, which were drawn up on the beach, they defied our force.

"While they were in this almost impregnable situation, the admiral Floreski, who had hated me from the moment that I had interfered in his behalf, determined to put me in a situation from which it was scarcely possible I could escape with life; and on the fourth night I was ordered with a party, scarce consisting of half the number of the enemy's forces, to land and attack them.

"I saw the malicious intent of this command, as did every one else, and I was repeatedly advised to decline it; but such advice I spurned at, and on the fourth night we steered for the shore.

"The difficulty attending this hazardous undertaking seemed to make my people the more anxious to perform it. We landed, while a small party who were ordered to fire their galleys, having performed that duty, we attacked the astonished Turks by the light of their burning vessels—drove them from their works, and before the morning dawned, the prisoners doubled the number of my party, and the ground was strewed with the bodies of the slain.

"Floreski maddened with vexation when the next morning he saw the banners of Tancredi waving on the dismantled walls of the enemy's works, and heard my courage and good conduct extolled by all around; he landed, and as soon as I saw him on the shore, I determined on having satisfaction for his base conduct. On pretence of consulting him on some subject of importance, I drew him away from his people towards a small wood, where, when we had entered, I thus addressed him:

'Now, Floreski, I can in your face deny your base assertions, and dare you to repeat them at the risk of that life which you owe to my aim.'

"Floreski, disdaining to reply, drew his sword, and suddenly aimed a thrust at my heart. Provoked at his treachery, I rushed on him. In my eagerness to be revenged I left myself unguarded—twice I was wounded: the sight of my blood provoked my anger, and Floreski fell beneath my arm.

"His wounds were, however, not mortal; he was conveyed on board his galley, and soon after returned to Italy.

"No doubt for a time the good Tancredi was afflicted at the reports he raised to my discredit; but truth is mighty, and will prevail. For near a year I was employed in difficult enterprizes in Dalmatia, and in all I was successful. I heard by every opportunity that occurred from my adored Angelica; her letters contained protestations of her love—her anxious fears for my safety—and prayers for my speedy return.

"Before the walls of Scardona I reaped fresh laurels. On that dreadful night when the assault was made, I was the first that entered the breach, and standing on a heap of the enemy who had fallen by my sword, I encouraged my men to perform those acts of desperate valour which gained us the victory.

"It was shortly after this that I heard of the death of the good Tancredi, and that Floreski had succeeded him in the government of Otranto. My affliction at this intelligence was lost in the fears I entertained respecting Angelica, who was now without the protection of a parent, and I determined, the first opportunity that presented itself, to return to Otranto.

"Overtures made for a peace by the Turks afforded me a pretext for an immediate return: but, oh! what horror seized me—what agonies unutterable tortured my frame, when, on entering Tancredi's castle, her weeping domestics informed me that Angelica had been missing for the last two days!

"All my inquiries were fruitless; no intelligence of my heart's adored could be gained. For many months I wandered about in a state almost bordering on madness; night after night have I passed in a small wood near the castle, where, in past happy days, I had often strayed with my Angelica, calling on her loved name, and listening to the echoes which mournfully repeated it.

"My suspicions at length rested on Floreski. Without reflection I repaired to his palazzo, and, in the presence of the nobles, openly taxed him with it. He denied the charge, and taking advantage of my threatening language, sent me to the galleys; and the son of the brave Romellino, the bosom friend of Tancredi, the intended husband of his beauteous daughter, was chained to the oar amongst the vilest and most abandoned of the human species!

"My desire of revenge alone made me endure life in such a horrible situation; I panted for an opportunity to escape, when I intended to have imbrued my sword in the heart's blood of Floreski.

"Near two years had elapsed since the time that Angelica was missed, and still she was unheard of, and I was still a slave; when one day, as the galley I was on board of was conveying some ransomed soldiers from the Algerine coast, I saw one who had fought by my side at the well-recollected night of the taking of Scardona.

"In spite of my miserable appearance, and my haggard woe-worn countenance, the soldier, with an exclamation of aston-ishment, recognized in a galley-slave his former commander;

but he suddenly checked himself, as he was hastening towards me, and withdrew from my sight.

"This circumstance reminded me of the baseness of my situation, when even a common soldier seemed to disdain to be thought to have a knowledge of me. It was too much for me to bear.—Curses, deep and soul-breathed, on Floreski, escaped from me; I gnashed my teeth, and bit my arm so dreadfully, in the emotions of my rage, that the blood poured in a stream from the lacerated limb.

"The loss of the sanguine tide of life somewhat abated the violence of my passion, and I remained in a lethargic state the remainder of that day.

"At night the vessel was anchored near the shore; and while the rest of the miserable wretches in my situation were slumbering after the toils of the day, I lay awake, sadly ruminating on my woes, when I heard some one approach the bench to which I was chained, and softly repeat my name.

'Who is there,' said I, 'that would now claim acquaintance with the wretched Romellino?'

'It is Paolo,' returned the voice.—'Alas, that I should ever see you in this dreadful situation! But I was not surprised, after what I had heard from the princess Angelica."

'Angelica!' said I—'what of her? Say—tell me what you do know of my Angelica?'

'Be comforted, comte,' returned the man, 'or we shall be observed. It was the fear of that circumstance which prevented me speaking to you this morning. I have a tale to tell you.'

'Be quick, then,' I replied; 'for the name of Angelica has roused my utmost expectations!—Tell me, first, where is she?'

'In captivity, near Algiers,' replied Paolo.

'In captivity!' I exclaimed—'my Angelica a slave! exposed to worse than death!—Oh, Heavens! be merciful, and let me die!'

'Rather live,' said the soldier; 'rather live to rescue her, and revenge yourself on your enemies.'

'But how? see these galling ignominious chains—there is no escape from them.'

'Can you swim?' demanded Paolo.

"I replied in the affirmative, and he seemed overjoyed.

'Ever since I saw you,' continued he, 'I have been pondering how I could effect your deliverance; by the greatest good fortune I found out who had the key of your chains, and when he was asleep, I fortunately obtained it: I have now the watch, and if you can swim as far as the shore, I will liberate you; and happy will Paolo be, if he can procure your liberty at the risk of his own.'

"A gleam of comfort now began to illumine my sad thoughts. Paolo freed me from my fetters; I embraced the honest veteran, and, impatient to leave the vessel, I only contented myself with having obtained a trifling knowledge of the situation of Angelica's residence, and cautiously descending the galley's side, I committed myself to the waves, and soon reached the shore in safety.

"I travelled the whole of that night as fast as the feeble state of my body would permit, in order to evade the pursuit that would doubtless be made as soon as it was known I had escaped. In the morning I lay down in the most retired part of an extensive forest, and rested myself till the shades of returning night enveloped the surrounding objects.

"Where I had landed was on a retired desolate part of the Calabrian coast. I had not seen one cottage, nor indeed any signs of inhabitants, and I began to fear that I had only escaped from slavery to perish with famine; still the hope of rescuing my adored Angelica gave me strength to proceed, and in the morning, when I had with excessive difficulty laboured up a steep mountain, I saw afar off a few peasants' huts, and exerting my yet remaining strength, I slowly crawled towards them. They compassionated my miserable situation, and gave me food.

"I remained a short time with them, and having recovered my strength, continued my journey towards the opposite coast, where I hoped I should be able to find some opportunity of crossing the Mediterranean, and reaching Algiers.

"In such an undertaking, which to others would have

appeared the greatest madness, as it was hardly possible but that as soon as I came there, I should be made a slave, I saw no difficulties; it would even have been a mournful consolation to me to be a slave in that country which contained my Angelica.

"From Calabria I crossed over to Sicily, begging a subsistence from day to day from the humble peasantry; such were the painful means by which I contrived to exist. Money I had none; for when I was sentenced to the galleys, my estates and possessions were instantly confiscated, and the vile Floreski enjoyed them.

"After a long day's journey, towards the evening I came to the base of the fiery Etna: I had ascended half way up its steep side, in order to view the country I was going to travel, when, worn with fatigue, I sat down, and soon after fell into a deep sleep. About midnight I was awoke with the dreadful convulsions of the ground on which I lay: I could hardly stand, when a shower of hot ashes had nearly formed my grave. I looked towards the summit of the mountain, which emitted volumes of flame and smoke, and oftentimes with hideous roar large stones were ejected from its fiery mouth, which threatened destruction on all beneath them; I thought that dreadful night would be my last, and I offered up a prayer to heaven for my Angelica.

"The love of life is, for great and wise reasons, deeply implanted in our natures—miserable as I was, I still set a value on my existence: I endeavoured to descend the mountain, and had almost accomplished it, when looking up, I saw a stream of liquid fire precipitately rolling towards the very spot on which I stood.

"Horror-struck with the dreadful death that awaited me, I was unable to move—every moment I expected to be annihilated: in that case my Angelica would have had my last prayers. I besought Heaven to bless and to extricate her from her miserable situation: the torrent approached me, when a gentle rise in the side of the mountain averted its course, and I escaped a death which I thought inevitable.

"Leaving the mountain, I journeyed across the island with

many a weary step, rendered still more fatiguing by the idea that perhaps after all my trouble I should not be able to procure a passage to Algiers: but, alas! I was destined to more miseries, to which those I had endured were light in comparison. Oh, Heavens! when I reflect on the scene that shortly after I beheld, I wonder that my senses ever returned—that I did not dash myself to pieces, and end a miserable existence.

"I was fortunate enough, when I arrived at the coast, to obtain at the price of my labour a passage to Algiers, in a felucca which belonged to some Jews who resided at that place, which it seems they had left by stealth, in order to vend their merchandise in Sicily, a thing prohibited by the dey. I confided to them my desperate undertaking, and it seems that they had seen my Angelica, and told me the name of the Algerine merchant who had purchased her.

"Alas! do I live to write that word—my Angelica *purchased!*—her beauties, no doubt, extolled by the savage wretch who sold her, in order to procure a higher price! Years have rolled away since that period; but at the revived recollection my brain again maddens, and furies possess my senses.

"After a prosperous voyage we landed at Algiers. I had taken the precaution to disguise myself in the garb of a Moor, agreeable to the advice of the Jews, and without delay I proceeded through the city of Algiers, according to the directions they had given me, and about midnight arrived at the residence of Hamet, the name of the merchant who possessed the jewel of my soul.

"Alas! when the morning dawned, and I surveyed the building, I began to despair: it was erected on an island situated in the midst of a lake, and the only communication to it was by means of two boats; these were always kept at the island, and when any of the people who resided there had occasion to go into the country, a Moor always waited in the boat that brought them over till they returned, or if their stay was expected to be long, the boat was taken to the island again.

"The dangers I ran of being discovered were great; the Jews had given me a small sum of money, and with it I purchased provisions, which safety obliged me to procure only at those retired places where I had a chance of escaping if pursued.

"Frequently did I pace the solitary shores of the lake, often directing my eyes towards those walls which enclosed the idol I adored, without being blessed with a sight of her. At length, observing that the Moor who always rowed the boat over would sometimes, while waiting at the shore, land, and amuse himself with walking about till they returned, I formed in my mind a plan to secure it, and which I effected in the following manner.

"Concealing myself in a hedge near the waterside while he was absent, I softly stole to the boat, and contrived to bore a hole in its bottom unperceived; I then retreated to my hiding-place, and shortly after saw it fill with water and sink.

"The Moor did not return for some time, and when he found that the boat was gone, he concluded that some person had crossed the lake to his master's residence in it, and he waited some time, expecting they would bring it back: meantime the persons he had brought over returned, and after repeated signals made by the Moor, the remaining boat was rowed across.

"Their surprise at his account respecting the loss of the boat was excessive; the shores of the lake were searched, but without effect, and they returned to the mansion.

"It was then late in the evening, and when it was sufficiently dark for my purpose, I approached the place where the boat lay, and stripping off my clothes, easily brought it to the surface of the lake; I then threw out the water that was in it, having stopped up the hole I had made, and dressing myself, stepped into it, and paddled myself over to the Moor's haram.

"The darkness of the night favoured my undertaking. I landed unperceived, and surveyed, as well as I was able, the place where my Angelica lived: it was a large palace, situated in the midst of a garden. I loitered about the place as long as I could with safety, and when the crimson tints in the eastern horizon shewed the approach of day, I returned to the boat, and crossing the lake, sunk it in the same manner as before.

"That day I purchased a larger quantity of provision than

usual, and at night returned to the island; I then sunk the boat, and hid myself in the gardens.

"My hope was, that I might perhaps see Angelica, who if she really was in the haram, would doubtless sometimes walk in the gardens. I had secreted myself behind an arbour in an almost impenetrable thicket, where, without the least danger of being discovered, I could see every one who entered the gardens.

"The whole of that day passed, when, towards the evening, two females approached me: trembling with anxious expectation I surveyed them, but neither was the lovely form I sought: they soon retired, and no one appeared after them.

"The next evening I trusted I should be more fortunate: the two females again entered the garden, and shortly after another followed them. How my heart beat against my side! for soon I recognized in her my long-lost, my adored Angelica!

"I could scarcely restrain myself from leaving my place of concealment and making myself known to her: prudence, however, had some influence on me. I observed that she did not join the two females who first came into the garden, but walked with a melancholy air by herself, till at length she entered the walk which led to the arbour behind which I was concealed. I scarcely breathed—I could hear my heart throb. Fortune favoured me, for Angelica, approaching the arbour, seated herself in it.

"The two females were at some distance from me; the present moment seemed propitious, and I ventured, in a soft voice, to repeat her name.

"Angelica started up.—'Who is it that calls me?' she said, in a terrified tone, 'Good Heavens! how like it was to Romellino's voice.'

'It is your Romellino,' I softly said: 'do not be alarmed, Angelica: seat yourself again, or you may attract notice.'

"Angelica, who seemed scarcely conscious of what she did, sunk down almost lifeless on the bench.

'Where are you, Romellino?' said she, in a faltering voice.

"I put back some of the branches which formed the arbour.—'Here,' said I, 'is what remains of your fond, your adoring lover.'

"Angelica shrieked. Alas! my misfortunes and Moorish dress had so altered me, that no traces remained of what once she remembered was Romellino. At her exclamation the females turned round and hastily approached her.

'Angelica,' said I, 'recover your terror, or else my endeavours to release you will be of no avail, and you will cause my being discovered, and certain death will be the consequence.'

"Angelica felt the force of what I said, and when the women came up, made some excuse for her exclamation, and they left her.

"I now asked her if she could not contrive to stay till it was dark in the gardens, as I had no doubt in that case but that we might escape?

'Who are you?' said she: 'the voice is the voice of my Romellino, but the features I recollect not.'

'I have disguised them,' said I, with a deep sigh, 'to prevent my being known; perhaps, too, my grief for the loss of my heart's adored may have brought on a premature old age. But perhaps Angelica does not wish to remember me—perhaps she loves another?'

'Cruel man!' said the weeping fair; 'no hour has passed wherein your image has not appeared to my mental view—no hour has passed in which my tears have not flowed on your account, since that cruel day when we parted.'

'Forgive me, my angel,' said I, 'my harsh language! Happy days may yet await us: the moments now are precious; can you stay here without observation a short time longer?'

'Yes,' said Angelica, 'Harriet's absence will enable me to do so. But how can you contrive to escape from this place, or how could you indeed enter it?'

'You may, perhaps,' said I, 'have heard of the loss of the boat; that was effected by me: no one but yourself knows of my being here; with its assistance we can leave this place, and I trust before this time to-morrow you will be in safety.'

"The approach of the females now interrupted our discourse. I understood little of their language, for they were Moorish women; but I believe they asked her to go in, which, however,

Angelica for the present deferring, they shortly after left
her.

"I did not dare to emerge from my place of concealment till
it was quite dark. In embracing my adored Angelica, I almost
forgot the perilous task I had yet to perform, and which, as my
preparations required some time, I could not set about too soon.

"Having learnt from Angelica where the remaining boat
was, I cautiously advanced to the place, intending to have taken
her away in that, which would add to our security from pursuit,
as Hamet's people could not then leave the island; but to my
mortification I found it was fast chained to the shore, and I was
unable to loosen it; I however found means to sink it, by which
we should gain time, and then repaired to where my boat lay.
Some time elapsed before all was ready, when with Angelica I
left the island.

"I rowed as swiftly as I was able, to the farther end of the
lake, which terminated at the foot of a chain of lofty mountains; amidst the obscure recesses which I doubted not were
among them, I hoped to find a place of concealment for myself
and Angelica till the search that would be made after us had
ceased.

"When we landed, I sunk the boat, lest it should serve as
a direction to our pursuers of the road we had taken, and we
began our journey up the steep side of a hill which it was necessary we should cross before the day broke.

"With Angelica leaning on my arm, I was insensible of
fatigue. The nocturnal lamp with her silver beams illumined
our path, and directed us to avoid the crags and precipices
which else would have menaced us with destruction. When we
stopped to rest, we saw beneath us the lake, whose clear bosom
reflected the beams of the moon, and brightened the distant
walls of Hamet's residence.

"At length we gained the summit of the mountain, and
descending on the other side, the lake and island were soon
obscured from our sight. The crimson streaks of approaching
morning were now visible in the east, and we hastened towards
a forest which thickly shaded the vale below, where we hoped

to conceal ourselves during the approaching day. Soon after we had gained it, the sun threw his broad beams over the world. I now opened before Angelica my small stock of provisions, which fortunately I had brought with me, and of which that loved possessor of my affections thankfully partook.

"As soon as Angelica had recovered from her fatigue, I requested her to inform me by what means she had been brought to the dreadful situation from which I had so happily rescued her, and she related her tale in the following manner:

'Reports, sent by your enemies to your disadvantage, daily reached Otranto, and the good Tancredi sunk beneath the pressure of his cruel disappointment, in the sanguine hopes he had formed respecting you; his health was gone, and he was apparently hastening to the grave. He often gazed on me with tears in his eyes, and would exclaim—"Poor Angelica! when I am gone, what will become of thee? I thought, indeed, my aged eyes would have been blessed by seeing you united to a hero deserving of you; I thought, too, that a son, as well as a daughter, would have watched my sick couch, and when I sunk into the arms of death, you would have closed those sources of my grief: but Romellino is unworthy of Angelica, and all my fond hopes are blighted."

'Such was often the tenor of Tancredi's discourse, till at length the principality resounded your praise. Your conduct and valour, in attacking and destroying, with a handful of men, the whole Turkish fleet, excited universal admiration; but that glorious victory was sullied by the reports of your enemies, who represented your conduct with respect to Floreski in the light of a common assassin, and asserted that you had decoyed him into a wood, and there had basely stabbed him.

'The admiral's return, still suffering from those wounds, confirmed those reports beyond a doubt, and my father, exasperated, would have recalled you from the army; but in this he was opposed by Floreski himself, who, with a generosity that excited admiration, besought him to allow you to continue, extolled your gallant achievements, and publicly forgave your conduct to him. Tancredi, at his request, therefore permitted you to remain. Alas! at that time I had my suspicions that there were some dark plots forming against you, and which, I found after, were, fatally for me, but too well founded.

'Your conduct, my dear Romellino,' continued Angelica, 'in Dalmatia delighted every one. Floreski, who was now recovered of his wounds, would often converse with me about you. The only one of the many invidious reports which were raised against you, and in which I could place any credit, was that of your conduct with respect to him, since not only his wounds, but his forgiveness of the injury, confirmed it. I admired Floreski for the nobleness of his conduct, and I took a pleasure in his society; but that pleasure was resulting from my attachment to you, for you were the dear theme of our conversation. Alas! at that time I knew little of his real designs; I could not penetrate into his motives; deeply versed in hypocrisy, he easily succeeded in gaining my esteem, who, ignorant of the wiles of men, was led by appearances, which, when too late, I found were deceitful.

'The good Tancredi now drew near his end; his lamp of life was nearly exhausted, and the flame now doubtfully hovered round the wick. On the morning of that day in which his soul winged its flight to regions of immortal glory, as I was sitting weeping by the side of his couch, the news arrived of your having taken Scardona; a momentary smile was perceptible on his features, which before were convulsed with pain.

"My dear Angelica," said he, "Romellino is worthy of you: may you be happy together! Tell him that I forgive him all the uneasiness he has caused me, and that had I lived I would have joined his hand with thine. Angelica, farewell!—my moments are numbered. Before the throne of Heaven shall I soon offer up an earnest supplication for your happiness. Angelica, adieu!"

'Such were the last words of Tancredi: covered with years and honours, and lamented by his people, he sunk into the peaceful arms of death. To describe my grief at this event to you, Romellino, who know how much I loved my parent, would be needless; perhaps it would have been alleviated by your presence, but I had no one to pour the healing balm of consolation in my bosom; my grief was also augmented by your being so far away, and the uncertainty there was of my seeing you before the conclusion of the war.

'The admiral Floreski was chosen to succeed my father in the government of Otranto; and soon after I began to develope his real character and designs.

'One evening he came to the palazzo, and to my repeated questions when he thought there might be a probability of your return, he remained silent. Astonished at this, and fearing that you had fallen a victim to your too-desperate valour, I demanded the reason, requesting him to let me know the truth, when, after much solicitation, he at length replied—

"Perhaps, fair Angelica, if I do not candidly declare what I am informed of concerning the comte Romellino, I shall not act as a friend towards you; you know how much I have interested myself towards one who has acted so basely towards me—who has not only endeavoured to rob me of my glory, my renown, the greatest treasure in a soldier's estimation, but sought to deprive me of my life (which indeed, without the other, would be of little or no value): but that I have forgiven; I scorn retaliation; I have endeavoured to wash away the remembrance of those acts, not only from my own mind, but also from the minds of the people, lest they should imbibe any prejudice against him. You will judge from these circumstances how greatly it must pain my feelings when you force me to tell all I know concerning the comte. To Otranto he never will return: fear of my anger, and of being obliged to perform his promise towards you, Angelica, will keep him away; for sorry am I to say that another possesses his affections, and a Turkish lady of high birth, who became his prisoner at Scardona, now holds captive that heart which once was pledged to Angelica."

'Though shocked almost to fainting at this relation, yet pride made me restrain my sorrow before Floreski.—"It is well," said I; "the comte Romellino's conduct has cured me of what affection I might once have entertained for him; he was then a man of honour, one whom I thought would ever have scorned to do a base act; as such I loved him, nor do I blush to own it, for a parent sanctioned such a disposal of my affections; now that he is no longer what he was, I regard him with that contempt which he deserves, as having deviated from the paths of honour, and becoming no longer worthy of my recollection."

'Floreski appeared delighted at my speech.—"Such a resolution," said he, "is worthy the daughter of prince Tancredi: but I fear it was too quickly formed to be permanent; and should the comte return—should he be prevailed on by my assurances of his safety to revisit Otranto, perhaps the princess Angelica would forget her hasty resentment."

"Impossible!" I replied: "were he to arrive this moment, I would not see him; he should be denied admittance at the palace gates, and he might return to his Turkish inamorata without causing one sigh to Angelica."

"May I then," said Floreski, throwing himself at my feet, "presume to hope that time and my unwearied attentions may procure for me that place in Angelica's affections, now vacant by the infidelity of Romellino?"

'I started at his speech, for this sudden declaration of Floreski's made me instantly suspect that what he had just said concerning you might be only to gain his own ends: a gleam of hope entered my breast that it might be so, for I could not bring that heart which had ever been yours to forget you in a moment; I could not think you were capable of such deeds as were attributed to you, yet I own that Floreski told his well-concerted tale in such a plausible manner, that had he not acted as he did so directly after, it might in a short time have obtained implicit belief.

"My heart," said I, "is too deeply afflicted with the severe loss I have sustained, to be capable of admitting another passion; it is indeed vacant, and I trust will ever remain so, for after Romellino's conduct, in whom can I place confidence?"

"Promise me, at least," said Floreski, still retaining his suppliant posture, "that should Romellino return, in spite of what he may urge in his defence of what I have imputed to him, that I shall not have to look on him as the cause of Angelica's denying my suit."

"No," I returned; "I cannot make such a promise, for perhaps you have been deceived respecting the comte's conduct: to give him an opportunity of declaring his innocence would be but just; should he seek it, it will make me conclude that it is the base contrivance of his enemies to injure him still more in your opinion as well as mine; and if he does not, it will be a tacit acknowledgment of his unworthiness."

"But what I have told you," returned Floreski, whose anger I could well perceive was excited by my answer, for he hastily rose from the ground and bit his lips—"what I have told you, when I affirm that it is true, I conclude you will no longer doubt; and lest you should, after what I have advanced, give Romellino an opportunity to cheat you into a belief of his innocence, and, won over by his hollow protestations of affection, consent to a union, I shall consider it as a duty I owe the memory of prince Tancredi to prevent such an opportunity, by banishing the comte Romellino from the principality of Otranto."

"Such a conduct," I returned, "would ill suit with the kind intent you have pretended to take concerning the comte Romellino: a true friend would be happy both in giving him an opportunity to rescue his character from the odium that hangs over it, and in the event of his doing so, to see him united to the object of his affections; but you are actuated from interested motives, and your well-formed tale is, I trust, not founded on truth."

'Floreski's rage at my speech somewhat alarmed me; he stamped on the floor, and seemed unable to give vent to his passion.—"'Tis well," said he; "I recall the pardon of my injuries; I will have revenge, and you may perhaps feel the effects of the insult you have offered me."

'Having said this, he left the apartment, and me to my ruminations. Notwithstanding my anxiety respecting you and myself, I felt happy in thinking that Floreski's assertions had no foundation, and that you had every reason to be as dear to me as ever, for I now was certain the well-contrived story of his wrongs was as false as the rest he had advanced.

'That evening a vessel arrived from the fleet, and by it I had the dear pleasure of hearing from you. Your letters breathed the same expressions of love and constancy; and while I was assured that there was no alteration in your conduct or affection, I execrated the base designing Floreski. I was anxious about you when I found you intended coming to Otranto, for I feared that your life was endangered, and that your bitter enemy would himself commit the crime he had imputed to you, and seek an opportunity to assassinate you, for I little feared his threat of banishment, being well assured that the nobles, who were your friends, would strongly object to such a measure, which might occasion a revolt among the troops who were under your command, whom you had so often led to victory; and if it really had taken place, Angelica had too much love for Romellino to refuse sharing with him whatever hardships fate had destined him to bear.

'Such was my resolution: anxiously did I each day, from the highest turret of the palazzo di Tancredi, gaze on the ocean where the distant waves seemed to join the clouds. Sometimes I imagined that I saw the vessel which contained you—sometimes a distant wave, with its head of foam, I mistook for the white sails of your galley. I watched the clouds to see if the wind was propitious to your voyage; but your coming was delayed, and each hour I grew more unhappy.

'One evening, to dissipate my grief, I walked in that wood where we had often vowed for each other eternal love; I sat down on the same bank which had often witnessed our protestations of the passion which occupied our bosoms; scarcely, however, had I seated myself, when three men, each wearing a mask, rushed from a thicket, and before I could cry for assistance, one prevented my speech by putting his hand before my mouth, while another held me: after some deliberation they carried me to a carriage, which was waiting in the wood, and I heard the voice of Floreski, directing the men to convey me to the beach.'

'And was it then,' said I, interrupting Angelica, 'the base Floreski through whose accursed arts you became a captive slave to a Moor? Oh, may Heaven blast him with its deadliest fires! But no—may I at least revenge myself on him! that will be some consolation, some retaliation for our wrongs.'

"Angelica continued—'When I had arrived at the seaside, it was nearly dark: I looked around me, but no mortal was near whom I could implore for assistance; I was put into a small vessel, which instantly proceeded on its destination.

'We had not, however, proceeded far on our voyage before we were overtaken by a storm, and which the next morning increased to an alarming height: the black billows threatened each moment to overwhelm us; the raging gusts of wind had torn to pieces all our sails; the water entered the vessel, and we expected every moment would be our last, when a large galley, seeing our dangerous situation, ventured near us, and scarcely had we got into her, when the vessel we had been in was swallowed up by the merciless waves.

'I now thought the moment of deliverance was at hand; and I determined, as soon as the galley was in sight of land, to make the commander of her acquainted with my situation, and entreat he would carry me to some part of the coast where I should be out of the power of Floreski till you arrived to protect me: but, alas! fate destined otherwise: the storm drove the galley far from the land, and when at length it abated, and the mists that had obscured the view were dispersed, terror-struck, we discovered at no great distance from us an Algerine corsair. To escape this formidable enemy, and a fate which to me was far worse than death, every exertion was made use of by the crew and some soldiers who were on board, but to little purpose; the corsair gained fast on us, and our people prepared to defend their vessel, as the only means averting the horrors of slavery.

'The combat was dreadful:—the cries of the wounded—the groans of the dying—the shouts of the men as they animated each other during the action—the sight of the miserable wretches who lay on the decks in the last agonies of death—altogether was more than my senses could bear: I sunk lifeless on the deck. When I recovered, I found myself in the rough grasp of a Moor. I immediately conjectured what my situation was, and rent the air with my screams.—Alas! they were of little avail, and I was conveyed with the rest of the galley's crew who yet remained alive, on board of the Algerine, who immediately proceeded for Algiers, having suffered considerably in the action.

'As none of the Moors could make themselves understood by me, they suffered one of the soldiers to attend me, who knowing something of their language, was my interpreter. To this man I disclosed the perfidy of Floreski, and conjured him, if ever he should escape, to seek you, and make you acquainted with the author of my misery.

'Oh, Romellino, what were my sensations when I landed at Algiers, and was exposed to sale!—do I live to mention it?—the daughter of prince Tancredi bartered for!—Hamet was my purchaser, and immediately conveyed me to his residence. For many months I laid in a state so nearly similar to one deprived of life, that they often thought I was no more. Hamet had every care taken of me that was possible, and at length my constitution triumphed over my miseries, which I hoped would soon destroy me, and I began slowly to recover. Hamet's treatment of me was such as I little expected to find from a Moor: never once was his language such as could offend the most delicate ears: he seemed to respect my misfortunes, and execrated the conduct of Floreski; and I once thought that he would have liberated me, on condition of my paying a large sum of money, but of late he has been silent on that subject, and his conversation to me has been of love: he offered to dismiss all the women he kept, if I would listen to his addresses. Latterly he has appeared irritated at my constant refusals, and heaven knows what would have been the consequences, if Romellino had not come to my aid, for the daughter of Tancredi would sooner have perished than have suffered the smallest indignity.'

"Such was the relation of Angelica, and which I often interrupted with execrations on the villain Floreski, the cause of such misery to us both.

'The time will come, lovely Angelica,' said I, 'when we shall be revenged of that monster; at present we must turn our thoughts to our situation, which is replete with danger;

but heaven, who aids the virtuous, will doubtless prosper our undertakings.'

"The sun had sunk behind the western mountains before Angelica had concluded her narrative, and we now commenced our uncertain course; anxious only, for the present, to increase our distance from Hamet's residence, we continued advancing through the forest, and when we had emerged from it, by the light of the moon we beheld before us a long chain of mountains, whose rugged sides were brightened by her rays.

"A thousand cares possessed my soul for my Angelica, when around us we listened appalled to the roaring of the savage beasts. I had no means of defence, for to have carried any arms, I well knew would excite suspicion, and therefore we should have become an easy prey if we had been attacked.

"Long before the morning, Angelica, too weary to proceed, sat down beneath a tree, and, whilst I watched, resigned herself to a short repose. Ah! what happiness I then had in viewing her beauteous face! Her fatigue had stolen the roses from her cheeks, but her lips still retained their lovely bloom. Little did I then think on what would soon follow—that those beauteous, those resistless charms—But I will proceed.

"Angelica was refreshed by her slumbers, and partook of the remainder of the provisions I had brought with me. A new and dreadful anxiety pervaded my mind, for as the rising sun dispersed the mists of night, I looked around me, but nowhere could I discover any signs of human habitation, where we could procure a fresh supply. Angelica pressed me to eat; but I refused, alleging that I had already taken some while she slept, for I was fearful that we should not meet with any village or hut that day, and, if so, there would not remain any for Angelica: fortunately, not far from us was a stream, where I slaked my thirst, and the sweet companion of my toils did the same, and we again set forward.

"In these deserted places we had little fear of pursuit, and we determined to proceed as far as we were able that day, in the hopes of finding a shelter for the night in some hut. Vain hope! for as often, disconsolate, on the summit of some mountain, we cast our eyes on the valleys below, no sign of human habitation met our longing anxious gaze. A silence like that of the grave seemed to reign over the hills and vales: no distant watchdog, no lowing herds or bleating flocks, gladdened our ears; but a continued range of mountains appeared around us, whose summits closed in the horizon.

"This day Angelica was often obliged to stop and rest, for her tender frame was unable to bear the dreadful fatigues she was forced to undergo. I did all I could to cheer her, but her spirits were gone. Still a small portion of the provision was left; I offered it to her; she ate a little, and entreated me to take the rest, which I promised to do while I ascended an eminence which lay before us, to see, before the night closed in, if there were any hopes of succour.

"Deeply did I sigh as I gazed on the dreary prospect around me: a valley lay at the bottom of the hill I was standing on, along which ran a stream of water; I anxiously examined the banks where it appeared likely the peasant might have chosen to fix his residence; but still I was far distant from the busy haunts of men: that stream presented an obstacle not easy to be overcome, for as to cross it with Angelica was impossible, it remained for me to judge which way it would be best to direct our steps when we had reached its banks. As the river widened to the right, I resolved to proceed in that direction the next morning, and then hastily advanced to Angelica, who was resting her exhausted frame on a small hillock.

"She raised her languid eyes as she saw me coming; but, alas! I had no pleasing intelligence to sooth her agitated mind. I began to suffer myself from the want of rest and food, and felt that I should scarcely be able to travel the next day: the scanty morsel of food that remained I treasured up for Angelica for the next morning; that dear angel anxiously demanded if I had ate it, which question I continued to evade, and entreated her to endeavour to sleep. She rested her lovely head on the side of the bank, and I watched for a short time over her, but at length, worn out with fatigue, I closed my eyes, and for awhile forgot my miseries. When I awoke, I found Angelica sitting by my side: the moon was hid in clouds, and the morning was fast approaching. Ah, how bitter were my waking thoughts!—no hope, no comfort, was near!—mournfully I arose, and my adored Angelica leaning on my arm, with many a weary step we gained the banks of the stream. It was here I entreated her to take the last of our provision.—'No, dear Romellino,' she replied, in feeble accents, 'I do not need it; here is my last resting-place on earth—I shall never proceed farther.'

'My adored angel,' I replied, 'do not rend the soul of your Romellino!—Savage wretch that I was, to take you away to perish amongst these mountains!'

'Do you love me?' said the dear maid; 'and is it possible you can regret taking me from the abode of infamy, where it is likely before this I should have been my own executioner? Sweet will now be my last moments, for Romellino will close my eyes.'

"O God! what were my sensations when I saw the once beauteous eyes of Angelica, now robbed of that lively expression they once possessed! Pain sat upon her brow—her lips were pale—her cheeks sallow, and her whole appearance indicating the truth of her speech. I knelt; I entreated, with tears fast flowing from my sorrowful eyes, that she would take the remnant of provision.

'What purpose, dear Romellino,' she replied, 'would it answer for me to eat? Would it not be protracting my moments of anguish for no use? for if I did take it, I should not have strength to proceed further, and perhaps too might then have the agony of seeing you depart before me. No, loved of my soul, eat it; it will give you strength to perform the last sad rites to your adoring Angelica; and when I am laid in my humble grave, let my soul be wafted to heaven on the tender sigh to my memory, which will depart thy quivering lips before the moment of thy dissolution arrives.'

"What agonies seized me! The powers of description are feeble to give an idea of what I felt, when I beheld Angelica lying almost motionless on the earth, her strength every moment decreasing, and she evidently striving to conceal the pangs of death, lest she should add to my griefs.

'Adieu, Romellino,' she with difficulty uttered, after a long afflicting silence; 'let us bid each other adieu in this world: it is but a few pangs, and our souls, divested of those earthly trappings, will again meet, never more to part. Death now hovers over me, eager for his prey: my love, stay not long behind me, for my felicity will not be complete without you.—Once more adieu!'

"Angelica, groaning, sunk from my bosom, on which I had rested her head, and all that remained of that once lovely maid, adorned with every external and mental accomplishment which adds dignity and grace to human nature, was now a lifeless pallid corpse.

'Fair angel,' said I, 'soon I trust we shall meet again; the pains of death would be sweet in comparison to what I now endure; may they be hasty in their approach! Thy sweet remains shall be entombed by my hands—I will form thy grave, and strew it with the simple flowers of the field.'

"With trembling hands I raised the earth, and gently laid her pale form in the shallow grave. I was astonished at myself; no tears came from my eyes—my brains appeared convulsed. When I had completed my mournful occupation, I stood in speechless agony. Long I surveyed her pallid features, when the name of Floreski suddenly came to my tortured remembrance.

'Infernal villain!' I hoarsely exclaimed, 'may my curses wither thy vile carcase!—This is thy doing—thou art the cause of that angel's death—of my misery!—Eternal tortures be thy lot;—When I die, my last breath shall curse thee. Die, did I say? and Floreski live? No, I will away; I will traverse the globe—hunt him to the verge of the world—revenge shall be mine!—I will mangle his limbs, and tear his heart in pieces!—Furies of hell seize on my senses—make me able to commit the most horrible acts to torture Floreski!—His dying pangs will be comfort to my soul, and it will then contented quit the world.'

"My recollection extends no further, for my senses forsook me: where I went, or what I did for two years I know not; but about the end of that time I awoke, as if from a sleep, in which I thought I had been dreaming of a scene similar to that I have now related. I was in a dark place, my feet and hands encircled with heavy chains, and my body fastened in a similar manner to a wall. I groaned aloud—'In what place am I? Ah, good Heavens! was it then a dream? Pray Heaven it is! for I thought I was but this moment standing by the grave of Angelica, and imprecating curses on Floreski; but now that I am awake, I find myself a prisoner, more strongly bound than would be the most outrageous maniac.'

"The sounds of my voice echoed through my dreary abode, and shortly after a door opened, and a man entered with a lamp. As soon as I beheld his features, I instantly recognized one of the Jews in whose felucca I had sailed from Sicily to Algiers.

'Is it true,' said he; 'did I not hear you speak?'

'Why that question?' I returned.—'For what purpose am I confined here? Is it not sufficient that I have lost my heart's delight, my lovely Angelica?—that the grave will for ever hide her beauteous form from my sight? But perhaps I am speaking to one of Floreski's agents. Yes, it must be so; this is his damned deed. But why does he not put me out of my torture, and complete his villanies?'

'I am glad,' returned the man, 'to hear you talk so rationally; I trust your senses are returning, for it is now near seven months since you were confined here, during which time no other words have you ever uttered than the names of Angelica and Floreski.'

'Couple not that saint with that demon of darkness,' I replied. 'Seven months, do you say? Is it seven months since Angelica perished?'

'It must, as I conclude,' returned the man, 'be nearer two years since we first heard that a person, whom we concluded by the description to be you, was wandering about the mountains. You lived on the grass, bark of trees, and what animals you could catch.—Twice you crossed the lake to Hamet's residence, and twice escaped their endeavours to seize you. We were fearful lest through you our voyage to Sicily might be discovered, and, after a great deal of trouble, found you busily employed in tearing to pieces a young kid, calling it Floreski. Fearful of coming near you, we watched till you had concluded your horrid repast, when you lay down and fell asleep; we then cautiously advanced, and before you were sensible of what we were doing, secured, and with great trouble brought you privately to Algiers, and then concealed you in this subterraneous place, which is beneath our residence.'

"Such was the relation of the Jew, and which my lacerated form confirmed. I trembled as I viewed the large scars which appeared all over my body, my limbs shrunken and hardly covered with skin—'And this,' I said, 'is all Floreski's doing: does not this cry loudly for revenge? Alas! before this the mortal remains of Angelica are mouldered away—gone for ever! never will her beauties again glad my sight!'

"My feelings were excited by these reflections, and for a long time I shed bitter tears. The man, leaving his lamp with me, went in the interim to call his companions, who entered and beheld my grief. I found myself greatly relieved by the flood of sorrow, and answered all their frequent questions with that propriety which made them conclude that I was no longer deranged; but when I entreated them to liberate me, they were fearful of my complaint returning, and requested that I would not deem it a useless precaution if I remained as I was a few days longer. To this I assented with a degree of willingness which made them the more ready to believe me entirely recovered: and in order to make my situation somewhat bearable, brought me clothes and provisions, liberated my hands and feet, leaving the chain only which confined me to the wall. In this state I continued for four days, during which time they repeatedly visited and conversed with me; and at length, convinced there was no danger, set me at liberty; and as I was urgent with them to procure me the means of leaving Algiers for Italy, glad, no doubt, to be rid of such an incumbrance, they provided a passage to Calabria; and having furnished me with money, which I promised to return as soon as I had reached Otranto, I set out, gloomy and wholly intent on the revenge which I was determined to take of Floreski; and fearful of being disappointed, as soon as I landed, I travelled with the greatest circumspection, lest he should have any intimation of my arrival: such a precaution was, however, needless, for misery had so completely disguised me, that my features were unknown even to myself.

'At length I entered the principality of Otranto, where I learnt that Floreski still held the reins of government, but that, being the object of universal detestation, a revolt was every hour expected. He had in the first instance incurred the people's hatred by his conduct with respect to me, and after that by repeated acts of cruelty and oppression. This intelligence hastened my arrival at Otranto, and lurking about his residence, I soon learnt when it was likely I could surprise him.

"It was his usual custom to repose during the heat of the day in a pavilion which was erected in the gardens of his palazzo, and that was the place I determined should witness my just revenge.

"With great risk of being observed, I at length contrived to effect an entrance into the gardens, where, concealing myself near the pavilion, I awaited the coming of Floreski.

"At length I saw him approach—Oh, how my blood boiled in my veins! I could hardly prevent myself from springing on him before he had reached the pavilion; but as in that case he might have escaped, I waited impatiently till I concluded he was asleep, when with cautious steps I entered the building, and approached the costly couch on which reposed my intended victim. I could hardly speak, so great was my agitation when I had a sight of his features as I stood beside him; at length I exclaimed—'Floreski, awake!'

"He started up, and was going to call his guards, but I prevented him by placing a dagger to his throat.—'Dost thou recollect me?' I with difficulty demanded.

'No,' said he, trembling and looking at me; 'I never saw you before.'

'Villain, thou liest! Look at me again, and recall to thy remembrance what comte Romellino once was, and behold what he is now.'

"Floreski grew deadly pale as I declared myself.

'Angelica,' I continued, 'is dead; she died in my arms; these hands formed her grave, and these hands,' I exclaimed, while furious rage nerved each joint, 'shall sacrifice thee to appease her wrongs and my own.'

"Thus having said, I cast aside the dagger, which would have been too sudden an instrument of destruction, and seizing him in my strong grasp, I dashed him on the floor, tore him almost to pieces, and glutted my eyes with the sight of his limbs yet quivering with life.

"I then became calm; my vengeance was now sated; I left the gardens, and proceeded immediately to the residence of the noble whom I had understood was likely to succeed Floreski as soon as he was deposed, and making myself known, avowed to him the deed.

"Scarcely could he credit my relation, for he had not the smallest recollection of me: but soon the death of Floreski was known, and I was embraced as the deliverer of the people; my estates were returned to me, and I was offered a post of high importance in the state.

"But my mind was too miserable to allow me to think of life with any degree of comfort: Angelica dead, I was dead to happiness. I sought out the soldier to whom I was indebted for my deliverance from the galley, and amply recompensed him for that service. I then left Otranto, with a resolution of never again visiting a place which recalled to my remembrance those days when I was happy, and which only added to my present sorrow—to seclude myself in some remote monastery, where the tale of my woes was unknown, and where I determined that I never might be recognized by any one, and never again hear the name of Romellino—to hide my features from view, to live by myself, to dedicate my thoughts to Heaven, and await with patient resignation my dissolution, when I hope to be united to my Angelica in regions of eternal joys."

Such was the conclusion of Romellino's misfortunes; and Rosalina, when she had perused them, sighed deeply at the relation; many parts of it indeed had so much affected her feeling heart as to excite tears. She thought she could now account for the peculiarity of his conduct, as resulting from the many calamities he had undergone. But that the duca should make choice of such a man for a confessor, or that he indeed would accept of such an office, appeared to her a perfect mystery.

Fatigued with the perusal of the papers, and anxious to dissipate the melancholy ruminations they excited, she retired to her couch, where sleep soon lulled her senses to repose.

The next morning she heard from Carletta, that Grimaldi resided in those chambers in the eastern wing of the castello where her father had confined her, in order to force her to a marriage with the prince di Manfroné.

She could not help smiling at the miraculous tales of her domestic, who related to her many wonderful stories concerning the monk, knowing how void they were of truth; but the servants had repeated them to each other so often, that at last they were persuaded that the weak chimeras of their own brains were facts that really had occurred.

She was anxious to see Montalto, to inform him of Grimaldi's being appointed confessor to the castello, since she had in a former conversation related to him the singular conduct of the father, and she determined to go to their usual place of meeting, namely, the chapel of Santa Maria, the next evening.

The narrative of Romellino she immediately sent with many thanks to the venerable abbot, as from what he had said, and was expressed in the latter pages, she did not think herself justified in detaining it after she had perused it.

That her father either knew the monk, or had some private reason for his actions, she could no longer doubt, when she heard the singular stipulations he made (and which were now no secret in the castello), of living so retired and apart from those whom it was his business to instruct.

She pitied Romellino's sufferings from the cruel perfidy of Floreski, but shuddered at the dreadful revenge he took of his inveterate enemy, which she thought ill agreed with his pious intentions of devoting himself to religion; for the heart which aspires to the service of Heaven must be free from all worldly passions—must be endued with charity, benevolence, and philanthropy; but she feared that the monk had not yet forgot the pleasure he seemed to reap from his horrible revenge, which she thought she should recollect whenever she saw him, and which could not fail to inspire her with unpleasant sensations, for whenever he raised his hands to heaven, her fancy would depict them stained with the blood of Floreski, and him exulting with savage delight over his mangled form.

When, however, Rosalina further considered her father's conduct in offering him a residence in the castello, and the solitary way in which he was to pass his hours, she was certain it was not his intention that he should officiate in the religious duties daily performed in the chapel of the castello; and in this idea she was confirmed by the attendance of the father who had officiated there since the death of the lamented Augustino: time, however, she trusted, would unfold the duca's designs, and the incomprehensible motives of Grimaldi in being so particular in his conduct towards her.

CHAPTER IX.

The marchese di Montalto had been unwearied in his endeavours to procure an interview with the mysterious monk, whose words and actions had so greatly astonished him, and led him to suspect that he was privy to the death of his father: but all his solicitude was in vain, for he never could meet with him. He frequently inquired among the monks for a person of his description, but from none of them could gain any information. Grimaldi had been pointed out to him as the only one who seemed likely to be the person he sought, and whose singular conduct made it a matter of probability; but Montalto, at the first glance, was well assured that it could not be him, from the difference of his height and figure, though, like him, the other monk had concealed his features.

He had frequently seen his adored Rosalina, and had as frequently lamented with her the impossibility of his visiting at the castello till the mystery of his father's death was unveiled,

because all his suspicions, from many concurring circumstances, centered entirely on the duca; he freely forgave the
wrongs he had received from him, which, however, only served
to strengthen his suspicions almost to conviction, that the duca
was not entirely innocent, and that the consciousness of guilt
had made him act as he did on hearing that he suspected him.
Still, however, before he took any further steps, he was determined to be well assured that his ideas were well founded.

It was on the evening after the monk Grimaldi had taken
his abode at the castello, that Montalto, according to his
usual custom, was pacing the long-drawn aisles of the chapel
of Santa Maria, his thoughts intently fixed on what he had
collected concerning his father's death, and all the meaning
sentences which the monk had uttered, and scarcely conscious
of his actions, he stopped opposite to a tomb which bore marks
of great antiquity, and was perhaps coeval with the building
itself: on it the sculptor had rudely endeavoured to portray a
youth kneeling before an altar, clasping an urn; the inscription,
which had been designed to convey the meaning of the above
to posterity, had been effaced by time: while Montalto was
gazing at it, though perhaps, unconscious of what he was doing,
it formed no part of his thoughts, he was suddenly disturbed by
a deep voice uttering the following words:

"The monument, marchese, which seems to occupy your
attention, was erected by a pious son to the memory of a murdered father."

Montalto started, and turning round, saw by his side the tall
figure of the monk Grimaldi; the words "a murdered father!"
hollowly vibrated on his soul.

"What father was murdered?" said he, hastily. "Was it certain
he was murdered?"

"Yes, signor, too certain; and when his son received intimation of it——"

"But how was he assured that the information was right?"
said Montalto, interrupting the discourse of Grimaldi, his
thoughts at that moment wandering on the words of the mysterious monk.

"It was proved beyond a doubt—the body of his father——"

"Was never found," again uttered Montalto, still thinking of his own parent.

"You know the tale then, signor?" said Grimaldi.

"What tale?" returned Montalto, who now awoke from his ruminations.

"The history that is related concerning that tomb."

"Your pardon, father, I do not; I was at that moment so deeply involved in thought, that I did not attend to what you were saying."

"And yet your answers were somewhat pertinent to the subject I was mentioning," said Grimaldi.

"Perhaps they might, father; yet now I remember you were talking about a murder."

"And you, signor, doubtless were thinking about one."

"What should make you suppose that?" said Montalto.

"From your answers—nothing else," returned the monk: "but perhaps I am intruding upon your meditations—if so, I will withdraw."

"Pray stay, father," said Montalto; "from your behaviour I should indeed almost conclude that you knew the subject that occupied my thoughts; but that is hardly possible; you mentioned something concerning that monument?"

"I did," said Grimaldi: "from its antiquity you will easily conclude that the tale attached to it is traditional. It is, as I am informed, the first monument that was erected in the chapel; as long as the inscription was visible, it recorded a most horrible murder, and when that failed, memory has still retained the tale.

"A signor and his son, travelling this way, were attacked by banditti; after an obstinate resistance, the signor, mortally wounded, fell, and his son long fought over the body of his expiring parent, till at length he was also overpowered, and both were left for dead. In this situation the bodies were discovered by a monk of this monastery, who, finding in that of the son some faint remains of life, had it conveyed to his cell, and his humanity was repaid by his recovery. Deeply did that son lament the loss of his parent; but he did not consume the time in inactive regret, for at the altar he solemnly swore to revenge his death; and having raised that monument to his memory, in which he is represented embracing the urn that contained the remains of his father, and offering up the vow, he set out, and having found out the haunts of the banditti, in a short time totally exterminated them, and then returned to this monastery, and having taken the vows, passed his life near the place which contained the ashes of his parent.

"What a noble example," continued the monk, "of filial piety—a virtue now almost dormant! A son hardly dreams of revenging his parent's wrongs: a father who fondly watched over the infantine years of his offspring, who looked on him as a blessing—a comfort to his declining age—a protection when his frame, degenerating to second childhood, needed it, now anticipates in vain the fancied harvest of his anxious cares; and he is condemned to 'feel how sharper than a serpent's tooth it is to have a thankless child.' Nay, there are even instances where murder has been committed, and where the son has loved the offspring of the vile assassin."

The feelings of Montalto, during the whole of the monk's discourse, had been greatly acted upon; but when he uttered the latter part, his pallid countenance shewed how greatly he was agitated, and he exclaimed—"Ah! your words are no longer riddles! I understand you, monk: you know, then, that Rodolpho has murdered my father."

"What," said the monk, "do I hear? what words are those which have escaped you? From what parts of my conversation could you conclude that I attached any crime to the duca di Rodolpho? It is as yet a mystery to me; but should it be so, can it be possible that the marchese Montalto, so famed for valour, benevolence, and philanthropy, can forget that he was a son—can lack that feeling which ought to be imbibed with his earliest sustenance? Alas! of what little avail are those virtues! they must be nominal—mere sounds, for filial piety is the basis, the sure foundation of all others."

"Monk, you torture me! you want to stretch my agonized feelings beyond their bearing, and then to smile over a being divested of reason by your insinuations—by your slow well-framed discourse. Tell me at once, while I have breath—while I am able to ask it without playing the maniac—tell me, do you know aught concerning my father's death?"

"Meet me at midnight, and you shall know more."

"More! Ah, it is then as I feared! Rodolpho, damned assassin! midnight murderer! thy heart's blood, drawn from thee by slow and excruciating torments, shall ascend to heaven as the sacrifice of a son to the memory of a murdered parent. My father murdered! Where in that moment slumbered the bolts of Heaven's wrath? where was a son, that he did not rush to a parent's aid, and intercept the blow of death? My brain maddens! At midnight, monk, did you say, I should know more? Where shall I meet you?"

No answer was returned, and Montalto turning about, found that Grimaldi was gone.

The tolling of the bell reminded him that it wanted two hours to the appointed time; but those two hours were an age to Montalto. At one time he hastily paced the gloomy aisle of the chapel, then leaving it, walked on the banks of the lake. At times gazing on the towers of Colredo, silvered by the moon's lucid rays, while the determined intents of his soul appeared in his rageful eye, Rosalina was forgot—Rosalina, whose remembered beauties would have soothed his rage, and lulled the transports of fury which shook his frame, was distant from his thoughts.

At length the time approaching, he returned to the chapel, and throwing his harassed frame at the foot of a tomb, awaited the arrival of the monk.

At length he came; the light of his lamp gleaming on the countenance of Montalto, shewed it flushed with the emotions of his bosom.

"You are come at last, father," said he: "I have been expecting you an age."

"I fear," said the monk, "my coming is of little use—you are too much the victim of rage to listen to the dictates of reason: and unless you will comply with what I shall exact, I shall depart."

"Any thing you wish I will do: be speedy in your determination; my anxiety to know my father's fate, increases with each moment."

"You will hereafter, perhaps, own the propriety of the step I am about to take. Marchese, I must bind you, by a most solemn oath, that you will not divulge the events of this night to mortal, and that you will not take any measures which may to you appear right, without my sanction. Unless you do this, your father's fate shall remain a secret in my breast."

Montalto hastily approached the altar, and bound himself by a most solemn vow, to do as the monk required: that done, Grimaldi conducted him through some passages, till they entered that chamber in which was the trap-door leading to the subterraneous passages beneath the castello di Colredo.

Montalto having raised it, they descended the stairs, and having passed through the long passage to which they led, he threw open the panel, and, guided by the monk, they at length arrived at the door of a dungeon.

Here the monk set down his lamp, and taking a key from his girdle, he said—"Now, marchese, recollect your oath; you will shortly have occasion for all your fortitude; you must be silent; perhaps my life at this moment depends on your conduct."

"How you torture me by your delays, monk! Do not doubt me; I feel equal to any scene of horror—my expectations are wound up to their utmost pitch."

The monk turning the key, softly drew back the bolts of the lock, and opened the door; he then took up the lamp.—"Now enter," said he, "and behold, stretched on the floor, secured by massy chains, that father you have long lamented as dead!"

Words are vain to describe the feelings of Montalto as he leaned over his father, who, notwithstanding his miserable situation, deeply slumbered. He spoke not: his hands were clasped together, his mouth open, his eyes almost starting from their sockets, his knees trembling, and scarcely able to sustain the weight of his body.

"There," softly uttered the monk, "there is a sight for a son! for a child who loves his parent, to see the author of his being the sad inhabitant of a gloomy dungeon, in want of liberty, of proper food—even the wholesome air but niggardly admitted to revive his fainting woe-worn spirits! Is not this worse than murder?—is not this a refinement on the momentary pangs of dissolution? Can Montalto see this, and not seek revenge?"

Montalto started, but as yet he could not speak; he faintly groaned.

"How is your generous nature affected! I thought it would be so," continued the monk; "I thought the son could never be so recreant as not to feel for a father's wrongs, when even myself, a stranger and a monk too, who ought always to consider forbearance as a virtue, could almost have revenged them: but that satisfaction I reserved for you, as a treasure too inestimable to appreciate."

"First let me liberate my father; let me restore him to liberty, and then I will dedicate myself to vengeance."

"That must not yet be," returned Grimaldi; "but you may revenge yourself on the author of your parent's wrongs this hour. See this dagger—it is a fit instrument for a son, whose father lies before him, chained to the earth, enduring all the horrors of imprisonment. Take it—it is the key by which you can free a parent."

Montalto seized the dagger; he felt its point—it was sharp, and the blade glittered in the rays of the monk's lamp; a ghastly smile illumined his pallid countenance.—"Lead me," said he, "lead me to him this moment; my father soon shall be restored to freedom."

"Unhappy prisoner!" said the monk, who seemed to gaze on the prostrate captive, "thy hours of misery are nearly concluded; sweet will be thy waking moments, when thou art clasped to the warm embrace of a son, at once thy avenger and liberator: and thou, haughty duca di Rodolpho, wilt from him meet thy due reward.—I will now," said he, "lead you to his chamber, where doubtless he is enjoying soft repose; or, delighted with his well-concerted plans of villany, is lying awake, contriving fresh plans to torment your guiltless father, or perhaps to get you once more into his power."

"But this night," said Montalto, "shall end at once his life and diabolical villanies—this night shall free the world of a monster who taints the air with his pestiferous breath."

The monk now left the dungeon, followed by Montalto, impatient to revenge his wrongs.

"Close the door," said the monk, "and give me again the key, or our being in the castello may be discovered by the castellain, who sometimes visits these places."

Montalto did as he was directed, though a deep sigh burst from his agonized breast as he drew the key out of the lock, and his hand still more firmly grasped the dagger.

The monk, who seemed well acquainted with the passages, led Montalto to a flight of steps, which having ascended, he found himself in a small apartment.

"We are now in the eastern chambers of Colredo—shortly we shall be in those inhabited by the duca: collect, marchese, all your resolution before you proceed further, for perhaps your arm, when you are on the point of seeking a just revenge, may be enervated by your fears, and your father, in consequence, remain a hopeless captive, calling in vain on a son who had not courage to do an act of justice to liberate him. Your own life, too, may be the forfeit of your terrors, as well as mine."

"You need not fear, father; my heart is steeled against reflection—I could wade in a sea of blood; my passions are roused—my nature seems changed, and in the office of a midnight assassin, which at another time might strike me with horror, I now anticipate the highest satisfaction."

Montalto looked all he said; his brows lowered—his teeth fast closed—his eyes unsettled in their gaze—his hand fast clenching round the hilt of the dagger—his step unsteady—and his whole demeanour bespeaking him bent on the accomplishment of his designs.

Traversing a long corridor, the monk opened a small portal, and after crossing two chambers, he touched a secret spring in the wainscot, and a panel silently retreating in its groove, disclosed a chamber, which was illuminated by a large lamp, which depended from the centre of the roof. At the further end was a lofty canopied couch.

The monk listened—"Your inveterate enemy," said he, "slumbers; heedless of the sighs and groans of his captives, he enjoys repose. Now enter, and release your father."

Montalto advanced through the aperture, and with noiseless tread approached the couch; he drew aside the silken curtains, and beheld the countenance of the sleeper, when suddenly Rosalina, so long forgot, rushed to his recollection. His hand was already uplifted, but he paused before he did a deed which would for ever make him lose all hope of a union with the idol of his heart; for could he hope that Rosalina would ever wed the murderer of her parent, however great the motives might be which urged him to such an act? Soon his arm, that was upraised, nerved with deadly rage, now hung motionless by his side; again he thought of his father, and feebly raised it—but love forbade the deed.

"Infirm of purpose!" lowly whispered the monk; "are you a man—are you a son? No, you are degenerated from the noble stock you sprung from. Away then from this chamber, where the utmost danger awaits our longer stay—away, and leave your unfortunate father to breathe his last in the dungeons of yon sleeper!"

"Oh, Rosalina!" thought Montalto, "but for thee I could have given liberty to a parent; my love renders me incapable of the deed by which it could be gained. How changed in a moment are my sensations! Is it possible that I could be so base as to take advantage of the silent hour of midnight—to descend to the conduct of an hired assassin! Montalto, thou art indeed degenerated."

The monk had by this time left the chamber, and Montalto soon followed him; he closed the panel, and silently returned through the chambers into the corridor which led to the eastern wing. Both occupied by their own reflections, for some time remained silent; at length the monk said—

"Your father then, signor, is to remain in his captivity?"

"Oh no! for pity's sake release him! It must be so—he shall have his liberty."

"It cannot be," replied the monk: "to that I refuse my con-

sent: but perhaps you have forgot your oath, and mean to procure your father his enlargement at the expence of forfeiting all
hopes of future happiness?"

"Ah, that oath!—Monk, how you have tortured my soul!"

"You have yourself to blame," returned Grimaldi; "you are
the victim of fear."

"Of fear! No, father; but I love—I adore Rosalina; it was the
idea that I should forfeit her good opinion, and become the
object of her hatred, which first stayed my arm, and reflection
on the unmanly act I was going to perform perfectly rendered
it useless."

"And could you indeed ever think of being united to the
daughter of your father's persecutor? Unworthy son of an
unfortunate sire!"

The monk paused, for they were now descending the stairs
which communicated with the dungeons from the eastern
wing. Montalto often sighed—the monk perhaps noticed it,
for he said—

"It is in my power, marchese, to render the situation of your
father somewhat better than it now is. I pity your situation—
you want resolution to banish from your breast a passion which
your better reason must disapprove; perhaps, too, it is not
mutual. Tell me, does Rosalina favour your suit?"

"It is the greatest happiness of my life to think that she
does," replied Montalto; "but as to a union—the existing circumstances forbid it."

"Marchese," said the monk, "you have every reason to believe
me your friend; perhaps I have it in my power to be essentially
so: do not then undertake any thing without my advice. It was
that you might liberate your father—that you might revenge
his and your own wrongs, that I afforded you an opportunity
to do it; at that moment I did not sufficiently consider the
strength of your attachment to Rosalina; it was, however, the
knowledge of that circumstance which made me require that
solemn promise of you, fearing you might want resolution
when put to the proof; my caution, I find, was necessary, and
I trust you will most religiously observe it—much depends on

your silence, which it is needless to unfold at present. Had I for a moment reflected on the power of love, perhaps I should not have acted as I have: but it cannot be recalled; you have, however, the comfort of knowing that your father is still in existence, and that you have a friend in me whenever you need one."

"You cannot give me a greater proof of your friendship," said Montalto, "than by alleviating the miseries of my father's confinement, and by advising me in what manner to obtain his release, consistent with my love for Rosalina, for, I blush to own it, she divides with him my fondest affections."

"And I blush to hear you say it," returned the monk; "for never was love so wrong placed. At present, and particularly under those circumstances, I am not competent to advise you, but I will consider what can be done."

They had now entered the chapel, and soon reached the outer portals, when the monk observing that he should, in general, be in the chapel either at or after the vespers, where Montalto might find him, retired to the monastery, and Montalto proceeded to his own residence.

Miserable indeed he was, divided between parental duty and his love for Rosalina. The one prompted him to demand instant satisfaction from the duca, and enforce the liberation of his parent; to make known to the world his base conduct, and to make him atone with his life for the injuries he had received from him.

Montalto started from his seat—"This instant will I repair to the capital, and there declare the vile uses which Rodolpho makes of his authority. My father's captivity—my own treatment—"

Montalto paused, for at that instant he remembered his oath, which prevented him from making known his father's situation. Restricted in that point, he found himself incapable of acting as he was instigated by his just resentment.

On the other hand, what would Rosalina think of his protestations of love, if he attempted any thing which could injure her father? Would she not believe him false, and as such, instead of loving, avoid him as her bitterest enemy? And such a conduct, how would it agonize his soul?

"The monk," thought he, "may direct me; for as to myself, the more I reflect on my situation, the more I am incapable of action. Impelled by filial duty, and restrained by love, I know not what course to pursue, to rescue a parent and preserve Rosalina's affection."

A thought at length occurred, and this was to endeavour to persuade Rosalina to a private marriage; her sentiments might then be altered, and she would consider the persecutor of her husband's father with more abhorrence than she could be expected to do while he was no relation to her; he would too, in that case, be certain of possessing the treasure of his soul's adoration: he determined, therefore, the next evening, when he expected to see Rosalina, to entreat her consent; and the monk Grimaldi, he thought, might be persuaded to unite them.

Such was, after many hours passed in debate, the resolution of Montalto, who now retired to rest, and his fatigued and harassed senses were at length lulled to repose by the kind influence of the gentle deity of slumbers.

It will now perhaps be necessary to relate to the reader the circumstances which induced the duca di Rodolpho to conduct himself in so base a manner to the old marchese Montalto, in doing which, the history must go back to a short time before that period when the duca led his forces to quell the insurrections of the northern banditti.

In so doing, the pen traces with regret the page descriptive of the vices of mankind. Much rather would it use its weak efforts to record to posterity those virtues which dignify human nature, which exalt the mind of the reader, and teach him to emulate whatever is praiseworthy: the reverse is, alas! the subject of these volumes; but may they inculcate an abhorrence of such deeds, and by shewing the true image of vice, and the baneful effects of indulging vicious passions and inclinations, in their proper colours, disrobed of their deceitful garbs, present a picture to youth, from whose deformity they may start with increasing horror!

Such indeed is the wish with which these volumes are written; and whether they answer that purpose or not, there is a consoling reflection which will ever remain to alleviate the disappointment, and which is, that their intent was good.

CHAPTER X.

THE duca di Rodolpho and the old marchese Montalto had been intimate friends, till a short period before he led his forces against the northern insurgents, when the marchese demanding of him the payment of large sums of money, which the duca, in consequence of his military preparations, had not the ability to restore, some words arose, which terminated in many revengeful expressions on both sides. The duca feared the rage of the marchese, who being in possession of many of his most important secrets, might, perhaps, be induced to take that opportunity of venting his malice by disclosing them; and therefore he determined to get him in his power, and, by a deed of horror, free himself from further anxiety on that head, at least as far as respected temporal concerns: as for the future welfare of his soul, the duca heeded it not, for his bosom, by the frequent repetition of deeds of darkness, was become callous to the stings of conscience.

It was a matter of some difficulty for the duca to execute his designs so privately as to elude the searching eye of suspicion, which, in consequence of the disappearance of the marchese, he was well assured would immediately glance at him. They were however effected in the following manner: Lupo, his trusty agent in his iniquitous plans, watched in secret all the movements of the marchese; and one evening, when his intended victim was riding by himself, assisted by a ruffian, who was hired for the purpose, he attacked, and with little difficulty seized the unfortunate marchese, who was unprepared for such an assault, and secreting him in the woods till midnight, brought him bound to the castello, and entering the private postern that communicated with the subterraneous passages,

secured him in one of the dungeons, and acquainted the duca
with the success of their mission. The hired ruffian as had been
before agreed on, disguising himself as a peasant, immediately
repaired to the late residence of the marchese, and related a
fictitious tale of his having seen him struggling in the waters of
an arm of the lake of Abruzzo, which he had rashly attempted
to cross. This account was credited, for the appearance of the
horse he had rode, whose arrival at the mansion first created the
alarm for his safety, proved that he had been in the water, and
during their search, the barette of the marchese had been found
on the banks of that part of the lake where the peasant reported
he had seen him perish.

Thus the duca securely triumphed over the marchese di
Montalto. He had him now in his power; his life was at his
disposal without fear of detection, and to rid himself of a troublesome charge, he resolved to ensure his safety by the death of
his enemy.

For this purpose he one evening sent for Lupo, whom he
wished to persuade to assassinate the marchese: he was at that
time walking in the hall of his castello; it was nearly dusk,
and no one but himself was in it when Lupo entered. He thus
addressed him—

"Lupo, I sent for you about an affair of importance to my
peace."

"Your excellenza knows that I am always at your service,"
said the castellain, bowing obsequiously.

"That affair of Astolpho was rather troublesome," said the
duca.

"Yes, your excellenza, he made a desperate resistance,"
returned the castellain, "but it was to little purpose."

"You took away the body, did you not?"

"Oh yes," returned Lupo; "the fish in the lake will tell your
excellenza that, if they could speak."

"I fear I shall not be able to reward you so much as I could
wish," said Rodolpho; "you have hitherto proved yourself faithful to my interests."

"It is my duty," said the castellain, again bowing.

"In this purse are some thirty or forty ducats; perhaps they may be useful to you."

"Your excellenza is always too generous," said Lupo, taking the money.

"The marchese enjoys his health, I think you told me the other day, notwithstanding his confinement?"

"Yes, he does, and talks in as high a strain as ever. This morning he said so many abusive things concerning your excellenza's conduct to Astolpho, and likewise about me, that I was almost tempted to——"

"To what?" demanded the duca, hastily.

"To put it out of his power to insult you," returned Lupo; "but I was fearful that you would not approve of it."

"I wish you had done it," replied the duca; "if he were dead, I should be at peace. This is the subject I wished to converse with you about: cannot you contrive it to-night?"

"What! in cold blood?" returned Lupo. "I wish I had known your excellenza's intentions this morning; but in cold blood to murder a man! I never did it but once, and that was to——"

"Well, it is of no consequence," hastily replied the duca, interrupting him: "you are always harping on that deed. But with respect to the marchese, am I to wait in anxiety for my safety till your passions are roused? I thought, Lupo, you had more regard for my feelings."

"The marchese is safe enough in his dungeon," returned Lupo; "but if your excellenza really wishes to have it done, I am willing: but then——"

"What objection are you now going to make?" said the duca.

"I should like to have some person to assist me; the marchese is strong."

"Whom can you have? Parozzi is by this time at Venice, and there is no one you can trust in the castello."

"If your excellenza would but stay at the door while I went in, and in case he should make any resistance——"

"I understand you," replied Rodolpho; "be it so. Shall we go now, or wait till night?"

"The night will be the safest, for then he will be most likely asleep," returned the castellain; "besides, his cries might be heard, and——"

Here a sudden noise in one of the galleries which were erected on each side of the hall disturbed their conversation; they both instantly looked up to the place from whence the sound had proceeded, but no object met their view.

"Our conversation has been overheard," said Rodolpho: "hasten to the place, and endeavour to find out who the listener was."

Lupo, as anxious as the duca, instantly left the hall by the door which opened on the staircase that led to the galleries, for his discourse, he was well convinced, had not been such as would admit of being made public. The duca following him, both arrived in the gallery at the same time, and his astonishment can be better imagined than described, on perceiving his daughter Rosalina lying motionless on the floor.

He raised her up, but she was insensible, and Lupo summoned her attendants, who carried her to her couch, where, for a long time, all their endeavours to restore her to life were without effect. The duca meanwhile had left the chamber, but remained in the corridor, which he hastily paced, greatly agitated, for he feared that his daughter had become acquainted with his murderous intentions respecting the marchese Montalto.

When Rosalina that evening was returning to her apartments, she passed near a door that led to the galleries of the hall; it was open, and hearing the voices of some people in conversation, curiosity made her stop to listen, when she discovered that they were those of her father and Lupo the castellain, and in that moment heard the duca's question respecting the body of Astolpho. Although she had ever deemed it wrong to pry into the secret conversation of others, yet an anxiety to know the purport of their discourse, created by her father's demand, surmounted every other consideration, and cautiously advancing, she entered the gallery, and trembling with indescribable emotions, heard their plans respecting the unfortunate marchese.

It was with the greatest difficulty that for some time she

could restrain her agitated senses from deserting her, but when she heard Lupo coolly observing that the cries of their unfortunate victim might be heard, she was no longer able to support herself, but with a groan, sunk insensible on the floor.

When she recovered, and found herself in her own apartment, she began to hope that what she had heard was in some dream; but when informed by her domestics that the duca and Lupo had found her in the hall gallery, alarmed lest she should incur his anger for listening to his conversation, she determined, if possible, to conceal her knowledge of it.

The attendants, according to the duca's order, now acquainting him with the recovery of his daughter, he instantly entered the apartment, and commanding them to withdraw, thus addressed her—

"Tell me truly, Rosalina, what was the occasion of your being in the gallery of the hall at so unseasonable an hour? did you see any one in it that excited your curiosity?"

"Indeed I did not," replied Rosalina, (which was the truth, for she was too well acquainted with the voices of her father and Lupo to render a sight of their persons necessary); "I was rather faint as I was crossing the corridor, and imagining the air of the hall, being less confined, might relieve me, I stepped into the gallery, and almost immediately fainted."

Though Rosalina was confused, as she evaded acquainting her father with what he was so anxious to know, yet the duca imputing it to her indisposition, was satisfied that his discourse with Lupo had not been heard, and shortly after left the chamber.

This then was the conversation so often alluded to in the first volume of these imperfect records, for though the name of the marchese had not been mentioned, yet she was but too well convinced it could be no other than him; and that her father could devise such a horrible act, was a circumstance which, whenever it occupied her thoughts, gave her the most lively sorrow.

It was now near midnight; the inhabitants of the castello had retired to their apartments, and were sunk in sleep, and the blast of night howled mournfully along the battlements, when the duca, thirsting for the blood of his intended victim, grasping a dagger, descended with Lupo to the dungeon of Montalto.

Stopping at the door, they listened, and heard him still pacing its dreary confines. On evil deeds fear is the constant attendant, and though two to one, and that one unarmed, yet they hesitated to enter his abode.

Thus, while conscience makes cowards of the guilty, virtue clads her votaries with impenetrable armour; peace and happiness await them, both here and hereafter. But the bosom stained with crimes never feels itself secure, though defended with thrice-tempered mail; in every breeze they hear the voice of an accuser, and in every shade fear an avenging arm; peaceful slumbers are strangers to their pillows, for when sleep does close their eyes, their disturbed senses produce to their mental vision scenes of horror and dismay.

While the duca and Lupo were listening to the paces of the marchese, they suddenly ceased, and a rustling amongst the straw convinced them that he had sought his wretched pillow; they now waited some time longer, when, concluding that he was asleep, they slowly opened the door, and Lupo entering, stabbed the unfortunate Montalto, who, though wounded, instantly sprung upon his intended assassin, and in a moment had wrenched the dagger from his hand, and was going to avenge the blow he had received, when the duca's sword prevented him, and he fell.

Lupo easily recovered his dagger, and having again plunged it in his body, hastily left the dungeon accompanied by the duca, both pale and terrified, looking continually behind them, expecting to be pursued by the bleeding shade of the marchese.

The duca did not stop till he had reached his apartment, where, having fastened the door, he threw himself on a couch, and covering his face with his hands, endeavoured to exclude thought, as well as the surrounding objects—but in vain, for in imagination he beheld the bleeding body of Montalto, while he thought he heard a voice say—

"Tremble, thou murderer! nor hope nor comfort awaits thee! Thine eternal jewel hast thou given to the common enemy of man, who will, before long, claim thee as his destined prey."

The reader may, perhaps, be anxious to know who the unfortunate Astolpho was, that fell a victim to the merciless rage of the duca.

Perhaps Italy could not boast a more accomplished cavalier. His courage was proverbial—his generosity and humanity were not to be excelled; but his possessions were small, and unequal to the wants of a liberal mind.

His heart was tenderly alive to the soft emotions of love, but for one only did it ever vibrate, and that one was the lovely Constantia, and who was not blind to the perfections of the signor Astolpho.

What happiness, what heavenly bliss emanates from mutual affection! The heart devoted to the object of its adorations swells with delight as it breathes forth the fond tale of love. Replete with joy were the days of Astolpho and Constantia; but soon an envious lowering cloud darkened all their comfort in this sublunary existence.

The duca di Rodolpho saw and became enamoured of Constantia. Who could see her and not love? With heart-rending grief the hapless maid beheld herself about to be sacrificed to the prevailing power of gold and its glittering appendages, and torn for ever from her Astolpho, whom shortly it would be a crime to love.

What pen shall describe the miseries of Astolpho when he heard the cruel intention of the parents of his adored! Oh, how his heart each moment throbbed with increasing agony! his respiration became difficult—his eyes poured forth no tears to relieve his bursting brain—his was not that grief which can alleviate its agony by the fast-falling drops of sorrow; the fever of his misery dried up those sources. Often was the point of his sword directed to his heart—but Astolpho's reason triumphed over his wish to end his wretched life.

Rodolpho knew the situation of the lovers; but so that his own wishes were gratified, he did not care how they were attained. He smiled when he heard of the misery of Astolpho, and with cruel exultation led his beauteous trembling bride to the altar.

Constantia, now the duchesa di Rodolpho, endeavoured to forget, in the duties of a wife, the love she had for Astolpho: her thoughts, however, too often for her peace of mind, dwelt on him; she wished to hear of him, for he had absented himself some days before her marriage, and no one knew where the hapless wanderer was gone.

In a lonely hut, concealed in the intricate bosom of a vast forest, dwelt Astolpho; there unseen he indulged in all the luxury of woe: insensible to the weather, in the most inclement night, when the storm howled through the branches of the forest, when the thunder shook the earth, and the frequent lightnings gleamed dreadfully around, was he often seated on some rocky cliff, resting his aching head on his arm, and often-times repeating the loved name of Constantia, while the rising gale rudely bore away the sounds of his voice the instant they proceeded from his lips.

Thus did Astolpho pine away his existence: he was become a living spectre; often had he watched the changing moon, and the sun had once encircled the world, when, feeling his page of existence drawing to a conclusion, he determined to take one look at Constantia, hoping in that moment, when his ravished senses were contemplating her charms, that the delight would free his soul from its earthly mansion, which then unconfined would hover round the dear object of its fond adoration.

How sadly beat his heart when from afar he beheld the lofty turrets of Colredo, where now dwelt Constantia! As he approached nearer, he saw the grey walls of the monastery of Santa Maria; a sudden thought gave to his bosom the only gleam of comfort he had experienced during so many long, long months of woe, and this was to fix his residence in its hallowed walls, to become a member of the church—"For then," thought he, "I shall have often an opportunity of seeing the angel I adore: we shall together offer up our prayers; I shall then be able to watch over her, to intercede with heaven for her happiness."

He was shortly after received amongst the holy brotherhood. He did not dare to ask after his beloved Constantia, for his confusion might have betrayed a more than common interest concerning her; and now that he had dedicated himself to heaven, and that the span of his existence was every hour contracting, to have made her acquainted with the fatal consequences of his love would have been to afflict her tender bosom with needless torture.

The first day he attended in the chapel, as his eyes wandered about, dreading, yet wishing to behold Constantia, he suddenly started at seeing her enter, and amongst her domestics was one who carried an infant.

At first all his senses, save that of sight, seemed deserting him; his eyes, opened to their utmost extent, were rivetted on the duchesa. There was an air of melancholy portrayed over her lovely features which somewhat pleased him, since he considered it as a proof that she was not happy, and that she had not transferred the love she professed for him to another. Strange sensation! but how true! Astolpho would have with delight laid down his life at her feet, if by so doing he could have procured her a moment's happiness. It was his constant prayer that she might be happy; yet in her present situation to have thought she was so would have been daggers to him, and sooner could he have reposed on their sharp points, than have laid his weary frame on the thrice-driven bed of down with the thought that Constantia was made happy by another.

But when the child met his view—when he thought to himself that it was the offspring of Rodolpho—jealousy, rage, and despair took possession of him; his senses, unable to support the dreadful conflict in his agonized bosom, happily deserted him for awhile, or reason might for ever have been hurled from her seat, and the unfortunate Astolpho levelled with the brute creation.

His weak frame, however, was unable to support the sudden shock it had received, and Astolpho, under the conviction that his days of life were nearly ended, determined to see Constantia, that he might bless her before he died, and, taking a pen, he slowly traced the following words:

"Before the attenuated thread which holds him to a mortal existence parts for ever, Astolpho, a monk of Santa Maria, earnestly entreats Constantia to see him: to comply with his dying request—to sooth the last pangs of mortality, can be no sin, though she is now another's."

When the duchesa beheld the well-remembered writing of Astolpho, she trembled and turned pale; all the love which she had so long strove to forget returned with increasing strength, and with an aching heart she left the castello, and soon arriving at the monastery, was allowed by the abbot to enter the apartment of Astolpho.

Stretched almost motionless on his pallet lay the victim of love. Constantia, when she recognized in the feeble form before her all that remained of the interesting, the handsome, generous, brave, and beloved Astolpho, could not restrain the impulse of her affection, which, so long dormant, now awoke with redoubled force; she shed bitter tears over him, which to Astolpho were like the gentle rain to the parched drooping plant which began to wither away, till the refreshing shower reviving it once more, its beauties gladden the eye, and its odours scent the passing zephyrs.

"Astolpho!" she mournfully exclaimed, "and is it thus we meet? Oh, cruel parents! who have robbed me of all my happiness—blighted all my joys, come, and behold your victims! My Astolpho, do not leave your Constantia! Oh, Heavens, have pity on him! How pale, how wan he is! his eyes almost closed in death's eternal slumbers! Look on me, Astolpho—bless me with the sound of your voice!"

"My adored Constantia!" Astolpho replied, in a feeble hollow tone, "thy dear solicitude has recalled me from the gates of death, that were opened wide on their eternal hinges to receive me! Do you then still love me?—is Astolpho still dear to you? Oh, repeat again those sweet words—they are a healing balm to my aching bosom!"

"As a dear friend Constantia must ever consider Astolpho: my heart has betrayed its feelings, but you know my situation—

duty calls on us to forget our mutual affection; you are devoted to the service of Heaven, and I am a wife; let us be friends, but let us forget that we have been lovers."

"You are right, Constantia," replied Astolpho, with a deep sigh, "we must indeed forget that; and should I recover—should health once more revisit my frame, will Constantia endeavour to make me wish to live, by letting me have the happiness of seeing her often?"

"Indeed I will, but on the condition I have mentioned," returned Constantia: "live then, my friend; we shall have the felicity of offering up our prayers together to Heaven—of seeing and conversing with each other."

"Ah, that will be happiness indeed!" said Astolpho. "I will endeavour to live, that I may repay your intended kindness—that I may prove myself worthy of your friendship."

After this conversation the duchesa took her leave of Astolpho, promising to see him again shortly, and with a heart somewhat lighter than it had been since her nuptials, she returned to Colredo.

How quick is the transition from joy to grief—from grief to joy! how closely are the extremes of human passions connected! Astolpho, from being one of the most miserable of created beings, now on again seeing Constantia, on anticipating the blissful hours he should pass in her society, was the most happy; his health soon began to return, and in a few days he was able to leave that couch on which he so lately had expected to die.

Constantia, according to her promise, had again seen him, and was delighted with the rapid change in his health; but she feared that she was doing wrong, for in spite of all her resolution of never feeling for Astolpho any other sensation than friendship, she found herself unable to forget that she had loved, and that, fatally for her peace of mind, she still preserved that affection for him.

Astolpho, fearing that the duchesa would retract her promise of seeing him, ever cautiously avoided any other than the most distant behaviour that common friendship would admit of; she did the same; but alas! their eyes disclosed the secrets of their hearts, and both became unhappy.

Each wanted courage to tell the other that they were acting wrong—that they must part—that honour, virtue, duty, forbade their longer acquaintance: thus situated, Constantia was often in tears, and Astolpho often sighed.

At length he resolved to triumph over himself, and one evening, as they were walking near the monastery, after some hesitation, he thus addressed her—

"We must part, Constantia—miserable as it will make me, we shall be more so, if we do not: love cannot descend to friendship, and in spite of all our endeavours, we still love."

"Noble minded, generous Astolpho! how much have you deserved my thanks! Alas! my heart tells me the truth of what you say—it must be so indeed: religion and prudence dictate the necessity of such a step."

How miserable were both Constantia and Astolpho! They had, however, one consolation, which was, that they were acting right, and could with confidence pray to Heaven to strengthen them in their pious resolutions.

Both wished to delay the moment of parting, but soon it arrived: Astolpho's eyes filled with tears, as kneeling he took the hand of Constantia and pressed it to his lips.

"Adieu, Constantia!" he mournfully uttered: "surely it will be no harm for us to remember each other, and to ponder over the past in the hour of solitude; for though the recollection will occasion many a sigh, many a heartfelt regret, yet the fortitude we have evinced in this separation will doubtless extend itself to our future actions, and make us support our hard fate with resignation."

"Astolpho, farewell!" said the pale, trembling Constantia: "in all my orisons you shall be remembered, and let us, on each new moon, when midnight has usurped her solemn silent empire over the world—let us employ some hours in prayers for each other's happiness; we shall pray with greater fervour when we reflect that both are engaged in the same pious office."

Astolpho promised to comply with her request, and after

many tears on both sides, these sad lovers parted. Constantia, pensive and melancholy, returned to Colredo, where she secluded herself in her apartments, and gave way to all the bitterness of grief, and Astolpho sought the most secluded part of the forest, to hide his agony from every eye.

Unfortunately this last meeting was beheld by Rodolpho. Unable to divine the reasons of Constantia's holding so long a conversation with a monk, unobserved he drew near them, and, concealed by the thick underwood, listened to their discourse. He instantly recollected Astolpho, whom he had seen once before, and in that instant would have sacrificed him to his rage, but wishing to know how their meeting would terminate, he suppressed his horrible intentions for the present.

The noble conduct of Astolpho would have produced sentiments of esteem in any other breast than the duca's, but his pride was hurt by finding that the duchesa had dared to retain her former sentiments for Astolpho, and that he had sought an opportunity of seeing her. He smiled at their adieus, because he vowed to himself that they should be eternal, and when they separated, he soon after repaired to the castello, where to Lupo he entrusted what he had seen, and his intentions respecting Astolpho.

Lupo, according to the instructions he had received, instantly repaired to the forest, and after watching some time saw Astolpho slowly returning to the monastery.

Lupo drew his sword, and rushed on the unarmed mourner, who, perceiving his intention, started aside, and avoided the intended thrust, and at the same moment seizing the castellain, soon disarmed him; but Lupo, unperceived by Astolpho, drawing a dagger from his belt, suddenly buried it in his heart, and put a period at once to the sorrows and life of the ill-fated lover.

Lupo, fearing a discovery, then drew the body towards the lake, and as he was going to plunge it into its watery tomb, he saw a miniature that was concealed in the bosom, which, when he had taken out, he found to be that of the duchesa; this he kept, and then threw the body into the wide-floating waters of

Abruzzo, which instantly closing over it, his murderous deed was concealed from the eyes of the world.

The miniature he gave the duca, who, not long after, found an opportunity of adding to the misery of the unhappy duchesa.

Unconscious that he knew any thing concerning Astolpho, she endeavoured to conceal when in his presence the grief which sat heavy on her heart; but this deprivation made her indulge it the more in private, and the duca had often surprised her in tears: this added to the rage which he treasured up in his heart against her, and which he determined at some future opportunity should burst at once on her devoted head.

One evening when Constantia, who for a long time had not left the castello, and in consequence had not heard that Astolpho was missing, was, according to her usual custom, walking on the ramparts with the venerable father Augustino, in whose instructive converse, and her attentions to her infant daughter Rosalina, she passed the else tedious hours, the father mentioned the extraordinary circumstance of a monk of Santa Maria not having been heard of for some time, and that it was generally supposed, from some circumstances of his conduct which had been noticed, that he had destroyed himself.

Constantia, whose ready fancy conjectured that the person alluded to could be no other than Astolpho, hastily demanded his name, and on hearing that it was him, she turned pale, and seemed unable to support her trembling frame.

"Holy Mother!" exclaimed Augustino, greatly alarmed; "what is the matter, duchesa—you seem unwell? Has my conversation affected you? do you know the monk Astolpho?"

"Oh, father! too fatally for my peace of mind I do—he was my first, my only love. You have heard of that circumstance, and may judge of my feelings when listening to his supposed fate. Alas! he has not been equal to the trial he so generously, so fatally imposed on himself."

"My unfortunate daughter," returned the confessor, "how sorry I am that I should have caused you so much pain! But do not unnecessarily afflict yourself, for what I said was only surmise; no traces of him have been found—he may have gone a journey to compose his sorrows by change of scene."

"Alas! I fear he has indeed changed this earthly scene! but let me hope he is now happy in realms of eternal bliss. To-morrow, father, I will make you acquainted with some occurrences that have lately taken place between me and the unfortunate Astolpho, but now I am not able: your arm, father—I can scarcely stand."

Augustino supported the duchesa to the door of her apartments, and then, having entreated her not to give way to grief, particularly as there was no reason to make it supposed that Astolpho was no more, left her.

Constantia's tears now flowed apace, unrestrained by the presence of any one, when unfortunately at this moment the duca entered the chamber. He started when he saw her grief, which she hastily endeavoured to conceal.

"Constantia," said he, in a stern voice, "what is the reason of this private grief? A wife, I should imagine, ought not to have any secrets from her husband."

"A trifling indisposition," replied Constantia, rather confused; "I am better now."

"I am glad to hear it," returned Rodolpho; "and that you may be quite restored," added he, drawing from beneath his mantle the miniature which Lupo had given him, "the shade of Astolpho sends you this!"

Scarcely had the well-remembered painting met her gaze, than she wildly shrieked—"Oh Heavens! it is true then," said she, "Astolpho is no more!" Her grief then prevented her further utterance.

"Thou seest I have found out the cause of thy sorrow," continued the duca, regardless of her hapless state; "I witnessed thy last meeting with Astolpho, and your tender farewell was not given in vain, for never more in this world will you see each other."

Constantia was unable to reply, and the duca, exulting in his cruel revenge, left the apartment.

We shall draw a veil over the sufferings of Constantia, for

though the duca had not confessed the horrid deed which had been performed, there was little doubt in her mind but that the hapless Astolpho had been sacrificed to appease his rage, for well she knew he would rather part with life than the miniature which she had given him long before her fatal charms had attracted the notice of the duca.

Her child, the lovely Rosalina, alone reconciled her to existence; but her peace of mind was lost, and her constitution every year felt the fatal effects of her secret hoarded sorrows, and at length she sunk into the peaceful arms of death. When she was gone, the duca felt the greatness of his loss: he then, though too late, repented his harsh behaviour to her; but his repentance or his sorrows were of no avail—they were unable to call back her immortal soul to its earthly mansion; and that beauteous ruin, bedewed with the tears of her sorrowing domestics, was consigned to the silent tomb, whose sculptured marble told the stranger of her virtues.

Such was the fate of Astolpho, and such was the termination of the life of Constantia. Rosalina had often, from the venerable Augustino, heard the sad tale; but the real end of Astolpho, though she conjectured how it had been effected, yet never was certain of the truth of her surmises, till she had heard the conversation between the duca and Lupo, as related at the commencement of this chapter.

Rosalina, from that eventful night, could not look with that pleasure on her father which she had ever been accustomed to do; for Lupo she felt an invincible abhorrence; but feelingly alive to a sense of that duty she owed a parent, she by degrees endeavoured to erase from her mind the deep impression made on her heart by her knowledge of his cruel deeds, and in part succeeded, so far as to feel sorrowful when he left her to engage the northern banditti, and was pleased to see him return, though that pleasure was clouded by the events that had occurred between her and the young marchese di Montalto, and which renewed in her mind all the unhappiness she had experienced, and doubly so because she was indebted for her life to him whose parent had been deprived of existence by her own father.

Happily, however, the fates decreed otherwise, and Rodolpho had not his life to answer for among the many who, to appease his rage, or who interfered in any favourite plans he had formed, became his victims.

The duca did not consider that the vengeance of Heaven is sometimes suspended only that it may fall with increasing weight on the offending head, and give an awful lesson to a sinful world. He had plunged into a sea of guilt, and the more he struggled to disengage himself, the more he was entangled amongst its hidden quicksands, which to avoid he was forced to commit fresh crimes, fresh deeds of horror; and he at all times vainly hoped to ward off the unerring sword of retribution by future acts of piety and repentance, which, alas! were deferred from day to day, till his bosom became hardened to his crimes, and his ears deaf to the voice of conscience, and which made him forget all his good intentions; or if he did remember them, it was only to smile at his former vain fears, and so long as he could hide his deeds from the world, he cared not for the avenging eye of an offended Deity, to whom not only our outward actions, but the inmost secrets of our hearts, are known.

In our next chapter we shall present our readers with the development of certain mysterious events which were related in the first volume of this work.

CHAPTER XI.

THE unfortunate marchese di Montalto, contrary to the belief of his dark assassins, was not mortally wounded, though the loss of blood had caused an instantaneous and deathlike stupor, which had deceived them into that belief.

When he revived, he found himself alone, covered with his own blood, which now happily ceased to flow from his wounds; the door of his dungeon was open, and the hope of effecting his escape made him exert his remaining strength to rise, and if possible to find his way through the subterraneous passages to the postern by which he had entered them.

The glimmering light which entered the grating shewed the marchese that it was near the break of day, and he knew that the moments were now precious. Supporting himself by the walls, after much pain he at length reached the outer postern, for he had taken particular notice of the way by which he was brought to his dungeon, in the faint hope that should he have an opportunity of escaping, his observations might be of service to him.

The postern was secured on the inside by large bolts, which to draw out of the stone wall was an exertion beyond his present strength, and in the attempt, the blood again flowed from his wounds, as every moment he now grew weaker, and his death more certain. He became desperate by his danger, and again making the attempt, fortunately succeeded; the fresh breath of morning revived him, and he sat some time on the rock to inhale it, and collect strength to proceed as far as the monastery of Santa Maria, where he hoped to find a secure asylum till his wounds should be healed, and he was able to pursue measures for his safety, and also for the revenge which he was determined to take of his treacherous enemy, the duca di Rodolpho.

Fortunately for him he had not proceeded far before he met one of the monks, whose surprise was excessive when he recognized in the wounded object before him the marchese di Montalto, who was supposed to have perished in the lake.

The monk assisted him to the small tower at the extremity of the northern cloisters, where, having placed him on a seat, he hastened to the monastery to provide the necessary bandages for his wounds, after being strictly charged by the marchese not to divulge the events of that morning to any person, lest it should come to the duca's ears, who would not fail to employ every means in his power to effect the work of death which he had fortunately as yet not succeeded in.

The monk was faithful to his promise. The tower, being in a ruinous state, was scarcely ever visited, and promised to be a secure retreat for him till he should recover of his wounds. The friendly care of the monk was unremitting, and the marchese began, though slowly, to gain strength. During this time the duca left the castello on his expedition to the north, and the marchese, who was constantly brooding in revenge, determined still to remain in concealment till he should return, and his plans were ripe for execution.

From the monk he learnt the arrival of his son from Padua to take possession of his estates and title; but he was disappointed to find that, though he constantly lamented the supposed loss of his parent, he did not take any measures to satisfy himself whether he came fairly by his death or not.

He then determined to watch his steps, and whenever he had a fit opportunity to do so without fear of being discovered, to upbraid him. His astonishment and anger were great when he one evening perceived him intently gazing (while concealed behind a hedge) on the daughter of the duca, his foul and bitter enemy; he then advanced, and concealing his features with his cowl (for during his residence in the precincts of the monastery it was necessary for him to wear the dress of a monk, in order to escape being noticed whenever he left the tower), upbraided his son with his conduct, and bidding him shun the offspring of Rodolpho, instantly left the place, and, well acquainted with the mazy intricacies of the forest, effectually eluded his son's pursuit.

When, however, he had heard that his son and Rosalina had become acquainted, his anger increased, and he sought an opportunity of again warning him, which he effected as described in the first volume, by secreting himself behind a panel in the chamber of the monastery of Santa Maria, whither his son had pursued him, and denounced vengeance on Rosalina should he not instantly withdraw his ill-placed affection from her.

Illness now for a long time confined the marchese to his apartment, and perhaps his anger at his son's conduct not a little delayed his recovery. It was during that period, that as he was one day pensively sitting by the casement, with his eyes fixed on the floor, that he perceived the trap-door which communicated with the vaults and subterraneous passages of Colredo. Such a discovery greatly delighted him, for he could now at pleasure enter it, and thus be enabled secretly to prosecute whatever plans his desire of revenge should dictate.

By this passage, as has been before observed, he effected an entrance into the eastern chambers of the castello, which being remote from the inhabited parts of the building, he ran no risk in frequenting them.

The return of the duca made him somewhat more cautious in venturing from his abode, and in order to divert the time, he visited the eastern chambers more frequently, and made himself minutely acquainted with the subterraneous passages, which knowledge might perhaps be of service to him when his plans of revenge were matured.

One day, as he was sitting in one of the apartments, he heard several hasty steps advancing along the corridor, and had but just time to hide himself in the gloom of a deep recess on one side of the chamber, when the door was thrown open, and the duca di Rodolpho and Rosalina entered.

From his discourse with his daughter, he learnt the danger of his son, and that their love was mutual; and after the departure of Rodolpho, the declaration of Rosalina, that she never would wed any other than Montalto, left not a doubt of it. Greatly enraged that his son, notwithstanding the frequent warnings he had given him, should seek a union with her, he determined to end his solicitude on that head by the murder of Rosalina; and he was also instigated to it, because by such a deed he revenged himself of the duca, whose ambitious prospects of an alliance with the prince di Manfroné would thereby be entirely frustrated.

That horrible deed in his vindictive rage he would instantly have performed, but happily he had no instrument wherewith to effect it; therefore, fearful of being discovered, he contrived, while Rosalina was examining the further end of the chamber, to emerge slowly from his concealment, and reaching the panel, which silently receding as he touched the secret spring, he was soon out of the chamber.

Rosalina, however, had in the mirror observed his figure gliding along the wall, which had greatly alarmed her; but at length, after having surveyed the apartment, and becoming convinced that she was its only inhabitant, she concluded that it was the effect of her disturbed imagination, and by degrees recovered of her terror.

The marchese, determined to commence his work of revenge, resolved that night should be the last that Rosalina should know; and as soon as midnight had arrived, he silently entered the chamber where lay his intended victim, and unsheathing his dagger, approached her couch.

The bright beams of the moon darting through the ivy-clad casements, shone on the lovely countenance of Rosalina, and for a while stopped his suspended arm, till recalling to his too-retentive memory his injuries, he was about to complete his dreadful errand, when the tremulous sounds of Rosalina's voice supplicating for mercy, rendered him unable to perform it, and he retired from the chamber.

The next night, greatly astonished, he saw Rosalina descending the stairs that led from the eastern chambers to the subterraneous passages. He watched her, for he instantly concluded that she was endeavouring to effect her escape, and to fly to his son for protection, when, greatly astonished, he witnessed the scene between her and his son, who till that moment he was ignorant was Rodolpho's captive.

His hatred of Rosalina was now turned into admiration of her conduct; he beheld her as the preserver of his son, and he blessed Heaven that he had not the horrible crime of her destruction to answer for, and from that moment determined to take her under his protection as far as he was able.

Accordingly, when the next night he discovered the hapless maid wandering through the caverns, he took an opportunity of assuring her that she had a friend who would protect her.

He knew that father Augustino was too ill to perform the ceremony of uniting her to the prince, and he determined, hazardous as the undertaking was, to attend himself; and he no sooner saw Rosalina conducted by the duca towards the chapel, than he hastened through the secret passage to the monastery, and met the messenger whom Rodolpho had sent for one of the fathers, and immediately followed him to the castello.

The attempt was replete with danger, but the marchese was

determined to assist Rosalina, as she had preserved the life of his son. His success has been recorded. He trusted to the confusion and terror which the sudden view of his features would cause the duca, and he hoped then he should be able to escape; or if he could not, he had ready prepared, beneath the folds of his garment, a dagger, which he would, on the instant of his being discovered, have sheathed in the heart of Rodolpho.

Some time after this, as he was in the chapel, he beheld the monk who had caused so much uneasiness to Rosalina by his seemingly minute investigation of her features. Not knowing who he was, he watched his steps when he retired from the chapel, and soon, unknown to Grimaldi, gained a glimpse of his features, which he instantly well recollected. For what purpose he could be there in that disguise (for the marchese well knew religion was not the motive that had made him take his residence in that monastery), he could not conceive, unless indeed he was, like himself, seeking revenge.

Thus passed the hours that brought on that memorable night when the marchese was surprised in his fancied secure retreat by the duca and the padre Grimaldi. And thus have we accounted for the many mysterious occurrences which had taken place as related in the first volume.

The marchese, once more in the power of the duca, concluded his destruction certain, and was unable to conceive the reason of the delay of his bitter enemy respecting his assassination; but it will be seen that the padre Grimaldi had other designs in view than his death, and which made him enforce from the duca that solemn promise to ensure his safety; and though at first he was allowed no other provision than bread and water, and was cruelly chained to the floor of his dungeon, yet in a short time those chains were taken away, he had the liberty of walking about, and his food was of a better quality.

His gaoler was the mysterious padre Grimaldi, with whom, as he considered him as the author of his present situation, he never exchanged a word, and the monk was equally silent as his captive.

CHAPTER XII.

Rosalina was almost as impatient to see Montalto, as he was to urge his fond suit. She was anxious to inform him what she knew concerning the padre Grimaldi, of his residence in the castello, and various other circumstances which had taken place since they had last met. Montalto would likewise have wished to have related to her the miserable situation of his parent, but that he was restricted from so doing by his oath.

It was not till the second evening after he had seen the monk, that Montalto could find an opportunity of addressing, unseen, his adored Rosalina, when, in a retired aisle of the extensive chapel of the monastery, they contrived to escape observation; great was Montalto's astonishment on learning the conduct of the duca towards the monk, particularly as he knew the part Grimaldi had acted since that circumstance had taken place; and he saw at once, or at least thought he saw, his motives for imposing on him the solemn promise of not revealing his parent's captivity; for he began to imagine that there must be some secret plot against the duca's life, else why should the monk have acted as he had done, in bringing him into the chamber of Rodolpho, after having armed him with a dagger, and inflamed his mind to the perpetration of any act, however dreadful, and which, indeed, nothing but the recollection of Rosalina had prevented him from performing? Still, however, the motives of the monk might have been alone confined to the wish of letting a son revenge his father's wrongs. At all events, he had every reason to consider the monk as his friend, in whom he could with safety confide the most important secrets of his breast.

In the most tender and animated terms he urged Rosalina to make him the happiest of men, by consenting to a private union; but she thus addressed him:—

"To attempt to disguise my sentiments towards you,

Montalto, or that a union with you would not complete my happiness, is alike unnecessary; for you must be well assured of it. Such a step as you wish me to follow might, perhaps, in some measure, have been excusable, when the duca, my father, sought to unite me, contrary to my inclinations, to the prince di Manfroné; but now that he is no more, the situation is far different: time, perhaps, will bring about an event so much desired by us; but without my father's consent, Montalto must excuse my refusal."

"Oh, say not so, my angel!" returned the marchese. "Alas! did you know the fatal secret which throbs for utterance in my bosom, you would acknowledge the necessity of such a step: but that secret I am forbid to unfold. The least delay is attended with the most dreadful consequences—consequences which may separate Rosalina and Montalto for ever!"

"Forever!" faintly returned Rosalina. "What have you heard—what new discovery—what dreadful secret is this which you dare not unfold?"

"I am bound by a solemn oath not to reveal it," returned Montalto; "'tis indeed a dreadful secret, and horrible must be the consequences if you refuse to comply with my request; for I must commit a deed which nature's tie calls me loudly to perform, that will sever us for ever—that will imbrue my hands in blood, whose stain my own will, haply, for the termination of my sorrows, wash away; for never will I survive the deprivation of your society, nor shall I be able to resist the dreadful purpose of my soul, if Rosalina persists in her refusal. Oh, miserable wretch that I am! torn by contending passions, whose despotic sway I am not able to control! You, Rosalina, can avert this dreadful horror that impends over all of us. Your duty, as a daughter, compels you to grant my entreaty. Can I say more?"

The dreadful conviction of his meaning instantly flashed on Rosalina's mind; she trembled and turned pale.—"Complete," said she, "the dreadful sentence—unfold at once your secret, and tell me that Rosalina is the daughter of a murderer—of the murderer of your parent. Alas! I had always too much reason to suppose it. You have heard it. Leave me then, Montalto, leave me to my agonizing reflections; but do not, I conjure you, confound me with the guilty, for I am innocent of a parent's crimes."

"Perish that bosom that dares to harbour any other opinion of my adored Rosalina!" returned the marchese: "the duca is not quite so bad as you imagine; though, perhaps, death would have been better than——"

Here he paused, and Rosalina, who had eagerly listened to his last words, hastily said—"Complete your sentence; make me happy by exonerating my father of the dreadful crime which I have so long thought him guilty of."

"I cannot, Rosalina—I am bound by an oath; suffice it to say, his deeds call for retribution, and my arm must grasp the sword—but Rosalina can avert its deadly edge."

"Be not hasty, Montalto; you may have been wrong informed."

"No, lovely Rosalina, these eyes beheld—Oh, how horrible! how wild are my sensations when I reflect on what I saw! My brain seems on fire—delays are adding fresh torments—this instant will I go—yes, this shall be the hour of vengeance!"

Dreadful was the countenance of Montalto while he uttered these disjointed sentences—it bespoke the horrible agitation of his mind; he breathed short and quick, his eyes were distended, his brows lowered, a dark gloomy hue overspread his features, his hand firmly grasped his sword; already had he started from his seat, which was the marble surface of a tomb, when Rosalina, almost as agitated as himself, hastily seized his arm.

"Whither are you going," said she; "what is your horrible intent? Speak to me, Montalto! My father is the object of your vengeance! Pause—reflect on the deed you would commit, and know that the hand which is raised against him shall never press mine: the duca may be guilty, but he is Rosalina's father."

Her voice seemed to allay the furious rage of Montalto; he stopped and gazed on her, while his brows became less overcast, and his looks more composed.

"Too well I know that it will be as you say, Rosalina—too well I know that the deed I would perform, that the blow I meditate, would make thee fatherless, and would heavily revert on myself; for never would I survive the loss of thy affection, and the horror of reflecting on myself as the cause of your misery. Yet such is my situation, I cannot avoid committing the deed. Oh, Rosalina, were death to pay his chilling visit to my agonized form—were he at this moment to liberate my soul from earthly thought, how great would be the blessing! I should then expire without forfeiting Rosalina's love, nor would a——"

Here he stopped, and striking his forehead with his hand, awhile gave way to all the force of his heartfelt agonies. Rosalina was deeply affected; she trembled, and the tears started from her lovely eyes.

"What, oh Heavens!" said the terrified Rosalina, "What shall I do to avert these impending evils? Tell me, Montalto, tell me, I conjure you, while yet I am able to ask it?"

"I have told you," mournfully returned the marchese, "the only way by which it can be avoided. Let us unite our destinies, and by that you will become the preserver of your father's and your lover's life. Refuse and you are the executioner of both."

"Alas! what shall I do?" said Rosalina. "Montalto, indeed you are too precipitate, you act before you reflect. What secret is this which it appears has so lately been entrusted to you? How do you know but that your information may be false—fabricated, perhaps, to answer some hidden purpose of my father's enemies?"

"Alas!" returned Montalto, "I was myself a witness of the truth of the sad information; these eyes beheld the soul-harrowing sight, which, when but for a moment I reflect on, my senses wander, and my blood boils with rage against the author."

"And how would my consent to a secret union," said Rosalina, "avert the dreadful tempest of your passions?"

"Because it would be an excuse for my not doing an act of justice, and in time might happily reconcile the mortal enmity which otherwise must exist," returned Montalto. "Condescend, my adored angel," continued he, throwing himself at her feet, "condescend to make happy your Montalto!"

"Heaven direct me!" said Rosalina. "I know not what course

to pursue. Were my sainted mother living, I should not want an adviser."

"Alas!" said Montalto, "are not the existing circumstances of sufficient moment to induce you to comply? I will not take you from your father's abode; only consent to be united to me, and soon, I trust, the gloom that lowers over us will be dispelled, and days of happiness appear to our view."

"On that condition," said Rosalina, faintly, "I yield to your request; and in so doing, I am equally actuated by parental affection, as well as love for you; and may heaven forgive me if I am doing wrong!"

Montalto's countenance was illumined with the joy of his heart; for the first time he pressed the timid Rosalina to his bosom, while he said—"To-morrow night, my angel, contrive to be here; before that time I will procure one of the fathers to perform the ceremony."

"Be careful," said Rosalina, "in whom you place confidence: above all, avoid Grimaldi—he is the duca's friend."

"I think not," returned Montalto; "indeed I have every reason to suppose him firmly mine. His conduct has evinced him such."

"How then," replied Rosalina, "would he, in that case, have accepted of apartments in the castello? Besides, as I understand, the duca and he are frequently engaged in private converse."

"There is, most undoubtedly, something truly mysterious attached to his conduct; but he is, perhaps, at least as I have every reason to suppose, the duca's enemy: he indeed is the very person I meant to solicit, for he is no stranger to my sincere attachment to you."

"You know best," returned Rosalina; "only be cautious whom you trust, for if you are betrayed, our ruin is inevitable."

The gloom of evening had long reigned in the aisles of the chapel, and Rosalina, fearing her longer stay might excite suspicion, hastily bade Montalto adieu, and promising to be there at that time the next evening, hastened to the castello di Colredo; while the marchese, reflecting how he could obtain a conference with Grimaldi, had seated himself beneath the portico that was erected before the portals of the chapel.

He had not been there many minutes, before his attention was roused by the echo of paces in the chapel, the doors of which being open, he soon beheld a monk approaching the place where he was, and to his great joy, when he had advanced within a few paces, recognized the well-known figure of Grimaldi, whom he so much wished to see.

His cowl was, as usual, closely drawn over his features, his head bent towards the ground, and his arms folded and wrapped up in his long garments. Montalto, on perceiving that it was him, hastily arose from his seat.

"I wished much to see you, father," said he, "and but this moment was thinking how I might obtain an interview. You told me that in you I had a friend."

"Have I not given you the most ample proofs of the veracity of that assertion?" returned the deep hollow voice of the monk. "But you would not advantage yourself of the opportunity you had to revenge yourself on your enemy, and to liberate your parent; and if I recollect right, your excuse was love—that you loved the daughter of the man who had so deeply injured you, and on that account would suffer your father to linger in a wretched captivity! Such a tale would gain no credit, were I to relate it to the world; no one would believe a son capable of acting as you have done."

"Doubtless I merit your reproaches, father; but spare them for the present. Alas! did you know how great is the power of love, you would find in that knowledge an ample excuse for my conduct."

"You said you wished to see me," returned the monk, without appearing to notice his last words.

"I did, father. I have made you acquainted with my love for Rosalina. She has at length consented to a private union."

"A private union!" hastily returned the monk: "what! while the marchese, your father——"

"I know what you would say," replied Montalto. "Believe me, I have every wish to liberate my parent; but as the steps I must take to do that would endanger, if not totally prevent, my union with Rosalina, first let me secure that inestimable jewel, and then I shall better know how to act."

The monk did not return any answer; he seemed to be deeply ruminating on what he had heard, and after a short pause, Montalto continued—

"Now, father, I hope to find in you that friend who would perform the ceremony which will make me the happiest of men. You may depend on my gratitude, for I am amply possessed of the means of recompensing you."

"You forget," returned the monk, "that you are addressing yourself to one who has bidden adieu to the world, to whom riches are of no import. No, marchese, I have hitherto endeavoured to befriend you, not from motives of being rewarded, other than by that pleasing reflection which always accompanies friendly actions."

"Excuse my hasty speech—I own myself wrong," replied Montalto. "May I then felicitate myself on your consent?"

"You may," returned the monk; "but remember you must be silent as the grave. You know the duca—our lives would hardly appease his wrath. But when you are united to Rosalina, what do you intend doing with respect to Rodolpho? Is the sword of retribution still to sleep, or will you not then sheathe its deadly point in his heart, and give a parent liberty?—Rosalina, then indissolubly your own, cannot control your actions."

"My resolutions are not yet formed," returned Montalto; "but as it was in hopes of averting my deadly hatred against her parent that she has consented to our secret union, his life at least must be spared."

"I thought," returned the monk, "that love elevated the mind—spurred on the soul to noble achievements—gave each thought and each intent new vigour: but either I was misinformed, or in you its faculties are strangely perverted. So as that you can obtain the object of your wishes, a father may breathe his last in a dreary dungeon—his enemy proceed in all his dark and deadly deeds unhurt, and secretly triumph in all his plans!"

"You do me wrong, father, to conclude, that because I will not become the assassin of Rodolpho, I do not mean to pursue the proper steps to liberate my parent. The moment I am so happy as to call Rosalina mine, shall be the commencement of my plans."

"What! you mean tamely to request his freedom? to beg of Rodolpho to let you have your father?" returned the monk. "Such a proceeding would doubtless well become the haughty, generous, brave Montalto!"

"Father, your words are daggers to my soul! Need I repeat, that nothing but Rosalina restrains my revenge? Yet, do not suppose that I would stoop to assassination. No, I would dare him to the field, and my arm would doubtless prevail against the base oppressor. But then Rosalina, the idol of my soul, would be lost to me! I know not how to act: justice and duty impel me—but love, more powerful than either, restrains me."

"I pity you," returned Grimaldi, after a pause, "sincerely pity you; the noble energies of your mind are lost. But your union with Rosalina—when and where is the ceremony to be performed?"

"In this chapel, father; an hour after to-morrow's vespers she has promised to meet me. At that time there is little fear of interruption; but should you think it better, the time may be delayed till the monks are retired to rest."

"We must be guided by circumstances as to that," returned Grimaldi. "You may, however, depend on seeing me here at vespers. Rosalina of course departs with you?"

"No," returned Montalto, "she will remain at Colredo, till the liberation of my parent, and other circumstances, render it safe for her to reside with me. But in all this time I have not asked after my father. Have you, as you promised, alleviated, as much as you could, the horrors of his confinement? have you informed him that his son was a witness of his miserable captivity?"

"I am incapable of such a refinement on cruelty," replied the monk. "It is sufficient for him to endure the horrors of captivity (which I have lately, according to my promise, endeavoured to alleviate), than to have the heartbreaking reflection, that he has a son who tamely bears the knowledge of his situation, and instead of avenging his wrongs when he had the power, is now on the point of being allied to his enemy! How would he curse the moment of your birth! how would he curse himself for being the cause of your existence!—No, I would not add to your noble father's miseries by such an unkind disclosure. A moment's reflection, and you surely would not have put such a question to me. But enough has been said and done to rouse the most lethargic being. On this subject I shall not speak further: your future resolves will, doubtless, be guided by Rosalina; and thus your father has no prospect of release. Indeed I almost repent that I consented to unite you to her; but my word is passed, and may not be retracted. Farewell, the night wears away."

So saying, he left Montalto, who, though happy that his wishes respecting Rosalina seemed so near their accomplishment, yet the reproachful words of Grimaldi, all of which he felt he had deserved, sunk deep into his recollection, and marred his comfort. Dejected, and unlike a lover on the point of succeeding in his dearest hopes, he slowly proceeded to his residence, where, when he had arrived, he sat ruminating on what steps he should pursue; but he rejected every expedient of releasing his parent, as often as they presented themselves, for he could think of no mode of effecting it but what must deeply wound the bosom of Rosalina: nor could he ask her how he should act, because his oath prevented him from disclosing his father's situation. To request advice of the monk was useless, because he would doubtless urge him to perpetrate deeds which, should he listen to, then Rosalina's affections would be lost for ever; and as he could not be happy without her love, so neither could be happy while his father was wearing out his melancholy hours in the gloomy dungeons of Colredo, from whence he could only be released by his means.

CHAPTER XIII.

MONTALTO's gloomy ruminations at length gave way to the lively imagery which hope formed before his mental vision; but before this, the lark, soaring on the fragrant zephyrs, with his early notes proclaimed the approach of morning. Clouds of golden hue floated in the eastern horizon; and as the radiant colours deepen to the view, and spread around their blushing crimson tints, the nocturnal vapours begin to disperse, and the varied scenes of nature open to the view. At length the sun, broad rising, with his powerful rays chases away the shadowy veil of night, and nature, dressed in her golden beams, smiles in her renovated beauties. The choristers of the grove shake their variegated plumage, damp with the dews of night, which, resting on the leaves of the forest, they appear, in the refulgent rays of the sun, as if adorned with glittering gems. Night, that had for many hours held her reign over the hemisphere, has taken her gloomy flight, and her solemn sister, silence, soon follows in her train, scared by the lark's unwelcome notes, or the song of the peasant, who gaily rises to his daily labour. The busy hum of the animated world increases, and sleep no longer rests on the eyes of mortals. He too seeks another hemisphere, where the sun has ceased to shine, and spreads his drowsy influence abroad.

Montalto watched impatiently till the shadows of the western hills increased upon the tremulous bosom of the lake, and the sun ceased to glitter on its wavy surface: he viewed with sensations of delight the pale moon slowly emerging, as if from the bosom of a vast forest, which stretched its leafy tenantry on the sides of the mountains which skirted the western horizon, as silent and solemn it rolled along its mystic course, gathering its borrowed lumen from the declining sun.

"Thou bright planet," said he, "who hast so often witnessed

the tumultuous sorrows of my bosom, shalt witness also the happiness that this night awaits me—shalt witness the vows of Rosalina and Montalto!"

While indulging these reflections, he had advanced to the chapel: he entered it; the last strain of the monks and nuns had ceased to vibrate in the air, and they were slowly retiring to their cells. He looked around, but Rosalina was not there. He went to the porch, and cast his eyes towards Colredo, but beheld not the beloved object he sought. He returned to the chapel, which was now empty, and a solemn silence reigned in its dusky aisles, which was shortly disturbed by the opening and closing of a distant door, which soon after Montalto found was occasioned by the entrance of the padre Grimaldi, agreeable to his promise.

From the time that Rosalina had consented to become the bride of Montalto, her agitation had every moment increased: at one time she thought of retracting her promise, but then she recollected the danger that would in that case attend her father, for the marchese had so repeatedly declared that nothing but a union with her could afford him a pretext to stem the torrent of his rage, and which she knew to be but too well founded, and which even had a virtue in it, since it was caused by, as she supposed, the murder of his father! She thought that it was a duty in her to be watchful of the safety of the duca, since, let his crimes be ever so dreadful, it would nevertheless be a crime in her to forget that she was a daughter: she might indeed refuse to comply with Montalto's request, and warn the duca of his danger; but that could not be done without hazarding her lover's safety; there was therefore no choice left her; she was either to look upon herself as the cause of the destruction of the duca and Montalto, or else risk his terrible anger, should he ever know it while she was in his power, and be united to the man she adored.

Rosalina had, therefore, little difficulty in choosing the latter, but she had great difficulty in allaying the fears that every moment took deeper root in her bosom, and which, the more she reflected on what she was about to do, the more they increased, and the evening had approached before she had made her final resolution; but, however, greatly as she dreaded her father's rage, she dreaded still more the loss of Montalto; and throwing her veil over her lovely but pale features, she arose to go to the monastery; but her feeble limbs refused to support her, and she sunk on her seat, trembling with the indescribable sensations of anxiety and terror which pervaded her bosom.

She was fearful that her senses would give way to the agitation she endured, and that she should be obliged to summon Carletta to her assistance, in which case she could not have attempted, without exciting suspicion, to proceed by herself to the chapel; and whether she yielded to Montalto's entreaties or not, she wished to see him, since he might conjecture, if she was to fail in her promise of meeting him, that she had altered her resolution, and thereby might blow into a flame the kindling embers of his just anger.

This reflection served to make her exert herself; and when at length she was able to leave her chamber, her fears of being observed and followed gave her fresh powers to hasten through the corridors and to cross the courtyard which led to the castle-gates. Fortunately she did not meet with a single person, and, somewhat comforted by this circumstance, she slowly proceeded down the winding path which led to the monastery, often stopping to rest her trembling limbs, which the nearer she approached the monastery, the more she feared would cease to support her, for her agitation and terror momentarily increased. Her fears were indeed not without foundation, for, after with the greatest difficulty she had succeeded in reaching the portico at the gates of the chapel, her eyes grew dizzy, the objects before her seemed to turn round, and she staggered towards the stone seats which were on each side the portico, on which she sunk, and instantly became insensible to all her cares, which were far too much for her fragile frame to support, and which indeed had for a long time fatally warred with her tender constitution, which they were rapidly undermining.

The monk, when he entered the chapel, advanced towards Montalto.

"The signora Rosalina is not yet come?" said he.

"No, father," returned Montalto, "but the appointed hour is scarcely past. I am not fearful of her neglecting her promise; sinister events may indeed protract her stay at the castello, as she will of course be cautious of attracting observation."

"I know not how this will end," returned the monk; "it is a rash undertaking, and pregnant with evil. What will the sensations of the old marchese be when he hears of this union!"

"Father, you seem to delight in unpleasant anticipations: surely the evils we have to encounter are amply sufficient, without creating imaginary ones to torture us. Let us rather felicitate ourselves on the enjoyment of happy days: such a hope will enliven the prospect before us, however gloomy it may at present appear; and our minds, instead of being weakened by mournful ruminations, will be strengthened by our pleasing hopes, and be therefore better able to support the calamities which otherwise we must sink under."

During this conversation he had advanced along the aisle towards the grand altar which terminated it, when turning round in hopes of seeing Rosalina approaching, he beheld her tottering towards the portico, and soon after sunk apparently senseless on one of the stone benches. He flew towards her, and found that his conjectures were but too true, for no signs of animation were perceptible in her pale motionless form.

His tender assiduities at length restored her; and as slowly she became sensible of the sound of his voice, her eyes unclosed, and she fixed her languid gaze on her lover; but the tall figure of the padre Grimaldi, who stood motionless before her, without offering to render any assistance to Montalto, while it roused her to a recollection of her intended union, nevertheless filled her with alarms, for which she found it impossible to account. It was a sensation of fear, bordering on terror, which his appearance always excited, notwithstanding she had now every reason to conclude, from his past and present conduct, that he was the friend of her lover. Comforted, however, by his presence, she endeavoured to banish her uneasy sensations respecting him, and which was necessary to enable her to attend to the ceremony which he was going to perform, which would unite her in the indissoluble bonds of marriage to the man she adored.

Animated by this last reflection, her strength returned, and leaving her seat, she entered the chapel, resting on the arm of Montalto, preceded by the padre Grimaldi, who with his accustomed slow and measured paces, advanced to the altar.

A cloud had rolled its sable folds before the moon, and obscured her silver beams; a gloomy horror seemed to enwrap every object in the chapel, that was rendered partially visible by the faint lumens of the twinkling stars: the silence of the monk—the echo of their paces, which appeared to Rosalina as if they were whispered around—and above all, the consciousness of the ceremony that was going to be performed wanting a parent's sanction, terrified her, and once she was going to request Montalto to let her return to the castello, but she paused, for she feared to hear the sounds of her own voice.

At length, when they approached the altar, the monk turning round, desired Montalto to remain there while he went into the monastery to procure a lamp. The hollow tones of his voice startled Rosalina, and she watched his tall figure till it disappeared in the gloom, and she remained silent till the sound of a closing door hollowly echoing through the vast fabric, caused a sudden exclamation to escape her.

Montalto, who had been for some time engaged in pleasing anticipations, now endeavoured to sooth the perturbation of her mind, and those endearing expressions which came from a heart so fondly devoted to her as was his, had the desired effect. She now ceased to tremble, and exerting herself, waited with some degree of composure for the arrival of the monk, who soon after appeared holding a lamp, the feeble rays of which darting through the gloom, rendered visible the surrounding objects.

Both their eyes were fixed on the padre Grimaldi, but a low creaking sound in another part of the chapel made the fearful Rosalina look to the place from whence it seemed to proceed, when to her astonishment she perceived in one of the side aisles a door slowly opening, and which disclosed the gigantic figure of a man, who leaning forward through the aperture, seemed to watch their movements. Rosalina involuntarily clung to Montalto, who, surprised at her agitation, turned round, when she silently pointed to the man at the portal; but before he had found out the spot, the figure had receded, and the door was silently closed.

"My dearest Rosalina," whispered Montalto, "why do you seek to alarm yourself by fancy-formed objects of terror? What is it that you suppose you have beheld, which makes you tremble so?"

"It was no suppositious form that I saw," returned Rosalina in a faint voice. "Dear Montalto! danger is lurking around us: for Heaven's sake, let me return to the castello! I shall faint with the terrible apprehensions which assail my bosom, if we stay here any longer; another evening I will come—believe me, I will indeed!"

"Cruel Rosalina!" returned Montalto, "is it thus, when by your kind acquiescence you had elevated me to the summit of happiness, that you seek to hurl me from the fancied seat of bliss, and render me the most miserable of created beings?"

"The construction you have put on my request is unkind," returned Rosalina: "believe me it is not with a view or wish to retract from my promise, but I am overwhelmed by sensations which almost overpower my reason, and which indeed is occasioned by the certainty that we are discovered."

"A moment's reflection, my Rosalina, will convince you how ill founded such an apprehension is, since no one but the father Grimaldi is privy to our designs, and he, I am certain, would not betray us to the duca, for his life is in my power, were I to unfold to Rodolpho what I know concerning him—a circumstance of which he cannot be ignorant."

Rosalina, somewhat assured by this last assertion, became more composed; and now Grimaldi arriving at the altar, laid his lamp on it, when she again hearing the same noise which had alarmed her before, looked anxiously towards the aisle where she had seen the alarming figure; but the lamp was so placed, that its faint rays rested against some opposite columns, whose dark broad shadows obscured the recess where the portal was. The monk noticed her agitation.

"You seem alarmed, signora," said he; "has any thing occurred that could give rise to your terrors?"

"Yes," returned Rosalina, who was on the point of relating to Grimaldi the figure she had seen, when Montalto suddenly interrupting her, said—"The gloom of the place, father, and the noises occasioned by the wind, have alarmed Rosalina; hasten then, I entreat you, in the ceremony, lest her increasing agitation render her incapable of longer stay."

The monk then turning to the altar, slowly opened his missal, and Montalto and Rosalina advanced nearer to him: but scarcely had he repeated a few sentences, when an unseen hand struck Montalto, who staggered and fell back on the steps of the altar, and at the same moment Rosalina felt herself seized in the strong grasp of a man, who bore her instantly out of the chapel. Her terror depriving her of her senses, she happily was for a time ignorant of the horrible anticipations of what might befal her; and which, joined to the recollection of Montalto wounded, in the hands of his enemies, would doubtless have harrowed up her senses beyond their bearing, and perhaps have affected for ever her reason. This calamity was, however, for the present spared her.

In the morning of that day, the duca repaired at an early hour to the apartments where Grimaldi resided, and thus addressed him—"When I first had the pleasure of meeting with you, father, you told me you were not ignorant of my views respecting the principality of Manfroné, vacant by his death: how you came by that knowledge is not material; perhaps you knew that my mind was ambitious, and that I should not neglect so favourable an opportunity of aggrandizement; if such were your ideas, they were rightly formed. Sebastiano, the leader of the adverse party, has refused my offers of assistance, relying, as I conclude, on some trifling successes which he has lately gained over the partizans of the late prince. Now, father, I wish for your advice: shall I at the head of my forces enter the province, and under colour of aiding the adherents of Manfroné, attack Sebastiano's people? Our united force cannot fail of success, and of exterminating him: stratagem will likewise put the other troops in my power, and then the way seems easy to the regal seat."

"Your scheme is just such as I would have proposed," returned the monk: "but you must be cautious—collect your forces within the castle-walls with as much privacy as possible, and in small detachments march to the capital, taking care that your people will arrive there on a certain day; the astonishment of Sebastiano, when he hears of the numerous party that has thus in a manner invisibly collected, will spread itself throughout his forces, and prevent the effusion of much blood; for the loss of many vassals will be severely felt by you, when you attain the sovereign power, and perhaps expose you to the attacks of the neighbouring potentates, who doubtless are now on the watch, and only wait till the adverse parties have exhausted their strength, to fall on the conqueror, who, of course weakened by warfare, will be unable to make any opposition. You must therefore guard well against depopulating the territories of the late Manfroné, for, Sebastiano vanquished, his followers being little better than mercenaries, will gladly fight for him who pays them best. By these means you will not only be able to attain the sceptre of rule, but also to maintain it against all attempts that may at any future time be made."

"Your advice, father," returned the duca, "seems rather the result of mature deliberation, than of the idea of the moment, and gladly I shall follow it."

"Your operations may be rendered still more easy, duca," returned Grimaldi, "if you have courage to grasp a dagger, and terminate at once Sebastiano's ambition with his life. You start! but I have said I was your friend; I did not mention this plan without intending to share your danger."

"Such a friend indeed as you," said Rodolpho, "is rarely to be met with. But in what manner shall this be performed? No one ever doubted my courage: but this attempt seems to partake of rashness—we may be discovered before the deed is done."

"I pledge my life for its success, if you will be guided by me.

I would not risk myself unnecessarily, and you will be no more endangered than myself. This indeed is a subject on which I have bestowed much thought."

"And I have too good an opinion of your judgment," answered the duca, "to pause a moment in giving my consent. Shall I acquaint Lupo with this project? He is faithful, and may be serviceable in this affair."

"I think you had better not," returned the monk, "and for this reason: while we are away, he must attend to your prisoner; and the more secret we are, the more likely of success. But while we are arranging your affairs abroad, there is a business of no small import which calls your attention at home."

"How, father? at home! What is it your vigilant friendship has discovered?" said Rodolpho.

"Your daughter Rosalina is on the point of being married."

"Married! how? to whom?" exclaimed the astonished duca.

"To your bitterest enemy, the young marchese di Montalto."

"It is impossible! Rosalina never could consent!"

"It is but too true," returned Grimaldi; "I have promised to perform the ceremony myself this evening."

"You, father! indeed! How would that act agree with your asseverations of friendship?" returned the duca, rather in a hasty tone.

"The information I have given you is, I believe, a sufficient proof of them: it is true I have promised, but the reason I did that is obvious—that no other monk might be induced by hopes of emolument to undertake it: confiding therefore in me, they will not have an idea of applying to any other person. But it rests with you, duca, to prevent the nuptials."

"Forgive my hasty expressions," returned the duca; "I was indeed wrong to harbour for a moment a doubt respecting you. When then is this marriage to take place?"

"This evening, at an hour after vespers, in the chapel of Santa Maria," replied Grimaldi.

"It is well," returned the duca: "this evening shall be Montalto's last. As for Rosalina, she shall rue her disobedience in confinement till she weds a husband of my choice."

"Content yourself at present," said the monk, "with confin-
ing the young marchese in your deepest dungeons, and restrict
the signora Rosalina to the walls of the castello: for this I have
my reasons, and you well know, duca, that all my plans are for
your benefit."

"Of that I am well assured," said Rodolpho, "and it shall be
as you wish. To-morrow we will have another conference, for
we must be hasty in our operations; and when I once am fixed
secure in Manfroné's vacant seat, where will be the man more
honoured, and possessed with more authority than yourself?"

"The pleasure of being serviceable to you," returned the
monk, "is recompense enough for me—I seek no other."

They now separated; the duca, assisted by Lupo and two of
the soldiers belonging to the castello, secreted themselves in
the chapel till the ceremony was begun, when having rendered
Montalto incapable of resistance by a severe wound, they instantly conveyed him to the dungeon assigned him by Lupo.

Rosalina, when she recovered, found herself in her own
apartment, and Carletta standing by the side of her couch: her
first inquiry was concerning Montalto; her domestic could not
give her any information of him; all she knew was, that the duca
had followed the men who were conveying her to the chamber,
and that he appeared to be greatly irritated, and desired Carletta
to acquaint her, as soon as she recovered, that he should expect
her attendance the next morning in his apartments.

This was indeed a painful task for Rosalina to perform, and
she trembled on hearing Carletta repeat the dreadful mandate.
The rectitude of her intentions in complying with Montalto's
entreaties alone enabled her to support the trying scene, which
she was but too conscious, from her knowledge of her father's
outrageous passions, awaited her.

The morning was swift in its approach, and the much-
dreaded hour arrived, when Rosalina, whose countenance
shewed the agitated state of her bosom, with a slow trembling step, leaning on her attendant's arm, entered the duca's
apartments.

He gazed on her for some time with a stern malicious countenance, when at length, in a harsh tone, he broke his painful silence.

"It was not sufficient, Rosalina," said he, "that you should attempt to dispose of yourself without the sanction of your father, but you must make choice of the man of all others, my most implacable and bitter enemy, who, scoffing at the many advances I made to be on terms of friendship with him, even after he had dared to harbour suspicions injurious to my honour! He thought, I conclude, to revenge himself against me in the tenderest point, by seducing my daughter from her duty, in making her set at defiance her parent's anger: this indeed would have been a triumph for Montalto, but thanks to my lucky stars, I have for ever prevented his designs!"

"For ever!" faintly repeated Rosalina; "is Montalto then no more?—he who, at the risk of his own life, twice preserved me from the savage Manfroné—who rid you too of an enemy you so much dreaded? Surely you could not be so cruel as to commit so horrible a deed?"

"And why not?" returned the savage Rodolpho. "Do you think I would tamely bear so great an outrage—and from Montalto too?"

"Then hear me," replied Rosalina, whose wildly-looking eyes shewed that her senses were disturbed—"hear my last words, for I feel that nature will before long sink under the pangs which rack my bosom. Montalto would have been your friend, if you had not been the murderer of his father! You start! Alas! what are my sensations when I am forced to tell a parent such a dreadful truth! And by all the blessed saints I swear, that never would Rosalina have consented to be united to him without your approval, much as she loved him, but she did it to stop the sword of retribution from shortening a parent's existence: guilty though he might be, she could not forget that he was her father. You have completed the dreadful deed; the father and the son both have winged their flight to heaven, where dreadful will be their evidence against thee. But there is yet one more victim, and that is your daughter, for never will I survive Montalto! No—life without him would be a blank indeed.—Did I not say I would not survive him? Is he then dead? The generous brave Montalto, is he no more? Ah, yes! now I recollect I saw him, as bleeding he lay in the chapel. My brain, how it burns!—what a horrid scene was that! Oh, misery! misery!"

Here, with a long and mournful groan, Rosalina dashed herself on the floor, and raved in all the frantic ebullitions of insanity. The duca was moved by her sufferings: he had her conveyed to her apartment, and in order to calm her, repeatedly assured her that Montalto was still alive: but she no longer was able to comprehend him. She accused him of the murder of Astolpho, the marchese, and his son. The pale attendants gazed on each other as they listened to her words, and Rodolpho, to his astonishment, found that his dark deeds were not unknown to his daughter; he affected, however, to impute her exclamations as the consequence of the derangement of her senses, and desired all the domestics to leave the apartment except Carletta and a monk, whom he had sent for to attend his unfortunate daughter, and who vainly exerted his medical knowledge to calm the dreadful perturbation of her mind.

The duca shortly after left the chamber, and going to Grimaldi, requested he would endeavour to undeceive his daughter with respect to Montalto's death, which the monk promising he would, instantly repaired to her.

He found her in the same melancholy state in which Rodolpho had left her, except indeed that her exertions had considerably weakened her, and there were some hopes that the composing medicines which she had taken would have the wished effect: she still indeed raved, and accused her father; but her voice was somewhat faint, and after a time sunk so very low, that her disjointed sentences could scarcely be understood. It was then that Grimaldi, who had not before spoken, but silently appeared to contemplate the unfortunate Rosalina's sufferings, uttered in his deep hollow-toned voice—"Rosalina, do not give way to grief, for Montalto yet lives." At the well-remembered sound of his voice, she gazed on him, as if endeavouring to recall to her memory who he was, when he again repeated his former words, which she appeared to comprehend, for she shook her head in token of her disbelief of them, and as if impressed with the idea that he had betrayed her, waved her hand for him to quit the apartment.

Grimaldi however still continued to speak to her, and to assure her that Montalto was yet in existence, and at length succeeded in making her believe him, which happily contributed, with the assistance of the medicines she had taken, to lull her troubled senses; and a powerful soporific being administered, she at length sunk into a profound slumber.

Grimaldi did not fail to be present when she awoke; but then her recollection having returned, she openly taxed him with having betrayed the confidence that the unsuspecting Montalto had reposed in him, and acquainting the duca with the intended marriage; but after he had requested her to send the domestic from the chamber, he solemnly denied the charge; adding, that he was well assured that their conversation in the chapel, when Montalto endeavoured to persuade her to a union, was overheard, not only by himself, but also by another monk, who must have made the duca privy to it; and concluded thus—"You, daughter, have perused the eventful pages which were traced by my hand, trembling with the agitation of a bosom torn by contending passions, but none of greater force than love: judge then, could I who have endured so much—who have been so greatly a victim to the tender emotions of my bosom—and who, to nurse my increasing miseries, have entered on a life of seclusion—do you think that I could be guilty of so great a cruelty as that of separating two fond lovers? Oh no! at such an idea my heart recoils.—But that I may prove to you the certainty of what I advance, I will myself convey a letter to the marchese, who is confined in the castello: nay more, if you will but be discreet, I will almost promise that you shall shortly see him: but this must be kept secret from the duca, for though my existence is of no import—though life to me is now a dreary blank, yet I would willingly preserve it, that I may dedicate it to your service, and when I see you happy, death will be truly welcome."

The hope of seeing Montalto conveyed instant comfort to Rosalina's bosom. She felt hurt at her injurious suspicions of the monk, and no longer considered him as her enemy, or the author of her present misfortunes. She conversed for some time with him respecting Montalto, whose wound, she was happy to hear, was of little consequence, and in a fair way of recovery: she entreated the monk to name an early period for the desired interview, and he assured her that it should take place as soon as she should be able to leave her chamber. With this promise he left her, having first, however, repeatedly warned her of the necessity of her silence, lest, should it come to Rodolpho's knowledge, he might no longer be restrained from terminating his fears of Montalto in his death.

Rosalina, assured of Montalto's being in existence, soon recovered, and on the second day she was able to quit her couch, and to sit at the casement of her chamber, which commanded a view of the extensive courtyard in front of the castello, where, ignorant of the schemes of the duca, she was astonished to behold the military preparations that were going forward, and the armed parties that were continually coming in; while Carletta's relation of what she saw, and of what the domestics conjectured were the intents of the duca, instead of giving any idea of the reason of the troops being thus silently collected, only served to lead her still further from the real cause.

The duca, busied in the preparations for his enterprize, seemed almost to have forgot the late events: from Grimaldi he learnt that Rosalina was recovering, and, satisfied with his account, he forbore to visit her—perhaps indeed the presence of his daughter, now that he found she was not ignorant of Astolpho's fate, was not capable of producing any agreeable sensations.

At the close of the third day, the monk Grimaldi entered Rosalina's chamber; and having requested her to send away Carletta, thus addressed her—"As this is the last evening, Signora, that I shall be in the castello for some time, I will at midnight procure you the promised interview with the marchese Montalto, if you think yourself able to walk as far as the east hall; its remote situation will preclude the possibility of your meeting being observed, and by this act of mine you will doubtless be well assured of my wishes for your happiness."

Delighted with the idea of seeing Montalto, Rosalina was not backward in expressions of her thanks and gratitude for his kindness, and which indeed answered every end that the monk seemed to wish, for it entirely took from her mind the doubts which had still lurked there, that he was in some way concerned with having communicated the secret of her intended union.

Whatever were the designs which the monk had respecting Rosalina or Montalto, he seemed to be anxious that they should consider him as their friend, and certainly he could not have thought of a more sure method than that which he was now pursuing.

In the meantime, the young marchese pined away the hours in his dreary dungeon. His suspicions of the author of his misfortune at first fell upon the monk, but when he recalled to his mind what he had told Rosalina as a certain reason that Grimaldi would not betray him, he began to doubt that it could be him. He was more unhappy about Rosalina's fate—exposed to the fury of the relentless duca, than his own hapless situation, though he could hardly ever expect to leave his dungeon alive; and indeed he wondered that Rodolpho did not terminate his existence, when he was rendered insensible by the severe blow which doubtless was given him by his perfidious enemy.

It was while he was deeply immersed in these ruminations that the door of the dungeon opened, and the monk entered.

"Unfortunate man!" said he, "how greatly I pity you, who are not only the victim of your own impetuosity, but also have so deeply involved the signora Rosalina."

"Tell me, father," said Montalto, "before you proceed, how is that adored angel? has the savage Rodolpho, unmindful of her tender frame, persecuted her?"

"It is impossible to say what he would have done," returned Grimaldi, "if the greatness of her sufferings, caused by her fears on your account, had not caused her senses to wander."

"Her senses to wander!—Oh God!" exclaimed Montalto,

"this is too much! My own hard lot I could have borne, but to think of my lovely Rosalina bereft of her senses—a raging maniac! the reason that illumined the beautiful structure gone, and in its place a gloomy, horrid void, like chaos before the world was formed!"

"Do not distress yourself unnecessarily," returned Grimaldi; "it is true, for a time her state was melancholy indeed, but now she is better; her senses have returned, but their absence, though short, has shook her delicate frame."

"Go on, monk; I know what you would say; you are prefacing the sad tale of her dissolution. Go on, and annihilate me with the truth."

"You are too impetuous, marchese," returned the monk: "had you been less so, your conversation in the chapel, when you pressed the signora Rosalina to give her consent to be united to you, would not have been heard, and at this moment, instead of being a prisoner in the dungeons of Colredo, Rosalina would have been your bride. I have exerted every means in my power to comfort Rosalina, and have in part succeeded, for she now is anxiously counting the tardy moments till midnight, when, at the risk of my life, I have promised to procure her an interview with you."

Whatever suspicions Montalto might have formed of the monk Grimaldi, all vanished when he heard his intentions. The blissful idea of again beholding Rosalina was a soothing balm, which healed the deep sorrows of his breast; and when he had acknowledged his sense of his kindness, he inquired how soon the happy time would arrive?

"It now wants an hour of midnight, the time I have fixed on as being the safest; but you must promise me, signor, that you will not advantage yourself of my wish to alleviate the horrors of your situation to effect your escape, a circumstance which would endanger my life; for if it had not been for some services I have rendered the duca, you know him too well to doubt but that my punishment would have been as severe as yours."

Montalto readily acquiesced with the monk's desire, and faithfully promised to return to his dungeon as soon as he should conceive it necessary. Grimaldi then saying he would be with him in an hour, to conduct him to the eastern hall, proceeded to Rosalina, who having ordered Carletta to retire to rest, sat full of impatience for his approach.

"Now, signora," said he, "if you will follow me, I will conduct you to the place I have fixed on for your interview with Montalto. Be sure you tread softly along the corridors, or you may disturb the duca or some of the officers who now reside in the castello."

"I am ready, father," said Rosalina, who now, in compliance with his request, trod with caution the silent corridors as she followed his slow paces. The inhabitants of the extensive pile were buried in sleep, and unobserved Rosalina reached the east hall, where, on a table in a recess at the farther end, burnt a solitary lamp.

"Direct your steps," said the monk, who had not spoke since he first entered Rosalina's chamber, "to that lamp, and remain there while I proceed to Montalto's residence."

Rosalina did as she was desired, and the monk crossed the hall in another direction.

In the pleasing anticipation of seeing the object of her love, the fears which her present situation might naturally excite in a female breast were disregarded; the hall was situated in a lonely and unfrequented part of the castello—in a part, too, where she, when confined there by the duca, had twice witnessed a fearful sight; but she did not allow herself to be terrified either by the recollection of them, or the sounds of the midnight gale, as it rustled past the casements, or rushed along the passages in hollow gusts. This hall had formerly witnessed many a splendid spectacle, for the ancient possessors of the castello had generally resided in the eastern wing; the lofty columns were still loaded with the spoils of the field, and the torn banners waved silently to the wind. Rosalina seated herself near the marble table on which was the glimmering lamp, whose tremulous lumen she each moment feared would be extinguished by the passing breeze.

At length she heard some paces approaching her, and beheld

a lamp at the further end of the hall, which, as it came nearer, she found was carried by the monk, and gleamed on the loved form of Montalto, who accompanied him. She hastily arose from her seat, and in a moment was clasped to his bosom; but the pleasure of their meeting was greatly alloyed by the change which each found in the other since their unfortunate separation. Montalto was pale, and his countenance was indeed but too expressive of the pain and misery he had endured; while Rosalina still laboured under the consequences of her severe illness. The presence of Grimaldi was rather a restraint to their conversation, and after they had enjoyed each other's society till the rosy-tinted morning glowed in the east, the monk reminded them that they must part.—"I am now," continued he, "almost immediately going to leave the castello; you must, while I am absent, make use of your resolution and philosophy, and guard against the ill consequences of giving way to useless regrets, and when I return, perhaps an opportunity may offer of uniting you: meantime, Rosalina, you need be under no apprehensions respecting the personal safety of the marchese Montalto; but I charge you both on no account to let Lupo, the castellain, know that you have ever met, or ever entreat him to permit you to do so, for you may rest assured that he is too faithful to the trust reposed in him by the duca, and you will thereby expose yourselves not only to a refusal, but your request will be made known to his master, which may perhaps be attended with fatal consequences: against this I warn you as a friend, and if hereafter you should neglect my admonition, you will only have yourselves to blame."

Rosalina and Montalto promised to comply with his advice, and now with many sighs they separated. Montalto repaired with Grimaldi to his gloomy dungeon, and Rosalina sought her own apartments, where, somewhat comforted by the promises of the monk, she resigned herself to the composing influence of the somnific deity till she was roused by the shrill tones of the trumpets and hollow cymbals, and hastily rising from her couch, she beheld from her casement, the duca in the courtyard, surrounded by his principal officers and attendants, surveying the troops who thickly thronged the spacious area; they were afterwards divided into several parties, and from the actions of the duca, Rosalina concluded that he was giving his final orders to the officers respecting their future operations, which she could not avoid feeling anxious to obtain a knowledge of.

After some hours were passed, the men were dismissed from the courtyard, and the duca still remained in earnest conversation with the officers, some of whom indeed looked rather like leaders of banditti than of regular troops, as indeed afterwards she found they were, for Rodolpho had engaged a considerable number of those savage outlaws at a vast expence, and it was on their well-known desperate valour that he placed his greatest reliance. Unlike the others, these men listened with an air of savage independence to his orders, and frequently seemed by their gestures to be debating among themselves respecting them. Rosalina shuddered as she viewed their ferocious features, and one in particular, who, instead of attending to the conversation of the others, leaning on his battle-spear, gazed on the lofty towers of Colredo, and the form of Rosalina attracting his notice, he fixed his eyes on her till she hastily retreated from his rude observance. There was some thing in the features of this man which was familiar to her recollection, but at the slight glance she had of them she could not at that moment remember where she had seen him; and when she ventured to return to the casement again, he was walking with some of his savage-looking companions at the further end of the courtyard, and the plumes in his military hat shaded his face. While she was looking at him, the door of her apartment opened, and Carletta entered.

"Oh, signora! at last I have heard all about the great preparations which have filled the castello with such a number of soldiers: the duca is going to make himself master of all the territories which belonged to the prince di Manfroné, and they say he will then be a prince, and you, signora, will be a princess, so Pietro says: but poor Pietro is going along with them to the wars; now, signora, if you would but speak one word to the duca, I am sure he would let him stay behind."

"If you were to consider one moment of the circumstances that have so lately taken place, you would see the folly of making such a request," returned Rosalina; "I should not only risk a refusal, but perhaps my father would be irritated against Pietro, as concluding he wished to stay behind; so you would have cause to repent my acquiescence. Do you know if the duca goes with the troops, and when they are to leave the castello?"

"I believe to-night," returned Carletta, in a mournful tone; "there are great preparations for a banquet in the hall, where all the officers are to dine, and after that, Pietro says, they are to leave the castello, and the duca——"

Carletta's conversation was here interrupted by the entrance of an attendant, who informed Rosalina that the duca expected to see her in the hall at the banquet.

Rosalina at first hesitated in her answer; she wished indeed to have been excused, but on finding from Carletta that the duca meant to accompany the troops, she could not refuse with any degree of propriety, and therefore desired the messenger to inform her father she should attend.

Rosalina was not sorry to learn that her father was going, because her fears for Montalto's safety would cease when he was absent. From Carletta she learned that the father Grimaldi had quitted the castello early in the morning, and she hoped that he would return before the duca, for she was firmly persuaded that he was not only a sincere friend to her, but also that by reason of the influence he seemed to have over him, had it greatly in his power to be so.

When the hour appointed for the banquet arrived, Rosalina descended to the hall: the confusion she felt at being exposed to the gaze of so many strangers, with whom it was crowded, increased the tint of the rose, which since her late illness but faintly blossomed on her lovely cheek, and added to her charms. Her fine dark hair was braided, and otherwise fancifully ornamented after the Sicilian mode, and her Grecian robe was confined to her taper waist by a girdle, which was richly studded with precious stones. Every eye was fixed on her as the duca introduced her to some of his particular friends, with whom he was in conversation when she entered, and a general whisper of admiration ran round the hall.

Rosalina hardly dared to raise her eyes during the repast, for whenever she did, she was sure to find herself the universal object of contemplation, from which her native modesty revolted. The conversation turned unceasingly on the business which was so shortly to be commenced, and Rosalina was shocked at the sanguinary schemes which were proposed by some of the leaders, and which appeared to gain general approbation.

She found that the enterprize they were about to be engaged in, it was imagined, would be but of short duration, and that they expected to return, crowned with victory, before a week had elapsed; for no one appeared to entertain even a momentary doubt of their success, and even derided the united forces of Sebastiano and the partizans of the late prince, so confident did they appear in their own strength.

The duca di Rodolpho, as soon as the banquet was concluded, arose from his seat, and filling a large goblet with wine, drank "to the success of the expedition," which was re-echoed from every part of the hall, and the hollow sounding cymbals and sonorous horns floated on the air their martial notes, which inspired every bosom with military ardour. The ruby-coloured vintage rose frequent in the capacious vases, and the music and voices of the guests, which now increased every moment, were far from giving sensations of pleasure to Rosalina, who found her situation becoming extremely unpleasant, for the leaders of her father's forces, who had been before restrained only by their fears of attracting the duca's observation in their conduct towards Rosalina, now emboldened by the intoxicating juice of the grape, eyed her with such an appearance of insolent familiarity, and some even attempted to address her, that she hastened from the hall as soon as possible, and gladly sought the welcome retirement of her chamber.

The sounds of mirth and rude merriment which prevailed for some time longer in the hall, at length suddenly ceased, and as soon as the shades of evening had closed in the views of nature, the trampling of steeds and noise of men was heard in the court-yard, and Rosalina saw the troops collecting in it previous to their departure.

Some of the officers appeared quite inebriated as well as the men, and increased the confusion and wild uproar that reigned, till the duca made his appearance, which soon silenced them; and when at length all was ready, the parties silently marched through the wide-opening gates, and as soon as they arrived at the bottom of the hill, Rosalina discovered by the light of the moon, which was reflected on their bright arms, that they separated, some continuing their course through the valley, while others wound along the paths made on the steep sides of the mountains. The duca did not depart with them, but remained in the courtyard in earnest conversation with Lupo for some time, when he returned to the castello.

The beauty of the night, and the various thoughts which agitated her bosom, took from Rosalina all wish for repose, and she still remained at the casement, where obtrusive memory brought to her recollection past hours of bliss enjoyed with Montalto, while to her mental vision appeared his loved form stretched on a miserable pallet, in a damp unwholesome dungeon, without the consoling voice of a friend to cheer him under the unmerited wrongs which were heaped on him by her father. Such were her sad thoughts, and the tears excited by them often rolled down her lovely cheeks; the beams of the moon glistened in the pearly drops of sorrow, and alone witnessed her griefs.

"And thou, soft rolling planet," thought she, "illumine with thy silver radiance the drear abode of my love—comfort him under his sad captivity, and reflect in thy bright orb the sorrowing form of his Rosalina, that he may view the object of his love, weeping at his woes!"

These reflexions were disturbed by a noise in the courtyard, and Rosalina looking down, beheld the well-remembered form of the duca, though he was disguised in his dress, and by a large mantle which he closely drew around him. One attendant only was with him, and both mounting their horses, were soon far distant from the castello, the gates of which were closed, and silence once more resumed her melancholy reign amidst the lofty towers and extensive halls of Colredo.

Rosalina was too well convinced of the propriety of Grimaldi's advice to speak to Lupo respecting Montalto, and she waited with no small impatience for the arrival of the monk, when she hoped that he might be persuaded to assist in procuring his liberty.

Excepting the female attendants, and a few soldiers who were incapacitated either by age or wounds from being of any service, the duca had taken with him every one who was able to bear arms, the castellain excepted, and who Rosalina rightly concluded was left at the castello to attend on the unfortunate victims of his deadly hatred.

She would often, when Lupo was away, traverse the subterraneous passages of Colredo, and sigh forth the loved name of Montalto, in the hopes of being able to discover where his dungeon was; but her efforts were useless, for Lupo, with his usual foresight, had taken care to close up those passages that led to it.

Carletta was little able to afford any comfort to her mistress, for she continually lamented the dangers to which Pietro was exposed, who it seems had long been the possessor of her affections.

It was near the close of the fifth day from the departure of the troops, that as Rosalina was sitting pensively at her casement, watching the declining rays of the setting sun, which now feebly darted on the earth, that she discovered a cloud of dust rising amidst the passes of the distant mountains, and as she watched it, once or twice thought that she saw the beams of the sun glancing on some bright object; at first she imagined that it might be the forces of the duca returning, but then, as the object she was viewing drew nearer, she could easily discover that they were indeed armed troops, but the smallness of their number convinced her that her conjectures were wrong; on their still nearer advance, however, she saw that they waved on high the banners of the duca. On this she immediately sent for

the castellain, who having viewed the party, was unable to conclude what was the motive of their return, or the apparent haste
they made to reach the castello; but they soon unfortunately
found out the reason, for a second troop appeared, preceded
by some horsemen, who soon overtaking the first party, an engagement instantly took place, which was fatal to the soldiers
of Rodolpho, for they betook themselves to flight, and having
dispersed, were no longer visible, while the victorious party
still continued to advance; and the castellain concluding that
their intent was to attack the castello, which, incapable as it
was of making any resistance, must soon fall into their hands.
He communicated his fears to the terrified Rosalina, and both
awaited the result in the most anxious state of suspense, when
the shades of night enveloped the enemy from their view, and
rendered their situation still more distressing.

Another hour had now elapsed, when the few soldiers that
had escaped were seen slowly winding up the path that led to
the castello, their strength seemingly entirely exhausted; they
were instantly admitted, and Rosalina, anxious to know the
particulars of what she had partly been a spectator of, went
down to the courtyard, where she found Carletta, who was betraying the most extravagant emotions of delight, for amongst
the few who had returned was her dear Pietro.

The account they gave was sufficient to excite the greatest
terror in the minds of the inhabitants of the castello. It seems
they had, according to their orders, marched towards the
capital, where all the parties were to meet on a certain day: but
when within a few hours' journey of the appointed rendezvous,
as they were passing through a forest, they were suddenly surrounded, and it was with the greatest difficulty that a very small
part of them escaped with life, all their officers having been
slain, and ignorant of the road they should take, and anxious
to avoid their enemies, who were endeavouring to trace their
steps, they thought it best to return to Colredo, in doing which
they were pursued, and in the last engagement, which Rosalina
had beheld, many more perished.

All that night the inhabitants of the castello were on the

watch, expecting every moment to hear their enemies at the gates; but their fears happily proved vain, for when the morning beams opened the surrounding country to their view, no traces of them were visible; and from the neighbouring peasantry they learnt, that after some consultation they returned the way they came, probably concluding that there would be danger in approaching the castello, which they could hardly suppose would be left in so defenceless a state as it was.

We will now return to the monk Grimaldi and the duca di Rodolpho, and endeavour to give a detail of their operations against Sebastiano; and in so doing, still more of the mysterious conduct of the monk will be related, who, it will seem, did indeed only assume the religious habit he wore, as a cloke to the forwarding of his unfathomable schemes; for the accomplishment of which, his remorseless and cruel disposition shrunk not at the perpetration of the most horrible deeds.

CHAPTER XIV.

GRIMALDI, when he left the castello, proceeded with as much speed as possible to the plain where Sebastiano and his people were encamped: arrived there, he demanded to have a conference with him, and was instantly admitted to his tent.

As soon as Sebastiano beheld him, he ordered him to throw back his cowl, but this the monk positively refused to do, and the haughty usurper was going to compel him, when he said— "It is well, Sebastiano: if it is thus you treat those who come to you with intelligence of the utmost importance to your safety, may you never know your danger till too late to guard against it, for I solemnly protest, that if you dare to offer violence to my person, I have not only an arm to resent my wrongs, but in one instant I would confound all your schemes. Now then I wait for your decision—treat me as a friend—give me a private hearing, and I will not withhold from you the important knowledge I possess."

Sebastiano, awed by the bold determined behaviour of the

monk, and instigated by curiosity to know what was the purport of his coming, dismissed the officers who were in his tent, and for a long time was in close conversation with Grimaldi: what the intelligence was that he had to unfold is unknown, but at parting, Sebastiano gave to him a ring.—"This," said he, "will at all times procure you instant admission to me, and whenever you may hereafter think proper to make yourself known, and I should fortunately succeed in my present attempt, which has hitherto been attended with success, you may depend on the most grateful return for the important service you have rendered me."

The monk took the ring, and bowing, departed; he then proceeded to the place where he had appointed to meet the duca, who travelled disguised, both that he might not be known, and on account of his personal safety, having only one attendant with him.

The fourth day was the one appointed for a general rendezvous in an extensive forest, near Casolo, which was within two leagues of Sebastiano's camp. The duca and Grimaldi arrived there early in the morning of that day, and Rodolpho anxiously awaited the coming of the several parties which composed his army, for he meant the next morning to attack Sebastiano, whom he had little doubt of conquering. With the friends of the late Manfroné he kept up a correspondence, and their forces arrived in the wood at the appointed time; but none of his own people appearing, he began to be very uneasy, and towards midnight dispatched several messengers in quest of them; and as every moment increased his anxiety, sleep fled his eyes, though his frame was wearied by his late exertions.

Early in the morning the messengers returned; but great was the surprise, terror, and confusion that their intelligence occasioned, for they brought an account that the several parties had been attacked by the enemy, who, taking advantage of their knowledge of the country, had secreted themselves in certain defiles through which they knew they must pass, and as they had no suspicion that any enemy was near, unprepared for resistance, they were easily surrounded and cut to pieces, very few escaping to bring the sad intelligence to Colredo, where Rosalina still remained, though in hourly expectation of an attack, and in a state of the greatest anxiety respecting her father's safety, of whom, or the padre Grimaldi, no one of the men who had escaped were able to give her the slightest information.

When Rodolpho heard this afflicting intelligence, he remained for a long time speechless with vexation; a panic suddenly seized the forces that were with him, who, expecting every moment to share the fate of Rodolpho's people, consulted their own safety, and dispersing, hastened back to the capital, where they awaited the coming of Sebastiano's army, who, flushed with victory, would perhaps have gained an easy conquest over them, disspirited and terrified at their enemy's success.

The duca still remained in the forest with Grimaldi and a few adherents; conscious that nothing could now be done, he was on the point of returning to Colredo to collect what yet remained of his scattered troops, and to stay there till he could procure fresh levies, for he foresaw the extreme danger there was of an attack being made on that place during his absence; but the monk endeavoured to dissuade him from an immediate return.

"How would you," said he, "bear the disgrace of returning vanquished to Colredo, without having attempted to revenge yourself for the losses you have sustained, and which you may place to the imprudent steps you so very unadvisedly of yourself pursued, in endeavouring to persuade Sebastiano to admit you as a sharer in the spoil? It was this act which roused his vigilance, and from that moment he doubtless employed spies to watch your proceedings, whose faithful intelligence has enabled him to act so successfully as he has done."

"It is to little purpose now," said the impatient duca, "to endeavour to find out the causes of the dreadful calamity that has befallen us, when the effects demand instant consideration: while we are thus inactive, Colredo may fall—Montalto and his son may escape—their vassals will doubtless be added to Sebastiano's forces, and thus, instead of gaining an increase of territory, which I fondly imagined was within my grasp, I shall lose what I before possessed."

"Your anticipations are certainly founded in probability, and are, therefore, not to be despised," returned Grimaldi; "but the means to avert so ruinous an event are perhaps not yet out of our reach: we must commence at the fountain-head—Sebastiano must die!"

"And who is there so weary of existence," said the duca, "as to undertake such a scheme, when there is not the remotest hope of success, but certain destruction? Sebastiano, in the midst of his people, need not fear the dagger of the assassin. If he were dead, I should indeed yet entertain hopes. Your project, father, is good in theory, but the practice, I fear, will surpass your ability."

"Had that been my opinion," returned Grimaldi, "I should have restrained my speech. Are you willing to try whether it is possible or not to effect it?"

"Certainly, in whatever way you propose to commence your plan, you shall not find me backward," replied Rodolpho. "I would this moment give half my dukedom that my dagger were planted in Sebastiano's heart."

"We will try if it cannot be done on more reasonable terms," said Grimaldi. "The shades of evening are now mantling around; we will instantly depart, for the delay of another day may be attended with fatal consequences. Sebastiano is now at his camp, which we shall reach about midnight."

"But have you considered well what you are going about?" replied the duca; "such an undertaking requires much circumspection and forethought."

"The love of life is innate," said the monk, "and though mine has been only a series of increasing calamities, yet I shew that I prize it, by consenting to prolong it. The difficulties we shall have to encounter will greatly depend on our own conduct, and if you will be guided by me, I can promise, that if we do not succeed, that our lives will not be endangered; the only risk is in effecting our escape after the deed of death is done."

"All my alarms," said Rodolpho, "arose from the fear of being prevented, and ignobly perishing without attaining our ends;

but Sebastiano no more, I care not for the consequences—my revenge will be sated, and I should die happy."

During this conversation they had begun their journey, and were traversing the extensive forest. The few that remained with them after the desertion of the troops, had directions to repair instantly to Colredo, where the duca promised soon to join them.

It wanted near an hour to midnight when the duca and Grimaldi passed the towers of Casolo, which was distant from the camp another hour's journey; and when they had arrived near it, they alighted from their horses, which they tied to a tree, and walked slowly forward to the first outpost, where, when they arrived, they saw the centinel fast asleep.

The duca, unsheathing his sword, was on the point of perpetuating his slumbers, when he was restrained by the monk.

"The death of that man," said he, "would be our certain destruction: we will awake him."

"What!" returned the duca; "how then are we to enter the camp?"

"Fear not," said Grimaldi, "that I can effect with ease and security; but be careful to preserve the strictest silence; your voice may be remembered."

The duca promised to comply; and the monk, going to the sleeping soldier, awoke him.

The man started up, evidently alarmed.

"You need not fear," said the monk; "none are here but friends: we wish to pass into the camp—see, here is your commander's signet."

The man having slightly viewed it, permitted them to go forward; and as they were proceeding, Grimaldi demanded if the count Sebastiano visited the guards during the night.

"No," returned the soldier; "we are secure from any apprehensions of an enemy. To-morrow we march in search of the duca di Rodolpho, for the count means to surprise Colredo, as he has learnt to-day that it is but slightly guarded. Yonder is the path; you will not meet another centinel. Good-night, friend."

"This intelligence," said the monk to the duca, "is of no

small importance; it promises success. You doubtless, are astonished at my conduct: know, then, that the reason of my early
departure from the castello was to endeavour to obtain a sight
of Sebastiano's signet, which I knew would greatly tend to facilitate our plans: and in doing this, I was well assured no time
should be lost, for Sebastiano's caution and vigilance would
be increased as soon as he should hear of your preparations;
happily I succeeded, and have obtained one so nearly similar to
it, that there is little fear of a discovery, and particularly during
the night; but it is probable, from what the man said, that we
shall not again want it."

They now entered the camp—no sound was heard—sleep
and silence prevailed around—Grimaldi silently pointed out
the tent of Sebastiano, and the duca grasped his sword.

It was at this moment that hasty footsteps approached
them; the duca started, but Grimaldi in a whisper bade him be
silent.

An officer now advanced with several men—"Stop," said he,
"and explain the purpose of your traversing the camp at this
silent hour."

"The purport of my coming I shall explain to no one but
your leader; but to shew that I am no unknown intruder, no spy
upon your actions, the evidence of this ring is amply sufficient."

The officer happened to be one of those who were in the
tent of Sebastiano when Grimaldi first entered it; and instantly
recognizing him, and seeing at the same time his commander's
signet, said—"Shall I conduct you to the tent of the count?—
he now sleeps, but I will awake him if you have any thing of
consequence to disclose."

"It matters not till the dawn," returned Grimaldi, with his
usual deliberate and hollow tone; "my business does not require
haste, but to prevent observation, the covert of night was most
apt for my purpose. If you have a vacant tent, lead me to it, for
myself and my companion require rest."

"I fear I shall have some difficulty in doing that," returned
the officer, "our prisoners are so numerous; but you are welcome
to mine, father; I am going to visit the guards, to see that they

are vigilant, and that none of Rodolpho's vassals escape, and probably shall be absent till the dawn."

"Your attention I shall not fail to mention to the count," said Grimaldi, "and I accept your courteous offer."

The monk, followed by the duca, who was hardly able to restrain his rage at the speech of the officer, were conducted to the tent, and there left to repose.

"Thus far we have succeeded," said Grimaldi; "but I must own I had my fears, from my knowledge of your impetuous disposition. Every thing bids fair for the accomplishment of our project; the men will shortly be far distant, and then for revenge!"

"Which I no longer doubt will be ours," said Rodolpho; "yes, my friend, to your steady coolness, which, I must confess, filled me with wonder, have we evaded suspicion: the glory and credit of this enterprize will be wholly yours. When Sebastiano is gone, cannot we endeavour to give freedom to my captive troops?"

"The enemy's vigilance in that quarter will render it impossible; besides, they are unarmed; and while they were seeking weapons of defence, supposing that we silenced the unwary guard, the camp would be roused, Sebastiano's fate would be discovered, and we should perish."

"You are right, father; another time we may perhaps attempt this, when we have with us a few resolute auxiliaries—it would indeed be a glorious act."

They now emerged from the tent, and cautiously looked around, but no human sound met their ears; the moon brightly illumined the camp, and the breeze displayed the standard which distinguished the tent of Sebastiano.

Leaving the tent, they cautiously advanced, and when they had arrived at the door of his superb residence, they listened, but no sound was heard, and the duca slowly drew aside the silken drapery which concealed the entrance.

A lamp was burning within, by the light of which they discovered their intended victim lying on a couch in the soft and still embrace of sleep.

"The moment is now fast approaching," said the monk, "which you would lately have given half your dukedom to have at your command; now then enter, and reap the harvest of your toils."

The duca drew forth a dagger; he felt its point—his countenance was ghastly pale, but it was deadly hatred, black and horrible revenge, which banished the colour from his cheeks; he entered the tent, and at length held his naked weapon over the unconscious Sebastiano.

The monk stood by his side; there was no danger of their victim escaping—his life was in their power—the irresistible fiat of fate was for the duca to perform.

"Mark how securely he sleeps," said the monk in a low voice; "how changed is now his situation from what it was a few short hours ago! Then, exulting in his success, fancy had already placed Manfroné's sceptre in his hand, and he conceived himself striding in Colredo's lofty halls, and giving orders to the subjugated vassals of Rodolpho; but soon the fond dream which spurred him on to deeds of blood, which incited him to thin your territories of their most trusty defenders, will vanish with his existence. Thus it is with man, who, while he thinks himself at the summit of his wishes, is suddenly hurled from the aspiring pinnacle, and all his fond hopes in a moment blighted."

"But that," returned the duca, "at least as far respects my present pursuit, shall not be my lot—let what will happen, this revenge is mine."

So saying, he raised his hand armed with the shining blade, and with a black demoniac look, thrice pierced the bosom of the slumberer, whose body heaved with a slight convulsion, the last efforts of departing animation, and the sleep of life suddenly became the eternal repose of the grave.

Both contemplated with satisfaction the bleeding corpse; and when they had glutted their eyes with the horrid spectacle, their own safety became their next object: they left the tent, and looked around; but the pale moon was alone conscious of their dark deeds—no mortal eye beheld them; but the angel, who in his sable volume marks the evil actions of mankind, started with horror as he noted down the dreadful deed of blood, and closing the eternal pages, dropped a tear, while looking forward into futurity, he saw the horrible punishments that awaited the murderer.

Silently they stole from the camp, and avoiding the spot where they had seen the centinel, regained their horses, and hastened onwards to Colredo.

Soon the morning dawned; nature blushed as the early sun dispersing the blue mists, gave her beauties to the view; but little could they please men who delighted in the opaque shades of night to curtain their deeds from the world.

Great was the confusion which reigned in the camp when the murder of Sebastiano was discovered. That it was perpetrated by the two men who had been seen wandering about during the night, hardly admitted a doubt, and a search was instantly commenced after them, but without success. Thus situated, the troops dreading to be found in arms without the countenance of their leader, and no one appearing to supply his place, began to disperse; and in the course of a few days this formidable army, which so lately had terrified the partizans of the late prince, totally disappeared, and their captives, freed from their chains, hastened back to Colredo.

Such was the termination of Sebastiano's efforts to attain power; his ambition was fatal to him as well as the duca, who though he escaped with life, yet had to regret the loss of many of his best troops, and which left him exposed to the attacks of the neighbouring potentates, who he well knew would gladly seize so favourable an opportunity of increasing their possessions.

He arrived in safety at his castello, and Rosalina, who began to fear some sinister event had befallen him, could not behold his return without an emotion of pleasure, and which was increased by the arrival of Grimaldi, whom she most anxiously wished to see, as she hoped by her entreaties to prevail on him to liberate Montalto; but he either was too much occupied with the duca's affairs, or else perhaps anticipated her request, and knowing his inability to accede to it, kept himself from her presence.

The duca di Rodolpho was gloomy and tortured with apprehensions for his safety; it is true indeed he had revenged himself on Sebastiano, but that was little comfort when compared with his losses; and when the troops who had been taken returned to the castello, he busied himself in making preparations for its defence.

Hope alone served to support Rosalina, but that was now becoming fainter every day: while Grimaldi was absent, it was her certain consolation, for she looked to his return as a period when she trusted that Montalto might enjoy the blessings of freedom; but now that the monk never approached her, she concluded that her hopes were delusive, and many were the sighs produced by that conclusion.

From her casement she frequently saw the duca on the walls of the castello, directing the operations of the workmen, and with him sometimes, but very seldom, was the mysterious Grimaldi, whose actions were seemingly so contrary, as if formed on the impulse of the moment, without a future design; but the monk was wrapped up in his own plans, which he sought to mature without the help of others, or rather perhaps, made others subservient to the accomplishment of his own schemes; whichever it was, the following pages will explain; but to Rosalina, his conduct was a mystery indeed.

Such was the state of affairs at the castello when an event took place which created the utmost astonishment, but which, as well as many other circumstances which we have related, could not in any way be accounted for, and filled the mind, not only of Rosalina, but also the duca di Rodolpho himself, with an unspeakable dread, for it clearly appeared that they had near them the most inveterate enemies, who, in their various attempts, constantly evaded discovery.

CHAPTER XV.

THE moon had some time emerged from the extensive forests of pines which skirted the eastern horizon, which now appeared a mass of indistinct foliage, and the breeze of night began to murmur around, but still Rosalina sat at her opened casement, pensively resting her beauteous head on her lovely arm, and often she raised her eyes and viewed the bright lamp of night encircled with myriads of scintillating stars.

The padre Grimaldi had been now more than a week at the castello, yet he never had been near her, whom he seemed to have forgot, as well as his promise concerning Montalto. Rosalina seldom left her apartments, for the castello was filled with strangers, and the duca was too intently engaged in completing its defences, which the security they had hitherto enjoyed rendered requisite, for the slow-moving hand of time had made many breaches in the walls, than to think of his daughter. She was indeed, in one sense, pleased at his conduct, for she wished to avoid being exposed to the gaze of the warriors, whose manners were as rough as their profession. Thus she never had an opportunity of meeting Grimaldi, or she would have solicited a conference with him. Sometimes indeed she thought that her father had terminated the life of her lover, and that the monk being privy to it was the occasion of his avoiding her presence, as not wishing to have so horrible a circumstance to disclose to her. Thus was she tormenting herself with her gloomy apprehensions, when her attention was suddenly excited by seeing three men slowly walking along the ramparts below, and station themselves opposite to the casement at which she was sitting.

The moon shining brightly on them, she perfectly recollected one to be the man who had so earnestly directed his attention to her on the morning that the troops were collected in the courtyard, and of whom she seemed at that time to have an indistinct recollection; but the others were so completely muffled up in their long cloaks, that she could not distinguish who they were.

They conversed for some time in low tones, and often directed their gaze to the turret which contained Rosalina's apartments, who, without knowing why, trembled with sudden apprehensions which assailed her: it is true, their long discourse, and the silent time of night which they had chosen for it, added to their frequent observance of her abode, was sufficient to raise suspicions in her mind of their intents; but then she could have little to fear in her father's castello while she was protected by him.

The men having staid a considerable time, during which they appeared to be debating some weighty matter, at length, with seeming caution, left the place, and turning round an angle of the wall, were hid from her view.

Having sat some time longer, and finding that they did not return, she closed the casement, and with a heavy heart sought her couch, and rested her weary frame on it: but sleep was far distant from her, with all his composing train of gentle slumbers and pleasing dreams, to steep her harassed senses into a forgetfulness of woe.

While she thus was passing the hours of night, she was disturbed by hearing some slow and cautious footsteps along the corridor to which her apartments opened. It was then past midnight; the moon was clad in mists, and her lamp was gone out; light clouds rolling before the stars obscured their feeble lumens; it was an hour too when visionary fears assail the bosoms of the superstitious; but Rosalina's mind was too well cultured to be alarmed at air-formed fancies, and she concluded the paces she had heard were caused by some nocturnal wanderers, whose intents were doubtless as dark as the time they had chosen for the execution of their schemes.

The steps ceased when opposite the door of her chamber, and Rosalina, who had risen from her couch, plainly distinguished a confused noise, as if occasioned by low whisperings;

these sounds, however, soon ceased, and again the low footfalls were heard traversing the corridor, and silence again resumed her welcome reign.

What the views of those people could be in approaching her apartments at that hour she was unable to form an idea of; but that they were connected with her she could not doubt, and she recalled to her mind that night when the daring attempt was made on her honour by the wretch, who, however, paid for his temerity in the loss of his hand: the ease with which he made his escape also occurred to her, but she was well assured that it could not be him, but some inhabitant of the castello, for he would hardly dare to appear in public, but rather endeavour to enter her apartments the way he formerly had done, which, however, was now impossible, as it was closed up. Her suspicions indeed all pointed at the man whom she first noticed intently gazing on her, and afterwards in close converse beneath her casement only a few hours before she heard the sound of foot-paces in the corridor.

At first she determined to acquaint the duca with that circumstance, and her suspicions of some plot being in agitation respecting her; but in proportion as the cheering light of day increased, her intentions and fears subsided, and she thought it would be better to wait till she had some certain confirmation of them, for the duca's conduct of late had been such, that she almost trembled whenever she approached him.

The morning heavily dawned; a murky gloom veiled the lovely scenes of nature; the clustering clouds moved heavily on, and the wind blew cold and comfortless. Rosalina's thoughts were as comfortless as the weather: she often sighed as she thought on Montalto, and her melancholy increased till she relieved her swelling heart by a flood of tears; an unusual weight of woe oppressed her bosom, and in order to alleviate her increasing sad sensations, she opened a volume and perused a few pages; but unable to give her attention to the subject, she closed the book, and taking up her lute, touched the responsive strings; but the sounds were discord to her ear, and she hastily laid it aside. Seldom had she been so melancholy as this day;

she ascribed it to the weather, and to her being disturbed in the night: but still she felt that neither the weather, nor the sounds she had heard, nor even Montalto's uncertain fate, were altogether the cause of her uneasiness; for there was another sensation, an accumulation of nameless fears, doubts, and surmises, without connexion—a mournful anticipation of some calamity, which, however, she could assign no reason for expecting.

Thus passed the day, which gloomily closed in. Rosalina was happy at its termination, and at an early hour retired to her couch, where her fatigued and harassed senses were soon lulled to repose by the welcome deity of slumbers.

Her dreams were as gloomy as her thoughts had been the preceding day, and towards midnight her wakeful senses were dreadfully oppressed; she seemed as if gasping for breath, and every moment expecting to expire, when she was awoke from her unquiet dream by a sudden noise at the portal of her chamber; and when she opened her eyes, what was her horror at finding her apartment filled with smoke, and the fearful cry of fire uttered by many voices in the courtyard below! Hastily she left her couch, and throwing on a few garments, approached the casement, when a volume of flames arose before it; and shrieking with the most dreadful apprehensions of instant destruction, she flew to the door, which was at that moment burst open, and two men rushing in, one of them hastily seized her in his arms, and running along the corridor, the end of which was in flames, he bore her from the dreadful fate which she thought must inevitably be hers, and reaching some of the distant apartments, his companion throwing a large mantle over her, carried her down some steps; and Rosalina, who from her terror had been unable to speak, or even to think of any thing else than her fears, now began to have a new alarm, and faintly demanded the reason of their conveying her into the subterraneous passages of the castello?

"Because, signora," said one of the men, "the courtyard is full of the flaming ruins, and the duca ordered us to convey you this way, as being the safest."

Rosalina's fears were somewhat appeased by this answer, but

when they reached the postern that opened to the wood, as the man who carried the torch was drawing back the large bolts, she had an opportunity of seeing his features, when she recognized him to be the same who had so lately caused her so much uneasiness.

It was now that she began to suspect that all was not right, and struggling to disengage herself from the man who carried her, she demanded to be conveyed back to the court of the castello.

"You do not reflect on the danger; in a few moments you will be in safety, signora," said he; "the duca's orders must be obeyed, and——"

A loud and dreadful crash above prevented his farther speech, and they hastily endeavoured to unclose the door, but the bolts being rusted, they had great difficulty in drawing them back.

"By St. Dominic, if we stay here much longer," said one, "the old castle will be about our ears—the tower has certainly fallen."

The door being now opened, Rosalina beheld the country illumined around with the flames of the burning pile. The men stopped, and seemed to be searching for something which they did not see—"Plague on it!" said one, "he promised to bring the mule here—what shall we do now?"

Rosalina, convinced by this that her fears were but too well founded, hastily disengaged herself from the man, who but slightly held her, and throwing aside the mantle, fled towards the monastery of Santa Maria; but her feeble limbs refused to aid her wishes, and the gigantic ruffian soon seized her.

The other man now came up, bringing with him a mule. Rosalina's screams echoed around; but at the castello they could not be heard, for the cries of the men assisting each other to extinguish the flames—the crackling noise of the consuming timbers—and the falling masses of the thick walls, completely drowned her fearful exclamations.

From the time that Montalto had last seen Rosalina, he had remained a close prisoner in his dreary abode, without ever seeing any other person than Lupo. He had, like Rosalina, looked forward to the return of Grimaldi, in the hope that their united persuasions would induce him to make them happy, and restore him to the blessings of liberty; but his hopes were vain, for the monk never after entered his dungeon.

If Rosalina was unhappy, what must have been his situation, when, to the affliction he endured on her account, was added the confinement of his father and himself, by the cruel and vindictive Rodolpho!

The little light that was admitted to his abode came through a small grating which was placed in the wall, near the vaulted roof of the dungeon, the thickness of which prevented him from seeing through, as he could not raise himself high enough to be on a level with it.

On that night when the castello was on fire, he was awoke by the extraordinary light which came into his dungeon, and from the exclamations he heard, soon conjectured the cause. How did he then tremble for the fate of Rosalina, particularly when he learnt that the flames were consuming that part of the castello where she dwelt, and which was above his dungeon!

The falling stones and timbers soon choked up the grating, which was filled with a stifling smoke, and Montalto breathed with difficulty; when suddenly the tower fell, and a large part of the roof of his dungeon gave way, and admitted the ponderous ruins. The door was burst open, and Montalto, who fortunately was standing near it, hastily ran out, and, lit by the burning timbers, rushed through the passage, and mounting some ruins, beheld the tower levelled to the ground. All hopes of his saving Rosalina were at an end, but he trusted that she was in safety; and now he bethought himself of his father, whom he resolved to restore to liberty, and then to leave the castello. As he was returning, he found several of the arms which belonged to the soldiers; and snatching two swords from the heap, hastened to the place where his father was confined, which was not far distant from his own abode, both being beneath the burning tower. He easily forced away the door, and beheld his astonished parent. There was no time for explanation; he gave him one of the swords, and entreated him to follow instantly.

"Another time, my dear father, I will explain every thing to you—at present the moments are precious; let us endeavour to gain our liberty, for Rodolpho's cruelty has been extended as well to the son as the father."

Well acquainted with the way that led to the postern, they soon arrived at it. Both were surprised to find it open; and concluding that they might possibly meet some of the duca's people, who would oppose their escape, they drew their swords from the scabbards, which they cast away, and darted out of the postern, when both distinctly heard the screams of a female, and forgetting the necessity there was for their instantly seeking their own safety, rushed forward in the direction of the cries, which Montalto soon distinguished were uttered by his adored Rosalina.

Before the man who held her could take measures for his defence, Montalto darted on him, and soon his blood stained the garments of the terrified Rosalina, who retreated from his faint grasp, and beheld her well-known deliverer. The other man would have fled, but the old marchese stopped his intentions for ever; and thus freed from her enemies, she endeavoured to compose the terrors which her late fearful situation had excited.

"To see you at liberty, Montalto," said she, "and to be rescued by you, is indeed a blessing which I was fearful it would never be my lot to enjoy, and repays all my sufferings and the horrors of this night: but to what happy circumstance do you owe your liberty?"

"To yon flames," returned Montalto, "which opened me a passage in my dungeon, at a moment when I expected to be numbered with the dead. My escape was miraculous—the saints protected me, and this happy night has given to me a father, and made me once more the preserver of my Rosalina."

"Your father!" she returned—"Oh, repeat that again! The duca, then, was not so guilty as I feared. Is that the marchese who now advances? Lead me to him—But no—I fear to approach one so greatly injured."

"Your fears are needless, fair maid," said the marchese, who had overheard her last words—"you are innocent. I have long been a secret admirer of your actions; nay more, I am grateful to you for being the preserver of my son's life, when unknown to me, he was confined in the dungeons of Colredo. You seem surprised, signora, but though you do not recollect me now, you have seen me before. Do you not recollect the circumstance of the monk who refused to unite you to Manfroné?"

"Perfectly, marchese," said Rosalina, greatly astonished.

"That monk was no other than myself," continued the marchese: "At the hazard of my life I did you that service, as a token of my gratitude, though you then little imagined who your friend was: but the time is precious and must not be delayed in converse—we must depart."

"And you, dearest Rosalina," said Montalto, "you doubtless will now accept of my father's protection, and avoid the many snares which seem to surround you.—Join with me in entreaties," continued he, turning to the marchese; "for you that have been so near an observer of our actions, must doubtless know how great is my adoration for Rosalina."

"Believe me, it pains me greatly to refuse your request," returned Rosalina; "but my situation at present will not admit of my doing what perhaps for many reasons I might almost feel justified in, but respect for your fair name prevents me."

"How is that, dear Rosalina?" said Montalto mournfully.

"When it is discovered," continued Rosalina, "that I am fled with you, will not my enemies ascribe the flames that are now consuming the castello as caused by me, to facilitate the means of my escape and your liberation?—an event which indeed appears so wonderful, that the hand of Providence alone was able to bring it to pass. Montalto, or I am greatly deceived in him, would ill brook such injurious reports of the woman he loves. No—suffer me to return to the duca; those ghastly forms of my conquered enemies will tell the authors of this outrageous act, and if his heart is not formed of adamant—if he is not dead to the voice of gratitude—if indeed his daughter is yet dear to him, he will no longer refuse me the happiness of being united to one who has so well deserved me."

"The signora Rosalina is right," said the marchese: "seldom have I beheld so much rectitude of conduct in one who, besides her youth, is doubtless swayed by love. Return then to the duca, and if he still refuses to consent to your happiness, but renders you miserable by his tyrannous and oppressive acts, then know that you will find in me a fond father, and in my son a husband, whose chief delight I am confident will be to render you happy."

"Oh, my adored Rosalina!" said Montalto, "and must we be again separated? Heaven knows what will happen before we meet once more, for you have too much reason to see that not even your father's presence is able to protect you against the secret plans of your enemies. Every moment I am from you will add to my misery; for independent of what farther designs the duca may have respecting you, and too well I know him to doubt that he would to-morrow unite you to any one, if so doing would promote his ambitious or interested views—have I not then every reason to fear that each coming moment may see me for ever deprived of all I love, of all I hold dear in the world?"

"You see, dear Montalto," returned Rosalina, "how greatly, in every situation where I needed his assistance, has Providence been my friend: dismiss then your fears; you have every reason to place the greatest reliance on my fortitude and resistance to any act of oppression which a parent is not warranted to use to his child; in such case indeed I do sincerely promise to accept the protection which the marchese so kindly offers me, and with it the hand of my loved Montalto. My longer stay endangers your safety. Do not let vain fears alarm your peace. If possible I will be in the chapel of Santa Maria in the evening of the third day from this, when I shall probably be able to inform you who the authors were of this night's outrage."

So saying she bade them adieu, and winding up the rocky path which led to Colredo, lit by the still burning ruins, arrived at the gates, through which she passed, and presented herself to the astonished duca, who imagined she had perished in the flames.

For once he shewed that he had not quite forgot the feelings of a parent, for he embraced her with real delight.

"When the fire is quite extinguished, my child," said he, "I will listen to the mournful relation you have doubtless to tell me—But, Rosalina, that blood! Good Heavens! are you hurt?"

"No indeed," returned Rosalina—"that horrible stain is the vital stream of a wretch, whose base intents were punished with his life—but I will reserve the relation till you are more at leisure."

Thus saying, the duca bade some of his domestics to attend her to a distant part of the buildings, which was free from the disturbance the fire had created, promising to be with her as soon as possible, and charging the men not on any account to leave the place where she was unguarded.

The news of her arrival soon reached the ears of Carletta, who was bitterly bewailing the supposed death of her beloved mistress; and she was soon joined by that faithful attendant, whose artless expressions of unfeigned joy, and the traces of the deep sorrow she had endured, greatly affected the tender heart of Rosalina.

The efforts of the people who were in the castello soon reduced the violence of the flames, but not till they had entirely consumed the tower, and the communication from it to the other parts of the building being pulled down, all apprehensions for the safety of the pile ceased: and the duca, anxious to find out who were the perpetrators of this act (for there was every reason to conclude that the fire was the effect of design, not of accident, as the men who watched on the walls affirmed that it burst out from three or four places at once), as he concluded Rosalina might perhaps be able to solve the mystery, he was going to her, when Lupo coming up, acquainted him that he had ordered people to search the dungeons where the old marchese and his son were confined, who had found them empty, and that it was plain that they had escaped, because the private postern that led to the wood below was found open.

"Escaped!" said the duca; "nay then it is plain that they were the vile incendiaries, and by that daring act sought at once to destroy both me and my castello, and to carry off my daughter. Go instantly and tell my people to arm themselves, for before the sun which is now rising shall have travelled one quarter of the hemisphere, their residence and themselves shall be a heap of ashes."

The castellain departed, and soon the war-trumpet echoed around its hollow-toned brazen notes. Every one started who heard the well-known sounds, and hastily arming, assembled in the courtyard, expecting to hear that an enemy was approaching to attack the castello, now that it was in a state of confusion.

Rosalina had retired to an apartment in the north wing, and was sitting there with Carletta, while the attendants, as ordered by the duca, remained at the door to guard her during the disturbance, when she heard the trumpet, and terrified with the idea that the castello was going to be attacked, she bade one of the attendants to learn the occasion of that signal for the troops to arm, who on his return, relating to her the intentions of the duca, she rushed out of the apartment, and, accompanied by the astonished Carletta, reached the courtyard, and falling, almost exhausted by her fatigue and fears at the feet of the duca, besought him to spare her preservers.

"What preservers, Rosalina?" said the duca; "sure you cannot mean the marchese and his son, the perpetrators of this villanous act?"

"Oh, if you knew what they have done, you would blush to suspect them. They protected me at a moment when I thought my destruction certain, and killed my enemies, whose blood has dyed my garments. Do not proceed farther until I have related the whole. The wretches who would have torn me away (who doubtless set the castello on fire to render their attempts easy and unsuspected), you will find dead in the forest, killed by those whom you now seek to destroy, and through whose means I am restored to you."

"Indeed, Rosalina, is this true? But I cannot suspect you, since I never found you guilty of an untruth. Retire to your apartment; I will inquire farther, and before I proceed to acts of hostility which I might repent of, I will again see you and hear the particulars of this night's events."

Satisfied with this promise, Rosalina, leaning on the arm of Carletta, left the duca, and again entered the apartment, where she staid in momentary expectation of his coming.

Meanwhile the duca, attended by some of his people, hastened to the forest below, where they found the breathless bodies of the two men, whom to his wonder he recognized to be those of the leaders of the outlaws whom he had hired to increase the number of his troops.

It was on viewing the ghastly wounds through which their dark souls had found a passage, that the duca, recalling to his mind the former acts of Montalto, felt ashamed of his conduct; he had persecuted the very man who had so repeatedly preserved his daughter, and he determined for once to do an act of justice, and endeavour to make amends for the wrongs they had sustained: and indeed in this there was great policy, for if he was once more on friendly terms with them, and his daughter was made happy by his consenting to the so much wished-for alliance, their vassals added to his own, would free him from the fears of being attacked, as he would then be able to defend himself.

He now returned to the castello, and sending to the padre Grimaldi, requested he would meet him at the apartment where Rosalina was, for he wished him to hear her account of what had happened, that he might be the more able to advise with him what course had best be pursued, in order to find out whether there yet remained any more of their secret enemies.

The troops were now ordered to unarm and to clear away the ruins, while the workmen had instructions to rebuild the tower.

He entered his daughter's apartment a few minutes before Grimaldi, who when he saw Rosalina, evidently started.

"You need not be alarmed, father," said the duca, observing his emotion, "the blood on Rosalina's garments is that of her enemies."

"Of her enemies! I rejoice to hear it," said Grimaldi; "I did indeed fear that she had been hurt. Your escape, fair daughter, must have been wonderful indeed; we thought you lost to us for ever. Who was it that protected you, for the duca spoke of enemies?"

"Rosalina will relate the whole," said Rodolpho, "and you will be no less surprised at her tale than myself, for what I already know has so much astonished me, that I could hardly have credited it, if I had not been an eye-witness to the truth of her words."

Rosalina then related every circumstance which the reader is already acquainted with, and to which Grimaldi and the duca listened with profound attention; and when she had concluded, Rodolpho said—"Now father, what is your opinion? there are doubtless more accomplices than the two wretches who are dead."

"I should rather imagine not," returned Grimaldi: "if there had been, they would most assuredly have left the castello together, or indeed have been awaiting the coming of their comrades with the signora; in such case, they could not possibly have arrived at the castello without being observed; indeed such a step, if they had learnt the failure of their schemes, they would have feared to take, for the men whom the marchese and his son destroyed might with their dying breath have disclosed who they were."

"But Rosalina," returned Rodolpho, "seems positive that there were three men on the ramparts the night before the fire, and that one of them was the person who was killed as he was dragging her towards the mule."

"Perhaps the men, when in the agonies of death, might, to ease their guilty consciences, have disclosed to the signora whether they had any accomplices or not, or what their views were in carrying her away?"

"No," returned Rosalina, "I did not hear them speak one word."

"Or the third person whom you say you saw on the ramparts might have been ideal—some shadow perhaps; or if it were a dark night, you might have been mistaken."

"No, father," said Rosalina, "I am certain there were three, for I beheld them for more than an hour."

Grimaldi now left the chamber, and the duca followed him. The monk did not utter a word till they had gained a remote part of the walls, yet seeming by his gestures to have something to unfold, the duca still continued talking beside him.

"I wish," said the monk, "that I had not persuaded you to let the marchese and his son live."

"How!" returned the duca: "in that case, what would have become of my daughter?"

"My extreme anxiety," continued the monk, without seeming to notice what he said, "to preserve your peace of mind, has made me neglect the caution of a friend. And are you really so easy to be imposed on? Rosalina indeed has been well in-structed in her tale. How the marchese and his son contrived to set fire to the castello remains to be discovered; but their reason for so doing is obvious—they wished to ingratiate themselves with you as the preserver of your daughter, if you escaped the flames, and induce you in common gratitude to consent to the wished alliance: doubtless they were observed by the two un-fortunate men, who became their victims in consequence. Reflect only for a moment, duca; those men in all probability had scarcely ever seen your daughter, and is it likely that they should endeavour to possess themselves of her—men whose hearts are steeled by their profession against the tender emo-tions of love, and whose whole delight is in rapine and plunder? The idea of the third person was well imagined, because it was calculated to take away suspicion from your mind."

"I scarcely know what to think, father," returned the duca; "but in this instance it is possible you may be wrong in your conjectures; Rosalina never could frame so artful a tale, so well calculated to impose."

"Supposing that she could not," said the monk, "do you doubt the ability of her lover to do it for her?"

"But how could he leave his dungeon?" observed Rodolpho.

"You seem to have great confidence in Lupo—are you certain he is worthy of it?" said Grimaldi. "Do you think he could withstand the entreaties of your daughter, when I myself, so much attached to you, who made every wish of your heart my own, was not able?"

"How, father, in what respect?" said the duca, rather surprised.

"When Rosalina was so greatly disturbed in her senses, at the supposed death of Montalto, you may recollect that it was by your desire I visited her, in order to undeceive her in that idea; it was then that, won by her prayers and entreaties, I gave a reluctant assent to her seeing Montalto, and this indeed I was led to do, in the hope that it would tend to restore her health, so much impaired by her illness."

"And she saw Montalto, did she not?" demanded Rodolpho, whose brow lowered as he spoke; "doubtless it was then that this scheme was planned. As for Lupo's obedience to my orders, I have known him long enough to banish the smallest suspicion of his fidelity."

"No," returned the monk, "at their meeting, which was but a few short moments, I was present. I marked every word—every gesture, and could stake my life against the possibility of their even having an idea then of what they have so lately done. You seem very positive about Lupo, but recollect the opportunity he had during your absence—no one to observe him; few in a dependent's situation are insensible to the potency of gold."

"My opinion of Lupo is not easy to be shaken," said the duca; "but certainly, if they ever did meet, it must have been then—but no, it is impossible."

"It is a weakness to imagine ourselves in a state of security; nay, it is dangerous in every sense. You are too confident of Lupo, duca, even though he were as faithful as you suppose. It is true, I have only observed what might have happened; I wish not to accuse the castellain, though indeed I should conclude his feelings more easy to be worked on than mine, since he is assailable by means which would not avail with me. Certainly I never have observed any thing in his conduct which could lead to suspicion; but then how could the events of the last night have been so completely arranged, and so well carried into effect?"

"There is certainly," said Rodolpho, "a great mystery, as well in this as in several other circumstances which have occurred. I think I told you of the villain who found means to enter Rosalina's chamber, and to escape, though with the loss of his hand. Might it not be him, think you, father, who has contrived all this?"

"Such an undertaking would be impossible," returned the monk, "because he never could enter the castello without being observed: but did you examine the bodies of the men who were slain?—that would convince you."

"I did, father, but their limbs were entire; the third person, however, whom Rosalina affirms she saw, might have been him."

"Far be it from me," returned the monk, "to set at variance the parent and the child. No, duca, I will imagine what I really and fervently pray may be the case, that Rosalina is candid and sincere—that she is all you can wish her—that even the most violent love could not induce her to perform any act contrary to the wish of her parent; I could even excuse her intended marriage with Montalto without your consent, and attribute it to what she declared it was—the desire of preserving the life of her parent, though indeed, surrounded by your friends and guards, the weak attempts of a single man must be obviously futile; but perhaps the eyes of love might magnify them to a host."

"Let a few days pass over," said the duca: "have a wary eye around you, my friend. I wish to think it was as Rosalina has told it, for you know my dangerous situation—nothing have I concealed from you. I have reflected about the probability of permitting this alliance; it would make Rosalina happy—I should also be able to increase my forces, and the count Florelli, the near relation of the marchese, would become my friend, and with their assistance, perhaps yet the principality of Manfroné may be mine."

"The desire of increase of territories and power is, I believe, generally predominant in every breast; the count Florelli may be equally as anxious as yourself to press the vacant seat of rule:

it is true, such an undertaking would be now difficult, for the death of Sebastiano has restored peace in the province, and those who enter it as enemies will have to encounter all its forces. But pardon me, if in my zeal for your service I utter what may be displeasing to your ears, but you really have astonished me by your sudden intention. What! is the duca di Rodolpho so lost in resources—is he become so greatly the slave of his own fears—he who never trembled—who dared boldly to enter an enemy's camp, and terminate the life of an hostile leader—shall he, to gain a handful of vassals, which he must sue for, give his daughter to his deadliest foe?"

"You are too warm, father—but it is caused by your attachment to me, and I excuse it: but would it not be better for me to consent to the union, than before the close of this week, see my castello beset by the united forces of Montalto and Florelli, and disgrace myself by a surrender, or perish on the walls? Think not I fear to die; but the seat of Manfroné holds out those charms to me which make me wish to live. Thus you see it is not any other idea than ambition which goads me on with its powerful impulse."

"But I, who calmly look forward to occurrences that are founded on probability, see but little hope now of your attaining your wishes. Might I advise, you would instantly march your troops against Montalto—exterminate both—seize on their possessions, and with their hoards of gold, troops will never be wanting—men who set dangers and death at defiance—to whom the shedding of blood is a trade. But rather than tamely let Montalto be united to your daughter, I would sooner see Colredo in flames, and you, duca, a lifeless corpse on my expiring body."

"Perhaps it would be more glorious—more worthy of me," returned the duca; "but our present forces—do you think they are sufficient for the purpose?"

"Yes, if you march them instantly to the place of attack, there is little doubt of success," replied Grimaldi: "the marchese and his son just returned after so long an absence, all will be in a state of confusion; their troops will be few in number, and those probably without leaders; they will be surprised before they have time to collect. You need only send a detachment—remain yourself at Colredo; but I repeat again, to ensure success, and prevent any serious loss on your side, you must be hasty in your resolutions."

"They are formed—the death of both of them is resolved on, and with their possessions Colredo shall be rendered secure against any attack. Let us go and hasten the preparations; the night will be the fittest for the deed of death; and before the morning dawns, I shall be secure from that quarter. Lupo shall command the troops; he is a man of courage and skill, and besides well acquainted with the weaker parts of Montalto's castello, having often been there with me, and therefore the most proper to be employed."

"If you are confident you can rely on him, he certainly is," returned the monk; "but strictly caution him not to let the marchese or his son escape; and to urge both Lupo and the troops to exert their utmost, tell them that it was owing to their secret machinations that their lives were endangered by the intended destruction of Colredo."

The duca and Grimaldi leaving the retired place in which they had been conversing, now advanced to the grand hall, where they found Lupo, to whom the duca issued his orders; and the men who were appointed to go, leaving their present employment about the ruins of the tower, hastened to refresh themselves, and make the necessary preparations against the evening, when under covert of the deepening gloom they were to leave the castello.

Carletta soon heard of the intended expedition from Pietro, and she hastened with her sad intelligence to Rosalina, who was dreadfully agitated on receiving the unwelcome news. To remonstrate with the duca, she conjectured, would be now of little use, as he seemed determined to put his present designs in execution; and when she found that he did not mean to accompany the party, she was not long before she resolved on doing an act, which would be some small return to Montalto for the many important services he had rendered her; and this was, to acquaint him with the intentions of her father, that he might guard against them. It is true indeed, the manner in which this was to be done was as yet unknown to her, as a messenger must be found whom she could depend on, to carry the important information to him.

The possibility that she might perhaps be able to persuade Pietro now occurred to her. From Carletta she learnt that he was not going with the party, and she determined, at all events, to make the trial, trusting that the certainty of the great reward which Montalto would not fail to make him, would be a powerful inducement for him to be faithful to his trust.

The greatest difficulty which appeared was, that as he was the admirer of Carletta, she would object to his running any risk, particularly as it would not be safe for him to return to the castello, and she now resolved to put Carletta's attachment to her to the proof, since she was confident that it all depended on her.

"Carletta," said she, "it is now in your power to render me a most important service."

"Ah, dear signora, name it; how happy shall I be!"

"That, Carletta, I much doubt.—You seem to be very fond of Pietro."

"Ye-e-s, signora, I will not deny it," said the girl, blushing; "if it had not been for these disturbances, we meant to ask your leave to marry."

"Doubtless, then, you would be very miserable to be separated from him?"

"Oh, very unhappy indeed," sighed Carletta.

"And yet the service I wished of you would have been to persuade him to leave the castello on a business which it is of the greatest importance to my peace he should perform."

"Ah, signora, how happy you make me! I am sure Pietro would do any thing to serve you, and your poor Carletta would part with life to make you happy."

"But perhaps, Carletta, you might not see Pietro for some time."

"But I shall see you happy," returned the affectionate girl, "and that will comfort me in his absence."

"Well then," returned Rosalina, "tell Pietro to come to me immediately; and if he consents to what I wish him to do, he will be no inconsiderable gainer by it, and shall be farther rewarded for his services with you, Carletta."

Carletta now left the chamber in order to see him, and Rosalina remained in a state of hope and fear as to the success of her endeavours, which had the important intent of preserving her generous defenders; and in acting as she did, she felt a consciousness that she was doing right.

Every minute that Carletta was absent appeared to Rosalina an age, for she feared that the smallest delay would render Montalto unable to take the proper steps for his safety, and in spite of all her solicitude and anxiety, he would fall a victim to the unaccountable and cruel resolution of her father.

CHAPTER XVI.

AFTER Rosalina had waited some time longer, Pietro made his appearance, accompanied by Carletta.

"I was informed you wanted me, signora," said the man. "I am ready to undertake whatever you wish me to perform."

"I trust indeed you will, Pietro, but I am not without my fears; you must, however, promise, if you should not wish to do me the service I require, that you will not disclose it to any one."

"You may rely on my fidelity," returned Pietro; "let me then know, signora, what I am to do?"

"Oh, pray tell him," said Carletta; "I am sure he will not refuse—he promised me he would not."

"Well then," continued Rosalina, "you know, Pietro, the intentions of the duca towards the marchese Montalto and his son; their destruction is resolved on, and this night is fixed for it. At the hazard of their lives they have protected mine, and I think common gratitude obliges me to inform them of their danger, that they may avoid it. This is what I wish you to do, Pietro: hasten then, that my intentions may not be frustrated by the caution of the duca, who probably may order the castle-gates to be closed, to prevent the possibility of his designs being known; and if you think there may be danger in returning here, I am certain you will be protected, and amply rewarded by the marchese; and Carletta shall go to you there. Are you now willing to undertake this important service?"

"Yes, signora," returned Pietro, "and with pleasure: but as I do not think it will be safe for me to return, I hope you will not object to letting Carletta come to me."

"You need not fear but I shall prove, in every way I possibly can, my gratitude to you, Pietro; and let what will happen to me," she added, with a sigh, "I shall not forget your comfort: in the marchese too, you will find a generous friend, or I am much mistaken."

"I shall instantly depart then," replied Pietro; "and, signora, you may set your mind at ease, for you need not doubt my fidelity."

This having said, he hastily bade Carletta adieu, and left the chamber, greatly pleased at so good an opportunity of leaving the service of the duca, in which nothing but the love he had for Carletta had detained him, for she was too much attached to her mistress to leave her, even for Pietro. He contrived to pass the castle-gates without being noticed, and soon was quickly proceeding towards the residence of the marchese.

Rosalina was now somewhat more composed, and in full confidence of Pietro's performing his mission, she lay down on a couch to give repose to her exhausted frame.

The duca waited impatiently for the evening, full of the sanguinary project to which he had been excited by the deep-scheming Grimaldi, and in imagination beheld himself enriched by the expected spoils, which he doubted not of obtaining; still, however, he was not satisfied with what the monk had asserted respecting Montalto's having, either by himself or his agents, set the tower on fire, in order to carry away Rosalina; he was indeed well assured that there had been a regular concerted plan, in which the two men who had attempted to carry away his daughter were accomplices, and the third she affirmed she had seen, in all probability was the principal, whom he, however, trusted he should discover.

Night slowly drew her shadowy veil over the hemisphere, as the descending sun diminished in his lustre.

And now the brazen trumpet gave to the gale its martial notes. Rosalina started at the sound, and Carletta endeavoured to compose her agitation by assurances of Pietro having long before that time acquainted Montalto with his danger. She slowly walked to the courtyard, which was now filled with the impatient men, who were eager to be gone on an expedition which promised both plunder and success. She ascended to the rampart, from whence she beheld them marshalled for the march, and at length saw them winding down the rocky path, and continuing along the margin of the lake, till night hid them in her deepening glooms.

When the marchese and his son arrived at their castello, great were the rejoicings of their domestics, who scarcely could be persuaded at first that their long-regretted lord was yet in existence; but soon they crowded round him, and expressed their honest joy in loud acclamations.

The marchese, who was no stranger to the vindictive spirit of the duca di Rodolpho, wasted no time in collecting and arming his vassals, for, ignorant of the late events, he thought he had every thing to fear, and that he would now openly attack him whom he had so greatly injured; and he sent to the count Florelli, acquainting him with the late events, and requesting the assistance of his vassals, not to act against the duca (for that he was determined to forbear, in consideration of his son and Rosalina), but to defend himself in case of necessity.

Whilst in the midst of these active preparations against the expected efforts of Rodolpho, the trusty Pietro arrived, and related the message he was the bearer of to the marchese, who could not sufficiently admire the grateful attentions of Rosalina, and from that moment determined to use even force, rather than his son should be deprived of such an inestimable blessing. The weak state of the ducal troops, which he learnt from Pietro, gave him no concern about the meditated attack, for the vassals he had so hastily been collecting far exceeded Rodolpho's whole force.

Montalto was delighted with the dear attention of Rosalina, which he fondly attributed to her love for him. He instantly took Pietro into his own service, and in his liberality far exceeded his most sanguine expectations. He was however greatly enraged with the duca's conduct, and requested to have the command of a party to oppose his troops, resolved that none of them should return to Colredo, at least not till he pleased: for this purpose he posted two detachments, one at the entrance of a narrow pass through which the enemy must march, and the other about the centre of it: the first party had orders to secrete themselves, and to allow the duca's people to pass on, while he at the head of the second meant to attack them.

Such was Montalto's plan, and when the night had shaded all objects from view, he had prepared every thing that was necessary, and soon his scouts brought him intelligence that the duca's party were silently approaching.

The moon partially gleaming through the trees that hung over the winding path, at length shone on the arms of the hostile party, when Montalto and his men rushed on them and commenced the work of death. Confused and terrified by this unexpected attack, many of them fled, while those that remained made but a feeble resistance. Montalto soon found himself opposed by Lupo, whose attack was furious at the onset; but his strength soon failed, and he was doomed never more to behold the lofty turrets of Colredo, for the sword of Montalto freed his soul, which flitted through his wide wounds to another world.

Such was the termination of Lupo's sinful existence. With all his sins unrepented of, he was sent to give an account of them, and to be confronted with the appalling spirit of the unfortunate Astolpho, one of the many whom his murderous arm consigned to the shades of death.

Those who had hitherto resisted the attack of Montalto's people, learning the death of their leader, sought their safety in flight, but were met by the first party and made prisoners. Thus, of all the chosen troops which the duca had sent on his cruel errand, no more than two escaped, who, climbing up the rocky sides of the valley, hid themselves till the victors had retired from the place, and then hastened with the sad intelligence to Colredo.

Frantic with rage, Rodolpho learnt the failure of his schemes—the loss of Lupo, and of his men. His situation was now desperate—every moment he expected to see the forces of his justly-incensed enemies at the gates. To oppose their entrance was impossible, and all his anticipations of future greatness fled, never more to return.

Unable to confine his vexation, he vented his rage on all around, and soon found himself alone, for the terrified domestics fled at his approach. He then bethought himself of the padre Grimaldi—he who had urged him, though contrary to his wishes, to attack Montalto; and with unequal steps he repaired to his apartments.

"Confusion!" said he, as he entered. "All is lost—two men of the party only are returned; the rest are killed or made prisoners. Lupo too is dead. Cursed fool that I was!—This is the consequence of following your counsel, Grimaldi: in every thing you have advised me I have been unsuccessful. What could persuade me to listen to you I know not: had I acted as I had planned, I should have evaded the certain destruction that must follow—now I am ruined, totally ruined. With a handful of men in the castello, and those incapable of service, I expect every moment the victorious followers of Montalto! This, all this, is the effects of your advice."

"And who," replied the monk, in his usual tone of voice, unmoved by the agitation of the duca, "who could foresee what has happened? Do you imagine that I am gifted with the knowledge of futurity—that when I was advising you for your interest, your glory—for every thing that is dear to a man of honour and ambitious principles, that I could foresee that Montalto would have been so soon prepared? I merely spoke the words of friendship: but the duca di Rodolpho is alone to blame, who, used to the wiles and intrigues of warfare, should have provided against a surprise."

"It is well, father," returned the duca, "to heap on me the blame. You well know it was my wish to endeavour to repair the breach between the marchese and myself, and which, through Rosalina, might easily have been effected: but, doubtless for some hidden views of your own, you worked on my feelings, and in fine hurried me to my destruction. Such is the result of your boasted friendship: would I had been without it!"

"I expected no other return," replied Grimaldi: "such is the fate of those who interest themselves for others. I am accustomed to ingratitude, and therefore fitter to bear it than many who unfortunately are in my situation: but though meek in spirit—though *my* passions can be restrained by the powerful voice of reason, yet, duca, when you accuse me of having views of my own which instigated me to give you wrong counsel, I must assert my innocence, and declare your asseverations to be wrong founded. A worm when trampled on will turn on its oppressor, though it has no means of retaliation; but your accusing me, and venting on me your anger, may perhaps tend to compose your spirits—if so, proceed: but such a conduct—how ungenerous, how ill does it agree with the exalted opinion I had formed of the duca di Rodolpho! When I delivered up to him his enemy who was planning his destruction—when I prevented the well-concerted marriage of his daughter—when I shared with him the danger of being discovered when Sebastiano breathed his last—had I any interest in all these acts? Are my coffers full of your munificence? No, duca, you had my friendship; all my powers, mental as well as corporeal, were devoted to your service. But now I shall mislead you with my advice no more; I shall again return to the monastery, and to my other misfortunes I add the ingratitude of the duca di Rodolpho."

"And would you then desert me at the moment when I most need a friend?" returned the duca. "Forgive my hasty expressions—I scarcely know what I say or do; you see the distraction of my senses, and yet you make no allowances for me: you must excuse me. What shall I do in this dreadful emergency? A few hours, and all will be lost! Shall I consign the towers of Colredo to the flames, and perish in them, or die in their defence?"

"I am always ready to forgive," returned Grimaldi, "and your situation admits of many excuses. You are not entirely without hope: Montalto loves Rosalina—that will restrain his revenge."

"Do not you think I had better consent to the alliance?"

"What! and expose yourself to the scornful refusal of the old marchese? He is not in love, whatever his son may feel; and though Montalto may prevent his father from any hostilities, through fear of hurting Rosalina's feelings, yet the marchese may disapprove of the union. However, duca, it is time enough to treat when the enemy is at your gates, for by this time they are fully acquainted with your defenceless situation. Wait awhile; a few hours may bring with them maturer considerations; you see they had not resolved on attacking you, or they would have been here before this. But there is one thing, duca, which seems not to have excited your attention—Have you learnt how it was that Montalto became acquainted with your schemes? Depend on it, he must have had early information, and that from some of your own people."

"You are right, father, it must have been so. I will cause an inquiry to be made, and indeed my mind misgives me that Rosalina is privy to that circumstance; if she is, there will be a victim to appease my wrath."

It may be remembered that the duca had ordered a guard to be stationed at the portal of Rosalina's apartment, in order to protect her during the confusion that reigned in the castello; that guard had not yet been removed, and the duca, resolving to demand of them who had been with Rosalina during the day, left the apartment of Grimaldi, who, from his last speech, seemed to dread his sanguinary intentions, for he said— "Recollect, duca, that even should your daughter be guilty, it is only through her that you can hope to avert the wrath of Montalto; therefore I conjure you to spare her life, for in so doing you will preserve yourself."

The duca passed hastily on towards the northern wing, and when he was crossing a courtyard, absorbed in distracting ruminations, he for the first time noticed that the morning had some time dawned, and that the mists of night were dispersed. Anxious to know if any more of his men had escaped, he altered his intention of going to Rosalina's apartment, and went towards the castle-gates; but no one had entered since the two fugitives, the bearers of the unfortunate fate of their comrades.

The duca ascended the walls, and looked towards that part of the country where lay the residence of the marchese; but no human being caught his eye, and it was but too certain that all his men had either fallen, or else were captives to the hated marchese. Such a total annihilation of every hope he had formed was almost sufficient to deprive a man (of such violent passions as the duca) of his reason; all his pecuniary resources had been expended in the endeavour to attain the sovereignty of Manfroné, or else indeed he might have hired fresh parties of banditti—but without money that was impossible.

He now indeed began to form some hopes that it was not the intention of the marchese to attack Colredo, or he certainly would not have let a moment pass without putting that design in execution, as he thereby would give him an opportunity to collect troops to enable him to make a resistance.

After some time passed on the walls, and in giving directions to his people to keep a strict watch, he repaired to the apartments of Rosalina, and demanding of the guard if any person had entered them during the preceding day, was informed that no one excepting Pietro had been there, and that only for a few minutes.

The duca then ordered Pietro to be sent for, intending to know what it could be that his daughter could want with him; but after his messenger had been some time absent, he returned with the information that Pietro was not to be found—that he had entered his apartment, where it appeared he had not been during the night, and that none of the domestics had seen him since the preceding morning.

Rodolpho, now satisfied that Rosalina had betrayed him, opened the door that led to her apartment, which he entered, and beheld her reclining on a couch in the soft embraces of sleep.

To him, whose mind and whose intents were savage as the Hyrcanian tiger, and wild as the howling blast of night, the beauties of his lovely daughter were insufficient to stop the sable purposes he meditated. Her head was reclined on her lovely arm, far whiter than the marble form of the Medicean Venus; the leaf of the rose was on her cheek, its fragrance in her breath; the powers of fancy had depicted some happy vision to her mental view, for she smiled. Ten thousand furies seized his soul, as he rudely caught her by the arm.

"Awake," said he, "thou serpent, whom I have nurtured in my bosom to sting my heart! Tell me, where is Pietro? Quickly unfold the reason of his leaving the castello, nor seek to hide the truth, lest I instantly open passage to your heart, and search it there."

The terrified Rosalina grew pale as the lily, which, trod down by the careless traveller, withers in the cold hollow blast of night. She raised her timid gaze, and beheld the wrathful coun-tenance of her parent, in which she read her own destruction, since she found that he knew of the cause of Pietro's absence: his lips quivered—his hand was on his sword, and the pressure of his grasp increased. The horrors of her situation were beyond her bearing; she trembled—lifted up her clasped hands for mercy, but utterance was denied her: the duca grew impatient.

"Answer me directly," said he, "lest I for ever render you in-capable, for methinks your blood flowing from you would cool the fever of my rage."

"Oh, my father!" said Rosalina, exerting all her fortitude, and which she found increased with her endeavours, "if it is your wish to murder your child, you are the author of my being, and I submit; but before you put your dreadful design in execution, hear me: it is true I informed Montalto of your designs, that I might preserve that life which had so often been endangered in defence of mine: such was the utmost of my offence; and if Montalto has escaped, it will be a comfort to me in the last agonizing pangs of dissolution."

"Montalto has then escaped," said the duca; "but mark the consequences of your information; all my troops are slaughtered—Colredo is defenceless, and every moment I expect to see its gates beset, and myself a prisoner in my own dungeons. Such are the consequences of your information. But, Rosalina, you shall not live, and, united to Montalto, smile with him at the anguish of a captive father!—No, that satisfaction you shall not have; the present moment at least is mine, and I will employ it in revenge."

"Strike! Oh, my father," said Rosalina, "end at once the life and sufferings of the unfortunate offspring of Theodora! Oh, my sainted mother! too much do I resemble thee, in being so early the sad inheritor of thy sorrows. May the dreadful deed which this hour will witness be forgiven thee, my father! but, oh, I fear that the blood of thy guiltless child will haunt thy sleepless hours!"

"And dost thou really think, Rosalina, that Rodolpho will survive the ruin of his fortunes? No, I will bury myself in the ruins of Colredo—its crumbling walls shall be my tomb as well as thine; and Montalto, when he comes, shall stalk, full of love and revenge, over the smoking pile; but neither shall his love be gratified with the sight of thee, or his revenge be satiated with having his enemy for his captive. By Heavens, this is a noble thought—worthy of Rodolpho! it is I that shall then be revenged; and thou, false dissembling wretch!—thou that art the cause of all this woe, prepare, for the moment of thy dissolution approaches. Fury, rage, and despair, nerve my arm and seize my senses; my brain burns with agony, and I long to do the deed of death—and die thou shalt, with a father's deepest malediction on thy devoted head!"

"Oh, my father, do not curse me!" said the almost inanimate Rosalina; "the horrors of death are sufficient, without that fresh misery."

Here she ceased—her increasing agonies held motionless the powers of speech; she sunk on her knees, and held the duca's trembling hand; but he flung her from him, and with a look, dark and determined, drew forth the thirsty weapon of death. Rosalina closed her eyes and awaited the murderous blow, while her frame trembled, and cold drops of water stood at every pore, when suddenly a confused murmur, which increased to a wild uproar, seemed approaching the apartment; the duca, whose arm was raised, stopped and listened, when repeated cries of "the enemy! the enemy!" and the trumpet's blasts being heard between the pauses of the distracted shouts of the people, he rushed from the chamber, and hastened to the courtyard.

The terror of the inhabitants of the castello had kept them continually on the watch, in expectation of the coming of the marchese and his troops; and that they might have the earliest information possible, a soldier was stationed on the highest turret of Colredo, who seeing a party winding along the distant hills, blew his horn, which instantly occasioned the disturbance that prevented the duca from doing the horrible deed he meditated, in imbruing his hands in the blood of his hapless daughter.

As yet from the walls, the party could not be discovered; and the duca having waited some time, began to hope that the man had been deceived, when a distant horn was faintly heard, and shortly after, the sunbeams glanced on the arms of the men.

The duca, whose feelings were not to be described, sent for Grimaldi, who soon after ascended the rampart where Rodolpho was standing, looking towards the party who were approaching.

"You see, father, it is as I said—yonder is the marchese, and Colredo must fall."

"Where is the signora Rosalina?" demanded the monk. "You have not, I hope, duca, committed the fearful act you meditated?"

"No," replied Rodolpho; "but I have found out that it was owing to her that Montalto was informed of my designs, which in consequence he was enabled so successfully to frustrate."

"I scarcely know how to advise you; wait till they approach, and demand a parley, and when we know their strength, we can better determine what should be done. The party which I perceive does not appear to be very numerous."

"That doubtless," said Rodolpho, "is the vanguard; the main

body are not yet in sight. Count Florelli's troops have joined the marchese before this; indeed his own forces are sufficient now to reduce Colredo. However, as nothing else appears better to resolve on at present, I shall gain some time in the way you mention; and if they persist in the attack, I will drag Rosalina to the walls, and they may pierce her body with their winged messengers of death. Colredo too, shall fall, and with it Rodolpho."

"The party is far distant from the vallies, and yet I do not see any more. Had you not better send one of the men to the loftiest turret, and bid him wind his horn, if there are no more in their rear?"

The duca immediately commanded one of the soldiers to go up; and when they saw that he had arrived, and was carefully viewing the country around, their suspense was great; but at length, to their astonishment, they heard the welcome tones of his horn.

"There is yet hope, duca," said the monk; "the party we see you have no reason to fear, for the number of your troops must yet surpass them."

"This indeed is an astonishing and unaccountable circumstance," said Rodolpho; "Montalto must have been better informed of our situation, than to think Colredo would surrender to a mere handful of men."

Various were the conjectures of the beholders as the party approached; but when at length they had arrived at the foot of the rocks on which the towers of Colredo rose, they recognized them to be some of the men who were supposed to be either dead or prisoners.

Great was the astonishment of the duca as he surveyed them. One person only was unknown to him, and he rode before the party; his vizor was down, and the bearings on his cloak denoted him to belong to the marchese.

The party were instantly admitted into the courtyard of the castello. The by-standers, lost in astonishment, preserved the strictest silence, when the cavalier, without raising his vizor, thus addressed the duca:—

"The marchese Montalto, unwilling to punish the men for

the cruel intentions of their master, sends back the prisoners made last night, and the wounded shall, as soon as they are able, follow them. Colredo might before this have been in his possession, but he scorns to take advantage of the duca's weakness as much as he despises retaliation."

This said, before the duca could reply, the cavalier had repassed the gates, and was on his way to the estates of the marchese.

Rodolpho was some time silent; he was indeed ashamed of his past conduct, and which was greatly excited by the generous forbearance of his enemy. At length he said to the monk—"It is resolved—Rosalina shall be united to Montalto—such a conduct merits such a return from me. How happy am I that my arm was stopped! Yes, father, another moment and Rosalina had ceased to exist. I cannot see her yet—go to her, and tell her of my new-formed determination."

"Which perhaps you may yet alter," said the monk; "and I should wish to preserve the signora Rosalina from the misery which such a step would cause her."

"I am now, father," said the duca, "determined to be guided by my own ideas; and in resolving to permit the alliance, I am urged both by my former wishes, as well as the noble conduct of Montalto; your advice is therefore needless."

"I will not pretend to advise you, duca," returned Grimaldi, "but I would caution you against being too precipitate. May there not in this wonderful conduct of Montalto's be some deep-laid scheme? I have my suspicions—but no matter, it is useless in me to unfold them."

"At this time it is, Grimaldi," returned the duca; "but how cold—how unfeeling—how contracted must be the sentiments of your breast, when you view with suspicious frigidity the noble conduct of Montalto! Indeed, father, I am often tempted to believe you have some deep design in view, though of what nature I cannot pretend even to form an idea."

"I wish you were as suspicious of your enemies as you are of your friends—but I have done. You will repent, duca, of your present intentions, when it is too late."

So saying, he slowly left the duca, who, eager to prosecute his plans of offering Rosalina to Montalto, went (though not without feeling conscious how dreadful he must appear in the eyes of his daughter after the late horrible scene) to assure her of his forgiveness—to endeavour to re-compose the cruel agitation she must have endured, and which he doubted not but that he soon would be able to effect, when she knew his present intentions.

He now approached her apartments: the guard he had placed there were gone, for imagining that they would be required to defend the castello, they had instantly obeyed the well-known signal of the warlike trumpet. He entered Rosalina's chamber, but she was not there: he called her repeatedly, but no one answered; and having entered all the apartments, and being satisfied she had left them, he returned to the hall, and summoning the domestics, bade them seek for his daughter, and to tell her that he had some pleasing intelligence to communicate to her.

The domestics, delighted with the message they had to take to Rosalina, who was greatly beloved by them, hastened away, and traversed the castello in search of her—but to no purpose; and greatly alarmed, they returned to the hall, and reported their ill success to the duca, declaring that the signora Rosalina was not to be found.

"Not to be found!" returned Rodolpho: "hasten away, nor dare to return with such an answer. Go find Carletta, her attendant; she will inform you where her mistress is."

"We have also inquired after her, your excellenza, but she cannot be found either."

"Peace, fools! she has ascended some of the turrets," said the duca; "she cannot have left the castello, for have I not been at the gates all the morning?—and Carletta is of course with her."

The men now departed, and Rodolpho, throwing himself on a seat in the hall, anxiously awaited the coming of his daughter, for he imagined that she had secreted herself through fear of him, and he was very unwilling that his late conduct should be known, as he now wished much to be on terms of friendship with her, that when the alliance between her and Montalto had taken place, she might be the more ready to interest herself on his account.

After the men had been gone near an hour, they again returned, but with no better success.

"Are you certain," demanded the duca, "that you have searched all the apartments?"

"We have indeed, your excellenza, and we even got the keys which Lupo had left with Gomelli, and opened all the chambers in the north wing; but we could not discover any traces of the signora."

"There was little occasion to examine apartments that were shut up," replied the duca; "but, now I reflect, she may possibly have fled for security to the subterraneous passages when she expected the castello to be attacked; go and search all of them, but be sure to tell her that there is no cause for fear, and that I wish anxiously to see her."

The men again departed; and having entered all the passages, returned fully convinced that Rosalina was not in the castello.

If Carletta had not been missing as well as her mistress, the duca would have been alarmed lest in her terror she had precipitated herself from the walls of Colredo to the terrific vallies below; but the idea that her attendant was certainly with her served to allay his fears, and he trusted that she would soon be tempted to emerge from her place of concealment, of which there were many in the castello that almost defied the most vigilant search.

But the whole of that day passed, and neither his daughter or her attendant made their appearance, and Rodolpho was now tormented with the idea that Rosalina had resolved rather to perish for want, than approach her father who had threatened her life; and he knew that Carletta was so greatly attached to her as to partake of her fate, rather than betray the secret of her present abode, which, if she appeared, would have been forced from her.

The night came, and still Rosalina was absent from her apartments. Greatly perplexed, the duca determined to see

Grimaldi, if he still remained in the castello, for he was uncertain whether he had not retired to the monastery.

The monk, however, was still in his slumber, and when informed of the wish of the duca to see him, followed the domestic.

"My calamities, father," said Rodolpho, as Grimaldi entered his chamber, "are, I think, never to have an end: Rosalina, now that I intended to have made her amends for my harsh conduct this morning, is missing, nor is there the smallest trace of her to be discovered."

"Missing! did you say? Surely, duca, you terrified the hapless maid into some rash act."

"I should almost fear that myself," returned Rodolpho; "but her domestic is also absent, and that circumstance is a certain proof (at least I wish to consider it so) of her safety."

"I hope it is," said the monk. "Has every part of the castello been searched? Perhaps she is concealed in the subterraneous recesses."

"They have also been examined," returned the duca. "I indeed almost fear she has been carried off: but then Carletta being absent also——"

"Is a sufficient reason to conclude that she is not," returned Grimaldi. "Perhaps, indeed, she may have fled to Montalto, and accepted of his protection, when safety no longer existed beneath a father's roof. If she had, then indeed he has sufficiently revenged himself of you, and you are justly punished for refusing to listen to my advice when I entreated you not to alarm your daughter."

"I cannot but admire my own folly," said Rodolpho, "in coming to you for consolation, for you seem to take a delight in torturing me. You see then that I did not take your advice, which it would have been happy for me if I never had: and perhaps Rosalina is in consequence of that gone to Montalto. All this I am aware of, and therefore could not come to you for information. What I wanted to know is, how to act; but you are content with reproaching me—with adding to my inquietude, without seeking to do any thing that could allay my anxiety."

Thus saying, he left the apartment, enraged in the highest degree at the cool torturing conduct of the monk, and ill at ease, sought his chamber. He had no friend now to consult with: Lupo, his trusty long-tried confident, was no more; from the monk he met nothing but reproaches, and his own thoughts were far from being friendly to his peace.

Such was now the situation of the duca di Rodolpho, who, when he was his own friend, when his conscience disturbed not his repose, was blessed with the amiable Theodora, with power, rank, riches, and honour: but when murder, with all its train of concomitant sins, increased the catalogue of his offences, then every evil began to assail him: the loss of his lovely wife—then gradually of his possessions; and, frustrated in every attempt, he was at last reduced to the most hapless situation; and, incapable of taking repose through the long cheerless night, he paced his chamber, while at each hollow blast of wind that shook the casement or moaned in the galleries, he started and looked around, expecting to see the shade of some unfortunate victim to his cruel, revengeful, and ambitious pursuits.

Wished-for morning came at length, and shed over nature a gay and joyous look, but it imparted no pleasure to Rodolpho. To the monk he disdained to speak, for he had not forgotten his late conduct; he therefore sat alone in his chamber, gloomy and irresolute what course to pursue, when a packet was brought him, which he hastily opened, and attentively perused.

The contents did not appear, by his features, to be productive of pleasure, for he often turned pale, started, and having re-perused it two or three times, he arose and inquired where the messenger was who had brought the packet, and being informed he was gone, he instantly hastened from the castello without acquainting his people, and totally unaccompanied, was observed winding down the path, and hastening along the road, seemingly greatly agitated, for he often put his hand to his forehead, and evinced other emotions of distress.

CHAPTER XVII.

ROSALINA'S senses were on the eve of deserting her, when the duca, alarmed by the sudden disturbance and cries he heard, hastily quitted the apartment. She listened to his receding paces, but had not the power to open her eyes. Carletta, who from an adjoining apartment had tremblingly listened to the dreadful resolutions of the duca, now ventured to come forth and endeavour to comfort her beloved mistress, so providentially, though perhaps only for a short time, preserved from death.

Rosalina lay almost motionless on the floor; the feeble panting of her bosom, as she with difficulty respired, alone told she existed, for her countenance was as wan as the silent dweller of the tomb.

"My dear mistress!" said Carletta, as kneeling by her side she gently raised her head—"Oh that I should ever live to see this day! How cruel, how unnatural a father, to render miserable so dear, so affectionate a daughter!"

Rosalina here uttered a deep sigh, and slowly opened her languid eyes.—"Is that you, Carletta?" said she: "is my father gone? Am I indeed still in existence? Oh, merciful Heaven! have pity on me, and end at once my miserable life; but let it not be by the hand of a parent! Spare him the guilt of so horrible a crime to answer for at the dreadful day of retribution!"

"I pray the saints to soften his hard heart!" said Carletta. "Do, dear signora, endeavour to compose yourself; you sigh so piteously, it breaks my heart to hear you."

"Ah, poor Carletta! you will soon lose your mistress. No matter, I shall then be happy in heaven."

"Do not talk so, I entreat you," said Carletta weeping, "but try to rouse yourself. Let us leave this horrid chamber, and hide ourselves from the duca."

"Alas! I have scarcely strength to move," said Rosalina; "the dread of death has almost annihilated me."

"Take a little wine, signora," said Carletta, as she raised a glass to Rosalina's lips; "it will help to revive you. I know of a place in the chambers above where we are sure of being secure, and perhaps in a short time his passion will abate."

"Alas! I fear there is little safety for me in the castello," said Rosalina; "every part would soon be explored: but if I am so fortunate as to be capable of walking, I have hopes that I should then escape the horrible death that awaits me."

"I hope you will, signora," said Carletta; "you are stronger now: take a little more wine. Holy mother! do not tremble so."

Poor Rosalina's efforts at last conquered the dreadful perturbation of her mind, and leaning on Carletta, she left the chamber.

"If my strength does not fail me," said she, "and I can once reach the monastery, I am certain there of being protected. Have you courage, Carletta, to accompany me through the subterraneous passages, for I know a way that leads to it, but without your assistance I shall never be able to traverse them?"

"Alas, signora! I will never be separated from you; and if the cruel duca sees us, I hope he will kill me first, and perhaps the sight of my blood would quiet him, and he might spare you."

"I trust I shall not have so great a proof of your attachment," said Rosalina, "though I believe you would indeed part with your life to save mine. Our way lies through father Grimaldi's chambers, and if he is there, or the doors are fastened, I know of no other way that leads to the passage below."

The trembling pair now stopped at the eastern suite of apartments occupied by the monk: the outer door was open; they listened, and not hearing any noise, they entered the first chamber, and with cautious steps crossed it; the next room was also empty, and in that was the well-known panel which communicated with the entrance to the vaults beneath.

Rosalina, as she cast her eyes around, beheld lying on the couch a sable mask; and Carletta, when she saw it, immediately said—"There, signora, you see I was right; that is the very mask which the monk wore when I told you I saw him—Oh, how it frightened me! I am sure I have never been able to forget it since; for whenever I look at his tall figure, I always tremble as if it had but just happened. Ah! Pietro used to say that there was something very strange in the pains he always took to hide his face, and to eat alone; and so I thought too, for those who do right need never be ashamed of shewing their faces."

Rosalina was too agitated to attend to the ready speech of Carletta, and having touched the secret spring, the panel opened, and she passed through, and Carletta following her, she again closed the panel.

Her success hitherto had greatly contributed to cheer her woe-worn bosom, and her strength returning, she proceeded with somewhat quicker paces down the steps, and along the vaulted passages, which drearily echoed to their hasty paces.

When she arrived at the postern which opened near the northern cloisters of the monastery, Carletta drew back the fastenings, and they emerged from the dark subterraneous recesses beneath Colredo.

The convent of Santa Maria was governed by an abbess who had long been famed for her piety. She was now on the verge of eternity: her thoughts and actions seemed already to partake of the purity and benevolence of sainted spirits. To her Rosalina directed her trembling steps, and as she entered the Gothic archway that led to the parlatory of the convent, and heard the iron gates closing behind, she almost wished that they might for ever shut her from a world from which peace and happiness seemed to have fled for ever. Within these walls dwelt tranquillity, holy meditation, and uninterrupted repose. Religion, with awfully sublime and smiling countenance, seemed to invite her to fix her residence in those hallowed abodes, where she would avoid a father's dreadful anger, wean her thoughts from Montalto, whom she had so little hopes of ever being united to, and gradually render herself worthy of eternal happiness.

Her resolutions to do so were quickly formed, and shed a mournful tranquillity over her agitated bosom.

She was at length informed that the abbess desired to see

her in her own apartments, to which Rosalina proceeded, accompanied by the nun who brought her the message.

"You seem to be very unhappy, signora," said the nun: "has any thing happened, for we heard that the castello was in danger of being attacked?"

"Alas! I do not know," said Rosalina, sighing; "whether it has been or not; my own calamities have so greatly absorbed every other consideration, that I am ignorant of that circumstance."

"There is little happiness in the world, dear sister," said the nun affectionately; "I was the victim of misery, before these walls kindly enclosed me from the turbulent cares and anxieties of life; since that period I have hardly known an unhappy hour."

"I almost envy you," returned Rosalina; "but soon I hope that like you I shall devote myself to the duties of religion, and be happy."

They now arrived at the apartments of the abbess, where the nun leaving her, she entered, and was received in the kindest manner by the venerable mother.

"Welcome, fair daughter," said she. "I ought to chide you for not oftener seeing me; but why are your cheeks so pale? what has happened? I am all anxiety till I know."

"Holy mother, I am come to you for protection: the tale of my sorrows is long—part indeed is already known to you; but the rest—oh, how miserable I am in being obliged to expose my father's dreadful and outrageous passions, which have endangered my life!"

"Your life, my poor Rosalina! thank Heaven you are safe!" said the abbess. "Here you may divest yourself of fear; but another time acquaint me with the particulars, for I see your spirits are unable to the task."

"You must not refuse the request I am going to make, holy mother," said Rosalina, "for I feel that if you should, I shall yet be unsafe, and a stranger to happiness. I wish never to leave these walls—to devote myself to Heaven. I shall then be safe from my enemies, safe from a father's deadly wrath; and knowing that Montalto then can never be mine, I shall endeavour to forget that I had ever loved: permit me then instantly to make those irrevocable vows of seclusion which will sever me from the world."

"My dear daughter," said the abbess, "I can hardly wonder at your present request, when I consider the motives that have induced you to make it. Believe me, I long have sighed at your unhappy situation, and in my prayers you were not forgotten. But I should be wanting in the friendship I owe the memory of your sainted mother, and have for you, my dear Rosalina, if I consented to a wish so hastily formed, the consequences of which you have not had time to consider. If, however, you do not alter your resolution before the third day, I will acquiesce to your wishes; but without your having time for reflection, I must decline giving my assent. In the meantime, be assured that you are perfectly safe while under my protection. Remember, my dear daughter, that a life of religious retirement does not give happiness to all: some are formed for the active scenes of life, for social duties; to them the seclusion of a convent would be a continual torment. Such instances are by no means unfrequent, and I should always most severely regret if you, Rosalina, should at any time hereafter repent of your vows."

Such was the resolution of the abbess; and Rosalina having remained some time longer in converse with her, at length retired to the apartment which she had ordered to be prepared for her young friend, and where Carletta was permitted to attend her.

Though the duca's conduct to Rosalina had been such as totally to banish filial love, yet she could not even now consider him in any other light than a parent, and she sat down to write to him to acquaint him with her intentions, and to assure him of her sincere forgiveness for the dreadful deed he seemed so fully resolved to perpetrate. In doing this, the frequent tears often effaced the letters she slowly formed with her trembling hand, which was scarcely able to guide her pen. The following were the contents of her letter:—

ROSALINA DE RODOLPHO TO THE DUCA DE RODOLPHO.

From the Convent of Santa Maria.

"This is the last letter you will receive from your unfortunate daughter while she belongs to the world. Alas! am I so deeply immersed in woe as to be obliged to tell a parent, a father, that I have fled from him in order to prevent the perpetration of the most dreadful of crimes? Surely it was not so, and my senses deceived me. Oh, grant, kind Heaven, that it was but a dream! How gladly would I return, and seek a father's blessing! But still I hear your enraged voice denouncing curses on the woe-claimed Rosalina—see your sword upraised to shed my blood! But praised be Heaven that you did not! No more will I wound your peace by my presence—no more will you be disturbed on my account. To-morrow I take the veil—to-morrow I shall be secluded for ever from the world. I shall not seek to palliate my offences: but as sure as every word, thought, and deed of mortals is known to the Ruler of the Universe, so certain it is that my intents in being united to Montalto were to render you secure against the efforts of a much-wronged enemy. A daughter, I will own, ought not to seek to counteract the designs of a parent; but with respect to the information I gave to Montalto, perhaps I had a right to do so. It is true I am indebted to you for my being—but did not he often preserve my life? and from that circumstance he had a right to share the duty I owed a father. Love does not now guide my words, for I must endeavour now to forget that I ever loved: but that I have a parent shall never be absent from my thoughts, and whenever I prostrate myself before the altar, that you may be happy here and hereafter, my dear father, shall be the constant prayer of your

ROSALINA."

Such was the letter which the duca received, and which affected him in the manner we have described, and made him instantly resolve to proceed to the convent of Santa Maria, and endeavour to dissuade his daughter from her intentions, which would destroy his new-formed hopes.

Arrived at the convent, he was conducted to the parlatory, which was divided by a gilt screen of curiously wrought iron, where the professed were allowed to converse with their friends, who occasionally visited them.

When Rosalina was acquainted that the duca wished to see her, she trembled and turned pale. But the abbess, to whom she immediately repaired on receiving the intelligence, besought her to compose her agitation, and by no means to refuse to see her father, adding, that the screen would effectually prevent him from using any violence towards her, and that in all probability his intention was to endeavour to be reconciled to her.

With a slow hesitating step, Rosalina at last entered the apartment, and beheld the duca hastily traversing the other end. He stopped when he saw her, and approaching the screen said—"Forgive, my dear Rosalina, my late dreadful intentions; believe me, I have most sincerely repented of them. I feel I am a father, and hope you will consider me so, when I promise sincerely that my future conduct shall be such as will make you happy; and as a proof of it, I here pledge my solemn promise, if you will leave the convent, to consent to your union with Montalto—nay, more, will even exert myself to forward an event which will make you happy, and be some amends for my late unkind treatment. I ask your forgiveness, my child—do not refuse your father!"

Rosalina melted into tears.—"My father," she said, "you have your Rosalina's forgiveness, her love, duty, obedience, every thing that a child can render to its parent: I could withstand your commands when harshly given, but when you are kind I could give up my existence, if so doing would be of the smallest benefit to you."

"I was not wrong," returned the duca, with pleasure in his countenance, "when I placed a reliance on the gentle complying heart of my Rosalina: yes, my child, you are far dearer to me than ever, and sorry indeed am I that I have been so unworthy, so cruel a father to such a deserving girl."

"Do not think of it, my dear father," said Rosalina; "all the past is forgot. I wish to give you an early proof of my compliance to your wishes. Shall I return to the castello with you?"

"Do, dear Rosalina," said Rodolpho, "But first acquaint the abbess with your intentions. Believe me, I long to embrace you, and shew the world that I can prove myself a kind parent."

Rosalina flew to the abbess and related all that had passed, while the joy and delight she felt was visible in her countenance.

"I congratulate you, my dear Rosalina," said the good mother, "on the prospect of felicity which I trust you have now in view. You now, my child, are no doubt glad that I resisted complying with your wishes yesterday."

"Most assuredly I am, holy mother; but when I made my resolutions I had little idea of ever again enjoying the affection of a parent: your kindness to me shall be the constant subject of my grateful thoughts."

Rosalina then taking leave of the abbess, hastened to her father, and in a few minutes was tenderly embraced by him; and when on the way to Colredo, he repeatedly assured her of his intentions of making Montalto acquainted with his compliance to their union.

Carletta accompanied her mistress, and the greatest delight prevailed amongst the domestics of the castello when they understood that Rosalina was returned; Rodolpho, too, appeared to be happier than he had been for some time; and the inhabitants of Colredo, on whose pale countenances terror and dismay were so lately depicted, now wore a gay and joyous look.

Grimaldi alone seemed not to partake of the general hilarity, for when acquainted with the return of Rosalina, and that the duca had consented to the long wished-for nuptials with Montalto, he uttered not a word, but kept himself in the retirement of his apartments, not even emerging to congratulate the duca on the recovery of his daughter.

From the traits of his character and disposition which have hitherto been delineated, it is probable that his dark savage mind was brooding plans of revenge, for it will be seen, that as he not unfrequently excited others to acts of savage cruelty, it was very unlikely he would tamely bear the insinuations of the duca, when he hinted that he had some design of his own in the advice which he gave him.

The duca, that he might assure his daughter of the sincerity of his intentions, determined as soon as possible to commence the pleasing work of peace and friendship, in which he was no less anxious than Rosalina, while Carletta partook of the joy of her mistress, for then she would be united to Pietro.

Rodolpho was so completely disgusted with the conduct of Grimaldi, that he never approached his residence, or even condescended to make any inquiries about him.

He determined, on the second day from the arrival of his daughter, to send a message to Montalto, expressive of his feelings excited by his conduct, and to offer to repair the breach and end all animosity by giving him his lovely daughter.

Such was his intention; and he fondly in idea beheld the accomplishment of his hopes: but the future is veiled from our sight—predestination belongs only to the Supreme Disposer of events, and oftentimes he smiles on weak-minded mortals, who, blind to the events which the next moment may produce, build airy structures of fancied happiness, which are often destroyed, almost before they are formed, by the blasts of disappointment.

CHAPTER XVIII.

How transitory, how delusive are human joys! when we think we hold the phantom happiness in our grasp, it vanishes! Always in pursuit, yet we never attain it: from the court to the cottage, if we continue our search, we shall find that happiness is rarely known. True felicity, indeed, is not to be enjoyed on this side the grave; and this deprivation is for the wisest of purposes, for our mundane affections would be so great as to exclude all wish, all longing after heavenly delights. The misery we endure below awakens all those delightful anticipations of a future recompence for the anxious cares and miseries of life, which urge us to continue its toilsome paths. Still, however, we fondly look forward, and in fancy see the air-formed gorgeous temple of human happiness rising stately before us—we see its wide-folding portals open to receive us—when, alas! we suddenly awake, and find it was but a mere delusion of the brain—a delusion which made us mindless of the wide-yawning gulf, on whose dreadful brink we totter, and often are lost.

What various roads do mankind take in the pursuit of pleasure, and what various forms does it assume, according to their capricious turns of fancy! Some place their delight in the accumulation of riches, in honours, in the gratification of sensual appetites; some in tormenting their own species; and a few in acts of charity and benevolence. Not of this last was the monk—he seemed to take pleasure in acts of cruelty and black and horrible revenge: such was his delight, and of which indeed the pages of this work contain too many sad instances.

Fame, with her many tongues, soon brought to the delighted ears of Montalto the resolution of the duca di Rodolpho, before he had expressed it to him; and anxious to see his adored Rosalina, he repaired to the chapel of Santa Maria, where it may be remembered she had promised to meet him, before she took her leave to return to Colredo, on the memorable night which witnessed the destruction of the tower.

Gentle spirits of love and sympathy! ye who wake the soul's tender emotions, and ye who render it sensible of the joys and sorrows of those around you, teaching the breasts in which ye deign to dwell to be joyous with the gay, and never to behold the fast-flowing tears of misery without mingling them with your own, and seeking to alleviate the woes of others! assist me to describe the happiness which both Montalto and Rosalina felt when they met! Now, too, that they no longer feared the resentment of a father, or were tortured with cruel doubts and fears, what sweet anticipations of happiness dwelt in each bosom! Alas! could either of them have foreseen the events of a few hours, how different would have been their sentiments! But Heaven conceals from the eyes of mortals the volume of fate; the evils of the present are sufficient, without foreseeing unavoidable calamities.

Rosalina communicated to Montalto the intention of the duca to propose the alliance to him the succeeding day, and which was indeed generally known throughout the castello, for the duca did not conceive it necessary to conceal what would so shortly become public.

"To-morrow, then," said Montalto, as he parted from Rosalina at the portico of the chapel, "to-morrow I shall have the blessing of again seeing you. Sweet expectation! How long will the intervening hours appear! But they must roll on, and the happy moment will at last arrive."

When Rosalina was gone, he stood watching her graceful form as she proceeded to the castello; and when its ponderous walls hid her from his view, he sat down on the marble bench to enjoy the cool breeze, which glided over the tremulous bosom of the lake. The leaves of the aged pines and larches rustled against each other, and the fragrant lily bent its lovely head as the gentle zephyr passed along; light and airy clouds slowly moved their fleecy forms in the wide aërial expanse; and as the scenes of nature faded to the view, imagination, with all her train, supplied the vacancy of sight. The soul of Montalto, calm and full of content, communicated its repose to its mortal habitation, and the happy lover, slumbering, became unconscious of what was passing around him—became unconscious of a dark savage form that hung over him, and who, putting his hand within the folds of his mantle, drew from thence a dagger!—

Ah! where was then the guardian spirit which watches over the safety of the virtuous? Was he far distant, or employed on some more important mission, that he did not protect the sleeping Montalto, and turn away the hand which now grasped the instrument of his destruction?

Twice was the murderous dagger upraised, and twice did it drink the blood of Rosalina's fond lover!—Groaning, he sunk on the pavement, and the shades of death encompassed him.

The cruel perpetrator of this barbarous act was on the point of repeating the blows, when a hasty footstep was heard approaching through the aisle of the chapel, and unseen he slunk away and concealed himself in the forest.

A monk who had been praying in the chapel, alarmed by a groan which hollowly echoed through the pile, hastened to the portico from whence the sound had proceeded, and found the bleeding body of Montalto. Life was ebbing fast from the deep wounds; the powers of speech were already gone, and the assassin seemed to have been successful in his dark purpose.

The monk raised up the senseless form, and, tearing off his garments, found the wounds: he endeavoured as well as he could to stop the effusion of blood; and having alarmed the inhabitants of the monastery by his repeated calls, the monks, hastening to the place, soon bore the unfortunate Montalto to a couch, and sent to the marchese to acquaint him with the almost hopeless condition of his son.

The attentive care of the monks soon prevented the effusion of the stream of life; and as it slowly glided through his veins, Montalto's senses returned, and, opening his languid eyes, he was endeavouring to speak, but was restrained by the monks, who were fearful that the least exertion would cause the blood to flow, and render their endeavours of no avail.

Great was the grief of the marchese when he arrived, and saw the lamentable situation of his son, and which he immediately ascribed to the well-known perfidy of the duca di Rodolpho; and though he had hitherto been restrained, both by his son's entreaties, as well as his affection for him, and the wish he entertained of seeing him happy in the possession of Rosalina, yet now he determined that nothing should stop his revenging himself in the severest manner.

Although it was almost impossible at that early period to form any opinion respecting Montalto, yet such of the fathers who had made the cure of wounds their study, thought favourably of his situation; and the marchese being very anxious to have him conveyed to his own castello, both on account of his being more carefully attended when under his own inspection, and also of his intended hostilities against the duca being kept from his knowledge, which would be much easier to effect there than in the monastery—a circumstance which he feared would retard his recovery, because it would awaken all his anxieties respecting Rosalina.

As soon, therefore, as the morning dawned, he had his son placed upon a litter and conveyed by his domestics to his castello, and then turned all his thoughts on revenge. His people were hastily summoned to prepare for the dreadful business of war, who, with the party sent by count Florelli, formed a numerous army.

Montalto, who was placed in a remote part of the castello, where the trumpet was not heard, nor the loud neighing of the impatient war-horses, remained in total ignorance of his father's hostile intents, or, feeble as he was, he would have endeavoured to leave his couch to dissuade him from attacking the duca; or, if unable to do so, his anxiety might have cost him his life. He remained all that day so extremely weak from loss of blood as to be scarcely able to speak, but his wounds seemed to promise favourably.

In the meantime the marchese, full of rage, approached the walls of Colredo, whose inhabitants seemed to be in the greatest consternation. He had begun to wind up the rocky ascents to its lofty walls, when a hasty messenger demanded a parley, which being granted, the duca di Rodolpho advanced without any attendants, and thus addressed the marchese:—

"That your intents are of a hostile nature, marchese, there can be no doubt; but before we begin the work of stern resistance, I would know the reason of your appearing in arms, since by your late noble comportment I had augured so favourably of you and your son as to determine, as a hostage for our future friendship, no longer to withhold my consent to the wished alliance between our children."

"Dissimulation ill becomes the duca di Rodolpho," returned the marchese: "deep indeed were your plans, but Heaven, I trust, will not grant them success. Either I or you this day will cease to live. Shame on you, duca, to act the murderer, and seek the life of my son! At his request I had forgotten my own wrongs, and though able to choose my revenge, yet I forbore on his account, because he loved your daughter: now the tie is broken, and if he lives, he will, I trust, learn to forget the offspring of his deadly foe."

"If he lives!" said the duca: "what then has befallen him?"

"Does Rodolpho forget the events of last night?" returned the marchese.

"By Heaven, marchese, I know not to what you allude, when you mention your son and the events of last night! You speak mysteriously to me."

"What then, duca, do you mean to deny that you are ignorant of the base attempt that was made on his life? It is needless to declare your innocence: for when had he an enemy but yourself?"

"Now by the holy rood I swear," said the duca, "that I am ignorant of the deed! Some foul and bitter enemy hath laid it to me. You know me better, marchese, than to suppose I would stoop so low as to deny my acts; but if farther confirmation is wanting, know that this very morning I intended to propose to you the alliance between our families, instigated so to do by your treatment of my people, whom when ill advised I sent against you. But your son yet lives, you say; then I will go alone, unarmed, and appear before him: if he taxes me with the crime you impute to me, my life and person will then be in your power, but if not satisfied with such a proof of my innocence, declare it now, and you shall see Rodolpho will resent the imputation.— Yes, you may subdue me, but the prize you will gain will be the smoking ruins of Colredo's towers, covering the dead bodies of their defenders."

"My nature delights not in such sanguinary revenge, duca," returned the marchese. "I could indeed wish to believe you innocent, because I know how firmly my son's affections are placed upon your daughter. I shall be satisfied with the proof you offer to give. Return then with me to my castello, and if Montalto is not your accuser, neither will his father be."

"Marchese," returned Rodolpho, "I wish to be in amity with you, and will instantly accede to your wishes; and if you wish it, Rosalina shall accompany me."

"Alas! the sight you will witness," returned the marchese, "would be too agonizing for her gentle frame to bear; but if he recovers, Rosalina may hereafter shorten the hours of his confinement."

The duca now called to his people to bring him his steed, and when he was ready, he rode by the side of the marchese at the head of his troops, and proceeded towards his residence, greatly to the astonishment of the inhabitants of the castello, who, in total ignorance of the cause, were wholly at a loss to account for his conduct.

But the duca, conscious of his innocence, and more anxious every hour for the union of his daughter to Montalto, was not alarmed at putting himself in the power of the marchese, for after the proof he had received of his noble behaviour, he felt himself perfectly secure. When they arrived at the castello, and the marchese had conducted the duca into the chamber where Montalto lay, he was evidently shocked to behold his pale countenance and hollow listless eye.

"The duca di Rodolpho," said the marchese to his son, "in order to do away with the suspicions I entertained of his being the cause of your present situation, has come to deny the charge to yourself: tell then, my son, who it was that has acted this deadly part towards you."

"I know not," faintly returned Montalto: "the deed was done whilst I slumbered beneath the portico of Santa Maria, but I am certain of the duca's innocence."

"I have some reason to believe that the intended assassin is not unknown to me," returned Rodolpho; "and if I am right in my conjectures, I will deliver him into your power."

"Your so doing, duca," said the marchese, "will place me under an obligation to you. Your conduct, and Montalto's reply, have assured me of your ignorance of this cruel act: on his account do I forget the injuries I have received; and Rosalina shall unite us all in amity."

"Such, I trust, will be the result," said Rodolpho; "and as you are satisfied of my innocence, I will instantly return, and endeavour to find if my suspicions are rightly founded; and if they are, before this time to-morrow the intended assassin of Montalto shall be in your power. Melancholy indeed will be the painful task I shall have to perform, to disclose to Rosalina the sad event which has befallen him; but I trust his wounds are not dangerous—and when he is able to leave his chamber, I will permit her to see him."

"That indeed will be a comfort to me," said Montalto; "and your promise, duca, I trust you will be mindful of, for it has animated me beyond expression."

"You may depend on me," said the duca; "for now I shall be ruled by the sentiments of my own breast, and not by the counsel of others, which has hitherto been my ill fate."

Thus saying, he took a friendly leave of the marchese and his son, and departed, revolving in his mind, on his journey to Colredo, what inducement the monk could have in seeking the life of Montalto, for it was on him his suspicions fell. And he resolved, as soon as he saw him, to tax him with it; and should it be so, to seize and deliver him to the marchese.

Rosalina, who had heard of the hostile approach of the marchese, and that her father was gone with him without any attendants, felt rather anxious for his safety, and ascending the battlements, long waited for his return, and at length was greeted with seeing him approaching hastily to the castello. She met him at the gates, and while her intelligent countenance spoke her joy on his return, her features were soon overspread with melancholy, when she beheld the agitation so plainly depicted in his; and as soon as he had dismounted, she silently followed him to the hall.

"Rosalina," said the duca, tenderly, "have you seen Montalto since the night he rescued you?"

"I saw him last night," she replied, blushing.

"Last night? Indeed! What, in the chapel of Santa Maria?" said the duca: "at what time did you leave him?"

"It was, I think," returned Rosalina, "about an hour after vespers. But you seem agitated, my dear father; has any thing happened to Montalto? Pray do not keep me in suspense, but let me know the worst."

"Do not alarm yourself so, my daughter; nothing has happened but what I trust a short time will rectify. Montalto was wounded."

Here the duca sprung forward to assist the trembling Rosalina, who, unable to support herself, was sinking on the floor, while her senses, unable to bear up against the indescribable emotions of horror which she endured, were deserting her. Carletta and the other female domestics were summoned to her assistance, and with their care, and the repeated declarations of the duca that Montalto's life was in no danger, she began slowly to revive; but her frequent tears shewed the greatness of her grief, and her sighs confirmed it. Rodolpho did all he could to comfort her, and even promised in a day or two to take her to see her lover. This promise served to allay the poignancy of her grief; and as soon as she was able, she slowly proceeded to her apartments, intending to write to Montalto a few lines expressive of her deep sorrow, and to acquaint him with her father's promise of permitting her to see him.

The duca immediately proceeded to the apartments of Grimaldi, which he found him slowly pacing, and instantly accused him of having attempted to murder Montalto.

"And who has given utterance to so vile a falsehood besides yourself, duca, for this tale could hardly be of your own invention?" returned the monk, in a tone of voice which told the passion that raged in his breast.

"My own surmises, monk," said the duca; "my knowledge of your hatred to Montalto; your dislike to his being united to Rosalina, and my acquaintance with your revengeful disposition."

"Your surmises, then, duca, were wrong—your knowledge of my hatred to Montalto equally so; but not so the dislike which you say I had to his being united to your daughter—that arose from my anxiety respecting the duca di Rodolpho; I could ill brook to see you stoop so low as to offer your daughter when you had refused her. You accuse me, too, of being revengeful: of whom have I been revenged but of enemies? Was it not at my instance that the life of the marchese was preserved, as well

as that of his son? Such acts are far from being proofs of a revengeful disposition. To ensure whose safety was Sebastiano
destroyed? Not surely the monk Grimaldi? he could have no
interest in such a deed: but the man he then called his friend
would have been endangered by his existence, and he fell! Could
the bones of Astolpho speak—could the voice of Theodora be
heard from the tomb—could all the accusing voices be heard
which one day will be raised against the duca di Rodolpho—
they would stun his ears with their long dreadful recitals of his
remorseless, bloody, and revengeful disposition."

The duca started and turned pale, but the monk, after a short
pause, continued—"I know of no one more likely to have perpetrated this deed you would impute to me than yourself; for
who is safe from the frequent gusts of your outrageous passions,
when, had but a few moments more time been allowed you,
Rosalina would have perished by her father's sword?"

"Peace, monk!" vociferated the duca, "nor torment me with
recapitulations of my deeds! And who are you that dare thus
to insult me—you whose mysterious behaviour excites general
observation—you who for some unknown reason veil your
features? But be careful, monk, lest I forget my promise, and
tearing away that cowl, see the face of my tormentor, which he
is so industrious to conceal."

"It would not surprise me," returned Grimaldi, "if the duca
di Rodolpho broke his promise; I have expected such a vio-
lation of my solemn vows long before this: but the crime will
revert heavily on you, for though you may suppose yourself
safe within your castle walls, the vengeance of the church will
reach you, and the power of the holy inquisition will make you
tremble."

The duca was silent, for he well knew that the inquisition
was a power which made even kings tremble, and but for that
fear, his passion might perhaps have prompted him to acts of
violence which he would in all probability have sorely repented
of.

"I will not," said he, "answer for my conduct if you protract
your stay within these walls, nor shall even the dreaded power

of the inquisition withhold my arm: thou knowest, monk, I fear not death."

"I know you fear not to inflict it on those who stand in the way of your ambitious views," returned Grimaldi—"Astolpho and Sebastiano are evidences of that."

"Dost thou again dare to repeat their names?" said the duca, his hand grasping his sword. "By Heavens, I could this moment open a passage for thy dark soul! Provoke me not again, monk, or thy life shall answer for it."

Grimaldi was silent; he stood motionless, and apparently unterrified before Rodolpho; his gaze seemed fixed on the ground. The duca viewed his gigantic form for some moments, and then left the chamber, secretly determining to find out who the monk was, before many more days had elapsed.

He had not proceeded many paces before he began to consider that he had done wrong to irritate the monk, who was in the possession of all his secrets, some of which were of a nature which shunned the glare of day; and he thought it would be better if he endeavoured to calm the storm he had raised. With this idea he slowly returned; and when he had approached Grimaldi's apartment, he stopped and listened to his slow footsteps as he paced its confines. The door was partly open, and as he looked through the aperture, he saw the monk, whose back was turned to him; his cowl was thrown back, and he waited anxiously till he should move, when he might see his features, which he had wished to do from the first moment of their meeting: but the monk's caution disappointed him, though his curiosity was much more excited, for when he turned round, a sable mask veiled his countenance; and the duca leaving the place to prevent being seen, soon altered his resolution, for what he had proposed to do in the moment when he was agitated by his fears, his proud and haughty spirit now made him incapable of; he however determined the next morning to pacify the monk, which he doubted not could be easily effected, and then passed on to his apartments.

It was now the hour when the sun ceasing to shine on this hemisphere, leaves the clouds tinted with his radiant beams,

and the moon slow rising in the east shews her pale form.
Rodolpho threw himself on a couch, and anticipating the time
when Rosalina would be his bride, began to form visionary
schemes of satiating his restless and ambitious disposition, to
effect which he little cared for the cries of the wife deprived of
her husband, or the mother of her son, perhaps her sole support
and comfort; these were ideas which never disturbed his rest.
To increase his forces, he determined to depopulate his territories, and then with the aid of the marchese, and the count
Florelli, he little doubted but that he should be a more powerful claimant for the principality of Manfroné, than any of the
neighbouring rulers who might attempt to seize the vacant seat.

Such were the ideas which agitated the bosom of the duca,
till the shades of evening increased the lustre of the moon,
and nature was sunk in silence and repose; he then sought his
pillow, and, fatigued by the exertions of the day, endeavoured to
close his eyes in peaceful slumbers; but in vain, for the remembrance of his cruel deeds, which the monk's conversation had
brought more forcibly to his recollection, tormented him till
long after the castle bell had told, in iron notes, the division of
night and morning; then, and not till then, could sleep weigh
down his eyelids, and for a few short moments blunt the unceasing sting of conscience.

CHAPTER XIX.

ROSALINA, when she had reached her apartments, sat down
and wrote the following lines to Montalto:—

"DEAR FRIEND OF MY HEART,

"Are our griefs never to terminate in this vale of sorrow? is
the prospect of happy hours which was so brightly opening, excluded our view for ever, by the sable clouds of fresh calamities?
What enemy can it be who thus invisibly haunts our steps?—
who has endeavoured to deprive you of your Rosalina, and me
of my Montalto? Alas! how do my tears flow when busy fancy

depicts you to my view, suffering from the anguish of your wounds! When we last met, how happy we were! We thought, fondly thought, that the season of sorrow was past—that a sweet tranquillity would attend our future days! how changed, alas! is now the scene! But I will not despair, for my father has assured me that your life is not endangered, and has promised that I should see you in a few days. Perhaps he has only done this to comfort me. Alas! how much do I need consolation! He has behaved most kindly to me, but comfort will be a stranger to my bosom till you are recovered. Let my messenger be acquainted with the state of your health, and rest assured of the unalterable affection of

"ROSALINA."

Such was the billet which she hastily penned with a trembling hand, and immediately sent by a domestic; and then to rest her weary frame, reclined on a couch; but her anxiety respecting Montalto prevented sleep from composing her agitation, and she soon after arose, and sitting at the casement, watched for the return of her messenger.

Night had some time ruled the hemisphere before the welcome sound of his horse's feet was heard on the drawbridge, and soon a packet was delivered her by Carletta, who had hastened to the courtyard to receive it: it contained a few lines from the marchese, assuring her that his son's life was not considered in danger, and that her kind attention in writing had greatly delighted him; and concluded with hoping, that as soon as he was able to leave his couch, she would make him happy by her presence.

This letter, as it convinced her that the duca had not represented Montalto's situation more favourably than it really was, which she feared he might have done to assuage the greatness of her grief, contributed much to her comfort; and full of hopes and happy anticipations, she closed her eyes in sleep.

But the fearful visions of the night blustering around, deprived her of the composing influence of the somnific deity, and when it was past midnight, terrified by a dream, Rosalina suddenly awoke; the particulars of her vision rested not in her memory, but the effect it had on her long remained.

The moon dimly gleamed through her casement, she arose; and beheld her encircled in mists, and at times totally obscured by passing clouds; the wind was high, and howled mournfully through the forest below; the melancholy owl was heard from her cheerless residence in the hollow of some time-worn tree, and the croaking raven, perched on the battlements of Colredo's towers, gave to the blast his harsh discordant notes.

Rosalina's melancholy increased—a heavy weight seemed to oppress her bosom, which she ascribed to her dreams and the cheerless scenes which the grey dawn gave to her view, for now a heavy rain descended from the clouds, which, borne on the strong bosom of the blast, dashed against the casement; she again sought her couch, but sleep was far distant from her.

Thus heavily rolled the hours till the sun broke on the dreary scene, and drove away the stormy clouds. Rosalina was sitting at the casement, her thoughts fixed on Montalto, and in endeavouring to form conjectures of their enemies, when suddenly a confused noise heard in the corridor which led to her chamber; she started from her seat, and listened; the steps seemed approaching, and at length she heard the voice of Carletta calling her.

Terrified and confused with her sudden anticipations of some fresh calamity, Rosalina had scarcely strength to draw back the fastenings of the portal, when she beheld a crowd of the domestics, whose pale countenances shewed how greatly they were agitated.

"Good Heavens!" said Rosalina, "what is the matter? what has happened?"

"Oh, signora! my dear mistress!" sobbed Carletta, at length, for the others seemed struck dumb with terror. "Oh, the duca! the duca!"

"What of my father?" said Rosalina; "speak, some of you—you alarm me; I will go to him!"

"Oh, no! no!" said the domestics; "pray, do not go! it is so horrible a sight!"

"A sight, Carletta!" said the pale Rosalina: "let me know the worst, I conjure you, if you have any friendship for me."

"Oh, signora! the duca is—is murdered!" said the weeping Carletta.

Hardly conscious of what she was doing, Rosalina flew to the apartment of her father, followed by the attendant and rushing in, beheld a sight which for a while rendered her speechless and immoveable.

The breathless body of the duca lay stretched on his couch; the bosom was bare; a dagger was deeply planted in the breast, the hilt of which was encircled by the ghastly fingers of a skeleton hand, and the clothes of the bed were dyed with the blood of the unfortunate Rodolpho.

Such was the horrible view which presented itself to the distended gaze of Rosalina: by the side of the couch stood the padre Grimaldi, who had been made acquainted with the murder of the duca the moment the deed was discovered by his domestics, and had immediately hastened to him; but it was too late to attempt any means for his recovery, for death had forever claimed his mortal part.

Rosalina, unable to support the dreadful sight of a murdered parent, fainted in the arms of Carletta, when Grimaldi turning round, he reprimanded the attendants for permitting her to enter the chamber, and directed her to be conveyed to her own, and the proper means to be used for her recovery.

Slowly they conveyed away the grief-stricken maid; and when she was gone, the monk, stretching forth his hand, disentwined the fingers from their bony grasp, and drew forth the dagger, which he attentively examined, and apparently started.

"There is some deep mystery in this," said he; "this dagger is the duca's, and well I remember to have seen him wear it. Were the castle gates securely fastened last night, and the private subterraneous passages?"

"I can answer for that, father," said the castellain, "for I secured them myself——"

"Then the murderer must be within the walls of Colredo: go

instantly, and direct that no one have egress from them on any pretence—we must not rest till he is discovered."

His directions were instantly complied with, and the next step was the examination of the guard who held their watch in the corridor which led to the duca's apartment; but as they were all well known to be his most faithful and long-tried soldiers, it was impossible to impute the crime to them.

Silence and dark suspicion now reigned in Colredo: each regarded the other with distrust, and feared to speak their sentiments. The gates were closed—every part of the immense pile underwent frequent examinations—but nowhere could the assassin be discovered.

To attempt to describe the emotions of Rosalina for many hours would be impossible: yet as soon as she was sensible of her situation, she evidently endeavoured to combat with her feelings, that she might be able to take the proper steps to find out the murderer of her father. This was no time for grief— her duty as a daughter called for her utmost energies. She sent for Grimaldi, who immediately attended her, and in a faltering voice requested the particulars of the sad scene she had witnessed.

The monk complied with her wishes, and concluded by stating the means he had taken to discover the perpetrator: that it must have been done by someone well acquainted with the secret communications of the castello was certain, for he was assured that the fidelity of the guard could be relied on.

"But the horrid skeleton hand, father! will not that afford some clue to your researches?"

"I think, signora, that the late duca informed me of some circumstances respecting an attempt which was made some time back to carry you from your apartments, and that the person, whoever he was, being attacked by him, lost his hand ere he effected his escape. This is a circumstance I have deeply considered, and am confident, from the hand being placed on the dagger, that it must have been done by him—probably out of revenge."

"It must be so indeed, father," said the sighing Rosalina; "but surely it would be easy to find the wretch out if he is in the castello?"

"Do you know of any private communications with the duca's apartments?" asked the monk.

"No," returned Rosalina; "I never heard of any; but as the castello abounds with them, it is more than probable that there may be some."

"My reason for asking that question," said Grimaldi, "is because the assassin could not have passed the guard. He must therefore have found some of those concealed passages, and thus have effected his purpose without fear of observance, and probably by this time has completely eluded our search—indeed his escape before proves him well acquainted with the interior of Colredo. Nothing, however, shall be omitted to find out who it was—of that you may rest assured."

"I thank you for your intentions, father," said Rosalina, weeping, "and shall leave to you to make the necessary regulations for the interment of my father, as I mean to proceed instantly to the convent of Santa Maria, where alone I can hope to find security from the secret attempts of my enemies, as I shall doubtless be their next object; and I am convinced, on reflection, father, that you will be of the same opinion."

"No, indeed I am not," replied the monk, "for would it not be most reprehensible for you to leave the castello before the remains of the duca were consigned to the silent tomb: your future relatives will doubtless mark your present conduct: and would it not give them an ill opinion of your filial duty, thus to fly the remains of your father, when in a few hours the last proof of our love will be paid to him? But if, indeed, you fear to stay here, I will in that case hasten the sad ceremony, and the evening after to-morrow shall be appointed for it. The next day you may retire to the convent, and, in the society of the sisters, haply find a relief for the sorrows of your bosom."

"Let it then be as you think best, father," returned Rosalina. "If indeed there was no danger in my stay here, I certainly would not have thought for a moment of retiring to the convent till the last sad rites were concluded."

"For so short a time," said Grimaldi, "I should hardly think there was any, for whoever it is that has assassinated the duca di Rodolpho, he will not venture to approach the castello till the general alarm excited by his atrocious deed has ceased, and peace again is restored; then, in the fancied security that will reign within these walls, he will naturally conclude that he would more easily be able to effect his further schemes, if indeed he has any."

"That he has," said Rosalina, "can be a matter of little doubt, if you call to mind the late attempt that was made on me when the tower was destroyed. Indeed there is every reason to believe that the person who endeavoured to effect that deed was the intended assassin of Montalto, and the murderer of my father; his next attempt will therefore be against me."

"Your opinion and mine perfectly coincide," returned Grimaldi; "therefore, after the interment of the duca, or even before, if you should still wish it, after what I have advanced, I would certainly advise your removal to Santa Maria."

"No—I am resolved to remain here till then," replied Rosalina, "at all events, as I should be most unwilling to shew the slightest disrespect to the memory of my parent."

"Is there any thing you wish me to do?" said the monk; "your desire shall be attended to, if in my ability to perform it."

"I thank you for your attention, father," returned Rosalina—"I should wish the marchese di Montalto to be informed of the sad events of last night—his advice and assistance would probably be of service to me."

"In common prudence," replied the monk, "I should advise you to avoid making him acquainted with it, for should it come to the ears of his son, his anxiety respecting you will doubtless retard his recovery—and the counsel of the marchese can be of no service now; but this I only submit to you—you will act as you think best."

"Then I will defer it," said Rosalina, "for a few days, at least till I have taken my residence at the convent; Montalto then can have no fears for my safety."

Grimaldi then left the apartments, and immediately ordered

the necessary preparations to be made for the interment of the duca.

Rosalina mourned incessantly the loss of her father: she had always loved him, even when his conduct to her had been harsh and cruel; and had he ceased to exist on that day when he had threatened to destroy her, she would have shed tears at his death. But now, to be taken off, when he had conducted himself so kindly towards her, and seemed to make her happiness his study, increased her sorrows. She had indeed nowhere now to look for consolation but to Heaven; and when alone, she frequently entered her oratory, and there directed the fervent pious petitions of her spotless soul to the bright residence of the All-powerful.

Carletta watched over Rosalina with unremitting attention: she sat by the side of her couch during the night, and seldom left her in the day; but she witnessed the wakeful hours of her sad mistress, for sleep never closed her eyes—her cheeks were pale and thin—her strength was decreasing, and melancholy seemed to have claimed her for her own.

The evening at length came when the remains of the duca were borne to the chapel of Santa Maria, there to be deposited in the cold bosom of the tomb. Though hardly able to walk, yet Rosalina prepared to attend the mournful ceremony; and sadly sighing, leaning on two domestics, she followed the silent train.

The chapel, dimly illumined with torches—the long procession of monks, who entered by pairs into the grand aisle, and ranged themselves round the grave—the costly emblems and honorary trophies of the duca, borne by the soldiers, who trailed their pikes on the ground—and the view of the bier, on which lay his pale remains—all exhibited a scene which struck cold to the heart of Rosalina, and her tears rolled unceasing from her swollen eyes.

The service at length commenced; the deep-toned voices of the monks chanting the requiem, joined to the softer strains of the nuns, rose in grand and solemn chorus to the vaulted roof. The abbot performed the service, but his speech was often interrupted by the sobs of Rosalina, unable to restrain her grief.

When the service was concluded, and the remains of Rodolpho committed to the earth, Rosalina returned to the castello, and in the retirement of her chamber gave free vent to her sorrows.

Thus perished the duca di Rodolpho, unlamented by every one except his daughter; cut off in the midst of his offences, with all his long catalogue of crimes unrepented of—no atonement made with offended Heaven for the sable deeds performed in his days of nature, how trembling—how full of horror—how confused will his guilty soul appear before the awful seat of judgment, when he hears the dreadful punishment which awaits the murderer!

How quickly do the years which compose the short date of human existence roll away. Time is ever on the wing, and each moment gives a soul to eternity! each moment witnesses the last sighs of some one around us! Yet, such is the vanity of human beings, that they take no warning from the departure of others, to prepare for the inevitable journey they will soon be called on to perform, but delay it from hour to hour, from day to day, and, thinking all mortal but themselves, at length forget to repent of their errors, when death pays his chilling visit, and ends the busy scene of life for ever!

Or if, when on the bed of death, when we behold the swift approach of the relentless power, we look back on the sinful actions of our lives with regret, and endeavour to make a hasty atonement for them, how futile must be such a repentance! Caused by fear, how unavailing with Him who knows the most retired secrets of the human breast!

Grimaldi the next morning, in the course of his conversation with Rosalina, told her that as nothing now prevented her removal to the convent, he would impart her desire to the abbess, and let her know, as soon as possible, her answer. With this promise he departed, and she prepared for her removal.

By the death of her father, Rosalina became possessed of Colredo and the domains attached to it; there were therefore many things which called for her immediate attention, such as acquainting the marchese with the past events, which she instantly resolved to do, and also to dismiss the troops who remained in the castello, that they might return to their long-expecting families.

The ambitious views of the duca had almost exhausted his coffers, and the vast expence of so large an establishment would, by the above prudent measures, be avoided: the further direction of her affairs she determined to confide to the marchese, who, she was well convinced, would consider her interest in whatever he did.

When Grimaldi returned, which was not till the day was far gone, he informed Rosalina that he had seen the abbess, who expected her the next morning.

"And why not this evening, father?" said Rosalina; "you know my anxiety to leave these walls, where danger lurks unseen."

"You have from me, daughter," said the monk, "the answer of the abbess, who doubtless had her reasons for appointing the period I informed you of for your removal—perhaps some apartments were to be prepared for your reception; however, the cause I know not. Have you written to the marchese?"

"I have, father, and have also determined on some arrangements which I wish to take place directly, respecting the dismissal of the troops."

"Such a step convinces me of your prudence," replied Grimaldi; "but the marchese—has he answered your letter?"

"I have not as yet sent it," replied Rosalina; "I waited for your return before I closed it."

"You had then better let it be conveyed to-morrow morning—'tis too late now," replied the monk. "I am sorry, daughter, that I caused you to delay the forwarding of it."

"To-morrow will do equally as well," replied Rosalina; "it will, besides, save Montalto from an uneasy night."

After some further converse, the monk departed, and Rosalina was left once more to her sad ruminations.

CHAPTER XX.

ROSALINA was thus obliged, much against her wish, to pass another melancholy night at the castello. She was not, however, under any fears for her safety, for the monk had promised to direct that a guard should be placed in the passages that led to her apartments. Carletta would have remained with her, but that faithful attendant was already so much fatigued with the many sleepless nights she had lately passed, that Rosalina desired her to retire to rest—a command which she, finding her entreaties of no avail, reluctantly complied with.

Left to herself, Rosalina took her station by the casement, and viewed the bright planet of night, as it continued its wonderful course in the regions of air: she thought of her mother, the hapless Theodora—of her father, so lately gone—and, as if busy memory delighted to torment her, of Montalto.

She arose from her seat, and to dispel her unquiet thoughts, walked about the room, listening at times to the clash of arms which was heard from the castle courts, when the centinels were relieved by their comrades, and the long hollow tones of the bell, as it told the departing hours of night.

Rosalina felt no inclination to retire to rest, and she again placed herself at the casement; the moon, attended by myriads of scintillating stars, shed their bright lustre over the clear azure heaven; the waters of the lake of Abruzzo seemed hushed to repose; not a cloud was to be seen; the leafy summits of the dark forest scarcely moved to the light breath which passed over them. The distant mountains appeared tipped with silver, and the grey walls of the monastery below brightened to the view; scarcely a sound was heard; night now stood in her noon, and viewed at equal distance her steepy rise and her declining race; nature seemed to pause in her great and wonderful works, and to give peace to the warring elements; sleep resting on the eyelids of mortals repaired their toil and careworn frames, and the restless passions of mankind for a while slumbered; even the warbling bird of night had ceased to tune her love-laboured song, and no midnight sound called drowsy Echo from her hollow caves.

"Far beyond those rolling planets," thought Rosalina, "is the bright abode of my sainted mother: there, unconscious of the miseries of her child, she tastes heavenly joys, the reward of her virtues. Oh, if the spirits of the dead are ever permitted to wander on the earth, surely it would be in such a night as this! Would that I could see the airy form of her who first embraced me in her fond maternal arms, and taught my infant tongue to lisp her name! But no! the cares and miseries of mortals reach not those hallowed regions, nor are they permitted to know what passes on earth, else their happiness would be destroyed.—And thou, my father, where, alas! is thy immortal spirit? Hast thou atoned for thy crimes? has Astolpho supplicated for thy forgiveness? Oh, if the prayers of mortals offered up in thy behalf can procure thee pardon, each hour would thy daughter fervently petition for it—each hour should masses be performed for thy soul's repose—at midnight should the voice of intercession arise from the chapel where thy mortal remains are for ever laid: but, alas! the hired supplication can be of little avail!"

Such were Rosalina's melancholy thoughts, from which she was interrupted by the low sounds of the passing bell of the monastery: mournfully did Echo repeat the sad tones which announced a soul to be on the verge of its departure from its mortal abode.

"Some one approaches eternity," thought Rosalina—"a soul is now struggling for liberty; soon it will burst from its narrow confines, and fly to adore its Maker: with what contempt will it then look upon the mouldering tenement which so lately contained it, when mixing with the angelic choir, it joins in tuneful symphonies and songs of praise! Dilated in its ideas, it will, from the immeasurable heights of heaven, look down on this globe, and wonder that so small a space contained it; but much more will it wonder that the short and momentary stay it was constrained to make in it was not wholly devoted to the praise and worship of Him who can never be sufficiently adored: how contemptible will then appear sublunary grandeur, high sounding titles, and all the little pageantries of state which agitate human ideas, and give rise to the baneful passions which taint the soul!—Hark! the bell ceases, and now the frailty of mortality is evinced! Such is the end of all: how happy or how miserable it is, depends on ourselves; and in a few revolving months the period of my dissolution will arrive, when I shall be called on to render up an account of the deeds of life. Methinks that death's dark shades seem to lose their horror the nearer we approach, and form an inviting covert for the wretched, for there peace for ever dwells; no jealousies, no broils torment us; the poor, the prisoner, the mourner fly there for relief, and lay their burdens down; death is the great privilege of human nature, and life without it would not be worth the taking. But yet he ever flies those who wish for him, and though certain in his approach, he most delays it where most he is sought."

Rosalina's melancholy increased every moment; she felt that indulging such mournful reflections in her present state of mind was rendering her incapable of supporting her allotted portion of existence with that patience and resignation to the will of Heaven which it was her duty to do; and having no inclination to retire to her couch though it was past midnight, she took up a volume whose pages contained many an eventful tale, traced by the legendary pens of days long since past, and by beings who now slumbered in the grave. The book had been a present to the unfortunate Theodora from the good abbot of Santa Maria, and Rosalina, independent of the narratives it contained, took a pleasure in perusing its contents, because she had whiled away many a cheerless hour with their aid, and her thoughts and eyes were employed on the same subjects which had once excited her beloved mother's attention.

She turned over the leaves some time before she could fix on a tale for her perusal, when the singular title of one attracting her notice, and not recollecting that she had ever read it, she trimmed her lamp. Rosalina continued the perusal of the volume till the clock of the castello had sounded the solitary hour of morn, and the moon no longer shed her lustre over the hemisphere, for the vapours and exhalations from the earth veiled her bright form.

From her casement she could just distinguish through the mist, the centinel on the walls below, resting motionless on his battle-spear. He perhaps, no longer mindful of his duty, was oppressed by the heavy influence of sleep; or recalling to his mind the past busy scenes of his life, the loss of some beloved comrade, or some memorable encounter, when of those who went forth in the morning, full of life, elate with the hopes of success, almost confident of victory, he alone perhaps was left to bring back the sad tale of their defeat, while all the companions of his toils were heaped on the plain, deformed by ghastly wounds, whose sanguine currents stained the drooping verdure.

Such were her reflections when a noise in her apartment made her turn round, and to her astonishment she saw the portal open, and the monk Grimaldi enter.

"Good Heavens, father!" she exclaimed, somewhat alarmed, "what brings you here at this time of the night?"

"You are in danger, signora," said he; "you must instantly leave the castello; the soldiers are mutinous—they are now assembling in the eastern hall; their purpose is to plunder Colredo, and if their rapacity is not satiated, your life may answer it. Haste then with me to the convent, for there only can you hope for security."

"Send instantly to the marchese, father; acquaint him with my danger; he will, I am confident, instantly arm his people in my defence."

"It would be fortunate if I were able to do that," returned the monk, "but the gates are in their possession; our only means of escape lies through the subterraneous passages, and when you are in safety at the convent, you may then let the marchese be acquainted with the situation of affairs here: the moments are precious, signora; you must hastily determine whether you go or stay."

"I shall certainly not hesitate in repairing to the convent, father," said Rosalina, "and as soon as my attendant is ready, I will accompany you."

"You do not consider, signora, the danger there is of our being discovered; besides, I have brought only one mantle, with which you must cover yourself; Carletta's fears may overcome her caution: the time too she will take to be ready will subject us to the greatest danger."

Rosalina suffered herself to be persuaded, and taking the garment from the monk, hastily threw it over her; she then followed his slow and cautious footsteps along the corridor, and was greatly surprised at not seeing the guard there whose steps she had heard during the night.

"I perceive you are astonished, signora," said the monk, "at this alarming proof of what I have told you; for doubtless when they saw me pass just now, they concluded I was coming to inform you of the conspiracy, and are therefore gone to join the others: we must be hasty; this way leads to my apartments, through which there is a communication with the passages below."

Rosalina began to be much terrified, and in her haste to leave the castello, did not notice that all the doors through which they passed appeared to have been thrown open purposely for them, the trap-door and sliding panel were also drawn back; but when after some time they had traversed the gloomy passages below, the portal which opened towards the northern cloisters was likewise ready opened for them, she observed it to the monk, who said in a low tone—

"I forbore, Rosalina, to notice to you this extraordinary circumstance; but I have my fears that our intended flight is discovered: we will stay here a few moments and listen before we proceed further, and are rendered visible by the faint gleams of the moon."

At this moment Rosalina started, for she distinctly saw the form of a man gliding at some short distance from her behind the low underwood; she was silent, but pointed out to Grimaldi the cause of her terror.

"I saw the object of your fears," said the monk, "but I trust we are yet unobserved; in the dark covert of the portal he will not be able to discover us; you see he is now going towards the monastery, probably with a view to surprise us there. As soon as he is at some distance, we will leave this place, and winding beneath the rocks, enter the chapel gate which fronts the lake. You now see, signora, how fortunate it was that you did not bring Carletta with you; so many of us must have been observed."

Rosalina, still keeping her eyes fixed on the man, at length saw him bend his way towards the monastery; and when he was no longer visible, she proceeded with Grimaldi beneath the lofty rocks on which the castello was erected, every moment gazing around with sensations of the most lively terror, expecting to be seized by the insolent soldiery.

Her fears, however, were not realized, and they reached the rocks which were nearly opposite to the portico of the chapel; but before she emerged from the protecting shade, she cautiously looked to the dark recess formed by the huge columns, and again saw the same figure moving behind them.

The monk seemed perplexed what course to pursue, but at length he said—

"To attempt to enter the chapel now would be madness; we will therefore continue proceeding among these rocks, which lead to the shore of the lake, and there stay till the search which now seems to be making for you has ceased."

Rosalina, full of terror, silently followed the monk through the rugged paths made in the rocks, after looking back to see if she was followed, till at length she came in view of the lake, on the margin of which, to her astonishment, she beheld a boat, and a man sitting in it.

"We are favoured by fortune," said Grimaldi: "this man will doubtless for a trifling remuneration convey us to the opposite side of the water, and we shall then be in security."

Suspicion for the first time now glanced in Rosalina's mind; the singular circumstance of a man at that time of night being in the boat, proved that there was some preconcerted plan in view, and she resolved to refuse to enter the vessel, but in such a manner that Grimaldi should not imagine she had any suspicion of the rectitude of his intentions, though for what end he wished to convey her from Colredo was yet a mystery.

"I think we had better return to the chapel," said Rosalina; "the man may now be gone, and I shall then be soon in safety, but if we pass to the other side of the lake, our return might be attended with danger."

"It is impossible to return now," said the monk hastily. "You had better instantly step into the boat, and if we cannot get to the monastery, we will go to the residence of the marchese, where you will be sure of protection."

"No, father," returned Rosalina; "let what will happen, I will instantly return."

"That must not be," replied the monk; "if, Rosalina, you will not be prevailed on to take the prudent step which I advise, I shall be necessitated to compel you. Nay, start not, signora; my determination is made, and which hereafter you will thank me for."

"Your conduct, monk," said the terrified Rosalina, assuming all the composure she was able, "convinces me that your intents in bringing me to this spot are of a dark and base nature, and that you have fabricated the tale of the soldiers being in arms merely to draw me from the protecting walls of my castello; but you shall find yourself foiled in your endeavours, for if you dare to attempt to detain me, my cries shall alarm the watchful centinels, and their honest fury may cause you dearly to repent of your present insulting comportment."

"The season of dissimulation is past," returned Grimaldi. "My plans have succeeded, and you, Rosalina, are in my power."

"In your power! Oh, Heavens protect me! What shall I do—where shall I fly?"

"You may make yourself easy on that head," said the monk, "for your destiny is fixed: nay stay," said he, rudely seizing her arm, seeing that she was on the point of hastening away, "you go not hence."

Rosalina's entreaties and screams were of no avail; she struggled to free herself from the grasp of the monk, and at length succeeded, and as fast as she was able she ran along the path which led back to the castello, the monk following her; but she had not proceeded far when she saw the man who had caused her so much alarm advancing directly towards her.

"Oh, whoever you are," said the hapless maid, "protect me, I beseech you, from the vile monk! My gratitude shall be unbounded."

The man replied not, but caught in his arms, and throwing a mantle over her head, bore her back to the boat, in which he placed her, while the monk followed, and seating himself by her side, held fast her hands, that she might not remove the mantle, which prevented her screams from being heard.

The boat now swiftly cut the yielding waters, and when the men had rowed for some time, the mantle was taken off her face, and the unfortunate Rosalina looking around, beheld herself far distant from the shore, and far beyond the reach or hope of succour; Colredo's lofty turrets appeared to decrease in size and height, while the opposite shore rose darker to the view. She was silent, for her cries now would be useless, for no pitying friend, no guardian of the innocent, was near to afford her aid.

CHAPTER XXI.

THE mild beams of the morning glimmered on the summits of the western hills before the boat reached the opposite shores of the wide-spreading waters of Abruzzo.

Rosalina, when she had conquered the first emotions of the deep terror which had seized her, began to reflect on her situation: that the monk was her enemy was manifest, but still she thought it hardly possible that it could be him who had committed such atrocious acts as had lately been perpetrated; she therefore was sometimes inclined to believe that he was the agent of the person who had so mysteriously escaped from the castello with the loss of his hand; at other times, that he was ignorant of those circumstances, and acted from the impulse of some horrible intent, which he had formed against her peace. Full of her fears, she raised her eyes to the blue vaulted canopy of heaven, and fervently implored the protection of the Almighty in her helpless state.

Scarcely able to move, Rosalina was helped out of the boat into a carriage that was waiting on the shore; the monk followed, and soon the lake of Abruzzo was lost to the view, for the carriage rolling rapidly along, entered a dark and gloomy glen, where the faint gleams of morning feebly penetrating the overhanging trees, scarcely rendered the drivers able to see their way.

Grimaldi spoke not: wrapt up in his long monkish garments, and his features, as usual, concealed by a cowl, Rosalina conjectured that he was sleeping; she turned her thoughts towards her escape, but alas! there was at present but little prospect of that; excepting her persecutor and his agents, she had not seen a single person, or even a sign of the habitations of man, in the gloomy roads through which they passed. She was sometimes on the point of addressing the monk, of demanding the reason of his conduct; but her fears restrained her, for she trembled whenever she beheld him: but though seemingly surrounded by dangers, and in the hands of her enemy, Rosalina did not give way to despair; she fondly hoped that there would soon occur some opportunity of escaping; and as indulging her grief would only weaken still more her fragile frame, and render her incapable of the least exertion when an opportunity might offer, she endeavoured to compose her agitation, and to comfort herself with the fond hope that her prayers would not be unheeded.

The carriage now emerging from the deep vale which it had been some hours in passing, entered on an extensive plain. Rosalina surveyed the country before her, but nowhere did a passing peasant meet her gaze. The sun now glared fiercely from his meridian altitude, and the mules seemed weary, and almost unable to proceed. Still however, they advanced, till at length, having gained the outskirts of a small wood, they stopped, and unharnessed them. The monk then for the first time broke his

long silence, by desiring Rosalina to alight, which she tremblingly complied with, and he followed her.

Some provisions were then spread on the ground by the men,
and Grimaldi entreated his hapless captive to partake of them.

"Do not give way to your grief, Rosalina," said he; "it is unavailing: you will know me soon—I wish to be your friend."

"My friend!" said Rosalina; "restore me then to my home,
and I will consider you as such."

"What, to the arms of Montalto! No, Rosalina—never, never
will you again behold him. Whether he recovers of his wounds
or not, he is for ever lost to you."

"And what good," said Rosalina, "can result from your detention of me?"

"You will know," replied Grimaldi, "when you arrive at your
journey's end."

Disdaining to ask any more questions, and the name of
Montalto having aroused all the tender emotions of her heart,
which she had endeavoured to suppress, Rosalina turned aside
to conceal her tears from the relentless Grimaldi, and long remained indulging the weighty sorrows of her bosom, unheeded
and unpitied.

It was near sunset when the mules were sufficiently refreshed
to proceed on their journey, and Rosalina was again seated by
the monk. The beauty of the romantic scenery which she now
beheld would at any other period have delighted her: but the
cascade roaring amidst the piles of huge misshapen rocks,
sparkling in the rich tints of the declining sun—the luxuriant
plains which were stretched around the vast mountains, along
whose bases lay their winding road, lost their beauty when busy
thought recalled her to her hapless situation. Rosalina gazed
anxiously around her, hoping to see some village or city which,
lying in their route, might give her hopes of effecting her
escape; and as the last gleams of the setting sun brightened the
distant prospect, she beheld the spires of some buildings that
seemed to be on the verge of the horizon, which every moment
contracted to the view, till the shades of night shed their murky
veil over the face of nature.

After travelling near an hour in darkness, the carriage at length stopped at a small hovel, of a wretched appearance, at the door of which one of the men repeatedly knocked before he could gain the attention of its inhabitants. At length it was slowly unclosed by an aged female, who, in a shrill trembling voice, demanded what they wanted? But as soon as the man had spoken some words to her, in so low a tone of voice that the sounds became indistinct before they reached the ears of Rosalina, the woman hastily drew back, and the man entered the cottage.

After he had been there a short time, he came out, and telling the monk that every thing was ready, he assisted the trembling Rosalina to alight, and she went into the hovel, where she beheld the wretched inhabitant of it busied in preparing a fire.

"I did not expect you to-night, signora," said the woman, "for his excellenza—I mean the padre, was quite uncertain when he should arrive; but I shall soon have the fire made, and get your suppers ready, for you must be fatigued after so long a journey."

"It seems you know all concerning my wretched situation," said Rosalina: "if so, let me entreat you to aid me in my escape, and you shall be amply rewarded."

The old woman was going to reply, when the entrance of the monk prevented her, and she sat about preparing their supper, sometimes, when she was able, stealing a glance at Rosalina, who, noticing her manner, was not without hopes that she should be able to succeed in prevailing on her to assist her to escape; and in that hope she partook of the provision which was laid before her, for she was faint with fatigue and want of food, which her grief would not permit her to taste during the day.

Grimaldi partook not of the repast; but when Rosalina had concluded hers, he told her she might retire to rest as soon as she pleased, as they would set out on their journey before sunrise the next morning.

Rosalina, glad to have an opportunity of retiring, imme-diately availed herself of that permission, and left the room, preceded by the ancient hostess.

Ascending a narrow flight of stairs, her conductress opened a door, which disclosed a small chamber, in one corner of which was a bed; and Rosalina having carefully closed the door, thus addressed her—

"You seemed as if you were going to answer my request when my persecutor entered: let me entreat you now, in pity, to lend a favourable ear to it. Whatever the motives are which induced you to comply with the wish of my enemy in resting here for the night, whether dictated by fear, or from pecuniary considerations, believe me, my friends are powerful enough to protect you; and as for a reward, if you can procure my freedom I will double whatever the monk promised you. Reflect, you are on the verge of the grave. Oh, enter not into eternity, I beseech you, with the horrible reflection of having been instrumental in oppressing the unfortunate; but let the pleasing idea of the good deed you will perform in procuring my liberation from my mysterious enemy, be present to console and comfort you in the awful moment of your dissolution."

The old woman appeared affected by the earnest entreaty of Rosalina.

"What you wish me to perform," said she, "is, I fear, beyond my power to do; for as his excellenza remains below, the only way in which you can escape is through the casement, and immediately opposite to that is the carriage, where the two attendants will probably stay during the few hours you will be here. But as you are ignorant of the country, there is little doubt of your being overtaken. Besides, the casement is so high that I should think it almost impossible for you to reach the ground unhurt."

"At least I can venture, good mother, if you will afford me your assistance," returned Rosalina.

"That I am not able to do, as his excellenza—I mean the padre, will wonder at my long stay; but there is a rope beneath the bed, which you can tie to the iron bars of the casement."

"I thought I saw a town not far off," said Rosalina, "at sunset—if I could reach that, I should be safe."

"You might perhaps conceal yourself there for a short time," said the woman, "but in these parts you can never be safe. I have a son, who sleeps in the shed where the mules are; I will go to him, and try to persuade him to wait for you; and if you should succeed in leaving the cottage unobserved, he will conduct you to Contarino, which is the name of the town you saw. I must now go: be careful, whatever you do, not to let it appear that you acted by my advice, for if you should, my life would answer it."

"Do not fear," returned Rosalina: "if Heaven is so indulgent to me as to favour my attempts, you shall be the immediate object of my generosity."

The old woman now departed, leaving her lamp on the table; and Rosalina, after having taken out the cord, and affixed it to the bars, and put whatever furniture there was in the apartment against the door, to prevent any one from entering, extinguished the lamp, that her design might not be suspected, and, almost breathless with expectation, awaited till she might expect her conductors to be asleep, when she intended to commence her adventurous undertaking, and free herself from the horrors which seemed to impend over her devoted head.

She sat on the side of the bed for some time, listening attentively to the deep hollow tones of the monk's voice, as he was talking to the two men. The confusion of the woman, who once or twice called him by the title of excellenza, did not escape her recollection; but in the agitation she was in, and the few moments she remained in the apartment, she had no time to inquire who he was; but perhaps if she had, the old woman might have been cautioned against making her acquainted with that circumstance.

She now heard the door below fastened, and from her casement beheld the two men seat themselves on a bench which was immediately below her. Rosalina was greatly agitated; for the night being warm, she concluded that they meant to pass there the few hours allotted them for repose, for they soon forbore to converse—one of them fell into a profound slumber, as his deep breathing announced, and the other soon after arose, and, getting into the carriage, seemed to prefer it for his nocturnal abode.

Thus was Rosalina left without hope, for she conceived it would be utterly impossible to descend from the casement without awakening the man, who would probably slumber there the remainder of the night.

Nature was now hushed to repose; no sound, save the distant barking of a dog, or the sonorous flight of the beetle, was heard. The sleeper below never once moved—the past fatigues had closely sealed his weary eyelids; the waning moon shed her dim light on the earth, and a few twinkling stars appeared in the heavens. Rosalina now heard a light pace, and looking to the place from whence the sound proceeded, saw a peasant advancing from the back part of the house, whom she immediately concluded was the woman's son, for he looked up at the casement, and then at the sleeper below. She attentively watched him, and at length saw him sitting down at the foot of a tree not far distant, apparently in expectation of her coming.

But Rosalina did not dare to make the attempt then, and waited another hour, in hopes that the man below would awake, and join his companion. In this she was, however, disappointed, and she began to despair, when she was startled by hearing the monk moving below. The idea that he was coming to her chamber almost rendered her unable to stir; but at length, to her great delight she heard him draw back the fastenings of the door below, and presently after saw him walking in front of the cottage, and his form was soon lost to her view in the surrounding mists of night.

It now occurred to Rosalina that a favourable opportunity offered of leaving the cottage without fear of awaking the man on the bench, if she could remove the furniture she had piled against her door, and, passing through the room below, secrete herself behind some tree or hedge till the monk returned. With a trembling hand she therefore hastily began the fatiguing employ, and had opened her door, when to her sorrow, she heard Grimaldi's returning paces, and soon after the closing of the door below announced his having entered the cottage.

She again looked out of the casement; the man on the bench still seemed to sleep undisturbed by the movements of the monk; and as her last and only resource, she resolved to trust to her good fortune, and run the risk of awaking him.

She now, as silently as she was able, got out of the casement, and, holding by the rope, put her foot softly on the bench, which trembled with the agitation of her body: the man was, however, still undisturbed—and the next moment she stood on the ground. She then stepped lightly on, intending to go round the cottage, and so reach the peasant; but in doing this, she passed by a low casement, which was open, and at which, horror-struck, she encountered the gaze of the padre Grimaldi, whose cowl being thrown back, disclosed the sable mask he wore.

The monk, starting from his seat, hastened to the door, and Rosalina fled towards the place where she had observed the peasant had seated himself; but he was no longer there, and probably had fled on perceiving the approach of the monk, through a dread of his resentment. He advanced nearer to her every moment, and at length caught her by her garments, as they waved in the wind.

Rosalina, exerting all her strength, at length succeeded in tearing her garments from his hold; but as she was struggling with him, what was her horror on perceiving he had but one hand, and that his other arm was shorn at the wrist!

Her sensations at this discovery were far beyond the weak efforts of the pen to describe. To her distended gaze, she instantly imagined, appeared the vile assailant of her honour, the intended assassin of Montalto, and, to sum up the horrid catalogue, the murderer of her parent!

She wildly shrieked at seeing the dismembered arm, and, with a dreadful groan, fell senseless on the earth.

The men, disturbed from their slumbers by her screams, now approached the place where the monk was endeavouring to raise her up, and quickly conveyed her to the cottage, whither he followed, and the old woman being summoned, every means was used to recall her fleeting senses.

Slowly did the vital current creep along her veins; but, with animation, her recollection returned; and when her languid eyes fixed their dim gaze on the monk, she started, and in-

stantly closed them, whilst her convulsed frame shewed how
deeply rooted was the horror she felt at the sight of him, in
whom she beheld the most bitter deadly enemy that ever
existed in a human form. She was no longer at a loss to guess
the motives of his taking her from the castello: but the horrible
certainty of his intentions agonized her far beyond expression.
Had Death then wrapped her in his chilling embrace, how
would she have welcomed his approach! how happy would she
have been to have resigned her spotless soul to its Maker! But
her hour of dissolution was far distant, and the lovely victim to
the inhuman schemes of a base wretch bowed with resignation
to the will of Heaven.

Her tender frame was weakened so much by her sufferings,
which always were increased when she saw Grimaldi, that he
began to fear that he should be deprived of his prey, and therefore kept from the chamber where she was. This had the desired
effect; and no longer tormented by his presence, her youth and
constitution prevailed, and she slowly began to recover.

But though her corporeal sufferings were diminished, her
mental agonies decreased not: her eyes, once so lovely, so bright,
and full of expression, now robbed of their lustre, hollow, and
continually suffused in tears, were often directed to heaven,
while her trembling lips slowly articulated the fervent prayer
for pity.

On the third morning, Grimaldi ventured to enter her apartment. She shuddered at his approach, and her horror at seeing
him was so great as to deprive her of the power of speech. His
design in coming to her was evidently to find if she was able
to continue the journey, for he only staid a few minutes, and
then leaving the chamber, gave orders to the men to harness
the mules.

It was in this interval that Rosalina entreated the old woman
to inform her who her persecutor was; but she either was ignorant, or else had made a solemn promise not to disclose that circumstance, and Rosalina was summoned to the carriage before
she was able to become acquainted with what she so greatly
desired to know.

Again was she seated by the side of Grimaldi, who still concealed his features, and the carriage proceeded along the luxuriant plains, evidently avoiding the towns and villages which now frequently appeared scattered over the face of the country.

At noon they stopped in the midst of a gloomy forest, where the beams of the sun but faintly penetrated: there they staid but a short time, and again pursued their journey.

As Rosalina was surveying the objects around, she saw at the verge of the horizon an immense pile of buildings, which was erected on the declivity of a huge rock: the setting sun was brightly reflected on the casements, and his beams glittered on the surface of an extensive sheet of water which lay near it. She fixed her gaze on the castello or monastery (for one of them she concluded it was), till the winding of the road, and some objects that intervened as the carriage descended the hill from whence she had beheld it, obscured it from her sight. It was some time before she again had a view of the scenery around, but the mists of evening now veiled the distant objects.

The carriage proceeded for some hours, till all was enveloped in darkness, when, as it slowly rolled down a gentle declivity, one of the men blew a horn. Rosalina started at the sudden sounds which were echoed around, when a fainter blast was heard at a distance, and the carriage stopped. The light of a torch now gleamed amongst the foliage in the vale below, and soon the trampling of horses was heard hastily approaching them.

The mules were now unharnessed, and their places supplied by the horses which were brought up, and they again continued their journey on a more level road.

When the carriage again stopped, it was beneath an immense and gloomy archway; and on their entering it, a man hastened from a small portal with a torch, by the glare of which Rosalina saw at a distance a large portico, supported by a long range of columns, whose size far exceeded the Gothic solidity of the pillars of Colredo.

She was now informed that she was at the termination of her journey. She trembled as she alighted, and, preceded by the man who attended with the torch, she slowly entered a portal on one side of the archway, and beheld an immense hall, the roof of which was supported by long rows of columns, almost black with time, on whose vast turrets were hung ancient suits of armour and faded banners, which appeared to Rosalina, as the gleams of the torch rested on them, to be dropping to pieces. At the extremity of this hall was a large flight of marble stairs, which she ascended, and when arrived at their summit, looked back, expecting to see the monk behind her; but only one of the men followed, and her persecutor was not to be seen.

When they had gained the gallery to which the marble steps led, the man who was behind entered a corridor, and called out two or three times—"Jacquelina!" A voice answered, and soon Rosalina beheld a female approaching, whose appearance well denoted the gloomy office she concluded belonged to her. She was tall, seemingly long past the meridian of life; her skin yellow and shrivelled; a few scanty locks hung over her wrinkled forehead, and her nose was thin and hooked; in one hand she held some keys, and in the other was a lamp.

She accompanied the men along an extensive corridor, at the extremity of which she opened a portal, which was fixed in a deep recess, and Rosalina entering, saw a large apartment, the furniture of which was ancient, but still retained traces of its former magnificence. On the other side of the room was a door, which was partly open.

"These are the apartments, signora," said the female, "which we were ordered to conduct you to.—Roberto," said she, turning to the man who carried the torch, "put a light to those faggots: this part of the castello has been so long uninhabited that every thing seems damp."

The man having complied, Jacquelina set down her lamp on a table, and, telling Rosalina that she would soon bring her some supper, quitted the chamber with the two men, taking care to secure the door.

Rosalina, left to herself, took a survey of her apartment, which was now lighted by the blazing faggots on the hearth: two large casements were placed under a gloomy arch, the panes of which were covered with armorial bearings; the floor was of marble, as were also the tables. Several paintings adorned the walls, which, on examination, seemed to be the work of eminent artists. Between the casements was a large Venetian mirror, whose surface, covered with the damp vapour of the place, had long ceased to reflect any object. She now took up the lamp, and went into the next apartment, which was of the same dimensions as the first: its furniture was a lofty canopied couch, the hangings of which were blue velvet, fringed with gold.

In this apartment were several doors, all of which Rosalina endeavoured to unclose, but succeeded only with one, which opened into a small closet, evidently adapted for the purposes of religion, for beneath the casement was a table, on which was placed a small crucifix of silver, a missal, and a rosary; the panes of the casement were adorned with a Madona, holding in her arms a lovely infant.

Rosalina bent before the image of the Saviour of the World, and humbly intreated for fortitude to bear up against the evils which surrounded her; and while thus devoutly employed, a glow of hope animated her woe-worn breast. She was at length interrupted by the opening of the door of the outer apartment, and rising from her suppliant posture, took up the lamp, and entering it, saw Jacquelina busied in arranging her repast.

"Your apartments, signora, command a lovely view," said the attendant. "This part of the castello is built on a cliff, which projects over the waters of Celano: your time will be pleasantly passed in viewing the prospects."

"There is little pleasure," said Rosalina, with a sigh, "in seeing the beauties of nature, when the greatest charm in life— liberty, is denied."

"Oh, you will soon forget the loss of that, signora," said the unfeeling attendant; "besides, I have orders to let you walk in the courts of this end of the castello, and all the eastern ramparts, during the daytime; so you can scarcely conceive yourself a prisoner; and you are to have, besides, whatever you may want, either of clothes or books."

Rosalina replied not, but sat down to her repast, of which she sparingly partook, while Jacquelina waited, seemingly ill pleased with her office, and the taciturnity of her charge.

When she was gone, and Rosalina left to herself, she felt but little inclined to sleep, for she was not without her fears that Grimaldi might enter her apartment during the night; she well knew by sad experience, that his dark and savage soul would not hesitate to perpetrate the most horrible crimes.

It was now near the dawn of day, and Rosalina watched the vermeil tints of morning as they deepened into the glowing beams of the sun, which at length penetrated the casements of her apartment. Jacquelina had not misinformed her respecting the view which they commanded, for nature seemed to have exhausted her arts to combine the lovely, the picturesque, and the romantic, in the scene which now appeared before her, dressed in all the radiant glow of morning.

On one side, at the opposite shore of the waters of Celano, which rolled beneath the casement, was a vast heap of huge rocks, over whose craggy sides a cataract rushed foaming into them; and in the spray appeared all the glowing colours which adorn the mystic bow that sometimes is seen in the hemisphere. At the bottom of these rocks appeared large caverns, which stretched their vast mouths apparently to receive the waves which glided into them, and echoed back the roaring of the cataract in various gradations of sound.

From this romantic view, the eye reposed on the luxuriant plains around; the nearer groves and distant forests that clothed the sides of the hills which rose from the margin of the river, forming a vast amphitheatre, whose irregular heights were at length bounded by the horizon.

The lowing of the herds in the pastures, the song of the fisherman who toiled in the river, and the melody of the birds, soothed the sorrows of Rosalina to a pensive melancholy, which she indulged till the entrance of Jacquelina.

She seemed surprised on finding Rosalina up, and that she had not lain down during the night; but, however, she scarcely spoke, at which circumstance her captive was not sorry, for the manners of the attendant, and the settled smile of inveterate malice that constantly appeared in her features, were unpleasant, and even disgusting to her.

When she was taking away the morning repast, she asked Rosalina if she would like to walk on the walls? to which she assented, in the hope of finding some way of escape, or of learning who it was that had so completely overthrown the fair structure of happiness which her imagination had formed.

"You may then come with me now," said Jacquelina.

Rosalina arose from her seat, and throwing on her veil, followed her attendant to the hall below, from whence she passed through the archway into a large court, which was apparently seldom made use of; for there the long grass waved to the gale, and the thistle reared its lonely head. She looked up, and viewed with astonishment the massy walls of the towers, whose lofty embattled summits far overhanging their base, seemed to bid stern defiance to the weak assaults of man, or the more powerful hand of time. The walls were nearly black with age: and as she sighing looked on the dark battlements, she could almost imagine them the dreary abode of the Fates, who lurked unseen within their deep recesses, and held their death-dooming debates.

A long archway led her to the walls, where she again contemplated the lovely prospects which she had viewed from the casements of her apartment. Leaning on the stone parapet, she looked below her on the rapid waters of Celano, which seemed to roll so far beneath the cliff, that she was apprehensive lest the ponderous walls of the castello would bring down the rock on which they were erected into the river.

The white sail gliding along the wavy surface of Celano attracted her momentary attention, but her thoughts soon returned to the means of effecting her escape, which, alas! she was fearful was impossible, for no outlet met her view: the walls frowned on her wherever she turned her gaze toward the land side, and the hideous precipices and river rendered it impossible on the other.

Her feeble frame would not permit her to walk for any

length of time, and she returned to her apartment, the door of which was locked by Jacquelina, who had been a close attendant on her steps.

Scarcely had she recovered from her fatigue, when the door opened, and Grimaldi entered. She started with horror at his approach, but collecting all her resolution, awaited with chilling expectation the developement of his intentions towards her.

"Lovely Rosalina," said he, "would I could persuade you to banish the fears which blanch your cheeks at my approach!"

"When I behold," said Rosalina firmly, "the destroyer of my peace, when I think of my own wrongs—of the wounds of Montalto, and the murder of my father, is it so strange that my blood should curdle in my veins? or do you think me so lost to filial duty, and to love, as to have banished all those feelings?"

"Talk not of love," said Grimaldi, "at least when you mention the hated name of Montalto, for these walls shall for ever enclose you from his view. Remember, that by so doing you will accelerate his destruction. Yes, Rosalina, it is now time to declare who I am, and, when you know me, you will not wonder at the deeds I have performed, to which I was urged by love, jealousy, revenge, and all the passions which, concentrating their influences in my bosom, would have made me perform deeds, to which those I have committed are as the gentle scarce-felt meridian zephyr to the hollow roaring blasts of night. One victim only has escaped, and that is Montalto: his existence, Rosalina, depends on your conduct; transfer the love you have for him to me—make me the possessor of your hand—whatever the imagination of man can form which would render you happy shall be done: refuse me, and dread the worst. View this dismembered arm: it was that blow which caused Rodolpho's death: whenever I see it, my blood boils, and methinks I could dart into the midst of hell's fiercest flames to plunge again my dagger in his detested form! You now know the fierce ungovernable passions you have to resist, and if you would know in whose breast they dwell, view him."

This said, he cast aside his monkish garment, and disclosed

to Rosalina the too-well-recollected dark ferocious features of the prince di Manfroné, so long supposed dead!

Imagination must fail in portraying the terror-stricken features of Rosalina, and the pen is not able to describe her feelings: she hid her face with her hands, as if the form before her had been that of some horrible spectral form, or demon of darkness, while her frame shook with the dreadful sensations which tortured her bosom, like the leaf of the aspen to the invisible element.

"Doubtless," continued the prince, "you are astonished to behold one before you whom Montalto falsely reported as no more: it is true he had reason to believe it, for, whirling from the dizzy height of Salerno, the waves of Abruzzo rolled over my form; but at that moment one of my domestics who was on the shore saw me as I fell, and, plunging into the lake, dragged me to the land. I need not relate the adventures of that night, when I secretly entered your chamber: you know how I was foiled, but it was only for a time; I easily effected my retreat, and remained in a peasant's hut till my wounds were healed: it was there I nursed my well-concerted plans of revenge. I entered the monastery, and by a tale deceived them as to who I was. My face I determined they should never see, and imposed on their credulity by affirming that I had made a vow to conceal it from the world. While pondering in my mind how I should effect an entrance into Colredo, I one day strayed on the margin of the lake which was beneath the western front, when as my eyes were cast to the ground, I saw my lost hand rotting in the blast: I snatched up the bones, and, having carried them to my cell, solemnly swore that they should grasp the dagger whose point should be buried in Rodolpho's heart. Circumstances favoured my procuring an entrance into Colredo, and of making my intended victim imagine me his dearest friend: under that idea I made him the blind tool of my own purposes; all his people were destroyed in the attempt which I urged him to of endeavouring to grasp at my possessions. I amused myself for some time with his distress, and when I had foiled him in every thing he undertook, I completed my purposes by his death, and in conveying you away. The tower was fired by my order; but there the unlooked-for escape of Montalto prevented my plans; but that act roused my vengeance, and he now suffers for it.

"Thus have I accounted for the mysterious proceedings of the monk Grimaldi. Now, Rosalina, you must make your election; but be careful while you do it that it wars not against my wishes, else perchance force may be used, which I would gladly avoid: forget, then, all that has past—give your free consent to what you cannot avoid—and be the princess di Manfroné."

Rosalina during the speech of Manfroné had recovered the deep distraction which had seized her; she saw that all her hopes of comfort on this side the grave were vanished for ever; and, reckless how long she continued on the earth, and therefore fearless of exciting the rage of the prince, she thus replied—

"And is it after the horrid detail that you have given me that you can imagine that Rosalina can stoop so low as to think with any other sensations than those of the greatest horror and disgust on the man who has declared himself not only an assassin, but the assassin of her father? If this is the way that the prince di Manfroné seeks to woo Rosalina, he is mistaken. Never shall my lips give utterance to any words than those expressive of the horror and detestation excited by your conduct. Gladly would I enter the silent abode of the grave to avoid you; but if that consolation is denied me, I would rather become an inmate with the most disgusting reptiles that crawl the earth, than live in the highest state of worldly magnificence, and condemned to the misery of seeing you. If you think, Manfroné, that in Rosalina you have to deal with a timid wavering female, you are mistaken, for my resolution increases with the difficulties that surround me."

"That, Rosalina," said the prince, with a smile of malice and revenge, "I shall try. I give you till the third evening from this to decide on the course you will pursue, and if you do not then comply, I shall put your boasted resolution to the test."

"Take my answer now," returned Rosalina, "and produce your tortures, you will find them of little avail. My determination of to-morrow will be the same as to-day, differing perhaps only in having increased during that space of time. My love is not transferable; Montalto irrevocably possesses it—you, prince, my detestation; but you might soften the anguish you have caused me to endure, by giving me my liberty, which you have so basely deprived me of."

"Never while life exists," said Manfroné; "here is your abode for ever; to pass the confines of these walls is far beyond your power: these are circumstances which you must have time to reflect on. I will not listen to a hasty determination: at the time I have appointed, you will see me again; but I must repeat my caution to you not to excite the rage of a man whom your death only would not appease."

Rosalina made no answer, and Manfroné arose and left the apartment.

His last words, indeed, struck her with such terror that she appeared for some time as if bereft of her senses; tears at last cooled the fever of her brain: though a mournful one, it was some consolation that now she knew the worst—her enemy stood confessed, but one whom she little expected ever to have again beheld. Happy would it have been for her if it had been a dream—a delusion of the mind, for so indeed it at first appeared; but soon, alas! she was too fatally assured of the truth, and that the life of Manfroné was miraculously preserved to nip the bud of all her dearest hopes, and overwhelm her in the deep abyss of misery and despair.

CHAPTER XXII.

Rosalina's mind rose superior to her misfortunes, and she waited with firm resignation for the close of the third evening, which she concluded would witness her dissolution.

Freed from any apprehensions of Manfroné's visiting her apartments before that period, she retired to rest at an early hour, and enjoyed an undisturbed repose till she was awoke by the entrance of Jacquelina.

She arose refreshed by her slumbers, and was somewhat surprised to find that her attendant behaved with much more respect than before, which she rightly concluded was her having been informed of the prince having offered her marriage, which indeed was a circumstance little to be expected; but Manfroné now considering Rosalina as possessor of the estate and domains attached to Colredo, sought by a union with her to add them to his possessions, resolving, however, in case of her refusal, to get possession of them by force, a circumstance which he had already made easy, by betraying the designs of Rodolpho to Sebastiano, who, as already related, easily surprised and destroyed his troops. In that instant his schemes succeeded almost beyond his expectation, and Manfroné often smiled to think how easily he had duped his enemies, and turned their swords on themselves.

Jacquelina brought some clothes, which she accepted, and also some books, which served to while away the melancholy hours of her captivity, and prevent her from pondering on the probable consequences of her persisting in her refusal to comply with Manfroné's request.

She walked in the morning for a long time over the silent courts and walls of the castello, and, encouraged by the respect and attention which Jacquelina paid her, asked many questions concerning the immense pile of buildings.

"What you have already seen, signora," said the woman, "is scarcely a fourth of the castello; but this is the only part which is not inhabited, for the prince and his officers occupy the whole of the other parts, which are much grander than these old towers. You may see the north and western wings from the extremity of yonder wall, but this has the finest views, and the prince's father always resided here; but when he died, the apartments were all shut up, and so continued till I was ordered to get those ready where you live. I believe that this wing of the castello is not thought so safe as the others, for once, when it was attacked, the enemy contrived to get into it, but were every one slain, and buried under that vast heap of rubbish you see near yonder archway."

Rosalina shuddered when she looked on the burial-place of the unfortunate assailants, but anxious to know how it was they had effected an entrance, she asked the woman, who replied—

"That beneath that wing were large caves which had communication with some of the towers, and the enemy had contrived to get into them without being discovered, and so had opened a way immediately beneath the heap of earth by the arch, where formerly there had been a small passage down to them, which, when they were slain, the prince commanded should be filled up with their bodies."

During this conversation, Rosalina had advanced to the extremity of the wall, and was struck with surprise at the wonderful extent of the building, which presented a range of embattled walls and towers as far as the eye could reach. Those she now beheld were evidently the workmanship of later years, their structure being more modern and less gloomy than the eastern wing.

"Some of the caves below," said the communicative Jacquelina, "were formed into dungeons, where formerly the prisoners used to be kept; but one stormy night the waters rose to an unusual height, and entering the grates which were placed in the rock to give them air and light, they all perished."

"Poor creatures!" said the pitying Rosalina; "how cruel it was to put them in a situation where there existed a possibility of such a shocking event taking place!"

"Oh! as to that, no one thought of them long, for in war there is but little time for pity! Death becomes familiar, and loses all its terrors by being constantly in our view. The prince, however, ordered that those dungeons should not be used any more. Perhaps, signora, you would like to see the principal apartments which the late prince used to occupy?"

Glad to beguile the time, Rosalina followed her conductress, who entering the hall, turned into a large gallery, which was ornamented with full-length portraits of the ancient possessors of the castello.

Rosalina sighed when she viewed them, for she reflected that they existed no more on earth—that their forms were long since mouldered away: and all their haughty plans, their wide-spreading ambition, extensive territories, and unbounded power, could not detain them from the grave one moment longer than the poor peasant who dug it for them.

Rosalina could not forbear feeling a kind of awe steal over her, as she trod the silent chambers which once had resounded to the voices of those who long since had ceased to be remembered. Those which had been the residence of the late prince were magnificently furnished; but time was destroying the beauty of the embroidered tapestry, the colours of the paintings were fading, and the labours of the spider now covered those of the loom: every thing was enveloped in dust; but still they plainly evinced the grandeur of its former possessor.

When Rosalina returned again to her apartments, she sat down to the perusal of one of the books which had been brought her, and thus passed the hours till the gloom of evening obscured the characters of the descriptive page.

Often were her thoughts fixed on Montalto, but knowing so well as she did the revengeful disposition of her cruel persecutor, all ideas of ever seeing him again were fled; there was not the least gleam of hope that she should be able to escape from the castello—but amidst all the horrors of her situation, Rosalina still confided in the goodness of Providence.

The dreaded evening now approached. Rosalina trembled when its shades darkening the earth, confirmed the empire of night. She listened with fearful expectation of hearing Manfroné advancing along the gallery; but he came not. She threw open the casement, in order to hear the tolling of the far distant clock, and there sat till its faint sounds announced the midnight hour. Still fearful of his coming, she remained there some time longer, when concluding that he was happily prevented from torturing her with his presence, she retired to rest.

The next morning she ventured to ask Jacquelina, if the prince was still in the castello; and great was her joy indeed, on finding, that in consequence of an insurrection in a distant part of his territories, he had been obliged to go in person to reduce the mutinous to subjection and restore peace.

Such a signal interference in her favour, Rosalina could not help ascribing to the goodness of heaven, and she began to indulge the fond hope that even now she should surmount the difficulties which clustered around her; and thus comforted, her strength returned, and she every day grew more able to endure with fortitude her expected sufferings.

Confident that she could not escape, Jacquelina now no longer fastened her door, and she had free liberty to rove un-attended over the silent halls and courts of that part of the cas-tello. Rosalina frequently availed herself of this liberty, and during her wanderings examined those parts which she thought would lead to some outlet; but in vain, for every place of egress was too securely fastened for her to hope to remove.

A month had now elapsed, and still the prince did not return. Rosalina had recovered her strength, and used fre-quently to remain the whole day on a projection of the rock, which commanding a more extensive prospect than any other part, she liked to sit and read there, when not prevented by the heat of the sun.

One evening, when tired of reading, she was leaning her arm on the parapet which terminated the rock; perceiving a small boat approaching the castello, she kept her eyes fixed on it, till passing beneath the rock, it was lost to her view.

In thinking of Montalto, she had totally forgot that circum-stance, and was going to leave the place, when she heard a soft strain of music which appeared to come from below. She lis-tened for a while, first astonished and then pleased with the sounds, till at length the scenes around were enveloped in shade, and the music ceased. Still, however, she remained at her station, looking down on the river; but though unable to pene-trate the vapours that rose from it, she heard the oars of the rowers dashing on the waters.

The next evening she again repaired to the place, and again listened to the pleasing melody, which lasted, as on the preced-ing night, till it was dark. When she returned to her chambers, she mentioned the circumstance to Jacquelina; but she was unable to account for it, as there was no possibility of landing below, for the immense crags jutted far over the waters.

The music was a great indulgence to Rosalina, and she waited impatiently for the next evening, when she intended again to listen to the soft, but melancholy strains, which, mellowed by distance, and softly repeated by the surrounding echoes, seemed more the work of enchantment than the performance of mortals. The day proved extremely hot, and she staid in the castello till the sun was rapidly journeying towards the western waves: she then left her apartments, and had proceeded half way down the marble stairs, when she suddenly stopped, for to her terrified gaze appeared, when far remote from her thoughts, the prince di Manfroné.

She trembled, and as fast as she was able retreated to her apartments, whither she was followed by her persecutor.

"It gives me pleasure, Rosalina," said he, "to see the rose once more bloom on your lovely cheeks. May I trust that it is a proof that you are willing to accede to my entreaties, and that you will consent to this being the bridal hour?"

"You have yet to learn, prince," said Rosalina, who now had somewhat recovered from the terror his unexpected appearance had occasioned, "that time has no effect on my resolutions when once fixed: and with respect to you, they are the same as when we met."

"And you are determined not to accompany me to the altar?" said Manfroné, his countenance gleaming with rage.

"Such indeed are my resolves; never shall a murderer—the murderer of my father, call me bride! I am ready to die, prince! Hasten then the period of my dissolution, and Rosalina will thank you with her last breath."

"Then, as I have to yours, listen to my determination, Rosalina. Beneath these towers there is a dungeon dark and fearful, from which the pleasant beams of the sun, or the cheering views of nature, are excluded—that shall be your residence for a week; and at the end of the seventh day, if you are still obstinate, I will gratify by force the longings of my bosom, and then, Rosalina, you may die."

Rosalina trembled, for at the mention of the dungeon she

immediately concluded it was that where the unfortunate captives perished, and the idea of having it for her dwelling was more than she could support with fortitude. The prince observed the sudden paleness which overspread her countenance.

"You may easily avoid your horrible destiny, Rosalina, by consenting to be my bride."

"If there is no other alternative, Manfroné, that can save me from such a cruel fate than that consent, let me be conducted to my dungeon. My soul, secure in its existence, smiles at the sufferings you threaten my mortal form with. But do you not dread an hereafter? Do not the punishments which await crimes like yours shake your nature? Or are you so hardened in sin, that you reflect not on the enormity of your deeds?"

"Revenge," returned the prince, "is the deity I worship; whatever are its impulses, them I implicitly obey. Religion I consider as a mere bugbear, calculated to awe fools, and increase the revenues of crafty priests, who, by their well-studied cant, alarm the weak minds of mortals with tales of punishments hereafter, which they pretend to be able to obtain a remission of, and even set a price on the forgiveness of offended Heaven. I smile at these ridiculous fancies. If the soul is immortal, a spark proceeding from the Divinity, as they pretend, where can the harm be in obeying its dictates? or rather, would it not be criminal to refuse to do as it urges us? If such is the case, (and the world, we see, is not the effect of chance,) and that when the body is no more, the soul still exists and returns to its Maker—can he find fault with his own works? No—the whole blame must lie on himself, from whom proceeds the ethereal essence which animates our beings."

Rosalina shuddered while she listened to the speech of the prince, who again sternly demanded if yet she would relent, or that night be carried to her dungeon?

"No, prince," she replied, "let me see my tomb, for such I am determined it shall be. Pleasant will be the gloom which reigns within it; and if the cheering views of nature are excluded my sight, at least there I shall not be tormented with the sight of a being so abandoned, so lost to Heaven as yourself."

Manfroné grew furious: he started from his seat, and leaving the apartment, ordered Jacquelina to call Roberto.—"I will, at least, teach you," said he, as he re-entered the chamber, "to curb the insolence of your tongue, which but irritates me the more against you. Is it, do you think, after what I have undergone to have you securely in my power—after sustaining the loss of my hand, and listening to the insulting speeches of Rodolpho, that I will suffer myself to be foiled in my purposes? No, Rosalina; do not deceive yourself with vain hopes that I shall relent, or that the gates of my castello shall ever be opened to permit your egress. Not even my death should liberate you, for with the last efforts of expiring nature would I give orders for your execution."

Roberto now entered the apartment, and the prince ordered him to get a lamp, which Jacquelina soon furnished him with.

"Now, Rosalina," said he to the trembling maid, "will you follow the domestic quietly to your dungeon, or is force to be used?"

"There needs no force, Manfroné, when we act by our own choice," replied Rosalina, rising from her seat, and walking towards the portal.

The prince was evidently surprised at her resolution, and at that moment felt a glow of shame at his own cruel conduct; but a stranger to the smallest resistance to his will, he determined that Rosalina should feel the full weight of his rage.

Roberto going before, descended into the hall, and crossing some of the courtyards, followed by the prince and his lovely victim, stopped at the arch, by the side of which was the melancholy heap of earth which covered the bodies of the unfortunate warriors.

Rosalina had occasion for her fortitude to support her at this trying moment, for the man opened a small door which was concealed in a recess formed by two projecting columns that supported the arch, descended some steps, and Manfroné bade her follow him.

The steps were narrow, and slippery with the damps, and scarcely could she prevent herself from falling; but at length arriving at the bottom, she found herself in a cave whose height and size the feeble lumen of Roberto's lamp would not permit her to discover.

The man seemed to have been previously instructed where he was to go, for crossing the cave, he stopped at a door, and having set down his lamp, he forced it open, for the bolts were rusted in their holds, and so corroded by the damps that they fell to pieces.

Rosalina anxiously surveyed the interior; but, however, she was spared the misery of existing with the relics of the unfortunate beings who had perished, as Jacquelina had informed her, by the flowing in of the waters of the river. The dungeon was small, and at the further end was a grating, through which the breeze of evening blew cold and comfortless. What furniture had been in the dungeon was now rotting to pieces, and the prince ordered Roberto to bring some more; and as he was departing with his attendant, he said—

"You see, Rosalina, that I am resolved to do what I have threatened. I shall again see you at the expiration of the week; but if in the interim you should alter your imprudent resolutions, the domestic who will attend you with provisions will faithfully bring to me any message you may think fit to charge him with; but as to any further indulgence than a couch and the coarsest fare, do not expect it."

Having said this, he retired from the place, and the door being closed, Rosalina was left in the gloomy dungeon, listening to the melancholy dashing of the waves beneath the grating.

Leaning on the rock, she looked through the bars, and beheld the waves of Celano, which flowed darkly under the rocks, when, as she was pensively reflecting on the melancholy hours she probably was doomed to pass in that horrific abode, she heard the music which had given her so much pleasure; it appeared approaching her, but shortly after ceased, and she listened to the noise of the oars, and the rippling of the water, as the boat, swiftly gliding along, divided the waves.

Roberto soon after entered, bringing with him a pallet for her to lie on, and what she was truly thankful for, a lamp and a small supply of oil. As soon as he had deposited his burden, he left the place, having carefully secured the door.

Innocence has no fears. Rosalina, confiding in the protection of heaven, retired to her humble pallet, and there slept, though the blast of night sighed through the bars of the grating, and the waves hollowly beat against the rock.

It was near morning before she awoke. The moon gleamed brightly on the water, but soon retired at the approach of the sun; and the gentle zephyrs of morn, impregnated with the odours of delicious flowers, entered the dismal residence of Rosalina.

"At least," said she, "though the terrific rocks which stretch far over my abode shut out from my sight the smiling beauties of nature, they cannot deprive me of her sweet breath, which cheers and refreshes my senses. This is a comfort which my ruthless tormentor did not think of, or else it is likely he would have sought some means to exclude me from it."

In the course of the morning, Roberto brought her some provisions, which, when he was gone, she partook of, and even ate with appetite; but in proportion as the gloom of evening entered her dungeon, her fears increased, for the tide was now rising, and the waves came so near the cavity of the rock in which the grating was placed, that, as they dashed against it, the wind blew the light spray on Rosalina: her fears, however, of the water entering the dungeon were happily without foundation.

The music again approached; and while Rosalina listened to it, she endeavoured to make her melancholy abode discovered, in order that she might implore the pity and protection of the people in the boat, who she thought might perhaps be able to rescue her. She therefore lit her lamp, and placed it before the grating, in the hopes that its rays, which shone on the dark rocks above, might attract their notice: but the recess in which the grating was placed was either so far within the rock, or the musicians were so intent on their harmonious amusement, that she did not succeed in her attempt; and, after having remained their usual time, they retired.

Her days were now passed in the melancholy employ of

watching the rolling waves, as they broke against the rugged exterior of her dwelling, and in viewing the rocks above, amongst the crevices of which grew a few aqueous plants.

Four days had now elapsed, and the evening of the fifth hastily approached. The waves seemed unusually agitated, and the gusts of wind that rushed into Rosalina's miserable abode chilled her frame; darkness soon covered each object from her sight, but the loud roaring of the waters prevented her from being able to sleep. She lit her lamp, and, sitting on her pallet, anxiously awaited till the violence of the storm should abate; but each succeeding wave seemed to be impelled with greater force, and her fears for her safety now began to assail her, for the water rising above the grating drove into her dungeon, which it completely overflowed. Rosalina started up, and ran to the further end for security; her lamp had been overthrown, and the oil was lost, so that, to add to the horrors of her situation, she was left in total darkness. The waves continued flowing in at intervals, and she fully expected that before the coming morn, her eyes would be closed in the welcome slumbers of death.

What a night of misery was this for the unfortunate Rosalina to support! How long did it seem before the grey dawn dispelled the gloom, and disclosed her comfortless situation! The storm, however, had now abated, and the danger which threatened her ceased; but the waters of Celano, which, when she last saw them, were clear, and disclosed to her view the rugged rocks over which they flowed, now disturbed by the storm, rolled along their dark waves, which ceased to reflect any object on their sable bosoms.

When Roberto entered, he seemed alarmed at the perilous situation of Rosalina, and for once looked on her with an eye of pity. He requested her to go into the cave while he cleared away the water in the dungeon, which, when she entered, she was astonished at its immense size. The light of day entered it from a long cleft in the rock, which, when she approached, she found nearly level with the water, and broad enough to permit any one to enter. This was a discovery of no small importance, for if she could persuade Roberto to allow her the liberty of walking there, she might fortunately attract the notice of the people in the boat, if indeed they should come again, which, if the weather continued stormy, she feared would not be the case, for she had not heard them the last two evenings.

When she returned to her dungeon, Roberto had finished his work, and, encouraged by the mildness of his looks, she thus addressed him:—

"You see, Roberto, the danger I was in, and which it was not in my power to avoid. I do not believe it is the intention of the prince di Manfroné, cruel as his conduct is towards me, that I should perish in my dungeon; if therefore you will leave the door open, I shall be able to retreat to the cave when danger threatens me, and I will reward you for your acquiescence to the utmost of my poor ability."

Roberto hesitated for a moment, and then replied—"To be sure, signora, I do not think the prince would be angry with me for so doing, because, as you say, it certainly is very dangerous, for we may expect stormy weather now, and it is equally as impossible for you to escape from the cave as the dungeon; therefore, signora, I shall do as you request, only to-morrow evening, when the prince comes to you, as he said he would, be careful not to be seen in the cave, and if you will promise that, I will not fasten the door."

Rosalina, pleased at having so easily succeeded, readily made the promise he required, and, as a farther inducement, gave him whatever valuables she happened to have about her on the night she so unfortunately left Colredo; and Roberto departed, well pleased with his treasures.

When he was gone, Rosalina lit her lamp, in order to examine those parts of the cave which were enveloped in darkness, in the hope of discovering another outlet; but her search was not attended with the wished-for success.

She awaited anxiously for the evening, in the hope of seeing the boat approach, for she was pretty certain that the sounds of the music proceeded from that side of the rock in which was the chasm that gave light to the cave.

But, alas! Rosalina was disappointed in her fond hopes: the

boat never came, and when it was dark she retired disconsolately to her cell, and laid her agitated frame on her pallet.

The next evening was the dreaded one which Manfroné had appointed for his coming; and though the last night her dreadful situation had prevented her from enjoying a moment's repose, her horrible anticipations of the deeds which the cruelty of Manfroné might urge him to perpetrate kept her wakeful then—her thoughts were a chaos of distracting ideas, and the sounds of the prince's threats of the vengeance he would take seemed continually to vibrate in her ears. She had no hopes now of succour from the boat, for there was little prospect of its coming, and if it did, it might be when Manfroné was with her, and in that case she would not be able to attract their attention by means of her light.

Such were her reflections during the night, and when the morning arrived it did not dissipate her melancholy. When Roberto came, he reminded her of the prince's intention of seeing her, and again cautioned her not to be in the cave, lest he might incur his displeasure for the liberty he allowed her.

Evening was hasty in its approach. Rosalina often looked through the chasm but the boat was not to be seen: she then seated herself disconsolately on the steps that led to the courts above, that she might have the earliest information of the dreaded coming of Manfroné, and in order to retire to her cell in time to prevent him from knowing his domestic's indulgence.

Such was her situation, when a few plaintive notes from a lute gave notice of the approach of the boat. Rosalina started from her seat, and, hastening to the cleft, saw it at a distance, and the men apparently lying on their oars, and making preparations for their concert.

Rosalina endeavoured, dangerous as it was, to make herself heard, but the dashing of the waves against the rock prevented her feeble voice reaching them. Terrified lest the prince should approach, she desisted, but taking her lamp, held it as far out as she could, in hopes it would attract their notice: they had now commenced their amusement, which doubtless prevented them from seeing her.

A noise now made Rosalina leave her situation, and, trembling, she listened to the voice of Manfroné speaking to Roberto, seemingly at the entrance of the passage which led to the cave. As she knew that it would be some time before he could descend, she again ventured to approach the cleft; and she again holding her lamp there for a few moments, hastened back to her dungeon, which she entered just as the light of the torch which Roberto carried flashed on the sides of the spiral staircase.

The sound of their feet shortly after convinced Rosalina that the prince and Roberto were in the cave, and she listened to the words which Manfroné was speaking to his domestic, and his last sentence so greatly terrified her, that she felt herself scarcely able to stand, for he desired Roberto to await his coming at the door above, as his stay there might probably be of some duration: such a step convinced her that he was determined to put his threats in execution, and she sunk on her knees, and implored the protection of heaven from his vile intents. The hope that she might have attracted the notice of the boatmen now died away, for the music had ceased, and no sound met her ears but the dreaded paces of Manfroné towards her dungeon; and soon the door was opened, and her bitter enemy entered.

"Well, Rosalina, you have hitherto forced me to be severe, but I hope that your concession to my wishes will no longer render that necessary: reflect on the consequences of your refusal, which will put you in a situation truly dreadful; accept, then, the splendid title I offer you, and with it my hand and heart. Here you are in my power—it is not in the ability of mortal to impede my intents; why then will you hesitate—why will you provoke a man, the effects of whose vengeance you have seen so many fatal instances of?"

"Yet, prince, they have hitherto failed in alarming me, and I trust ever will: you reflect not that it is the black revenge which dwells in your bosom which has rendered you in my eyes the most odious of men, and the longer you pursue that conduct, the more those sensations, so inimical to your wishes, will increase. If you had tried to persuade me to an alliance, and used lenient measures, it would have been the only way in which you could have hoped to succeed with me; but to be forced to an alliance is a mode which will never win Rosalina."

"Then," said Manfroné, "I receive your final answer, and now, proud fair, I mean to possess the lovely habitation of your scornful soul; nor longer will I wait to reap the harvest of my toils."

Thus having said, he caught hold of the trembling Rosalina, and dragged her towards him: she screamed with affright, and long did she resist his dark intents; her agonizing sensations gave her fresh strength, and by a sudden effort she disengaged herself, and, opening the door of the dungeon, fled to the farther extremity of the cave: but the prince was resolved to perpetrate the dreadful deed which had long been the subject of his meditations, and he hastily pursued and brought her back. The strength of the hapless maid was fast decreasing, when suddenly the blast of a horn echoed through the cave. The prince started at the sound—hasty footsteps were heard—the door of the dungeon was burst open—and Manfroné, drawing his sword, prepared to punish the unwelcome intruders; but an arm, far superior to his in skill and strength, with a death-dealing blow laid his gigantic form on the ground, gasping for life.

CHAPTER XXIII.

Montalto rapidly recovered of his wounds, and, at the expiration of the fourth day, was enabled to leave his couch. Perhaps the idea that his adored Rosalina would be permitted to see him contributed not a little towards the re-establishment of his health.

The news of the assassination of the duca di Rodolpho soon reached the ears of the marchese; but, fearful that it might distress his son, he carefully concealed it from him, till Montalto, anxious to see Rosalina, demanded of his father if he knew the reason that she had not fulfilled her promise of seeing him?

It was on the morning of that day that the marchese had heard the distressing intelligence respecting Rosalina from Carletta, who, having passed many hours in the greatest agony, and, after having inquired of every one concerning her dear mistress, at length determined to let him know her absence; he scarcely knew how to reply to his son's questions concerning her, for he well knew that should he hear of Rosalina's absence, his present weak state would not detain him an instant from seeking her, and he perhaps might fall a victim to his precipitate conduct: he therefore evaded, as long as he was able, any direct replies to his son's repeated questions, but at length informed him of the death of the duca, and, attributing the silence of Rosalina to that mournful event, Montalto's alarm on her account was appeased for a time, and his health became perfectly re-established.

The absence of Grimaldi at first was not noticed, because he had of late been so seldom visible, and it was supposed that he had gone to reside at the monastery; but when the marchese learned that he had not been seen since the departure of Rosalina, he was greatly agitated, for it may be remembered that the circumstance of his refusing to marry Rosalina to him in the chapel of Colredo brought him acquainted with the person of Manfroné, which, to his astonishment, he again recognized while in the monastery of Santa Maria, after he had concluded that he had perished in the lake. It was evident to him that he had taken Rosalina with him to his castello, where he heard he now resided; and when he thought that his son was able to bear the afflicting intelligence, he imparted it to him as gently as he was able.

The grief and rage of Montalto cannot be described.—"Alas! my father," said he, "had you made me acquainted with the existence of the base prince di Manfroné, what evils might have been avoided! The death of the duca—my wounds—and, above all, the horrible persecution which my adored Rosalina now undergoes perhaps—but let me not ponder on a circumstance which would distract my soul, but, collecting all our forces, let us instantly march and attack the wretch, and rescue her."

"Your grief makes you talk wildly, my dear son," said the marchese.—"What are the forces we could raise, when compared with his numerous troops? Deeply, indeed, have I regretted not having informed you of the existence of Manfroné; but I will repair my involuntary fault, which was occasioned by the many circumstances which, after so long an absence from my domains, engaged my time and attention, by immediately repairing to the dwelling of the prince, and seek by stratagem to effect what our forces could not."

"No, my father," returned Montalto, "your years would ill suit with such an undertaking: but this hour will I depart, and, taking with me a few trusty followers, destroy the venomous serpent in his den."

After much persuasion, the marchese consented to this plan, and Montalto, selecting two trusty domestics, and Pietro, whom he had taken into his service, set out on his adventurous undertaking.

When he arrived at the residence of Manfroné, he learned that he was absent from his castello: but whether Rosalina was there or not, he was unable to discover. Pietro, disguising his features, mixed among the domestics of the prince, to endeavour to find from their conversation what Montalto so earnestly wished to know, and was well convinced that if she was in the castello they were ignorant of it.

Montalto, then, imagining that Manfroné, fearful of leaving her behind him, had taken her to the province which he was reducing to subjection, hastened there, but still could not hear any tidings of the adored of his heart. He then returned back to the castello, when he was informed by Pietro, whom he had left there, that he had been shewn the interior of the building by the domestics, and that if Rosalina was in them, she must be in the eastern wing, as that part was not inhabited by any of the household, and the gates which opened to it were constantly kept shut.

"But I found," continued Pietro, "that some one resides in them, for as I was prying about the castello, seeking out places from whence I could survey the courts and walls of the eastern wing, I saw a female domestic at one of the casements. My inquiries respecting her were, however, fruitless, and fearful of exciting suspicion, I was silent."

Montalto now felt almost certain that Rosalina was in the eastern towers of the castello, and many an hour did he employ in viewing their gloomy walls, but her loved form was denied to his longing gaze. He now procured a boat, and passing beneath the rocks on which they were erected, sought to excite her attention by the performance of some musicians whom he took with him, on pretence of enjoying the echoes among the rocks.

In one of those visits, perceiving the aperture in the rocks, he determined to examine it, and accordingly, entering with Pietro, discovered the cave and the steps which led to the courts above; but the door was too strongly fastened for him to break open, and whilst they were there, hearing the echo of footsteps, they retired.

It was on that same evening that Rosalina was conveyed to the dungeon; and at the very time she was approaching with the prince and Roberto, did her tender lover listen unconsciously to her paces, but unfortunately ignorant of that circumstance, he left the cave and entered his boat. He was now, however, well assured that the eastern towers were inhabited; and as he conjectured that the portal he had seen would procure him admittance to them, determined to come some other evening and force it open.

Having heard that the prince was returned, he was obliged to be more circumspect in his visits to the rocks on which the towers were erected, for fear of exciting suspicion, and delayed exploring them, in which he was also prevented by the stormy weather.

Thus passed the time, when having provided the necessary implements, he one evening approached the rocks, when struck with a light which gleamed through the chasm, he hastened towards the place, and distinctly heard the screams of a female. His fears immediately suggested it must be Rosalina, and in order to intimidate the wretch who was the cause of her exclamations, when he had leaped from the boat into the cave, he snatched up a horn, and blew that strong blast which made Manfroné start and let go his savage grasp of the almost senseless Rosalina.

Pietro and the other domestics immediately followed Montalto, who, directed by the cries, rushed to the dungeon, and in a moment sheathed his sword in the body of the prince, while Rosalina, recognizing her lover, almost fainted with excess of joy, and hung with rapture on his arm.

What a sight was this for the dying Manfroné! Frantic with rage, he collected his yet remaining strength, and taking an opportunity, when unobserved by Montalto and Rosalina, was on the point of wounding them, when Pietro suddenly rushed into the dungeon, and seeing the danger of his master, hastening to prevent it, unfortunately received the thrust intended for him, and in the next moment plunged his own sword in the heart of the prince, over whose senseless body he fell.

Thus perished the prince di Manfroné, and such was the fruit of his savage schemes: justice overtook him at the very moment when he was exulting in his success; and to add to his misery, saw those happy whom he had thought would never again have met in this world.

Gentle reader, reflect on the short-lived triumph of the wicked, and how dearly it is purchased. Seldom are they permitted to exult in the fruition of their wishes; or, if they do, they fall far short of their sanguine expectations. But whether they succeed or not, a certain punishment awaits them, and conscience with its sharp and deadly tooth destroys all their comfort in this world, till at length they sink unlamented into the grave—the gates of eternal destiny open to receive their guilty souls, and trembling they appear before the judgment-seat of Heaven without hope of mercy.

The attention of Montalto was suddenly directed to the unfortunate Pietro, in whose arm the sword of Manfroné still hung. He drew it gently forth, and raised him from the body of the prince.

"We are in danger," said Pietro; "the moment the musicians

you had hired understood your design was against the prince, whose vassals they are, they hastened into the boat, and rowed away, intending to alarm the castello."

Rosalina turned pale at this intelligence; but when Montalto, recollecting the portal above, determined to effect his escape that way, she tremblingly informed him that one of the prince's attendants awaited there his return.

"If we can secure him," said Montalto, "he will, through fear, or hopes of reward, shew us some way of escape. I will instantly make the attempt, for the moments now are precious."

Having said this, he called one of the domestics, and bidding the other go to Pietro and assist him, he took the prince's lamp, and ascended with Rosalina the steps, endeavouring to comfort her amidst her fears, for she trembled lest the gleam of happiness which now burst on her was on the point of being obscured for ever.

When they had nearly gained the summit, Montalto advanced alone; the door was opened by Roberto, who, when he saw a stranger approaching, struck with terror, fled; but Montalto soon caught him, and holding a sword to his breast, said—

"Shew me this instant a private way by which myself and friends can escape: the prince is dead, you need not therefore fear his displeasure. If you refuse me, this moment you cease to exist; but if you execute my wishes faithfully, you shall be rewarded beyond your most sanguine expectations."

There needed little to persuade a man to make an election between his destruction and the prospect of not only preserving his life, but also receiving a reward; and Roberto consented to endeavour to preserve them from the threatened danger, but at the same time represented the difficulty there was in the undertaking, as they must pass through the inhabited parts of the castello, all the portals which led out of the eastern wing being closed up, excepting the one which communicated with the interior of the building.

Rosalina now advanced, and shortly after Pietro, whose wound fortunately ceased to bleed. Roberto preceding them, crossed some of the courts of the eastern wing, and passed through the iron gates which led to the other sides of the castello, when suddenly a confused noise was heard, and the light of several torches glared on the walls.

"The men have betrayed us," said Montalto, extinguishing his lamp; "Manfroné's people are now coming to search the subterraneous parts for us. Is there any place where we can hide? or must we perish in our defence here?"

The terrified Rosalina had run to Montalto for protection, and was obliged to support herself by him, for her fears rendered her almost unable to stand; every moment the sounds increased, and the voices were nearer; and at length they saw a portal opposite to them thrown open, and a party of men, armed with swords and pikes, rush through it.

"Our only chance of escaping," said Roberto, "is to hide ourselves behind those projecting columns near yonder arch till they pass. In their hurry to descend into the cave, they may not perceive us; and when they are gone we must lose no time in leaving the place before their return."

Roberto's advice was followed, and a moment after the crowd rushed along, and darting down the spiral stairs, were out of sight. Montalto then hastily emerged with Rosalina and his people, and closing the iron gates which would retard the return of the party, proceeded with Roberto along the corridor.

But they were not yet in safety, for a few more of the attendants now crossed their path in their way to join the others, and observing them, stopped and demanded who they were.

Montalto replied not, but resolutely attacked them, and the first that had advanced being slain, the rest retreated. In this encounter Roberto assisted him, for knowing that as he was seen with him, his life would no longer be safe, chose rather to perish there, than risk being taken. His services were not unnoticed, and Montalto encouraged him by his promises to persevere.

The inhabitants of the castello were now in the greatest alarm: for ignorant of the numbers of the people who had got into the castello, and terrified by the exaggerated accounts of

those who had fled, now assembled in the spacious area in front
of the castello, and blew the war trumpet to summon every one
to it.

To this circumstance Montalto and his party were indebted
for their escape; for the halls and corridors through which they
were obliged to pass were all empty, and Roberto conducting
them to a side postern, they emerged from the castello.

It was now completely dark, and under the protecting covert
of the surrounding shades they pursued their way, Roberto
being their guide; and before the morning dawned were far
distant from the danger which they had so narrowly escaped.

It was a fortunate circumstance that Pietro did not delay
them, for though weakened by loss of blood, yet he was able to
proceed as fast as Rosalina, whose fears would not permit her to
think of rest till the heat of the sun made it necessary.

The party who first descended to the cave found the breathless body of the prince yet warm; every part was searched, but
no one was to be seen: and they at length were returning with
his remains to the portal above, when the men who had assembled when summoned by the trumpet, having forced open
the gates which Roberto had fastened, meeting the others, took
them for the assailants: and before the mistake was discovered,
it was fatal to many. At length peace was restored, and the body
of Manfroné, disfigured by being trod under foot, was found
amongst the rest, and brought into the hall.

Great exertions were made to discover who it was that had
committed the deed, but no one could tell: parties were sent
in search of them, but they fortunately did not succeed, and
Montalto, with his adored Rosalina, and faithful attendants,
arrived at Colredo, which was the nearest place of safety, and
immediately sent a messenger to the marchese to acquaint him
with their success.

Great was the joy of the inhabitants of Colredo to see their
beloved mistress, and when Carletta arrived (who had resided
by desire of the marchese at his castello till his son's success
should be known), it is hardly possible to conceive the extravagant joy of the affectionate domestic, and which perhaps was

not a little increased by the presence of Pietro, whose wound was soon healed; and now the castello di Colredo, which hitherto had witnessed so many scenes of sorrow, was no longer the abode of melancholy.

Roberto, who had been of such signal service, was amply rewarded, and Pietro and Carletta were placed far above dependance: but though Rosalina wished it, yet both of them refused to be united before that day which should witness her nuptials with Montalto, and which was unavoidably delayed on account of the recent death of the duca di Rodolpho.

The tale of Romellino, which Manfroné pretended to be a recital of his own misfortunes, and gave to the abbot of Santa Maria, in order the better to mislead and keep him in ignorance of who he was, was nevertheless founded on facts, and the unfortunate victim to love did indeed still exist in a remote monastery on the inhospitable shores of Calabria; time, however, had blunted the edge of his afflictions, and the burthen of life became at last easier to be borne.

At length the day arrived, so long expected, so much wished by all who knew the virtues of the illustrious pair, and the marchese, with the assistance of the comte Florelli, left nothing undone which could contribute to the magnificence and splendour of the nuptials.

The halls of Colredo were superbly adorned in all the splendid magnificence of that era in which the occurrences which comprise these eventful records took place. The several apartments and saloons of the immense pile were thrown open, and thronged with the friends of the deserving pair. At the time appointed for the ceremony, Rosalina having thrown off her sable attire, and put on a Grecian robe, which was compressed to her slender waist by a zone of brilliants, shewed the elegance of her form; her lovely hair, dispersed in braids and ringlets, after the Sicilian mode, was adorned with pearls, which displayed the beauty of her glossy tresses—entered the hall with the comtessa di Florelli. The splendour of her dress, and, above all, the blushing lovely wearer, created general admiration.

Montalto at the altar received his beauteous bride as the

greatest earthly blessing heaven could bestow. The ceremony was performed by the venerable abbot of Santa Maria; and as soon as it was concluded, the happy pair received the congratulations of the crowded assembly, who breathed their sincere prayers for the happiness and comfort of Montalto and his Rosalina.

And successful were their wishes, for heaven smiled on their union, and never did a pair enjoy more real felicity than they did. After their marriage, Pietro was united to Carletta, and thus completed the happiness of the deserving couple, who, however, could not be persuaded to leave the castello, but chose rather to attend on Montalto and Rosalina, than to enjoy the independence in which they had been placed.

Here the pen pauses: with its weak efforts it has endeavoured to delineate the vices of mankind, placing them in such a glaring view, with the hope of exciting in the bosom of the reader that horror and detestation which must make him studiously avoid giving way to those turbulent passions that vitiate the mind, and render it insensible to the charms of virtue; and may these pages, which shew him the misery attendant on evil actions, in all his researches after worldly enjoyment and felicity, deeply impress on his mind, beyond the prevailing power of vice to erase, the never-failing maxim, that

"To be good is to be happy!"

FINIS.